mastered

HONOR BOUND: BOOK EIGHT

ANGEL PAYNE

mastered

HONOR BOUND: BOOK EIGHT

ANGEL PAYNE

WATERHOUSE PRESS

Forever and always...for Thomas

And

*For all the readers who encouraged
me to "push the envelope":*

*Thank you for supporting the Boys,
even into this crazy adventure!*

CHAPTER ONE

Time had dictated a lot of Brynn Monet's life. Watching it, abiding by it, dancing to it...and praying to it for better things to come.

This was one of the prayer moments.

Lots of prayer.

No one confirmed that better than Shay Bommer, the husband of Brynn's best friend, Zoe, as he drove a fist into the living room wall of their Las Vegas suburban home.

But Zoe wasn't here right now.

The emptiness was symbolized to sickening perfection by the gaping cavity Shay left in the wall when he pulled his fist out of it and stepped back, snarling like a cornered animal at everyone in the room. It took a while. It was a full house tonight with eight other people in the room, five of them legitimately qualifying as humanized Mack Trucks. The men had dropped everything to fly here for the guy who'd once served side-by-side with them as part of the First Special Forces Group. Brynna stood nervously in an opposite corner with El Browning and Ryder Monroe, the friends she couldn't be without right now.

The hole Shay just created joined the other two he'd already made. Brynn doubted anyone would blink if he destroyed the whole wall.

Or maybe that was wishful thinking on her behalf.

Taking out a wall felt like a damn great idea right now.

Even better idea? Obliterating the bastards who'd kidnapped Zoe six hours ago.

"Shay." The word, hammered with command, was issued by the pirate hunk who stalked forward. Though Rebel Stafford didn't have an eye patch or a peg leg, the comparison fit in every other way. Those shoulder-length waves of jet-black hair. Those eyes, shot with Caribbean blue specks. That accent, laced with earthy Creole. Those tattoos covering both arms—or so she assumed. The form-fitting T-shirt he wore over his camouflage pants prevented final confirmation—not that her mind's eye hadn't already re-outfitted him in breeches, riding boots, a tricorn, and nothing else.

No time for the rest of that vision. Brynn would have been thankful for it too, if the reason was anything other than this.

Dear God. Why Zoe? Anyone but Zoe.

Except that no one but Zoe made sense.

A truth that ravaged every inch of Shay Bommer's face.

"What?" The man spun and glared at Rebel. "*What?* Have you come bearing any useful information about where the *fuck* my eight-months-pregnant wife is, Reb? If you haven't, then get the hell out of my sight."

A pulse ticked in Rebel's stubbled jaw. If she'd blinked she would've missed it, so formidable was the man's self-control. "Can't do that, man, and you know why."

"Fuck off."

"Not happening. You know I need to run through the details with you again."

Shay slumped against the wall. Brynn's heart broke for him. In this case, "the details" only meant one thing: the horrific sequence of events between his wife's bathroom break during their dinner date and the moment she'd screamed before being shoved into the back of a black van behind the restaurant. Shay had sprung to his feet, bursting into the alley in time to notice only two things about the van before it sped away. One, it had no plates of any kind. Two, the driver maneuvered the bulky thing like a seasoned pro.

"Damn it." Shay exposed locked teeth. "I've told you everything I know!"

"I know." Rebel squared his shoulders. "But I need you to sit down, take a shitload of deep breaths, and then tell me again. I need everything you can possibly remember."

Shay dropped his head. Dragged both hands through his thick chestnut hair, choking back a broken breath. "I...can't."

"Yes, you can. We need more to go on. Something. *Anything.*"

By "we," Rebel included the guy right behind him, whom he was rarely seen without. Rhett Lange, call-sign Double-Oh, served as their battalion's tech and covert-identity specialist. This was a fancy way of saying that on the team's most dangerous missions, his dependability was key. Nobody knew that more clearly than Rebel, who, as the "blow-shit-up guy," needed rock-solid intel at every turn of an op.

Brynn jerked her head, forcing the tangent away. Why the hell did she know all of that? Even worse, why did it give her the same adrenaline kick as her *Teen Scene* centerfolds wall from high school? Even right now. Especially right now.

Focus, Monet. Focus on what you can do to help. Zo wasn't just your dance captain for three years. She was your rock through all the shitty times—and the days that were worse than that. You have to be there for her now. You have to do something.

Another silent but desperate plea. She was going not-so-slowly insane, sitting here in helpless dread and disbelief...

A feeling she was no stranger to.

Good afternoon, Brynna. I'm Officer Feld and this is Officer Smythe, Vegas PD. Sorry to pull you out of rehearsal, but I'm afraid we have some bad news. It's about your sister, Enya...

She was saved from the memory in the nick of time—by the man who stepped up and pulled her back to safety—mentally, at least. Rhett Lange's effect on her body wasn't so simple. The man matched his friend for sheer physical potency—with one difference. He wasn't a pirate. No other comparison worked for Rhett but *Viking*. Though no wild hair tumbled to his shoulders, the red tips of his short blond spikes lent the Icelandic flair. His eyes, the color of North Sea depths, were bracketed by rugged creases that deepened as he focused on Shay.

"Reb's straight-up on this, Bommer. I can't do a thing with what you've given me. *Think*. You've been trained to do this. Close your eyes. Focus. Can you at least tell me which way the van turned at the end of the alley?"

Shay slid down the wall, *thunk*ed to his backside, and buried his head in his hands. "You mean as I watched them drive away with my helpless, screaming wife?"

The room fell silent—until a small sob stabbed the air to Brynn's left. She reached over, locking hands with El and Ryder again. The woman who'd danced with her as many years as Zoe, along with the male model who'd become the D'Artagnan to their Three Musketeers, joined their desperate grips to hers. The connection was comforting but didn't fill the void left by Zoe's absence. Nobody knew her as deeply as Zoe. Enya didn't count. Not anymore.

Stay strong. You have to stay strong. Zo would do the same for you.

She managed to keep from trembling—until a three a.m. breeze sneaked in through the patio, threaded with enough of a March chill to thwart her effort. El began to shake too. Ry yanked them both against his chiseled chest—again, a huddle missing a key player.

"Zoe." El's sob was broken with grief. "Oh my God...Zoe."

Her cry yanked Rhett's head around. As he took in their miserable clump, a grimace stabbed his soldier's veneer. "Fucking bollocks." The desperation in his voice, underlined by the accent clipped by both London and New York, reached into Brynn's heart. "We have to figure this fucker out."

Rebel stalked back across the room. "Damn it, Bommer. I get that this is hell for you—"

Shay surged up, a bestial sound bursting out. "You get it? Is that so? Then enlighten me, Moonstormer." The call-sign might as well have been hot oil on his tongue. "Tell me what the hell you *get*. You go through a different submissive each month. You flog 'em and fuck 'em, with aftercare barely over before you're eyeing the next skirt in line. Forgive me, asshole, if I have trouble believing how you *get* this."

Under other circumstances, the accusation would've earned Shay a black eye from Rebel, followed by the other guys in the room. Every one of them had dropped everything to be here for their buddy in his blackest moment. Rebel and Rhett had flown from Seattle with Garrett Hawkins and Zeke Hayes, where the four of them still served in Special Forces out of Joint Base Lewis McChord. Another former battalion-mate, Kellan Rush, had arrived an hour ago from Hawaii—an odd sight, since Tait Bommer wasn't with him. Shay's older brother was also Kell's best friend, damn near surgically attached to the man except for when he'd been hauled off for training in the middle of the ocean. Also taking part in that training were the battalion's captain, John Franzen, and language specialist Ethan Archer. While awaiting clearance for leave from the training, Franzen and Archer had joined Tait in calling every hour to check on Shay. The coincidence was very likely a blessing in disguise. Shay was already crumbling at the seams. Tait's presence would likely make that worse.

As if the assumption needed affirmation, Shay twisted back, trying to use his forehead on the wall. After three attempts, he gave up. The mountains of his shoulders heaved with his breaths.

Rebel filled in the other end of the composure spectrum. With barely a change to his stance, he calmly murmured, "Glad we got that covered. Do you want to talk about something that matters now?"

Shay's breaths stretched longer. "Left," he finally grated. "I think they turned left."

"That means they went south." Across the room, Rhett flashed a small smile. He'd clearly been hoping for that answer.

"Out of town, then?" Ryder queried. "To California? Or Arizona?"

"Not necessarily." El added her knowing gaze to Rhett's. Brynn looked on, hiding a bizarre bite of envy for their connection. Or *was* it that strange? El's mind worked like a hard drive, able to process a thousand pieces of information and spit out a conclusion in seconds. It was the key behind her impeccable dancing, why she always got audition callbacks before Brynn, who performed mostly from her gut. Two different routes to the same result—except when that outcome was impressing a man as incredible as Rhett Lange.

Focus! This is your best friend's living room, not a damn

cocktail bar. Phone numbers on napkins are not *why you're here.*

Getting Zoe back. It was the only thing that mattered—no matter what it took from all of them to do so.

"The airport." El's hazel eyes favored dark green, betraying her anxiety. "Shit. They could have been headed for the airport, right?"

"Air*ports*," Rhett corrected. "Not just McCarran. In this case, Henderson Executive fits that bastard's MO better."

"MO?" Brynn looked from him to Rebel, who nodded grimly. "What bastard?"

"Yeah," Rebel muttered. "It does."

"*What* bastard?"

El twisted her lips. "Homer Adler. He's the only one who makes sense. Right?"

Rebel's jaw hardened while throwing another glance at Shay—for good reason. Even the mention of Adler's name stripped the color from Shay's face. Could he be blamed? Brynn's gut wrenched, thinking of what that beyond-mad scientist had put him through as a "test subject" of the Big Idea, a secret human-animal genetics experiment. As the only victim who'd been dosed with the serum as a child, Shay had become critical to Adler as a grown man. After weeks of cutting him open to learn the secrets behind his animal strength and speed, Adler had Shay drugged into a stupor, preparing him to be the main stud horse for mutant superbabies.

A lot of the guys in this room had prevented that from happening, staging an off-books rescue worthy of a Hollywood adventure. The team hadn't failed—thanks to the secret weapon they'd brought along for the mission.

Zoe.

Who, beyond anyone's knowledge but her own, had

already been carrying the superbaby so important to Adler and his goons.

Important? As adjectives went, it barely dinged the bell—and was probably the only treat that could've enticed Adler out of whatever slime hole in which he'd been hiding for the last year. Clearly the worm had learned of Shay and Zoe's happy announcement and had gotten so eager to get his hands on the baby, he'd bounded back into the limelight with a damn ballsy leap. By grabbing her tonight, Adler had shot to the top of every government watch list ever conceived, including countries who weren't even friends with the US. Finding Adler and his minions meant finding Zoe—and the first baby of an entirely new race of humans. That meant a new breed of warriors. And, in fifteen to twenty years, an unstoppable army.

"Fan-fucking-tastic." Zeke growled it low and tight, exposing the dismal downturn of his own thoughts. Garrett scowled with similar intent.

On the couch, Kellan leaned forward, chin balanced on his clasped hands. "Those piranhas could have very well slithered back into the bog they came from, too. Vanished without a trace."

"With a gagged pregnant woman?" Brynn countered. They might have forced Zoe to stay on her feet, but no way would she be quiet about it.

"Valid point." While his tone remained at mission gravity, Rebel cracked an approving smile. "That narrows down the search."

His smiled widened. Brynn's heart flipped a little, and the reverberations didn't stop there. *Great.* She had her dread over Zoe *and* a throb between her legs to contend with now.

Rhett's nod coincided with his buddy's, doubling the

pressure of her frustration. The speed at which the two men processed things was as captivating as the packages their brains came in. "Right," he agreed. "We focus on Henderson Executive."

"Let me help." El scooped up her laptop again and then nodded at Rhett. "Amazing what a girl in dance tights and heels can get the guys in the Caesar's security office to spill during her break. I may know a few new shortcut hacks into the airport's security feed."

Rhett chuckled. "Legally, I'm not supposed to love every word you just said."

"Me neither." El shrugged, making the piercings along her right ear wink in the light. She tucked a strand of her pink pixie cut behind the row of jewelry. "But I hate everything about the reason I'm here, so it's a wash."

Rhett's full lips thinned into a commiserating line before he led the way back to the dining room. In their wake, nobody else had much to say. Brynn only had to take a glance around to know thick silence wasn't the norm for these guys. If they were working, conversation was likely all Spec Ops sarcasm between the soldier acronyms and radio code. If they were off the clock, it was probably more smack-talk, blended with their chosen off-duty "amusement"—a term Brynn was determined to leave alone right there. She'd overheard enough conversations between Zoe and her sister, Ava, as well as their cousin, Rayna, to figure out what those pastimes might be. Ava and Rayna, now both married to guys on the team, used expressions like *safe word, subspace,* and *aftercare* as if they merely chatted about the new flowers they'd planted or movie they'd seen. It hadn't escaped Brynn's notice that with Shay's arrival in her life, Zoe had joined that party.

What the hell? Had submissiveness become a virus?

If that was the case, Brynn vowed to get the vaccine right away.

It wasn't like she was a puritan. Being kinky, even deeply so, didn't transform her friends *or* their husbands into different people. If it made them happy—and she understood at least the sexual dynamite part of that equation—then why fault them for their consensual choices? Dan Colton, the boyfriend she'd met in this very room, had actually revealed himself as a Dominant by the time they went on their third date. By that time, Brynn had been so nuts about him that she copped out with flirtation, declaring his revelation "bold" and "sexy" but secretly hoping it was his way of simply stating a need for intensity between the sheets.

For almost a year, that had been just the case. By day, Dan had been attentive and sweet, enduring the steps of recovering from the explosion that had disfigured half of his face. By night, he was everything she'd ever fantasized about in a lover: forceful and powerful, the only man who'd ever met the mighty needs of her libido and still had passion to spare. Through it all, he'd never brought out one satin blindfold or pair of fluffy handcuffs. His "I'm a Dominant" Tourette's had seemed just that—or maybe his accident had changed more than his flesh. Whatever the reason, she'd been damn grateful—and giddily on her way to falling in love.

Until Dan confessed he wanted to take her to a BDSM club.

"Beginning of the end" had never fit a night in her life more aptly.

He'd tried a hundred poetic phrasings. Told her they'd take it slow, that he would explain things as they went, that she'd discover new parts of her submissiveness that she'd never known before—

At which point she'd rocketed off the couch and seethed her reply from across the room.

I'm not a submissive, Daniel. Nor will I ever be.

Why did Dan's answering stare still burn so brightly in her memory? His assessment, hard as steel but as fathomless as morning sky, had been potent to the point of brutal—and over six months later still confused the hell out of her.

Because you may have...liked...being stared at like that?

Because you may have truly knelt for the man, had he commanded it?

Never.

She was stronger than Enya. She could never be anything less. If she needed a reminder of the consequences otherwise, she could always take a quick drive to the Sandbells Psychiatric Facility...in hopes that her sister would say more than ten words in a row to her this time.

Nope. No kneeling in her future. Not for a man who commanded it, at least.

And wasn't that irony's ideal cue to come knocking?

She didn't care. As Shay slipped back down the wall and hunched back over his knees, she didn't think twice about dropping down next to him.

"Shay?" She squeezed his shoulder. "Hey, don't check out on us now, buddy. Come on. Stay strong."

Oh, sheez. *Stay strong?* She was really going with that? But if she didn't, who would?

Garrett, Kellan, and Zeke were a dark, darker, and darkest row of uncertainty, shifting weirdly on their feet. Under other circumstances, Brynn would've chuckled. Ask these guys to lead hostages from a hot zone, extract an emissary from an embassy, or haul a buddy from a battle trench, and they were aces for the job—but Shay's torment was a jungle they didn't know how to handle. Never mind that all three of them had slogged similar bogs of despair within the last two years—but as best as Brynn recalled, they'd also been able to act right away on the crises with their women. Zoe had been snatched from that alley nearly eight hours ago, and Shay didn't have even a step one.

No wonder his friends looked like prisoners. They were staring down their worst fear—and were shackled by it.

Ironically, the guy who "didn't get it" was the only one who came near. He crouched next to Brynn, presence still as huge as Blackbeard. "The woman has *beaucoup* brains as well as beauty, Bommer. Heed her, *mon ami*."

Shay raised his head, already glowering. Clearly, Rebel's unique mix of Creole 'tude and soldier drawl didn't impress him in the least. Maybe it was a guy thing, because all that musical French drawl was so sexy to Brynn, even her neck hairs tingled.

"*Merde*," Rebel spat. "Look. You're not doing Zoe a microsecond of good by giving up the ghost on your shit now." He bent over farther, meeting his buddy's glare, warrior to warrior. "I'm not going to insult you by coating this in weasel-speak. You know as well as I do that the condition we find Zoe in may not be pretty"—he gripped Shay's forearm when the guy grimaced and grabbed at his hair—"and she's going to need *you* all in one piece." He shook his friend hard. "I-Man? *Fuckhead?* You hearing me?"

No response came from Shay except an angrier coil of his hand, twisting deeper into his thick chestnut hair. Brynn's throat throbbed with emotion, and she wondered how the man hadn't fully scalped himself yet. The only thing worse than a loved one in trouble was being helpless to do anything about it. *"Enya, please let me back in. Let me help you through this!"*

"You can't, bibi. Nobody can help me through this except Peter, and he doesn't care anymore. He never will."

Of course he hadn't. And wouldn't. Someone newer, fresher, and shinier had entered the submissive program at Club Catacomb, captivating the bastard like an infant with a new shiny—the same way Enya had charmed him eight months prior to that.

No time for that bitterness now. She had to stay focused on keeping Shay sane.

"Why don't I make you something to eat?" She curled a little smile at the spark of interest in Shay's eyes. "I can't unscramble security video feeds, but I *can* scramble eggs. Are there some in the kitchen?"

Shay's forehead crunched, giving his face a uniquely boyish light. Brynn half expected him to rub the "sleep" from his eyes with a knuckle. "Yeah," he said softly. "I guess we do. I mean, we usually do. Zo goes to one of those farmer's markets on Tuesdays and Thursdays. She likes to get tomatoes and carrots and onions...and apples." His face contorted again. "Yeah. Apples. She loves those. Don't touch the apples, okay? She'll want one when she gets home."

It was a line worth waiting for. *When she gets home.* If he believed Zoe would survive this, then Brynn would too. If things like psychic connection really existed, she was certain Shay and Zo shared such a bond. Their love was palpable when they were in the same room, infusing everyone around with its magic. Brynn didn't harbor the illusion of finding such a thing for herself one day; cosmic connection required an emotional bridge she just didn't have anymore—but she could sure as hell jump on Shay's train and use *his* bridge this once.

She made sure he got the point by tightening her fingers around his.

Damn.

Beneath her grip, his skin was icy—or maybe her impression was skewed by Rebel's nearness. The man was a walking furnace. No wonder his eyes were always intense as blue flames and his nearness felt like a rush from the oven on a frosty morning.

And there she was, doing it again. Mooning over her personal fantasy pirate when there was a crisis to focus on—when the dearest friend she'd ever had was God-knew-where.

Zoe. Oh God, girlfriend. Hang on!

"Got it." She forced a small smile along with the reassurance to Shay. "No apples will be harmed in the making of Brynn's famous scrapple."

Shay laughed again—but this time, to her shock, seemed to mean it. "No, no, no. *Zoe* makes the best scrapple."

Brynn squeezed him one more time before rising with a tease of a glower. "We can settle it with a little friendly competition when she's back."

"Yeah." His laughter faded all too quickly. "When she's back."

Brynn swallowed down more rocks. They landed in the aching valley of her chest. Shay Bommer had been a warrior, a fighter, a secret operative, and a Spec Ops wonder, likely ordered to summon some crazy-ass courage for all those battles and missions—but none compared to the bravery demanded of him right now. Brynn had a sudden yearning to drop back down and hug him in encouragement.

Remarkably, Rebel beat her to the punch.

She looked on, wonderment growing, as Rebel embraced his friend with gruff ferocity. "You're going to get through this, Shay," he said. "You *and* Zoe. You hear me?"

Brynn giggled as Shay muttered, "Yeah, yeah. Fuck you too."

She turned to head into the kitchen but was stopped short as Rhett and El bounded back into the room.

"Got 'em!" El pumped a fist into the air.

"Thanks to I-Man." Rhett nodded toward Shay. "Sometimes it takes just a nibble of intel. You gave us the right bite, man."

El bounced forward again, face full of excitement. "After we determined the most likely route those assholes would take to Henderson Executive, factoring in traffic on Highway 15 and their need for *laying low* as much as possible, Rhett got onto the city's mesh network and searched for cameras that had any glitches in their feeds over the last eight hours."

Rhett set his laptop on the ledge between the living room and the entry foyer. A digital map of the city filled the screen, emblazoned with a glowing green path between the Paradise-area restaurant where Shay and Zoe had eaten and the tarmac of the Henderson Executive Airport. "They might as well have dribbled paint behind them," he remarked.

Garrett lived up to his call-sign by eyeing the monitor like a wary hawk. "Or maybe they left the digital breadcrumbs on purpose, to throw us off?"

"Excellent question." El nodded. "One *we* also asked"— she paused as Rhett clicked his tracking ball, bringing up a new image—"until we found this."

The buoyancy drained from her tone. The next second, everyone understood why. Brynn's gasp was smothered by the guys' F-bombs as a security-camera feed appeared, time clock in the corner, along with the words *Tarmac Two*. The footage wasn't so grainy to prevent everyone from recognizing an unconscious Zoe, her baby bump evident at the front of her tiny form, being carefully dragged from the back of the van by a pair of muscle-heads. The second they transferred her onto a rolling gurney, they stepped back and let a third man take over. Clad in dark dress pants and a crisp white dress shirt, he moved swiftly over Zoe, taking her vitals—and possessively clutching her round stomach.

CHAPTER TWO

Shay lunged at the laptop. Garrett and Rebel held him back. Nobody else said a thing, watching like they were subjected to a silent horror show. Though Zoe and the mystery man were fully clothed, it was torture to watch that stranger grope her as if the unborn child were his.

Brynn's teeth grated like nails on a chalkboard. If the footage made *her* feel like this, no wonder Shay had turned into a powder keg.

The bearded man stepped back and adjusted his glasses, nodding in satisfaction. The new angle allowed a better view of his features. He had close-cropped dark hair, a well-manicured beard, and gangly limbs, which added to the creepy vibe he gave off with every movement. He reminded Brynn of some rare spider, skinny but lethal.

At least Doc Man's distance from Zoe served to calm Shay by a fraction—until the man motioned to one of the henchmen, curling fingers in like a tarantula. The guard stepped forward and locked Zoe to the gurney with thick leather straps...

Officially morphing Shay from man to beast.

"Cocksucker!" His eyes bulged, his neck strained, and his body lurched, a bull at full attack. He seized the laptop and swung it over his head, preparing to hurl it across the room, but Rebel leapt and swept the device away in just enough time. His reward was an elbow in the chest, Shay's blow hurling him against the wall with a sickening crash. Brynn choked, barely controlling the urge to race to him, but Zeke and Kell had entered the fray, so she didn't dare. The pair grunted, fighting to restrain Shay from his own grief and fury.

"Cocksucker!" he bellowed again. "You perverted, pathetic, depraved dick of a cocksucker!" He snarled, kicked, writhed, and even bit Zeke's arm. Brynn winced, though Z barely flinched. Most importantly, he didn't relent his grip any more than Garrett or Kellan—a good thing, since Shay's wrath climbed higher by the second. "I should have killed you when I had the chance. I should have listened to my gut when it told me to drive that dagger through your neck, Royce. I should have listened. I should have *listened*!"

Rebel handed off the laptop to Rhett, the action as poetic as a pair of relay runners passing a baton, without wavering his stare from Shay. "Wait. You know that guy, Bommer?"

The question bordered on redundant. The four-way wrestling match clearly wasn't fun for anyone, especially Shay—though processing Rebel's words was the douse of logic he needed to tether at least part of the beast. Shay went limp before surrendering to a long groan.

"Nyles Royce." He seethed both syllables. "He's one of Adler's 'team,' though I'm pretty sure he snatched the Doc Wonder wear off of Costume-Crazy dot com. If that monster is a real doctor, I'm the Shah of Persia." He stopped, forcing down hard breaths. "The bastard knows his knives, though— and just how to use them."

With eyes closed, he ran a hand up under his shirt, lifting the fabric as he went. There was no way to miss the ugly row of scars beneath his trembling fingers. One, two, three... Brynn shut her own eyes after he reached six, remembering the night Zoe had tearfully told El and her about the cuts...which marred every part of his body.

"One day, he got careless. Left my arm unlocked while turning to clean off one of his blades—so I took the biggest one I could find on the tray." He let out a breath in stumbling spurts. "I yanked the bastard down. Had his face against my stomach. I could have slit his filthy throat, making him eat my balls as I did it. But I didn't. God*damn*it, I didn't!"

Another silence wrapped around the room.

"Fuck," Zeke finally growled.

"One way of putting it." Kellan wrapped a hand around Shay's shoulder. "It's all behind you now, brother."

Shay whipped his head around. If glares could turn into real fire, Kell would've been charcoal. "But it's not behind *her*." His raw rasp ripped the air. "It's *not* behind her. And Royce... likes to play with his food. A lot. He...gets off on it." He moaned and whirled back as if to add to the crater collection in the wall. Instead, he braced both fists to it, dropping his head between his shoulders. "His 'sessions' with me... Many times, we weren't alone. He'd call in a woman. Sibelle. Long red hair. He demanded she arrive with her hair down, wearing nothing else. He'd cut out his 'sample' from me and then fuck her. Wouldn't give me the painkiller until he was done with her. Sometimes not even then. He'd want another sample. Would watch me scream while he stuck his dick into her again. Then again. Over and over..."

"Shit." El sobbed it before rushing toward Shay but was stopped by Zeke, who shook his dark-haired head. Wisely, El conceded. When a soldier sensed a comrade needed their space, they were usually right.

"What's he going to do to her?" Shay grated. "What's that worm going to do to my tiny dancer and our child?" He withdrew his hand, only to let his bruised knuckles slide down the wall. "Let it be me again." His prayer bled out his soul for them even more. "Please. *Please.* Let it be me again. I won't even scream this time. I'll let them slice and dice all they want... for the rest of my fucking life...whatever they want...as long as it's not my beautiful girl...and my perfect, innocent baby..."

Rhett, now the closest one to him, pulled in a long breath. Without questioning how, Brynn discerned his intent as if it were her own and stepped over to take the laptop before he hauled Shay into a tight hug. Brynn clutched the laptop to her chest as if it could prevent a single tear from sliding down her cheeks. Still, she didn't move. Stood and lent Rhett the support he needed to pull his friend through the bleak, hard moment.

He smiled at her in thanks.

She smiled back.

Oh, *hell.*

Long story short: he stole her breath.

Forget about the brilliance of his smile, the fortitude of his jaw, and the twinkle in his dark eyes. Right now, his resplendence had everything to do with the energy he radiated. Tenderness and concern flowed from him, securing Shay in the invisible bond that only another man of valor could comprehend. It didn't matter that they served on different teams across the world from each other. Evil was evil—and right now, it only mattered that evil had gotten past the gates and then dragged two innocents into its shadows. Wrong move, if Rhett Lange or *any* of the guys in this room had anything to say about it.

And she wondered why men like this turned her self-restraint to mush? Maybe it had something to do with *this* shit, right here. Their shared character, honor, purpose.

Their understanding of the price their country asks of them. The men who slogged through the hard stuff, who forged the difficult decisions and then supported their brothers-in-arms when the boots were on the other feet, without conditions, definitions, or limits.

She and Enya used to have each other's back like that. Through Dad's desertion and Mom's withdrawal, through junior and then senior high, through college and first jobs and first loves, they'd hung in there together. Loving without question...

Until Enya pledged her submission to a Dom.

And lost the rest of herself in the deal too.

Crying over that train won't bring it back to the station. Don't be stupid.

Another stupid move: picturing what it would be like as the woman of one of these guys. To have all that devotion and passion showered on *her*...

Yep. Stupid.

Absurd. Impossible.

"Hey." Rhett gave Shay an affectionate shake. "We're going to get her back, man. You hear me?"

Shay dipped a hesitant nod. "Okay. *Okay.*"

"Good. But we still need your help." He tapped on Shay's forehead. "*This* gray matter, all the way in *this* game. Got it?"

"Yeah, man. Got it." Shay clawed a hand through his wavy russet hair. Stared at the room's opposite wall, only this time in remembrance instead of remorse. "Since Royce is involved, we have to assume he's answering to Adler, since Stock and Newport are out of the picture."

Everyone tensed—and rightly so. Cameron Stock and Kirk Newport had been Adler's allies after the government caught wind of Adler's unorthodox methods and yanked funding for the Big Idea lab—at least until the guys' rescue raid for Shay, in which Newport was apprehended. A court martial and prison sentence had followed. Stock had eluded capture for a few months longer, but Dan—indulging a personal vendetta that also wasn't too popular on Brynn's "quirky boyfriend traits" list—had found him in Mexico, bringing him to Zoe and Shay's wedding as what had to be the world's most bizarre wedding gift.

Kellan hitched a hip against the easy chair. "So that rules out Area Fifty-One as their destination."

Shay commented on that with a dark growl. Again, nobody faulted him. Newport had abused his military clout to get Adler a lab in a clandestine bunker inside the famous military base on the outskirts of Vegas, where Adler had turned the middle of the Nevada desert into the Island of Dr. Moreau— atrocities Shay had witnessed before helping destroy the lab. The experience had foreshadowed his own fate at Adler's hands.

"So they took her to the old facilities in DC?" Rhett ventured.

"Them." Arteries pulsed in Shay's arms as he fisted both hands. "Where they took *them*, damn it."

Wisely, Rhett withheld from responding.

Zeke lumbered forward, swarthy face focused. "When we were in Myanmar last week, Franzen mentioned that the DC warehouse hasn't been touched since the raid. It's still a possibility, though my gut says no. Homer baby is wily enough to know we'd consider it. He also knows we'd be able to request boots from Fort McNair faster than he could take a shit and Charmin-shine his ass. By the time he flushed, we'd have the building peeled open like a can of stewed tomatoes."

"Way to kill my appetite, Z—but yeah." Garrett sidled next to his friend but kept gazing at Shay. "There has to be another choice."

Everyone let out a collective breath when Shay not only nodded but did so with assurance. "Yeah. There is."

"And?" Zeke prompted.

"Austin."

"Austin?" Garrett scowled. "As in...Texas?"

Shay nodded again. "At the outskirts of town. The site of the old Verge Pharma building, or close to it. I learned the whole story last year, when Colton let us hide in the suite at the Vdara when everyone on the planet was looking for me."

Brynn couldn't help one small smile. Oh, how she remembered that week of holing up at the Vdara. It'd seemed like a luxury staycation, except for the times they were reminded that every law enforcement agency in the city—plus Stock, Newport, and Adler—were out to capture Shay any way they could. She didn't doubt that all the danger fed her attraction to Dan, the G-man just as commanding as his soldier friends—and mind-bendingly gorgeous to boot. The feeling had been heady and heart-stopping...

And temporary.

But, as she'd come to learn over the last few months, not worthless. Despite the heartache of the relationship's end, everything about her journey with Dan had brought her to who she was now. Clearer about why she'd made that mistake. More resolved to never make it again.

That determination prompted her head up again. "Learned it from who?" she asked Shay. "You and Dan were pretty picky about the suite's guest list." The two of them had been so bossy about the issue, she and El had nicknamed them "the old ladies." Zoe, already deep into the "yes, Sir" and "no, Sir" thing with Shay, hadn't joined the fun. While their dynamic wasn't nearly as intense as the shit Enya had gotten into with her Dom, it had still made Brynn giggle—and mightily razz her friend at every chance she got.

Get back here alive, Zo, and I'll never tease you again. I'll be too busy thanking God for you.

"Ghid Preston," Shay answered her. "You and Ry were watching a movie in the other room."

Zeke grunted. "Ghid. Yeah. Good man."

"He filled in some blanks for Tait and me," Shay offered, "about why our mother fell off the grid after the Big Idea project was discontinued. He told us about a site outside of Austin, supposedly the home of Verge Pharmaceuticals—but that was only what the building said on the outside. Inside, it housed Adler's new lab facilities. They abandoned the building after Newport got them cleared to move to Area Fifty-One."

As he spoke, El grabbed the laptop back, snapped it open, and clacked at the keys like a teenager in chat mode. "Got it," she announced ten seconds later. "Right here."

She turned the device so everyone could see the screen, consumed by images of a building that had, at one time, likely been an architectural showpiece. In the pictures El showed, the giant glass-and-chrome building was closed off by chain-link fences and was rocking the "overgrown decay" look. Rain had streaked the dirt from the roof down over the walls, and tall weeds rose up from the ground to meet the stains.

El scrolled to some links on the side of the page. "Looks like it's still registered to Verge."

"Only a two-hour plane trip from here," Kell filled in, "as

opposed to the five hours required for DC."

"Good point." For a second, Shay's face didn't look so ravaged.

"Feels like our best bet," Zeke concurred.

Rhett studied the screen more closely. "Especially because this complex isn't as helpless as it looks."

Rebel stepped in. "You're right," he murmured. "The weeds on the fence have only grown as high as this break point. They'd have overtaken the top if the wires there weren't still charged."

"And look at this." Rhett spread his fingers to expand an image. "Around the loading docks, in the back."

Rebel shifted closer, practically pressing his cheek to his buddy's for the better view. Nobody in the room flinched— Brynn imagined they all operated under close quarters when on missions—though she wondered if anyone picked up the new strain in Rhett because of it.

"That dust has been scuffed recently," Rebel murmured. "A lot of it, too."

"And there." Rhett pointed at the screen again. "Fresh tire marks?"

"Or some huge fucking slugs looking for a little shelter," Rebel countered.

"It's Texas," Zeke inserted. "You never know what Mother Nature's going to allow."

"No shit." The mutter was nearly indiscernible, issued from Rebel's thinned lips as he stepped away from Rhett— though Brynn wondered if he'd traversed a lot farther than that in his mind.

No matter what, the last minute had exposed a couple of truths to her. One, the waters of both Rebel Stafford and Rhett

Lange ran deeper than the world saw—and maybe, as the team's notorious rule breakers, that was how they liked it. Two, she shouldn't be so curious about grabbing her psychological scuba gear for those waters—especially not now.

No. Not ever.

What the hell had gotten into her about both of them, anyway? *Stay on the shore, girlfriend. Those waters are laced with your personal arsenic. Men like them are death sentences to your heart and spirit.*

If only Zoe were here to lend her willpower.

If only Zoe were here, period.

Rhett's comment sliced into her rumination. "There's some very fancy security hardware here too. The picture is fuzzy, so I can't catalogue it." He shook his head, making the red tips of his hair dance beneath the light. "This is going to take recon. Probably from the inside."

"Recon?" Rebel folded his arms and growled. "From the *inside*? Right. Because we have that kind of time?"

Rhett grunted. "So you vote for just blowing the lid off the place?"

"Sounds like a plan to me," Zeke drawled.

"Right." Garrett snorted. "That's a fine plan—unless Adler's fun little fairies have been hard at work building in some cute booby traps for wandering C-4 enthusiasts. Just to make things more interesting, yeah?"

Zeke narrowed his eyes. "You've been watching too many James Bond movies."

"And you've been to too many CrossFit sessions." Garrett caught enough of Rhett's commiserating glance to go on. "The ability to bench-press a tractor tire doesn't do you shit beneath a mountain of rubble or a lungful of sarin gas."

Rebel glowered back into pirate mode. "Better the guy who tried than the guy who stood around *strategizing* with his dick in his hand."

"So you're all dead," Rhett snapped, "and Zoe and her baby are still turned into Adler's human sushi."

That took care of any remaining stomach flips—and turned into Brynn's bravado for whacking the man's shoulder. "There's a word in the dictionary called *tact*, bozo. Look it up. And *you*"—she stabbed two fingers into Rebel's chest, cutting short his gloating snicker—"aren't any better."

Rebel glowered. "Huh?"

"Are you really licensed to play with explosives? Who do I write a letter to about that?"

Shay shoved from the wall and barreled toward them. "This bullshit's getting us nowhere. If I have to tear down that building brick by brick, I'll do it."

Zeke hooked him to a halt. "Negative." He shrugged in reply to Shay's snarl. "That's exactly what Adler's anticipating, not to mention your fun friend Nyles. Sorry, I-Man. If Zoe's their holy grail, you're their golden Arthur. On top of that, you've barely slept or eaten, not to mention the emotions that are fucking your game to shit."

"And *yours* wasn't when you went after Mua for taking Rayna as revenge for when you put his brother away?"

"I was way clearer than you." Z jerked up his chin and firmed his jaw. "I was also a lot less valuable to Mua than you are to Adler."

"And Mua was a moron," Garrett inserted.

Shay fumed into silence. Brynn winced again in sympathy. The guy had no other option. Homer Adler and "moron" didn't belong in the same sentence. The man was brilliant—to the point of daunting.

But while Brynn had sworn off soldier studs like these as lovers, she knew their fiber as men. "Daunting" was part of their job description, along with terms like "impossible," "risky," and "what-the-fuck-are-you-thinking." She could practically see the gears churning in their heads already about what they were going to do for Shay.

And Zoe.

As if the conviction of her conclusion drew him forward, Rebel moved to the middle of the room. But that was where things got weird. He didn't stomp forward; he sauntered. Like a gentleman pirate strolling the decks in the sun, he clasped his hands behind his back while glancing at Rhett.

"Hey, Double-Oh?"

"Yeah?"

"Weren't we about to hit up Franz for those two weeks of leave?"

Rhett closed the laptop with a knowing grin. "Do believe we were."

"Seems a good time to make that happen."

He grinned wider. Rhett mirrored the look.

"The mavericks haven't had an adventure in a long, long time."

"God help us all," Zeke muttered.

"Sending that the wrong direction, buddy." Garrett jabbed hands into his pockets. "With those two, we'll be posting bail money to hell." When he pulled a hand back out, a child's pacifier dangled from his fingers. His eyes softened, undoubtedly succumbing to a vision of his nearly two-year-old son, Racer.

"As long as they take care of recon on Texas first, I don't

give a shit."

"Amen, brothah." Kellan lifted his hand, wiggling a confident Hang Ten. "And while you guys are checking out shit in the land of longhorns, I can cross the DC warehouse off the list. Wouldn't hurt to check out LA, too. If Adler formed relationships with any of Stock's show biz buddies, he might be going that route, as well."

Z bumped a fist in his direction. "Good thinking. What better place to hide someone than the land of ultimate illusion?" His head jerked, a thought clearly piercing it. "You have any lines on where to find a discreet pilot?"

Kellan curled a wolfish grin. "Sam Mackenna just got into town."

Z chortled. "Mackenna! They really let that ape leave Scotland?"

"All six-foot-whatever of him." Kellan chuckled. "He's here for some cross-training between the air forces, only they've been delayed due to some bullshit red tape. He's sitting on his hands over at Nellis, going stir-crazy. Seriously, you'd think he'd been forced to hole up in a cave for years or something."

"Call him. Right away."

"Done."

Zeke cocked a wry look at Garrett. "I'm pretty sure Franz won't have a problem with our request for some leave, either."

"Under the circumstances?" Garrett returned. "No. But adding in the can of whoop-ass we unleashed on those drug traffickers last week *and* the fact that he's in training now?"

Z snorted ruefully. "Why training gives that guy a nonstop boner, I'll never understand."

"Don't bother to try," Kell interjected. "Just be grateful."

"Agreed, Slash-tastic. Agreed." Zeke's resilient tone reflected a newly buoyant mood among the guys—even Shay, who stood without the help of the wall or sofa for the first time in hours. "We'll put together the mission command center right in the next room so you can monitor everything that's going on, I-Man."

Shay growled. "If they find Zo, *monitoring* won't be all I do, asshole."

"Bridge to cross later." Garrett clapped a hand over the big man's shoulder.

El stepped forward again. "I can be here a lot too. Help out in any way you guys need with the tech."

Brynn frowned at her. "You're in *two* shows right now."

"One's dark for two weeks," El countered. "And they can grab someone to cover for me at *Papillon*. Thank God the Braneff Brothers believe in huge show casts."

"Outstanding." Rebel smacked his palms together. "And I've got a guy who can hook up Double-Oh and me into a place just outside Austin."

Rhett jogged up a brow. "Of course you do." He traded a look with his friend that solidified Brynn's earlier assessment. Deep waters. Both of them. *A lot* of them traversed together.

Which meant they didn't need company.

But some moments in life were just dominated by other forces. Maybe divine ones. That was the excuse she went with as a string of insane words spilled off her lips.

"And I can help you two with that part."

Both men looked up. The pirate and the Viking stared at her, scrutinizing with two distinct shades of deep blue that dared a girl to get lost in them. What an ideal match for the rabbit hole she'd surely just flung herself into.

Rhett's ruddy brows were the first to crunch. "With what part, peach?"

Okay, forget being entranced by his eyes. *Peach?* Had he really gone there? It seemed so—and in one syllable turned a dorky endearment into an all-hail for the deepest tissues of her sex. She stood there with the wet panties as proof, desperately praying she effectively hid the sexual cataclysm that had just struck.

Maybe going to Texas with him wasn't such a keen plan after all.

"El, Garrett, and Zeke have things handled here. Kellan's scoping out DC and Hollywood. So why don't I help you two in Texas?"

So exactly *why* was she pushing the point again?

"Please. I need to help find her too."

There it was.

It sure as hell didn't come easy. She wasn't wired to beg for anything in her life. Only when the moment really called for it did she flip open the circuit box and consciously decide to rewire her nature. But if any cause was worth it—if any*one* was worth it—Zoe Chestain-Bommer was that person. Brynna had a nonexistent father, a mother who might as well have been, and a sister who lived in fantasyland most days. Ryder, El, and Zoe were her only real family now. She'd be damned to stand by and just watch a monster rip one of them away.

"Please," she repeated, "I have to do what I can. You have to let me help get Zoe back—somehow!"

CHAPTER THREE

"Are you insane?"

Rebel might as well have thrown tacks at her instead of words. But the regret didn't stop his dick from *its* primal need, twitching against his camos after two seconds of impact from her huge, pleading eyes.

Her eyes.

Fuck.

From the moment he and Rhett had arrived to the sight of her on the couch with a desolate Shay, he'd prayed her gaze wouldn't be as huge and stunning and mesmerizing as he remembered—that he'd overly embellished things since seeing her at Shay and Zoe's wedding last August. He'd deliberately steered clear of her that day, knowing she was still hot and heavy with Dan Colton. The less he was around her, the easier it'd be to ignore how breathtaking she'd be once her turn at the altar came—as Colton's bride. Dan wasn't a stupid guy. He was probably just being polite about things, waiting for Shay and Zoe to have their special day before announcing he and Brynna would be celebrating theirs.

Or so Reb had thought.

Colton had been a dumb shit after all. Had let a treasure like her slip through his fingers.

But now, Rebel Masterston Stafford was going to be just as big a *couillon*.

Uh-uh.

This was *not* the same.

He wasn't letting her go as a friend and lover. He was simply informing the insane beauty that as sweet as it was, her noble gesture wasn't going to end up like some gal-pals retreat. No champagne breakfasts and pony rides, even if they did find Zoe.

And that was a big fucking *if.*

They were, in all meanings of the word except a few—like having the government's official blessing and even a shred of advanced intel—embarking on a covert operation. That meant risk. Lots of it. And danger. Lots of *it.* And if combining the two, the very real possibility that at least one of them wouldn't leave Texas alive.

If that shit went down for either Rhett or him, procedures were easy. He and Double-Oh had bent or broken the rules so many times, they'd memorized each other's wishes for what would happen after the formalities were taken care of, like making sure the world was told they'd been in an "accident" while on "vacation" and then notifying all the pertinent people for each other.

Ironically, the first half of those instructions was the harder part. Rhett's family was thrown to three corners of the world—his mom, dad, and brother lived in New York, London, and Shang Hai, respectively.

Then there was the issue of Reb's "pertinent people."

On paper, it all seemed easy. There was just Father, after all. But "second shack to the right, one mile into Terrebonne Swamp" wasn't an address one openly shared. Still, after a close call in Cambodia had slammed his mortality down his throat last year, he'd sucked it up and dragged Rhett on that dismal excursion. He'd barely cut the motor of their rented skiff, letting Rhett look his fill as they drifted by the place: two rooms beneath a tin roof on stilts that rose from mud-oozing duckweed, mosquitoes, and a shitload of bitter memories. He hadn't offered to take Rhett inside. Nor had Rhett asked for it.

Reb had been grateful for the tact but braced for the questions to come later. They'd never come. Rhett had simply known, in ways as mysterious as the bayou they'd just journeyed from, that parts of Rebel would always be like the mossy shadows of the place. Left behind and forgotten.

Things with Rhett had always been like that. Intimate but accepting. Hard but easy.

Brynn Monet was *not* easy.

She was ethereal and beautiful, generous and adorable— but at the edges of her composure, in places she fought to hide, she was wild, too. He'd never bought the voodoo tales about the *rougarous* who shifted from human to wolf, or the *feu follet*, dragonflies turned into mischievous fairies, but this woman gave him pause for thought—especially now, with the craziness that had just spilled from her delectable mouth.

And continued to as well.

"Insane?" she echoed. "About wanting to help get my best friend back here safely?"

Rebel forced down a calm breath. Damn it. She wasn't making this easy, with those copper flames in her eyes and the queenly flare of her nose. "Helping is an awesome idea." Unbelievably, he kept his tone reasonable. "Just not in the middle of Texas hill country with Double-Oh and me."

Her brows formed a pair of dark-ginger arcs—the perfect invitation for him to throw back with a heavy hand on the haughty. Instead, he shifted from foot to foot, wondering why his adrenal system had kick-started a soul-deep tangle usually saved for the shittiest parts of missions. What the hell? How was she turning his senses into sawdust and his equilibrium into a goddamn teeter-totter?

"You think I just want in on the adventure, is that it?" she charged. "That I'm just one of Zo's old dancing buddies who feels *left out of the fun* and doesn't understand the risks of what you're doing?"

He had a retort for that—but damn him if the words just jammed in his fucking throat. It had to be her eyes—again. It had to be how they took on an unearthly sheen, framed by those gold-tipped lashes, pulling every piece of reasoning out of his goddamn head.

"Do you know *anything* about me, Sergeant Stafford?" She swiveled her head back, combo'ing a nod and a shake, which should've given her a bitch-poser vibe. Instead, all Rebel thought of was an Amazonian princess, down to the question of whether he should take a knee and drop a bow. "Okay, I can't help hack into a security system like El or interpret five languages like Zo, but did you know that the reason I started dancing in shows was to make money for school? That I'm only four classes away from landing my criminal psych degree? That maybe, just maybe, I can help you read these guys faster and sharper than any computer readouts or artificial analysis?"

Behind her, El jabbed a fist into the air. "Point for Monet. Go, girl."

She hitched a no-shit shrug. "He gets a minor bye on that one. How could he have known that, without stalking me?" Her quick little glance would yield her nothing but his dark, guarded stare. *Oh,* mon chou, *if you only knew how close I was...* "But you *don't* get mercy for the rest, Moonstormer."

Strangely, a laugh tripped off his lips coaxed by the

magic of his call-sign on hers. Her voice...every word out of her elegant lips reminded him of home. It was sultry and smoky, knowing but innocent—and yes, unbelievably, the balance he needed to echo her words back with authority instead of stupidity.

"The rest, Miss Monet?"

He mocked—a little—with the words. If it bothered Brynn at all, her composure didn't betray it. As best as he observed, she really believed she could help her friend by doing this—no matter what it took. Her tenacity floored him.

And terrified him.

"You know only a few definite aspects of the situation you're dealing with right now," she said, "and Nyles Royce is one of them." A lengthy breath filled her lungs and then released. "And we *know* he likes redheads, right?"

A bizarre sound echoed through his brain. He identified the deafening *whoop-whoop* from the recesses of his past, watching reruns on the TV in the laundromat on his way home from school.

Code red, captain. Warp core breach eminent.

"Uh-uh." It tumbled out of him just like the chuckle of a minute ago, beyond his understanding or control. That was just fine. She needed to hear the vehemence in it. Everyone in the room did—especially fucking Rhett, who seemed to be giving her some serious consideration. "No way," he snarled before spinning fully at his friend, forefinger extended. "No *fucking* way, man."

His exclamation worked like the start bell to a prizefight, at least to Brynna. She shot forward, hands on hips, tossing back her hair—like he needed a reminder of the strands that made her perfect Nyles Royce bait—and leveled a withering glare. "You don't think I can do it."

He fumed. "I didn't say that. Or mean it."

"The hell you didn't." Her lips were perfect ribbons, even in her fury. "So Zoe could be drafted for a mission to save Shay, but I'm not good enough for your op to save her. Is that about right, Sergeant?"

Was she fucking kidding? That wasn't *about right*. Not at all. Didn't she see? Couldn't she tell? She really had to be some Amazonian goddess, meant to be worshipped in the center of a temple, not slogging through the Texas back country with a pair of knuckle-draggers like Rhett and him, seeking out scum like Homer Adler and Nyles Royce.

"Well?" She actually tapped her foot and cocked her head. When one was a demigod, they apparently could get away with that shit.

It also meant they could deal with a dose of their own medicine. He was sure as hell down with that. "Well what?" He cocked his own head, proving she hadn't invented obstinacy on her own. "You're not coming to Texas with us, damn it."

"Because you've given me a valid reason why not?"

"Because *you've* given me a valid reason to allow it?"

"Zoe—"

"Was drafted for a mission under very unusual circumstances."

One side of her mouth quirked. "And these aren't... unusual?"

Rebel stomped closer to her. Actually loomed over her. Channeling his outlaw ancestors like this had made more than a few *men* quake, but the saucy little wench just widened her eyes and tugged that sweet mouth a little higher.

"Stop it," he said from locked teeth.

"Stop what?"

"Looking at me like that." He added, after her breathless tone fully hit his consciousness, "And sounding like that."

"Like what?" She was goading him now, but there was no defense against it. The way she worked her lips together, dragging his stare toward them. The way she pressed a little closer, letting him inhale her essence, some light flowery body spray mixed with the earthier tang of her sweat. The way she reached across the inches between them, skimming fingertips over the back of his hand. "Like I don't *have what it takes* to keep my cool around a guy like Royce?"

Behind him, Z and Garrett snickered. To his right, Kell did the same. There was no sound from Rhett—yet. He imagined the assmunch just bided his time, waiting for the ideal moment to fire off his own ridicule.

He didn't care.

All he could think about was leaning deeper in, seizing the back of Brynn Monet's gorgeous goddess head, and positioning her to receive his tongue straight down the wet heaven of her throat.

Exactly what Nyles would do to her. And worse.

"The answer's still no."

Especially now, in this special moment of a hell and all the disgusting visions that had brought it on. Especially as she quit the come-fuck-me lips thing, opting for an incensed pout that was even more kissable.

"And that's still not an acceptable answer."

Kissing fantasies be damned. He tossed those aside. Replaced them with an image of marching her back into the bedroom, shoving down her cute yoga pants, throwing her over his knee, and reddening her taut little ass—at discipline-level impact. He was so incensed, the fantasy didn't even include a happy ending for them.

Almost.

Damn. He needed to curb his fucking libido—five minutes ago.

And as the appropriate saying went, sometimes the best defense was damn good offense.

"Hmm. Criminal psych, huh?" He purposely stepped back, jogging up his chin, yielding a much better view of her incredible swan's neck, blending into gracefully sweeping shoulders. *Winning choice, asswipe. Now keep your focus on the goddamn goal. Offense.* "So...this is what they teach in those courses? To act like a seven-year-old, refusing to accept answers besides the one you want, even if issued from the senior officer on your case?"

She paused before answering. Just long enough to make him worry.

"So it *is* my case now?"

Even Rhett couldn't help but join in the laughs at that one. Rebel braced hands to his hips and bolted his stare into hers—satisfied that he at least brought on her blush. *You want to play with the Moonstormer, lady? Then let's play.* He let his wildest interpretations of that run across his mind and his gaze. Though Brynn couldn't see the details, she at least comprehended the intent—every naughty, nasty detail of it.

Her blush darkened.

His smirk widened.

You like that, ma petite chatte? The innuendo of it, while stamping his cock with pain, filled his will with confidence.

"This isn't a decision I like making, Brynna." He told it like the truth it was. "But we're all going to be under a lot of pressure—"

"I can handle pressure."

El tapped a finger on the air. "That girl can handle the pressure!"

Brynn lifted her chin.

Rebel didn't make a secret of his frown.

"You won't be coddled."

She glared. Insulted? "I don't do coddled."

El lifted another finger. "She hates being coddled."

Rhett huffed. Snarled. Pressed over her again, nearly hunching his shoulders, feeling like a goddamn ape. The little fool only stared back with eyes full of Olympus's own lightning. *Fuck.* The only thing that seemed to faze her was the unspoken promise of spankings. *A lot* of spankings.

And now, every time his eyes closed, the only way he kept envisioning her.

And wouldn't *that* be a dandy way to start a mission with her?

You're not starting anything with her, you moron!

The charge stabbed into him enough to drive him backward, gaining the necessary distance from her for rational thought. Or so he assumed. Now standing next to Double-Oh again, he grabbed his friend by the elbow and then jerked a nod over the path he'd just come, silently enlisting his friend to back him the hell up with their cute but crazy resident redhead.

Wasn't happening.

Rhett flung a stare like *he'd* chugged the bloody Kool-Aid, confusion twisting his all-too-pretty features. "Reb, I've always got your back, man...but what's this about?"

His jaw didn't drop often. He saved that special reaction for times just like this. "Are you fucking joking?"

"Are *you*?"

He forced his jaw back up, closing it on grinding teeth. Actually took his time about it, just in case Rhett wanted to let him in on the psych-out. "She has no fucking field experience!"

Rhett released an enduring sigh. "Not a stitch. But she *does* have a point. Neither did Zoe. But without her, Shay might still be the filet of the day inside that DC ware—"

Too late, the idiot realized what kind of a red cape that'd throw in front of the bull they were still barely calling Shay. Sure enough, Bommer swung fully around and kicked out, flipping the couch all the way over onto its side, then left the room by stomping up and over the destroyed furniture—

Not before burying one more fist in the wall.

Rebel expelled a hard breath. He admitted—very secretly—to a wash of confusion at Shay's torment. To have that kind of love for a woman...for *anyone*... What must it be like? He'd been alive for close to thirty years and was damn sure he'd never felt anything close to it or ever would. He'd never even missed it either. And wasn't *that* just poetic? The hell of his childhood had simply replaced its curse in his adulthood. Deeper scars were easier to cover. They were nothing like the pain he watched slithering up every inch of I-Man's back, sinking fangs deeper with every step Shay took through the dining room, to finally escape outside. Nothing like the clawed, desperate hand the man drove through his hair as dawn peeked over the crags of Red Rock Canyon, the sky's cheerful glow like a full-blown mockery.

No more confusion. The answer blared clear as the emerging light of the day. Loving anyone like that wasn't just an ability he didn't have—it was a burden he didn't want. Ever.

That did him no good with the problem of Brynna Monet.

And her goddess's magic.

And her wild-ass notions about what "helping" a friend entailed.

And the fact that she now walked over with an arm hooked beneath Rhett's—apparently enlisting *him* on her side too.

"What the fuck?" He glowered at Double-Oh as they stepped over. "I'm distracted for a second by I-Man hurling couches across the room, and you're now on her side?"

Rhett flashed his best blasé smirk. *Asswipe.* It was the same look he used to charm women right out of their panties, everywhere they went—but the idea of Brynn's lacy bits in Double-Oh's pocket made him want to puke.

"Just so we're all straight, I've always been on her side."

Rhett let him have it eye-to-eye without a chaser of wimp, but if the guy thought that got him off any easier, he was vastly mistaken.

"We're *not* all straight," Rebel snarled. "This mission—"

"Mission?" his friend rejoined. "I haven't heard anything about a *mission.* Last I knew, we were headed for some nice, no-stress down time out in Texas—especially if we have some extra support along in the way of getting on with the locals."

A few layers of his tooth enamel disappeared as he bit down. "You're seriously going with that, huh?"

Rhett didn't even give that a shrug of reply. "Brynn's come up with a good idea for mitigating your concerns about the situation."

He slid a wry look toward the sweet-smiling woman. "Is that so?" The big bad wolf gig wasn't gaining him traction. Maybe smooth panther was the way to go. Her continued geniality was definitely encouraging.

"You object to my inexperience, my unpreparedness, and

my...innocence." From the last, she visibly held back a giggle. "Is that all correct, Sergeant?"

Rebel thought fast, attempting to examine her answer from all angles. What was her end game? *Can't con a con artist,* cher. *I learned at the skirts of the best.*

"Yes." He firmed his stance. "That's correct. More or less."

"So what if I put your fears to rest—with a personal test?"

"What do you mean?"

She stepped away from Rhett and tilted a look of open challenge. "Why don't you step outside and find out?"

He let his laugh spurt out. Gave her—*and* the smirking baboon next to her—a look that meant only one thing. *Are you fucking kidding me?* "You're asking me to 'step outside' with you, Miss Monet?"

She twitched her head a little. Flipped her hair back again, only to gather the thick, waist-length glory into one hand and secure it into a ponytail. "Well, isn't that how you *boys* like to settle things, Sergeant Stafford?"

He opened his mouth. Nothing came out. What the hell kind of response was good for something like *that*?

Rhett didn't wait for him to decide. With a snort that became a smirk, he turned for the slider that led out to the backyard, tossing over his shoulder in the process, "This is going to be *so* good."

★ ★ ★ ★ ★

Eight hours later, the shithead wasn't any more tired of that annoying-as-fuck jam—demonstrated by the bellows of laughter from the tall ginger soldier waiting on the tarmac outside the private charter terminal at McCarran for him. RAF

Commander Sam Mackenna was a hardworking guy who got along with everyone he met, but in the years Reb had known the man, his laughter could never be qualified as bellowing—until now.

Well, wasn't that fucking special? Especially when a glance at his watch instantly narrowed down the list of who could be calling Mackenna at exactly this moment.

Take rocks. Dump into gut. Grind into acid. Stir. Repeat.

"Fuck," he muttered beneath his breath, though he kept his approach to Sam at a definite don't-mess-with-me stride. Didn't do him a short curly hair of good. As he got close enough to make his glare blatantly clear, Sam covered his mouth and dedicated himself to a very loud, very fake cough.

"Desert air drying you out, Braw Boy?" He growled both syllables of Sam's call-sign, a reference to the Gaelic slang for the rugged face most women couldn't resist. If the emphasis didn't get through to Mackenna, Rebel would be more than happy to illustrate further by "prettying up" that square jaw with an upper left hook.

God, he damn near prayed for it.

After the events with Brynna in the backyard last night, he was looking for *any* reason for a good dust-up. He watched a roadrunner skitter across the runway, tempted to call the damn bird out for a few rounds—especially as Sam pocketed his phone, barely able to control the quirks of his "bonny" Scottish lips.

That did it for niceties.

He leaned over, "patting" Sam on the back so hard, a lesser man would've tumbled into the brush. Sam stayed put but really did begin to choke. Reb clucked his tongue. "Damn. That sounds bad. Maybe you should go see somebody about that, boyo."

Sam added laughs between the chokes. "Not if I'm feckin' dead, ya lice-ridden oaf."

Rebel snickered despite his tension. "Haven't lost a damn bit of your touch, Braw."

"Better with age, Moonstormer. Like good Scotch and my very talented cock."

He groaned. "Oh now, *that's* a good one. You been saving that up the entire two years we haven't seen each other?"

Sam snorted. "I really *have* had better things to do."

"Like talking to Rhett on the phone?" He peered out toward all the mirrored buildings on the horizon. Sin City was oddly pretty in the late-afternoon sun. He wished he was in a better frame of mind to enjoy it. "That was him, wasn't it?"

Sam's back was turned as he inspected the five-seat Piper Lance they were taking to Texas, in lieu of anything available at the base. But if this "off-duty escape" was truly going to fly below the radar, so were they.

They...meaning Sam, Brynn, and him.

He still couldn't believe he was agreeing to this.

"Well, we didn't talk long." Sam's tone was suddenly matter-of-fact, lending the hope that *not long* was the honest-to-fuck truth and Rhett hadn't relayed anything about the startling events in the Bommers' backyard last night. But he didn't trust the Scot's nonchalance. Not for a second. "He, errrmm, just wanted you to know he's already unloaded at the landing strip in Austin and is getting ready to drive out to the complex you secured—*after* he stops at Hopdoddy for a triple-patty special. Wasn't sure if he meant that last part or if he said it just to taunt me."

"Both," Rebel supplied, though he allowed himself a

whoosh of relief past his small smirk. "Okay, then. That all sounds good. Real good."

"Hmm."

Something about the guy's *hmm* told him the relief had been premature.

"Yeah, well...he also wanted to know if you'd gotten all the air back in your lungs, seeing as how a sweet little lass named Brynna managed to—how'd he say it?—'flatten you like a pizza' three times in a row last night?"

Yeah. Really premature.

Rebel shot over a glare—only to have it smack the Scot's massive shoulders, which shook with distinct intent. Those muscles couldn't hide much, especially if Sam was laughing his ass off at someone.

"Damn it. She took me by surprise."

"Right." Sam sniffed against his mirth. "Because after four years in the Special Forces, you're not used to that or anything."

He spun, more than happy to show the guy what *his* shoulders were up to—a demeanor he was more than happy to bear out, in every coiled inch of his stance. "You want to tell me the shifty little heathen wouldn't have duped *you*?"

Sam shrugged. "Way I heard it, there wasn't a lot of shifty. She proposed her conditions, fair and clear. Three solid chances to prove she wasn't the little wilting violet you assumed." Sam swung out from beneath the wing, tugging at rivet points as he went. Whether the man was flying a jet, a helo, or something in between, he was famous for his personal aircraft cross-check. "And you know what happens when you *assume*, my dearie."

"I'm not your goddamn dearie."

"No. *She's* meeting me in a room at Catacomb tonight."

His ginger brows waggled. "And I guarantee she'll be calling me a lot more than *dearie* by the time we're done."

Reb chuckled. Couldn't help it. Forget trying to stay immune to Mackenna's charm, even as a guy. The man was like a fucking TV weatherman. One had to smile even if he brought news of raining cats and snow flurries. Worst part was trying to visualize the guy as a Dom. He'd heard tales about the guy's legions of dripping subbies back home. Nope. The gray matter wasn't going to cooperate with *that* image right now— especially as Sam's face brightened in an even more affable smile, as he looked somewhere over Reb's shoulder.

"Ah. This must be the 'shifty little heathen' now."

The Scot was right. Their new visitor *was* Brynna, a fact conveyed before Reb even turned his head. More important senses drove it into him with startling surety. The energy on the air, tautening every hair at the back of his neck. The uptick of his heartbeat, prepping everything else in his body for the joyous conflict of being near her again. Yes, even after last night—maybe more so because of it.

The extra exhilaration in his blood didn't take long to find its way between his thighs. Happened almost instantly, in fact, as soon as he pivoted to take her in once more, making him suddenly feel like it had been eight years since last seeing her, not hours. Per his growled command after she'd turned him into human pizza for the third time, she was dressed for purpose, not prettiness: a khaki work shirt tucked into skinny jeans, leading down to sturdy hiking boots with green-and-pink-striped socks bunched around the tops. Her hair was styled just as practically, a single side braid roped over one shoulder. An Angels baseball cap covered the top of her head.

God*damn*. If anything, the attire enhanced everything

that awakened him sexually to her—even the fandom for the Halos. What woman wore attire for a trip to the wilderness but *still* looked like fucking Aphrodite?

This was definitely going down as his most uncomfortable op-that-wasn't-an-op.

Screw that. Off the books or otherwise, he was damn glad this was the first and last time he and Brynna Monet would be "working" together.

Shay strode onto the tarmac behind her, bearing her small duffel bag. He actually looked a lot better, though half moons of darkness still haunted the bottoms of his eye sockets. Though Brynn had come to an abrupt halt in her tracks, Bommer kept walking, holding out a hand to greet Sam.

"Braw Boy. Good to see you, you filthy Highlander."

"Same to you, drizzle shit." The weatherman was at it again. Insults that sounded like compliments. Shay didn't let that pineapple wither too long on the ground, though. He lobbed back a scorcher that somehow linked Sam's ass with nuclear fallout, but Rebel was beyond caring about the particulars...

Not when he noticed that Brynn still looked rooted into the blacktop. And stood more rigid than the damn light poles.

He approached her, wondering if the deer-in-the-headlights routine was just her elaborate setup for the verbal smackdown she'd surely been working on since last night— when doing the real thing to him. Three times in a row to be exact, as he'd been eloquently reminded by a very gleeful Rhett. But even as he stepped close enough to see the caramel ribbons that swirled through the chocolate of her gaze, she barely breathed, let alone spoke.

Correction. She breathed, all right. In harsh, tight spurts

that got sucked back in as fast as they escaped. At her sides, her fingertips trembled, in between tapping her thighs in a Morse code solely of her translation.

A frown pushed at his brows.

If he didn't know better, he'd peg her vibe as...afraid. Scared shitless, actually.

"Brynn?"

She jerked a glance over, though not in surprise or fear. Not at him, at least. So what the hell had her so *fugazi* she was tossing aside a perfectly good chance to rib him once more?

"Brynn?" He lightly cupped her shoulder. Her muscles were as stiff as steel poles. *"Ca vien, minette?"*

His prompt seemed to work on a little of her strange trance. She blinked fast, swallowed hard, and then pointed across the tarmac. "We're going to Texas...in that?"

"Would I have told you to meet me here otherwise?" He deliberately chose a lighter tone—out of concern, not cruelty. His sarcasm always seemed to bring out hers. Hopefully she'd grab the bait.

No chance.

"You told me we were taking an airplane."

The wobble in her voice only intensified. Hell, talk about a perfect chance for turnabout being fair play. But taking advantage of a person's fear was what terrorists did—a truth he knew through firsthand experience. Entirely too much of it.

He deepened his hold on her shoulder instead. "It's a sturdy machine, Brynna."

"It's an oversized child's toy." She yanked from his hold, hunching her shoulders in, starting to bite a nail.

His frown dug in deeper, coinciding with his confusion. "You've been on tour with shows before, right? Haven't you flown all over the country?"

"Not in glorified tin cans!"

Well, this was getting him nowhere—except, perhaps, to a clear way out of this whole situation. Sam could've been standing there in full uniform, a chest full of candy attesting to his expertise in the cockpit, but it wouldn't have made a difference to Brynn. She didn't trust anything about the Piper.

"Look. We don't have time to run through the safety record of the plane or for you to get therapy about this."

She pulled her hand from her face far enough to make it a fist. "Did I say I needed therapy?"

"Don't think you had to."

Shit. What was *that*, with the aw-shucks line straight from one of Franzen's lame musicals? Worse yet, what was this electric shock through his chest when his "sweet understanding" instantly turned her eyes into huge pools?

Wrong. This was all wrong. Her horror should've been *his* triumph. Her reticence, flipped into his golden opportunity. At the very least, he needed to be blasting fate a new asshole for withholding this loophole *last night*, when he'd gone hand-to-hand with the women and nearly ended up in traction because of it.

Now, his goddamn brain was in the sling instead—completely useless for lending his voice *any* kind of authority.

Thank fuck they were standing at the center of a tarmac and not the middle of a Catacomb playroom.

And just like that, his body didn't pay attention to any orders either. Was it expected to, when his imagination had suddenly populated Brynn Monet onto a St. Andrews cross, naked and bound and spread for him?

Goodbye, pansy musical dude.

Hello, Master Reb—the Dom who'd let entirely too much time pass since his last dungeon play session.

And now *really* needed to make sure this woman didn't get on a plane with him to fly to a ranch house on twenty acres in the middle of Texas hill country.

"Okay, so this is going to be a problem for you." *Much* better. Firm, decisive, final. "So no harm, no foul. Shay's still right over there. You can just leave with him, and—"

Her glare cut him short before her retort did. "Wouldn't *that* fix everything perfectly for you?" She huffed out a laugh, shaking her head. "Plays right into your wildest dreams, doesn't it?"

You do not want to know what my wildest dreams are made of, cher.

"My needs aren't important right now." He thinned his lips. "And neither are yours. We're wasting time bickering and biting our nails"—pointedly, he dropped his gaze to the finger she'd been tearing at—"when we should be getting clearance from the tower and getting our asses out of here."

Not a shred of Broadway Joe in that one, either. As a matter of fact, he should've been damn proud of every snarled syllable.

Then why did he feel like such a douche when her shoulders fell again...and her chin trembled, fighting back intense emotions? "I am extremely aware of our time constraints, Sergeant. There's not a second that goes by when I'm *not* aware."

Sam finally made himself useful by stepping over with perfect timing, saving them both from a surely awkward silence. "Greetings. You must be Brynna. You're famous already around here, you know."

She flashed a smile that never made it to her eyes. "Peachy. Great to meet you, errrr..."

"Sam." He picked up her hand and then bowed over it, brushing lips along her knuckles. "Commander Sam Mackenna, of Her Majesty's Royal Air Force. I'm on loan to the ruffians over at Nellis for a few weeks."

"But right now, he should be finishing his preflight inspection." Rebel all but broke in between them, disgruntled as hell to watch Mackenna turn on the courtly accent and the King Charles manners, a sure sign he was jockeying for some coo-coo-get-in-my-pants action. *No fucking way.* "Go ahead. Move along. Check the oil. Kick the tires. Lay out the peanut bags. Chop chop." He shoulder-butted the guy, hard enough to let Sam know he meant business—only to find himself pushed aside by the woman behind him, with the eyes of fear and chin of stubbornness that wrenched at his chest all over again.

"So you're flying this thing?" she asked—demanded—of Sam.

He bent over again, this time in gentlemanly deference. "Yes, ma'am."

"Good. Then don't fuck it up."

She whirled away from them both and marched toward the plane, head high and spine straight, not a trace of her terror showing from this angle. Rebel, battling to ignore what *did* show well from this view, caught up with her in time to help her step up into the plane. As he did, there was no escaping the sensations that slammed him—nor did he want to. He was... proud of her. And even more. Inspired.

The feelings weren't difficult to peg. They were part of the good stuff about being in Spec Ops, these moments where witnessing someone push past their internal walls outweighed the exhilaration of watching them scale real ones. Pride came from the honor of being part of the moment. Inspiration came from knowing that when *his* turn came for the wall leaping, he'd be able to use it as strength.

And God, did he want to remember Brynna Monet.

Every damn thing he could about her.

No sense in fighting that one anymore either. No matter what kind of flameout he'd suffer when this was over, there was no way to fight the searing lure of her now. Dan Colton's loss was absolutely his gain—and he was going to savor every last possible penny of this fortune.

But right now, nothing was about him. It was about parking his ass in the leather bucket seat next to hers. Examining the white expanse of her face, the dilated terror in her eyes, the taut coil of her hands. Reaching across her to grab the strap of her shoulder belt—a detail lost to the obvious whirl of her thoughts—and clicking it into the fastening on his side. Keeping himself turned toward her, one hand on her jiggling knee, and forcing her to take deeper breaths with the steady squeeze and release of that hand.

Finally, she seemed to get the idea. Her chest began to rise and fall with longer, calmer flows. Rebel remained silent, communicating with her simply through his touch—and his gaze. The latter couldn't be helped. Now that he had her locked in and to himself, he took greedy advantage of the chance to stare his fill. Those dark-red lashes, fanned over her cheeks with a little curl at the ends. The bright-red wisps escaping her braid, playing at the elegant slope of her neck. The contrast of her lips, the color of ripe raspberries, against her pale, pale skin.

Without notice, she blinked her eyes open. Peered at

him—and then actually cracked a fast smile. It was such a surprise, Rebel burst into a laugh.

"Not funny." Her chide had no rancor. If he pretended hard enough, he could almost imagine they were in bed together, after he'd spanked her into an orgasm and then fucked her into a couple more.

Not. Going. There.

Too late. His imagination had hammered down stakes and the tent of debauchery was on the rise.

"Of course not," he returned, all mocking smirk and teasing eyes.

"I'm serious, Rebel."

"So am I." And suddenly, he was. Even through the extended moment of thick silence between them. Even through the lift of his fingers, softly stroking those errant hairs off her neck as well. Even through the seconds he took to swallow with purpose before murmuring, "So what are we talking about here? Natural heebies about flying in a...'tin can'...or deep-seated childhood trauma I really *will* need to call the shrink about?"

She swallowed too. Leaned her head over a little, toward his hand, which he'd dipped just a little beneath the collar of her shirt. It was either do that or try to behave—in which case his gaze would've migrated toward her cleavage. Not that the work shirt showed it off well, though it was much better than her workout attire from last night. Damn sports bras. They needed to be renamed tit crushers.

"Can I pick something in between?" she replied. When he pressed his fingers to her nape in a wordless affirmation, she went on. "The last time I was in one of these, Enya and I were on vacation in Costa Rica."

"Enya?"

"My little sister. Well, not that little. Not so little that she didn't get a wild hair up her backside and sign us up for a *ziplining adventure* in the middle of nowhere. After that plane ride, I thought I'd be dying in the middle of nowhere too."

He compressed his features, hoping they spoke his commiseration. "Wish I could say I don't know how that feels." Even the world's finest pieces of military aircraft didn't make up for RPGs or missions in shitty weather conditions.

He was glad to see his reassurance sink into her—though bewildered by the rest of her reaction. With a little turn toward him, she leaned her head sideways against the cushion, as if settling in for a warm chat over tea. "Yet here you are, ready to do it again."

He couldn't help the new quirk of his lips. Well, imagine that. The smooth little psych major *did* want a heart-to-heart, disguising her question as observation. Did she know how thoroughly *he* knew this drill already? How many times he'd already had his head torn open by the base shrinks, being the guy on the team most exposed to the possibility of watching his guts blown out of his body as his last mortal sight?

But if this soothed her nerves for the flight, he'd be more than happy to oblige.

She wouldn't learn a thing he didn't want her to.

"In my line of work, you learn to live by fear or possibility," he offered. "If you want to keep serving your country and making a difference, you have to choose the latter."

There. That should give the little Freuds in her head something to snack on for a few minutes. He waited for the signs of it—the slight furrow in her brow, the tentative chew on her lip—though damn it, all she did was change the angle of her smile and reach for him too.

As she lifted her fingers, Rebel tensed. Shit. She was going for his face. *Not the goddamn face.* It wasn't that he hated it. He just didn't exactly...enjoy it. It was why he'd gotten so good at all the fun of bondage. Tie them down before the naked stuff started, meaning he controlled every inch of contact. Yeah, yeah. He'd seen the explanations on paper—mommy issues, intimacy issues, fucked-up-beyond-recognition issues—like any of that happy horseshit made them easier to deal with. Only one thing helped with that. Not indulging, period. Not allowing those special little female touches that all but sucked his soul straight to his eyes—and the pain back into his heart.

And yet...he let her.

Wanted to let her.

He flinched and tensed and grunted but sure as fuck went ahead and just let her move in, tracing one eyebrow, over the bridge of his nose, and across the next brow. Enduring—no, goddamnit, *enjoying*—the awakening of every cell beneath her questing touch.

Christ. Stop. Stop.

Don't ever stop...

She finally did.

Only to utter words that made his inner chaos even worse.

"That's what makes you a hero, Rebel Stafford."

His first temptation was to free a laugh. Correction: a bark. An angry, caustic bite of sound that would double as the bolt cutter on the lock of his control and let out the filth he didn't even reveal to the brain bakers. The reasons why he was nobody's fucking hero—least of all, hers.

He clamped back the laugh—and with it, the bark. The feat was a little tougher than usual but nothing years of practice couldn't help him achieve. When most of one's soul was off-limits to the world, it got easier to just add on to the fortress.

He spread a smile across his lips like a peanut butter ad. There. A much tastier way to approach things—especially now that Sam had climbed into the cockpit and started revving the engines. "Everyone buckled up?" the Scot called over his shoulder.

"Affirmative," Reb returned.

"Shit-shit-shit!" Brynn gasped.

Peanut butter still in place, he slid a hand into one of hers. "Hey. Just look at me, okay?" As she clamped her fingers around his, his pulse picked up. Instincts he could only call primal started to surge. As she complied with his command, the desperation in her gaze latched on to his and held on, backed by every tense muscle in her body. "Good," he praised, lifting his grin higher. "I got you, *cher*. I got you."

She attempted a nod but looked more like a broken bobblehead. As they taxied toward the runway, she flattened against her seat, her free hand grabbing the armrest near her window, knuckles bulging against her skin like marbles. "Ohhhhh, God. Oh God, oh God, oh God!"

Rebel lunged. No sense in trying to loosen her death grip on the seat, but he cupped her face, forcing her wide, wild stare in line with his again. "Hi," he murmured.

He almost chuckled when her eyes narrowed—if only for a second. "H-H-Hi."

"Remember that part about looking at me?"

"S-S-Sort of."

"It wasn't a helpful little hint, *mon chou*."

Her lips compressed. She squirmed a little. Not quite a fume but as adorable as one. "S-So...what? It was an *order*?"

Little fires burst in her eyes as she spat that. Damn. *He'd* be the one squirming in a second if she kept that up—though the ordeal would be worth it. He'd endure two full forest fires from her if it meant keeping her attention diverted from their accelerating speed and Sam's confirmation for takeoff from the tower.

He flattened a thumb across her cheek. Tugged her attention deeper with the tips of his fingers in her hair. "Would you like it to be one?"

He had no damn idea how she'd respond. A growing instinct had jabbed at his gut since interacting with her last night, even before she'd gone all bad-ass ninja on him. Until then, he'd assumed that dating a Dom as hardcore as Colton must've meant she was just as intense a submissive—but there was a defiant streak in her that all but dared a man to push at it. Maybe Dan had just been too messed up physically and emotionally to sort through that and missed his window of opportunity.

Or maybe her rebellious streak just needed another rebel to tame it.

The plane lifted off the ground. Climbed up into the sky.

Brynn's breath clutched. Hard.

He didn't give her a second to recover. With gravity his new best friend, he pressed over her, consuming her personal space. She wasn't a tiny thing like Zoe or El, but her size was... nice. *Very nice.* A stunning combination of curves and muscles, softness and strength...a womanly landscape he greedily studied now. Her jeans fit in all the right places, accentuating her gazelle-graceful legs. Even the work shirt was a thing of poetry at the moment, pulled taut across her chest due to her new position. He glimpsed her bra through a little break between the buttons. Who the fuck knew seamless beige could be so goddamn sexy? Then again, with her flawless pale skin underneath, even burlap was instant boner inspiration.

"I...I don't do orders, Sergeant."

He didn't react to that—at first. Simply evaluated her dilated gaze and slightly parted lips before letting his regard dip to the wild animal of a pulse still racing in her throat. After another long second, he slid his thumb down atop that thudding artery.

Her pulse instantly doubled.

So did his.

"So that's why you keep calling me *Sergeant*?"

She gulped, making his thumb rise and fall. And his cock bulged with new pressure.

"It's respectful."

They ascended higher. Did she notice the city getting tinier and tinier outside the window? Rebel could only account for himself. He didn't care if the landscape below suddenly turned into a nuclear holocaust zone. This woman already razed the same effect on his senses.

"*Rebel* is just as respectful. I'm not your commanding officer." He closed the gap between them, now near enough to inhale her. Soap and shampoo and that damn floral body spray once more. *Hell, yes.* If this was radiation poisoning, it was one awesome way to go.

"I know." She started to lick her lips but bit the move into submission, seeming to know just what an effect it had on him. "But Rebel doesn't feel right either."

He nodded. And actually agreed with her. Though his name was sultry music on her lips, it felt strange. Too intimate? Not intimate enough?

Wasn't like he had a decent alternative. Only one of those came to mind, and it sure as hell broke more protocols than his proper name.

That was when the Traitor roared through his head. His not-so-little buddy, doomed to live in his mind since the day Mama and Papa had taken the plunge and legally named him Rebel. The fucker sped in on his typical mental Harley, painted black and red save for the words emblazoned across the gas tank in bright yellow.

Fuck the rules.

Who was he to argue with the demon on the Harley?

He stretched his arm the rest of the way across her seat. Slid his hand off her neck in order to seal it over her fingers, still gripping the armrest like a life preserver. "Doesn't feel right," he echoed, softly but purposely. That yanked her gaze straight up again, and he opened up every spigot of sensual force to keep her locked there. "Then let's try something else."

Her mouth parted a little more. Her breaths, heated and shallow, hit his jaw at racing speed. Well, that confirmed it. His diversion was a success. She was distracted, capital fucking *D*.

Which didn't explain an ounce of his own reaction. Swimming senses. Head light as helium. Blood thick as oil. Hot, *hot* oil. He couldn't even blame the altitude. He'd flown in hundreds of planes across every corner of the globe. None of those flights had screwed him up like this.

It was her.

This woman who'd shot him into the ether from the moment he'd first laid eyes on her. Now she was beneath him, needing him...

Cranking *his* need for her...

He wondered if he could bribe Sam to veer their flight off-course by a few hundred miles. Fuck it; he wondered if they could just go to the moon. Not that he wasn't halfway there.

"Something else?" Her voice still tremored a little. From fear or arousal, he couldn't tell—and didn't want to. Like the depraved bastard he was, he liked the idea of scaring her. Even more, he liked the idea of arousing her. "Like what?"

Rebel slid his stare to her mouth. "Like *Sir*."

She gasped. For half a second. Before he stole her breath with the commanding, crashing, dominance of his mouth.

She moaned. He growled. Plunged in deeper. Took every pliant inch of her tongue with his. Sucked her in, all slick and wet, giving as much as he plundered, rejoicing in the best kiss of his goddamn life.

She let go of the armrest. Used that hand to reach for his face again.

Not this time.

He wrapped hard fingers around her wrist, forcing her arm to the cushion next to her head. "Keep it there," he snarled against her lips before dropping his hand beneath her shirt. "I want to explore. And you're going to let me."

Her eyes flared with shock. Rebel grinned. He was enjoying the crap out of this. Surprising her like this. Exposing her like this. Taking all those new arousals...and making them his.

Full justification—at least to him—for the harsher growl he let out when her eyes flickered toward the cockpit. Sam seemed thoroughly engrossed in the controls, despite how he'd leveled them off at full altitude in a crystal-blue sky.

She flicked her tongue nervously over her lips. "Sam—"

"Knows to mind his own business." To emphasize, he slipped his hand beneath her bra, pinching the perfect nipple that waited. As her eyes flew back to him, he turned on his evil grin. "I'd say he's even grateful."

"Grateful?" She made a play for outraged—at least with her tone. By the time she got around to considering a glare, she emitted a gasp instead. Could've had something to do with him scraping her erect tip with his thumbnail.

"Mmmhmm." He trailed his hand to her other breast. "Pilots appreciate it when the flight is kept peaceful."

Her breath snagged audibly. It had to be one of the sexiest sounds he'd ever heard. "I don't feel...very peaceful."

"Neither do I." He'd never meant anything more. "*You don't make me very peaceful, cher.*" He answered the question in her eyes by flowing his hand down her body, on top of her clothes, trying to memorize every inch of her curves even with that goddamn barrier. "I tried hiding it. Then I tried just avoiding the temptation altogether. You belonged to Colton... and I carried all these fantasies about touching you like this. Arousing you like this..."

"And controlling me like this?" Oh, how she fought for defiance with that one. Jerked up her chin, set her lips, rekindled the fire in her eyes. Did he dare tell her all of it only underlined her real need to him? Her true desire...to make him challenge her even deeper?

"You think I'm controlling you?"

She worked her lips against each other. "I think you're trying."

He pulled away for a second, searching the storage compartment behind them and finding exactly what he needed. With a quick flick, he had the fleece blanket spread over them both. As Brynn crunched a look of perplexity, he pushed close to her again, yanking her hand back into his beneath the soft cover.

Her gasp covered his lips as he formed her fingers around his crotch.

"You really want to know who's in control?" He let her watch his tortured swallow. "Christ, Brynn. You make me crazier by the second."

"Oh...my." She wetted her lips again. Gaped wide at him, appearing a little confused. He bit back a whoop of triumph. He had no right. This was dirty tactics. The blood of pirates and warriors ran in his blood, and his...finer attributes...matched that rugged heritage.

"That's because of you," he grated. "And I'm only half hard."

She stroked the strained denim, exploring his contours, gasping another time. "Oh, *my*."

"Want to test my point?" Her openness made him bold. He went for it, unsnapping the button and guiding her hand right in, over his swollen flesh. "Say it, Brynna. Just once. Call me Sir...and feel what you do to me."

Before she could climb back into her head and summon a protest, he kissed her again. Deeply. Thoroughly. Unrelentingly. Rolling their tongues together until they danced in unison and her sweet, perfect taste filled not only his mouth but every cell of his senses.

By the time their mouths left each other, her fingers had closed around the throbbing crown of his dick. She circled him tighter before rasping, "Sir."

He groaned. Precome roared up his shaft as his skin strained to hold the arousal that throbbed hotter, bigger. "Fuck." He pushed deeper into her grip and then ordered, "Again. Say it again."

Damn it. Her taunting little smile delivered another matchstick to his blood, tempting the flames of his lust *and* fury. "But you said only once," she sing-songed.

He inhaled hard. Again. God*damn*it. She had him in the palm of her hand—literally—yet who else could he blame for it but the desperate bastard reflected back from the ombre depths of her eyes, jaw grinding and nostrils flaring?

Maybe his estimation about her had been all wrong. Maybe the woman was born to be dominant herself. In which case, he was in a *lot* of trouble.

Nothing like a definitive litmus test to find out.

Raising his hand back up, he dove his fingers into her hair, compressing against her scalp and twisting the silken red strands...harder. Harder. Her gorgeous gaze popped wide again—for just a second. As her eyelids dropped heavily, her mouth went slack...setting free an aroused little gasp.

Oh...*yeah*.

He dipped his face over hers again. Let his breath mingle with hers again. But didn't kiss her again.

Instead, in a growl he summoned all the way from the heat consuming his balls, he commanded, "Say it again, *mon chou*. And mean it."

She licked her lips—as she looked down to his. "Or else?"

Just the barest of whispers...that grabbed his dick tighter than her fingers. Despite the torment, Rebel actually laughed and repeated, "Or *else*?"

One side of her mouth lifted. The sly little pussy cat actually thought she'd called him on his shit. "Simple question. But it's all right if you don't have an ans— *Ohhh!*"

Damn, her little yelp was cute, coming a few seconds too late to stop him from yanking down her jeans, after making short work of the button and fly. But because the fucking things were created to hug her curves, it took a second tug to slide them down far enough for the discipline he was determined to deliver. As he did that, she merely mumbled and grunted in confusion—until he swept his hand in, directly over the cotton-candy-colored boy shorts covering her crotch, and then drew back a little. A little more...

"Oh, hell n—"

He kissed the rest of it into silence as he swatted her pussy without mercy.

Brynn screamed into his mouth as he did it again, then again. Drew breath to unleash another shriek into him...

But moaned against his lips instead.

As he turned his next spank into a long, savoring caress.

Fuck. *Fuck*.

Her trembles.

Her gasps.

Her little jerks against his fingers, silently pleading for more...

Fuck. *Fuck*.

"Hey." Sam's shout from up front was edged with humor. Damn bastard had likely been waiting for the moment with calculated glee. "Everything all right back there?"

Brynn's face turned the color of her panties. Reb nipped at the crests of her cheeks, letting a shit-eating grin fly before yelling, "Yep. Fine. Okey dokey...asshole."

Sam chortled.

Brynn seethed. She bucked her hips, only to realize how that positioned her even better for his fingers. "Get your hand out of my pants, Stafford."

"Not a problem." He offered it as if she'd just asked him to pull his elbow off the armrest—while working his cock deeper into her grasp. "Ladies first. You cease and desist, and so will I."

"*I* never asked for a free grope!"

"Which is why you're still enjoying it?"

The fire in her eyes intensified. She took a second, formulating a comeback. Fatal mistake. Rebel moved faster, slipping his thumb beneath her panties, pressing in against the nerves that waited in trembling, wet readiness.

"Oh, my God!" she rasped.

"No." He brushed the word into the curve of her jaw. "Not exactly. But *Sir* will do just nicely."

She growled.

Moaned.

Seized into complete silence—as her clit vibrated beneath his touch.

Rebel lifted his head, watching her eyes roll back in her head. He angled his face over hers, unwilling to miss a single second of her descent to surrender...and then the ascent he'd bring her.

"So beautiful," he whispered to her. "*Ma minette doux. Take me higher. Surrender to me...deeper now...oui, petite chatte...oui.*" As his own senses were sucked into their sensual vortex, his lips and tongue surrendered to the language he'd first dreamed, babbled, and spoken in. The pressure in her sex drew out the need in his own, engulfing him in a haze of pulsing primal sensation, until he felt her body swooping and soaring on the same sexual currents. As she panted harder, so did he. As she edged closer to explosion, so did he. As she lost more of her mind, so did he.

Not yet.

Not...yet...

To emphasize the point, he spanked her again.

"Oh!" She breathed it more than anything, the sound husky and hot. "Shit. Ohhhh, *shit.*"

Rebel snarled low as he stroked her clit, circling steadily. "I'm so ready, *mon chou*. My cock wants to explode for you. Does your pussy want to come for me?"

"Y-Yes. Ohhhh, yes. Please!"

He kissed her, finishing with a long lick along her bottom lip. She was salty with sweat and sweet with desire. "Then say it. Just for me. The power is yours, Brynna. Say it and make us both fly. Now. Fuck! *Now!*"

Her pussy quivered faster.

Her head fell back farther.

Her lips opened on the most beautiful sound he'd ever heard.

"Sir!"

She came apart beneath his hand.

"Ohhhh! Sir! Yes!"

He came apart beneath hers.

"*Oui, minette. Oui. C'est bon. Je jouis. Je jouis...*"

The sky might have been zooming beyond the window, but his senses spun into heaven, occupied by one angel alone. White heat, blinding ecstasy, fulfillment like he'd never known, all inside this cocoon beneath one thin blanket, in one fleeting minute, with this one blazing surprise of a woman.

When he was able to process words again, he pressed in and kissed her...somehow needing to hang on to this feeling... to her.

What the fuck?

No. Uh-uh. That wasn't the way things worked. *He* wasn't the one who tried to "hang on." *Ever.* Sure, a purpose had been met. They were well into the flight now, and he doubted Brynn would care if they really were zooming along in a soda can— which meant it was time for a little sweet aftercare and a lot of emotional disconnect.

The safety of the thought pulled him away from her.

Only to gaze into the reticence already entering her gaze. Then turning back out as a blade...slicing smooth as a scalpel into his chest.

He smirked to hide the pain. Kissed her again—on the nose. "Thank you." At least he meant that part.

Brynn tilted her head, clearly confused. "Hrrrmm. I think that's my line...Sir."

He stiffened.

That still wasn't supposed to feel that good.

"Brynna...look..."

She smacked his chest, almost playfully. "Calm down, buckaroo. I was just ribbing you." She shrugged. "It was a diversion tactic, right?" She waved a hand toward the window. "And it worked. So...thank you."

While she spoke, he eased her jeans back up her hips and then offered a tissue for her sticky hand. Christ, even the act of helping her clean up fed something deep inside him, as if taking care of her was exactly what he'd been made for.

Lethal waters, Stafford.

The sharks are circling.

The worst sharks of all, too. The invisible ones...from the places he couldn't get to. The places best left hidden inside.

A warning that did him no damn good as Brynn tugged the blanket up, curled it beneath her chin, and then burrowed into the crook of his shoulder, her eyes blinking in slower and slower rhythm. "Yep," she murmured drowsily. "Very good.

Perfect plan. Nice idea, pirate hottie."

His heartbeat tripped. He didn't know whether to attest that to shock or pleasure—but why was a choice necessary?

He dragged his hand through the ends of her hair and brandished a provocative smirk. "*Pirate hottie?* Have you been digging into my pedigree, Miss Monet?"

"Hmmm? No. Just ogling your tatts. And your hair. And your ass. And maybe...a few other things."

He grinned into the top of her head. "And came up with *pirate hottie?*"

"Has a nice ring to it, *oui?*" She lifted a slow smile too, as if to complete the tease. Instead, she burrowed deeper against him. Rebel dropped a hand to her shoulder, holding her there. Funny little kitten. If he didn't know better, he'd peg her as drunk...or lost to subspace. Neither was remotely possible, though a sole truth surely rang true: the woman had enjoyed the hell out of what they'd just done.

I don't do orders, Sergeant.

If she weren't half asleep already and looking so goddamn delectable about it, he'd have laughed aloud in her face.

And I don't let subbies doze off in my arms, cher.

So today proved to be a first time for many things.

Now he just had to make sure there would never be seconds.

CHAPTER FOUR

"Thank fuck," Rhett muttered. The rumble of Rebel's rented SUV couldn't have come a moment too soon. For a guy who'd spent his childhood shuttled between New York and London, the conversation of tree frogs and cicadas was as stimulating as listening to paint dry.

On top of that, all he'd been doing for the last two hours was final tech checks, ensuring every machine and program in front of him was speaking correctly to the same on Kellan and El's end in Vegas. His brain was going to explode if he had to look at another line of security coding or wander around the ranch testing sound levels on mobile mics. Though as mission locales went, the only thing that beat this place had been their special-assignment digs in Iraq: a former sheikh's palace with fifteen bedrooms and a couple of pools.

The ranch only had one pool, but the thing came with a waterfall, swim-up bar, and private Lake Travis views along with an attached boat house—and that was before entering the main mansion, a true Texas sprawler with five bedrooms, four fireplaces, game room, recording studio, and spaceship-worthy workout space. *Damn.* Rebel may have been a man-slut, but the dude sure rocked the personal connections. In this case, his version of "I know a guy" referred to Dax Blake, a former Spec Ops operative who'd become one of the hottest country music stars in the solar system. This place comprised Dax's "Texas digs," not to be confused with his Antebellum place in

Nashville or his "vacation chalet" in La Plagne.

Blake's generosity perfectly fit their cover story of just being "some buddies and a friend" enjoying their leave in a beautiful part of the country—though as Brynn Monet climbed out of the car and gave him a cheerful wave, he wondered how he'd stick to the "friend" part of that scenario. The woman would've knocked even Blake out of his thousand-dollar boots, with that gleaming red ponytail, movie starlet lips, and an outfit that accented every luscious inch of her pinup-perfect curves. And what the fuck did *he* do about it? Jammed his hands into his back pockets, jerked his chin stupidly, and hoped like hell he covered up the dork who still lived deep inside: the guy before Sir Rhett finally surfaced, finding a safe arena for communication at last in his life.

Time to put away *those* kinds of thoughts as well. Far away.

"We made it." Brynna's cry broke into his brood, bringing needed energy to the air. Rhett cut loose with a grin as she bounced on her toes. His expression dropped when she remained next to the car, hanging back for Rebel.

What the hell?

Reb had barely been civil to her last night at the Bommers', after the triple takedown of legend. She'd barely seemed to care, only asking how fast they could get out of town and continue the search for Zoe. Now, she waited on Moon like—

Shit.

Like a subbie on a Dom.

"Okay, asshole," he growled beneath his breath. "Abort that launch right now, before you start seeing little green men too."

Luckily, no aliens of any color appeared, though the impression clung that Brynn still deferred to Reb. As Rebel yanked their luggage from the car, she turned and damn near fretted over him, despite how both bags were likely a fraction of what he humped through jungles and deserts on real missions. After Reb shirked her off with a laughing growl, she hurried up the curved paver walkway, a new smile in place for Rhett. His tensions eased further as she warmly embraced him.

Maybe he really had been alone too long. And maybe, hopefully, the two of them had actually come to a little truce during the flight down from Nevada. That had to be a good thing going forward, no matter what stupid vibes his gut threw out otherwise.

"Welcome to the shack." He grinned as Brynn giggled.

Rebel, approaching behind her, smirked from behind his Oakleys. "I'll relay that little feedback to Dax, next time I see him."

"Fuck you," Rhett jibed.

"*Boys.*" Brynn's tone joked equally, though ended in admonishment.

Course change.

"How was your flight?"

"Fine."

Was their rubber band snap answer, given in unison, really the evasion he suspected? *Note to self. No more solitary ops prep in the middle of nowhere.*

"It was fine." Rebel underlined the last word as if Rhett had disputed him. "Smooth and quick. Nothing major."

Brynn bobbed a firm nod. *My name is Brynna Monet, and I approved this message.*

What the *hell* had happened on that trip?

A little casual sleuthing was definitely in order.

"So Mackenna behaved himself, eh?"

"Affirmative," Rebel grunted, pushing forward into the house.

"Sure did." Again, Brynn rushed it out.

"Hmm." Rhett kept his tone noncommittal but his stare keen. "So...the internet meme quotes were all clean?"

She flashed a bright smile. "Every single one. Crazy, right?"

"Yeah. Crazy."

Sam didn't know any clean internet memes.

Brynn barely spared a glance for the sprawling main hall, the two-story granite fireplace, and the sweeping stone archways that laid a castle feel atop the cowboy chic. "So where's the good stuff?"

Rhett replied by flashing a look of his own—of bewilderment. This was her window to disclose her tease, if the question *was* one, but she only stared back, her stare intensified by expectancy.

"You *are* all set up, right?" she pressed. "The command center and all? Where is it? Have you connected to El yet?"

He felt his smile soften. Damn...this woman. They probably could've transported her to the foyer of the sheikh's place itself, and all she'd be concerned about was the effort to save her friend.

Brynn Monet was the real deal.

In the body of a too-good-to-be-true goddess.

Which meant the friend zone was really going to suck ass this time.

"I've been on all morning with El. We've been running tests on everything—and even had time to work on a little something else too."

He couldn't help winding a bit of mystery into the

statement, to be rewarded exactly how he'd hoped.

"Something else?" she repeated, lifting an intrigued smile.

"Awwww." Rebel hoisted the bags onto the ten-foot-long leather couch. "You baked, didn't you, honey? Please tell me it was your famous lemon bars."

"Fuck you." Rhett chuckled but fought the new twist in his belly. The joke about his abysmal kitchen skills, normally a stress reliever for them both, felt like a jab with an extra purpose today.

Brynn puckered her lips. "You want to show me sometime today, Double-Oh?"

He swept an arm toward the plank-floored hallway that led to the rest of the house. With the other, he hooked out an elbow to escort her. "Your wish, my command."

Rebel emitted a rumble while falling into step behind them. "Kiss-ass."

It was a step up from the lemon bars poke—or so he hoped.

The hallway paralleled the grounds, allowing for full enjoyment of the lake views while walking to Blake's huge office. Once in there, décor of leather, wood, and masculine comfort surrounded them. Along one wall of the room were half a dozen framed platinum records. The desk and computer systems consumed another corner, and one wall was comprised of two sliding-glass doors, opening to the terra-cotta patio Rhett had been spending a lot of time on today. He couldn't wait to show Brynna why.

"After you." He swiveled around the big rolling chair in front of the desk, beckoning her to sit. He offered the matching chair to Rebel, not missing how his friend rolled at least three inches closer to Brynn. When Reb propped an ankle to a knee, his other knee rested directly on top of Brynn's—a contact she seemed completely happy with.

What. The. Hell?

He barely wrestled away a glower. Not so successful when it came to the mental boot up his ass. He felt like one of those idiots in a cravat from some BBC period show, ready to call a "cur" out for daring to touch his virginal lady conquest. Thinking about Brynn Monet's "virginal" status was *not* a good idea. Containing his own dick around the woman was torture enough, let alone stressing about anyone else's. And "pistols or swords?" wasn't an expression that tripped easily off his lips.

No. Screw that.

Rock, paper, scissors, guys. Hand grenade beats pistol and *sword.*

Wait.

Shit.

Reb was the expert at those, too.

So he just had to start showing off *his* weapons.

He peered around, spying the item he needed on the desk behind Brynn. Leaning over without scooting around, he took an extra moment to savor his larger claim to more of her physical awareness. With his chest next to her face and his neck against her hair, it was a moment of tangible intimacy— one that, if he wasn't mistaken, affected her as potently as him.

Damn the knightly pledge. If they were alone, he would've gone for it. Tangled his free hand in her hair and tilted her head back. Gazed into her huge chocolate eyes for all the signs that she welcomed what he yearned to do: plunge his mouth over hers and then his tongue in along hers...

"Yo, pretty boy?" Rebel's prompt was a stab of impatience. "Sometime today? We don't all have time to sit and pick our zits."

"*Hey.*" Brynn jerked her knee up into his. "Be nice."

Rebel chuckled.

Huh?

It was *really* time for the Rhett Lange portion of this fucking operation.

He tugged on Brynn's chair, halting the knee fornication, before facing her toward the three huge monitors on the desk. One belonged to Blake so remained dark. A ton of coding consumed the screen next to it. He'd been double-checking the shit, ensuring their firewalls were up and the IP was routed through fifty other cities, in preparation for when Adler and his goons latched on to their chatter with Vegas. Yes, *when* they latched. No way in hell had Adler dared this superfreak move without anticipating there'd be some hot pursuit. The fucker had likely been ready for them for weeks.

The third monitor displayed a blue screen of death until Rhett jiggled the joystick in the box he'd just grabbed. After a few blinks, the screen "woke up" to relay a high-def feed from a mobile camera.

He grinned and swiveled the control stick.

Fewer things were more fun to a gadget geek than showing off new toys.

Brynna leaned forward, tilting her head as if to make sense of the image. "Is that...grass? And the underside of a bush?"

He pushed the stick forward and shifted his thumb over one of the two buttons on the pad, swiveling the camera around. "Ding ding. Prize for the beautiful lady."

"Wasn't hard," she replied. "The image quality is exceptional. But unless they've started making GoPros for mice—*whoa.*" She cried out as a structure appeared in the picture. "Isn't that...this house?"

Rebel supplied the answer to that. "Looks like it." He peered behind them. "That patio right there, as a matter of fact."

Brynn rose. Peered at the monitor, the patio sliders, then back again—before gasping as *she* appeared on the monitor. Her legs, at least.

"What the—"

The "mouse cam" appeared to roll over the threshold, into the office. Rhett chuckled softly as Rebel joined his perplexity with Brynn's, surging to his feet and staring at the floor—right where he should've been looking into the lens of a little rolling camera.

Reb shot him a frown.

Rhett bounced back a wicked grin. Maneuvered the camera until it practically crawled up Moonstormer's leg.

"Fucker." Reb jumped. The pound of his landing was joined by a metallic sound, as if an erector set had been tossed. The camera feed confirmed it, the image going nuts, showing the room's walls and ceiling before balancing again—with a close-up of Reb's boots. "What the *hell*, Double-Oh?"

The late-morning sun cast a strawberry halo over Brynn's hair as her head tick-tocked between the monitor and the floor. "Exactly what he said." Her gaze was huge with curiosity. "What's going on?"

He couldn't resist letting the mystery stretch for another moment. "Well...dielectrics have come a long way in the last few years. Let's say that much."

Brynn cocked her head, unwittingly becoming the world's most adorable kitten. "Huh?"

Rebel pushed out a dazed snort. "Shit. Of course. But the metasurface advances... They can conceal all the nooks and crannies of a camera?"

"When it's really the size of a mouse—and they've successfully tested a spray-on version of the stuff? Yes."

"Helllooo?" Brynn swept a hand in a wide arc. "Somebody want to break this down for the girl who barely understands the buttons on the TV remote?"

Rebel gave her an indulgent grin. "The camera's still there, *minette*. It's just invisible."

Minette?

Thank fuck Brynn kept stealing Reb's attention, her jaw dropping into an adorable gawk. "Serious?" she blurted, giving Rhett time to neutralize his features again.

"The technology's been in development for years." He rushed it out too fast but would be damned to let Reb grandstand through the subject of *his* expertise. "Using ceramic beads embedded into a thin layer of polytetrafluoroethylene."

Brynn blinked. "The girl who can't get to CNN without a guide, remember?"

"Teflon." He flashed an indulgent smirk with the clarification.

Rebel approached the camera again. "They had a lot of early success with it, but only with two-dimensional scenarios." Using the monitor as his guide, he stepped all the way around the device this time. "Never something like this. A moving object, in all dimensions, able to manipulate light waves on all sides." He pushed a fist against his chin and then shook his head. "This is a huge slice of awesome, Double-Oh."

Somehow, Rhett couldn't revel in his friend's praise. The verbal applause from Reb felt as it always did, generous and warm—but there *was* a difference to it now.

Because of what was added to the air now.

The palpable connection established between Brynn and him.

Rhett grunted against the knot in his throat. He wanted to think he was imagining things—but was punched by glaring evidence otherwise. Brynn stepped over, moving up aside Reb. Screw that. "Aside" didn't begin to describe it. The woman turned into female plaster, hooking her arm around Reb's elbow and then pulling herself close, wrapping at least one whole side of her body against his.

And the fucker didn't flinch one inch from it.

The knot tightened in Rhett's throat. Squeezed liquid fire down into his stomach. Didn't take a goddamn rocket scientist to burn off a conclusion from there—or to wonder where they'd both stashed their Mile High Club membership cards.

"This is perfect." Oh, yeah. All the signs were evident in Rebel's tone too. The silk of contentment. The thrum of confidence. The boost of his Creole drawl. All bore evidence to the obvious now. That asshole had recently gotten laid.

"For what?" Brynna prompted him.

"This is the mouse that's going to gather our cheese," Reb explained. "Our way inside the building, to gather initial intel. If Adler's goons can't see this thing, it'll have free rein of the whole building."

The acid eased by a few drops as Brynna jerked in surprise, the action peeling her back from Reb a couple of inches. Rhett would've been ecstatic with at least a couple more, but it was a start.

"Really?" When she directed the question his way, his tension softened again. "That's possible?"

He held up the box. "World's most fun RC car. It has a range of five hundred miles."

Her eyes warmed as her smile widened—and just like that, his muscles became taut rope again. Why'd she have to look that beautiful while feeling up the middle of Reb's rib cage? "Special Forces. One of the best places to be a tech geek," she cracked.

And goddamnit, why'd she have to call *his* ball with such accuracy?

"Okay, who's been feeding you our deep, dark secrets?"

He managed enough of a grin to turn it casual.

Hers faded in the shadow of her total sincerity.

"I don't know a remote from a radio wave, but I sure as hell honor those who do."

He had nothing for that. How could he, when she spoke with such a magical, heartfelt husk? When the sheer spell of her voice filled his brain with only one obsession now: the image of her "honoring" him in other ways? On her knees. Those huge eyes turning up to him. That strawberry sweetness of a mouth, opening to take his cock inside...

His spun back toward the desk, concealing his hard-on by pretending to check the monitor.

Was that what had enticed Reb to the about-face on his hostility toward her? Had it been the magic of her voice, even just asking him for something simple like a bottle of water? If they'd started talking and she started in on other subjects... *hotter* subjects...no wonder Rebel had been a goner.

Not the Zen candle of thought he needed right now.

"Of course, one of us will need to get in at first, to plant the camera." Rebel turned to pace toward the patio, though he threaded his fingers through Brynn's first, conveying he did so reluctantly. "It's a little less than an hour into Austin. I'll leave around eleven, get there about midnight, be in position to move on things about thirty mikes after that."

Well, that did wonders for dampening the boner. Setting down the controller with a definitive *thunk*, Rhett pushed off from the desk and paced outside too. "Who the hell says *you* get to have the fun?"

The sun bore down on the lake, casting Rebel's forceful features into silhouette as he looked out on it. "Because if I'm caught or killed, at least the camera's inside and you can drive it. If you're eliminated, mouse cam is dead and useless."

"Stop." Brynn stomped out now, hands flying to hips, hair fanning in the wind. "Nobody's getting caught, killed, eliminated, or dead." She exhaled with definition. "The three of us will go together."

Rebel angled a sharp stare back at her. Rhett clenched back a growl—and then a grimace. Growling wasn't usually his style—and if he indulged, it was motivated by specific circumstances. Watching Reb get his Dom face on was definitely not one of them. But never had he seen that look outside a kink dungeon before. Never did he think Reb would meet a woman who inspired it like that.

Or anticipated that he'd get so furious about such a connection.

"No." Well, that made it easier to bite out the word. "Moon's...right. He knows the skins and skeletons of buildings better than me." The concession tasted like sour milk in his mouth. "And it's best if he goes streamlined. We'll only bog him down."

Brynn spun, looking ready to challenge *him* to some hand-to-hand now. "You mean *I'll* bog him down."

He let her come, his feet planted and his jaw squared. The little brat didn't know it, but this was a huge fucking favor. An excuse to match her piss and vinegar? *Oh, bring it on.* "Let's get something clear, sweetheart. I don't say what I don't mean, and I don't expect to be questioned about it at every turn. Reb's going to bell this cat faster if he's on his own, instead of over-the-shouldering about us the whole time." He jabbed a finger back toward the house. "We can both be bigger assets to him from that office, feeding him information like traffic patterns and police chatter, than waiting for him in some field with our thumbs up our arses and our hearts in our throats."

Wait.

What the *hell*?

Our hearts in our—

Christ.

What the fuck's going on now, *asshole?*

That shit violated every last code between Rebel and him. It didn't matter that they were unwritten, unspoken codes; they just *were*. Chatting up garbage like their "hearts" was no-man's land—forbidden territory, no matter what tenor the conversation took. Just because the team mix was different didn't mean the rules could change. At least they weren't supposed to.

But they had.

Because Rebel had let them.

Exchanged things with this woman up in that plane. Things like bodily fluids.

So yeah, the rules were changing. He just wished to hell he knew which ones and how much.

Time to wing it, mate.

"Look." He met her gaze as he launched back in. "You belong on this op, Brynn. It was why I stood up to that wanker for you last night." A tick of his head indicated Rebel as the subject of the wanker reference. "You're going to get to do your part. You *will* help us find Zoe. But only if you're alive for it. For *that* to happen, Rebel and I call all the shots right now."

She pursed her lips. Really wasn't necessary. The hot spice of her eyes conveyed her frustration clearly enough. "So...what? Just sit down, shut up, and take orders?"

"In less than ten words?" he rejoined. "Yes."

"In less than *five* words, Sergeant, fuck you."

Karma was going to find some grand retribution for his reaction to that—but at least he managed to rein in his grin before it broke all the way free. How could he be blamed when she was so damn enticing, snitting at him like a tomboy denied a spot in the dodgeball game but stopping directly between Reb and him, hands coiled as regally as a princess?

When she stamped a boot down—holy shit, *stamped* her foot—he made Karma no more promises on his composure. He was saved by glancing over at Reb and catching the same struggle on his face.

Well...shit, part fucking two. He didn't even want to think about being on the same page with Moonstormer again. Man-slut Stafford didn't get to flash his damn charm and bounce off the shame hook so easily this time. But that wasn't getting addressed anytime soon. *Put it in the box—but keep it on top.*

At least focusing on that task cleared the way for a shot of calm. "Peach—" Which, apparently, didn't cover his verbal filter. The word begged to be let out whenever he looked at her, the color defining so much of her beauty. "We all do things we don't want to do, for the sake of the—"

She cut him off with a splayed hand to his breastbone. "For the sake of the mission?" she shot. "You're seriously going there? Let me save you the effort, Sergeant. I've heard that one before, in much more creative ways."

The calm was nice while it lasted. No way was it holding up to the confusion she'd just brought down in an avalanche. Out of pure instinct, he looked to Reb again. Once more, the guy's face mirrored his thoughts. *Step carefully.* Somehow they'd pinged a sensitive nerve—demonstrated to the hilt by her sudden shove back, finished by a bitter laugh.

"Yep. Heard them," she rasped. "Even liked them. Still do. That's my damn problem, isn't it? Let's see... *Embrace the suck.* That's a good one. Or how about *bite the bullet*? I also enjoy *watch my smoke, diehards get it done, bounce the rubble, push the hard deck...*"

"Damn," Reb uttered.

"Ditto." Rhett wasn't sure how to punctuate it, aside from a bewildered stare. Obviously, Dan Colton wasn't the first man who'd had to take off his gun belt before climbing into bed with her—though considering her in bed with some cocky-ass soldier boy was like biting a brick of gravel. It was hard enough to contemplate her getting horizontal with Reb in the plane. No. Scratch that. It was fucking impossible.

He chose to focus on the woman herself, despite how her backlash morphed from bitter to openly hostile. "I could regale you with more—but you know what? None of them matter *or* apply. I'm *not* going to *sacrifice for the mission* because to me this isn't a mission. This is my best friend's life. I'm not going to sit back and just wait to *hit my mark* when one of you tells me to. I have ideas to contribute too."

Oh, yeah. A sensitive nerve. Probably more than one.

But *which* ones?

He was on unfamiliar ground. And, as much as it sucked to admit it, was open to offers of help...

Even if it meant asking Rebel for it.

But by the time he looked back to his friend, Reb had already picked up the torch. At Brynn's side again, he wrapped a hand around her waist, pulling her in with the surety that spoke an undeniable truth. He'd already done it before. Sure enough, Brynn's body acquiesced like butter over a flame, softening against him—though her face conveyed a different story. She wasn't happy about the biological betrayal. At *all*.

Rhett's jaw constricted. *Feeling your pain, little peach. More than you know.*

"Your ideas are important, *cher*." Reb's voice was firm but intimate, another facet Rhett had never expected to surface beyond dungeon walls. "And we'll listen to every one of them—when the time is right. That time is going to be when we have more intel to work from."

More conflict sprinted across her features. Her spine stiffened. "So I really *am* supposed to sit down and shut up?"

Rebel let her push away, earning him massive points in Rhett's book. Rage was like diamonds on Brynna Monet. She was five times more gorgeous for it.

"You're supposed to stay calm and trust this process, Brynna," Reb ordered. "You're supposed to trust *us*." He tilted his head, as if seeing into her own. "Last night you dared me to trust *you*, that you could handle the pressure if shit went sideways out here. Well, you earned that trust—but now the scales have to balance back. If you can't tell us that your conviction is a hundred percent behind us, speak the hell up now. Double-Oh can get right back on the hot line, and Sam can be back in Austin with your ride home. Seeing as how I'm headed back toward town tonight anyway..."

Her mouth dropped. Definitely a good thing/bad thing.

While Rhett forgot about wanting to pummel Reb's chest like a victory drum, his distraction was delivered by the perfect *O* of Brynna's lips—causing other parts of his body to beat with twice the fury.

"You wouldn't dare." Her indignation only made everything worse. *So fucking gorgeous.* She was the kind of woman who immortalized redheads, Helen of Troy mixed with Ann Margret, sprinkled with enough Agent Scully and Emma Stone to ensure he forgot all about his longtime fealty to Scarlett Johansson. This was even worse because his mental boner for her was as mighty as the one between his legs. No wonder Rebel had jumped her during the plane ride—underlining the steel in the guy's fortitude now.

"We would, and we will." Reb scooped his stare from her to Rhett and then back again, building his conviction by the second. "Unless we have your assurance that we call the shots—for now."

She shifted from foot to foot. Drummed her fingers on her thighs. Finally slanted her head at him, full of taut wariness. "For *now*?" When Reb returned a smooth nod, she snapped, "What the hell does that even mean? What are the parameters on that? 'For now' isn't a clear—"

Rebel ripped her short by sweeping a hand beneath her chin. Gripped it so hard, she winced for a second.

"*Trust*, Miss Monet." He held fast as she tried to jerk away. "It's your choice. Balance the scale *now* or pick up your bag, walk out the door, and wait for me in the car."

Her nostrils flared. Her lips parted, exposing gritted teeth. After a grueling trio of those harsh breaths, she raised a hand, gripped his wrist, and thrust it away. "Fine," she seethed. "We do everything your way—for now."

For the first time, Reb's composure developed a crack. His breaths were far from serene as he pulled his hand to his side, fisting it. His stare narrowed as he charged tightly, "Because you trust us?"

"Because I trust you."

He exhaled with more calm. "There. That's not so hard, is it?"

She took a long moment to respond—if that was how one could label her wordless turn from Reb, followed by a determined stomp down the path through the tall grass, toward the lake. But in every stiff step she took, Rhett could interpret the words she'd left unspoken, the message hurled behind on the air like holy water tainted with a curse.

Not so hard?

That was probably one of the most hellish things she'd ever done in her life.

★ ★ ★ ★ ★

The silence also brought the waiting.

Because of course, as long as the subject of hell had come up, the Rhett Lange version deserved a visit too.

Hours' worth of it.

The recruiters never talked about this part of the job, even in Spec Ops training. Tumbling from a plane at twelve hundred feet? No problem. Navigating from a swamp without electronics or a compass? Piece of cake. Hand-to-hand combat with everything from an armed hostile to a rabid gorilla? Fuck, yes. But keeping oneself from tearing off their own skin while waiting for night to fall? Not a single manual on that. Not a word of advice to fight the insanity that crawled up a guy's bloodstream—or the memories that taunted his mind when there was nothing to fill it but time, stretched into torture.

At least that was how it had seemed...to his ten-year-old mind. Eight hours of a transatlantic flight, even filled with the coolest books, movies, and video games, were still eight hours to ask the questions he didn't dare voice aloud—for fear of the answers he'd get in return.

Why'd they even have me, if they can't live on the same continent?

Why do I have to be the ping-pong across the ocean every month?

Why don't I belong with either of them?

And the worst ones of them all...

Was I the one who caused this in the first place?

What did I do wrong to make them give up on each other?

He'd called them the ghosts: the demands that refused to go away, even when shoving them to the darkest places in his soul. But as the years went by, he was tired of letting the demons have that power. He fought them, chasing them to the reaches of his conscience. But it wasn't far enough—so he turned the whole world into his ghosts. He'd lashed out at everyone, indiscriminate in his choice of enemy.

Three years, twenty suspensions, and six expulsions later, Mother and Father had him transported to the Heritage Military Academy in upstate New York.

It was the best thing that had ever happened to him.

For the first time in his life, his anger received structure, his violence was transformed to effectiveness, and his loneliness was filled with seventy-five brothers, all as fucked-up as him.

And the ghosts?

Banished.

Washed away by the irreverent humor and easy Creole drawl of the force of nature they'd assigned as his roommate. Rebel Masterston Stafford was like nobody he'd ever met—or likely ever would. Their connection proved that opposites really could magnetize and repel at once.

A truth that'd held all the way to this day.

To this minute.

Though soaked with sweat from a run around the ranch's grounds, his blood still simmered, too hot for the hours left of this goddamn waiting game—still at the temperature it had boiled to when discerning Rebel's skank move from this morning. But what the hell, then? Go high and mighty and ask him what the fuck he was thinking, taking advantage of two solitary hours with Brynna?

Right. And brand himself a hypocrite in the doing.

Same opportunity? Same circumstances? You would've made the exact same move, asshole.

And God, could he imagine that opportunity. Those circumstances. The sky cruising by outside the window. Sam conveniently "occupied" in the cockpit. The engines vibrating through the seats. Brynna looking up with those wide chocolate eyes, breasts peeking from beneath that rough work shirt. Reb staring back, eyes glittering with black-violet dominance...

Shit.

Shit.

"Hey."

Wasn't *that* convenient. As if manifested by the force of Rhett's thoughts, Reb strolled into the kitchen, bare to the waist. He was sweating to the point of sheen, simply missing a ship deck and some Hessians to transform into one of the sea scoundrels from whom he was descended. Damn it, even the laces on his black sweats weren't tied.

Motherfucker.

"Where the hell have you been?" It was practically condemnation, and Rhett didn't care. Might as well get the agony of this over with. Reb enjoyed providing details of his conquests between the sheets, and Rhett doubted this would be any different. He pushed both hands against the counter, bracing himself for the guy's play-by-play of what had happened with Brynn, heartened by the knowledge that in a few minutes, the ordeal would be done.

Yeah. That was for the best. Get it handled and put away by the time Reb left for Austin tonight.

"I hit the gym," Rebel grunted as he wicked the sweat from his neck with a towel from a nearby drawer and then filled a glass from the water purifier. "Did you see the setup Dax has in there?"

"No."

"You need to. Dude's got the *American Ninja Warrior* trials going on in there. Truth. He's got a spider wall *and* a parkour run."

"Oh."

"You get in a run?"

"Yeah."

He peeled off his own shirt, able to dip his head into it, hiding the new color on his face. Christ. Was this for real? Was he stammering and blushing in shame, all because of where he'd assumed—with justification—where the dipshit had just been?

Or perhaps was headed now.

Of course. That had to be it. Made more sense, considering Reb's nature. To him, free afternoons weren't trips to hell but fields of opportunity. He'd have gone for a workout first, capped perfectly by a romp with Brynn. She was probably naked and ready for him right now...

"So where's Brynn?"

Which thoroughly justified blurting *that* out.

He prepared for Reb's innuendo-spiked reply. Instead, without anything but sincerity, the guy filled in, "Asleep. For a while, I think. Makes sense. She didn't leave Shay and Zoe's place until about four a.m."

"True."

He ducked his face again.

You're such a moron.

A moron with validation. Was he just supposed to ignore Rebel's whoremonkey antics—again?

Reb finished off his water and then slammed the glass to the counter with an ear-ringing blow. "Okay." He brought his palm down with just as much force. "Out with it, fuckhead."

Shit. Or...not. If a come-to-Jesus was what Reb wanted, that was what he'd get.

"Out with what?"

"The reason why you've been a spitting churl since Brynn and I got here. What the fuck, Lange?"

A laugh felt agonizingly appropriate. "A...*churl*?"

"You prefer shit fungus? Douche canoe? Wanker of the day?" Reb tossed the Brit slang at him with chin raised high. "You're still not getting a goddamn trophy for it."

The expression, one of the asshole's favorites to sling in their Heritage days, worked no nostalgic miracles now. Instead, it made Rhett think of how Rebel had treated women since the day they'd met, pouring on the bayou charm to get between their thighs as fast as he could. During their adolescence, it had made Reb a demigod in his eyes. Through boot camp, Special Ops courses, and Live Environment training, it was understandable as a pressure release—but in the last few years, as they'd learned about BDSM together, it wasn't cute anymore. It sure as hell wouldn't keep getting his blind eye. Starting now.

"Fine. Trophy's all yours, Moon. Congratulations." As the words spilled, so did his resolve. What the hell was the good of this? And why was he even doing this right now? Brynn had already proved she was able to physically handle herself, so why was he in such a fucking twist about protecting her emotionally?

Because it's not her *who needs the protecting?*

Yeah. It was so time to be done with this bullshit.

"I'm going to take a shower."

"The hell you are." Rebel caught him around the bicep and spun him back. "We're not done."

"That sounds like a personal problem, man."

"You haven't answered me."

Rhett ripped his arm free. "Does it matter if I do?" Dared raising his glare to Rebel's face. The bastard's gritty gaze and tight mouth betrayed what a shitty night's sleep he'd gotten, a premission norm for him. The guy needed to bathe and then crash. Badly. "It won't change a thing, Rebel."

Cords of tension twisted down Reb's neck and shoulders. "What's that supposed to mean?"

"That you fucked her."

Well, that was one way of blowing his strategy to hell.

"Fucked who?"

Now *that* was *really* funny. "I don't believe this. Who *else*, dipshit? You going to tell me Brynna was just practicing a new show number, draping herself all over you like that?"

The guy had the decency to finally drop the act. Thank fuck for small miracles. "I didn't fuck her."

And maybe he had to be more careful about the uptake on the miracle shit.

"So she went from kicking your ass last night to gazing stardust at you today because you...what? Let her use most of the armrest in the plane? Brought a copy of the rom-com starring the dude with the dreamy hair and sat through it with her? Gave her the best foot rub of her life?" A gape took over as Reb looked away, his expression clouding over. In return, Rhett took his own turn at confusion. "Christ. So what the fuck *did* happen?"

Rebel poured more water and gulped a giant swig. Elbows on the chopping block, he stared out into the herb garden. "She turned applesauce on me when she saw the Piper. Turned white as a ghost as soon as Sam fired up the engines. So I... distracted her."

"Distracted," he echoed. "Without your cock?"

Reb's fingers, flattened on the wood counter, compressed until the nail beds whitened. "I didn't say that."

A chuff escaped. "But you didn't fuck her."

Rebel shoved up. "Does it matter? I got her here, didn't I?"

He had no idea what resparked his rage more: the dickhead's callousness, or his righteous claim to it. Did it matter? His anger was back, blistering and hot, firing into his arms, ramming them into Rebel's shiny chest. "It does matter, you arrogant prick. In case you haven't picked up on it yet, Brynn Monet isn't a panting little thing who wants to bow at your feet and beg for your flogger."

Reb stumbled back but cocked a smirk through every step, his moves like an insolent rag doll. "Buddy, you might be very surprised at what that girl wants."

"Woman. She's a *woman*, damn you—one who's had her heart fucked with enough by players like you."

The guy stopped. No more rag doll. The grin fell away too. "Right." His eyes narrowed, all traces of color gone. "Because a catch like *you* is what she's looking for, huh? Love songs and long walks on the beach, with sex on the side? A Dom who's willing to settle on limits that keep her *happy* because the alternative just may be—oh, *gasp*—losing her and being alone. And God help poor little Rhett Lange if he's alone, discarded again by the world, wandering the earth in search of his lost, broken—"

One fist. Driving straight for that asshole's face.

Stopped midair, skin smacking skin, sweat exploding.

The monster who stopped him—

Now the friend who stared at him, unblinking and unrelenting.

Daring him. Like so many times before.

Drawing him closer. Like so many times before.

"Let. Go." His lungs shook on the syllables. He twisted his wrist inside Reb's.

Rebel just kept staring, with those eyes as fathomless as midnight. "I won't ever discard you, Rhett."

Rhett. Not Double-Oh or dude or dickhead. His name, so simple, nearly sanctified...rasped with that baritone intimacy. Yet asking for even more.

"I said *let go.*"

"Why?"

The fucker tugged harder, bringing him eye-to-eye.

Breath-to-breath. Heat-to-heat.

"Because I'm pissed at you."

"Pissed?"

He had the nerve to say nothing else. To say everything else. To arch one black brow, turning it into the curve of a question mark...without the finishing dot.

Beckoning Rhett to be that completion.

Firing every drop of his blood with the same goddamn need.

Making him wonder...once more...what it might be like. To reach out, to touch, to fill his senses with this sun who'd been lent to the earth as a man. Just once...

No.

A matching sound, low and vicious, clawed up his throat. He finally shoved free, chest laboring, eyes glaring. That was the trouble with dreams about touching the sun. They could only be dreams. Taken to reality, they incinerated a man.

He wheeled around, heading back toward the door out to the grounds. "Take a shower," he growled in the doing. "You stink, asshole."

His own plans?

He was going to jump in the lake.

And hoped, when he got out, that his mind *and* his cock wouldn't still be raging beyond any semblance of control.

CHAPTER FIVE

Peace in our souls.

Paradise in our hearts.

Brynn gazed at the framed needlepoint hanging on the wall in the little den next to the office and wondered whether to laugh or cry.

Or cut to the chase and scream.

The temptation bubbled from her belly into her throat as one of the guys—at this point, they were both being such ogres that it didn't matter which—slammed a door off the living room. It had been like this for hours between them, increasing as the afternoon turned to twilight, pushing through the whole house like a pressure cooker about to blow. She counted on the night bringing an equally murky mood between her mission mates.

What the hell had happened since this afternoon?

She certainly didn't have anything interesting to report. After stomping out on them, she'd found one of the guest bedrooms with the intent of sulking away her frustration for a while. Instead, a wall of exhaustion had hit.

Two hours later, she'd been yanked from half asleep to fully alert by the sound of skin smacking skin and then a duel of low growls. She'd been too far away to distinguish the cause of the fight, only knowing it ended in Rhett's escaping toward the lake at a jog, the tension in his torso turned to ironic beauty beneath the sun. Half a minute later, she'd heard rushing water and the clack of a shower door.

Process of elimination led her to think of Rebel beneath that spray—and the heated temptation to join him there. But unnerving instincts had held her back. She couldn't help but remember Shay's words from last night.

You go through a different submissive each month, asshole.

Though Shay's rage had spawned the words, Rebel sure as hell hadn't denied them—meaning the "diversion" he'd given her on the plane was exactly that for him. A pleasant way to pass the time. No more, no less.

But as the minutes passed, even that truth had been eclipsed by the cloud that spread through the house, undeniable and thick, the aftermath of whatever had gone down in the kitchen. The toxic aura was an affront to every gold and pink thread of the needlework on the wall. Brynn could practically feel the tenderness put into every inch of the piece and wondered what special lady in Dax Blake's life had created it. Mother? Sister? Wife? And what would that woman think about the way the males in this place were acting now, avoiding each other in stony silence—when they weren't grunting profanity under their breaths or abusing every piece of furniture they could?

Whump.

A lot like that.

She pegged the perpetrator of the cabinet slam as Rebel, since the *rat-a-tat*s on the computer in the next room could only be Rhett's. In the kitchen, plastic crunched. A soda can *thwopped.*

Rhett cleared his throat. "Hey. The Sriracha chips are mine."

The cabinet creaked. "There's two bags."

"Right. And they're both mine."

A gritted curse in French. Steps that pounded so hard, the walls jittered.

Brynn exhaled as the needlepoint bounced on its hanger. So this was what it felt like to referee three-year-olds.

She swung out of the chair, setting aside her e-reader. Just when she was getting to the best part of the novel too. The rock star and the geek scientist would have to deny their desires for a few minutes longer.

Maybe longer than that.

Deciding to hit Rebel first with the censure about playing nice, she rounded the corner into the office—

Just as Rebel entered from the other door, already dressed in head-to-toe black for his subterfuge tonight. He had a bag of Sriracha chips in each hand—that he suddenly turned over, raining the spicy contents onto the floor.

"What the hell!" She gaped at Rebel, who glared only at Rhett—who simply leaned back in the chair and rolled his eyes.

What the hell?

The internal echo didn't dilute the shock. Was this kind of shit *normal* for them?

"Here you go." Rebel tossed the bags back over his shoulder before whirling back toward the kitchen. "Have at it, pal."

"Rebel!"

Brynn hurried after him, catching up only after he'd stalked out the front door of the house itself. It was then, while pulling him by an elbow, that a wave of energy poured off him— jolting her with a crazy new awareness.

The violence he'd just hurled at Rhett...wasn't just violence. She knew it because he redirected all of it at her now, and a lot of it was already familiar to her. A force she'd already experienced once today—in the depths of his gaze and the magic of his fingers—during the flight down here.

"Holy shit." Her grip slipped from his elbow. She curled in her fingers again, trying to reestablish the hold, but the uniform's slick fabric was made for escaping much more determined attackers than her.

For a second, Rebel stared like she'd blurted that his dog died. But only a second. He erased the expression as fast as he'd brandished it, making her wonder if she'd imagined everything, until his vicious rasp cut down at her.

"I'm taking off."

He spun and headed for the car, his steps eating up the front walk. Only then did she notice the duffel bag in his hand—and the mouse cam's hard-sided case in the other.

"I'll get dinner in the city. Tell Double-Oh I'll patch in for a comm check as soon as I'm on the road."

"From the..." She scurried to keep pace, though it took three of her steps to one of his. "But that's not how you're supposed to—"

He halted her by whipping back around. "Do you think I give a fuck about the supposed-tos right now?"

A glower took over his face. His shoulders rose, hulking him up. Brynn glared right back, hating him for every breath that shook her rib cage. What was this? Where had the bold wonder woman of last night gone? Why wasn't she stepping forward to knock him on his ass *now*—at the moment it really mattered? What the hell had he done to her today, that all she could focus on was the tightness around his eyes, the sharp twists of his mouth, and the breaths that made his chest lurch in rhythm with hers?

"Yeah," she finally murmured, "I think you do." She edged a step toward him while digging her gaze deeper into his. "You care deeply about the supposed-tos, Rebel—the right kind of them. If you didn't, you'd be back in Tacoma right now, enjoying a beer, having wished Shay the best with finding his wife. No, not even that. You'd be in Louisiana, wouldn't you? Running a bar or a jazz joint, or maybe even a fishing boat—" She halted, caught off guard by the sudden spike of his tension. "Okay, not a boat. But something *other* than this, getting ready to risk your own hide because of your loyalty to the brother of a brother."

She lifted a hand to his face. Tenderly combed back a bunch of his inky waves, teased against his forehead by the approaching night wind. "Yet you're ready to walk out on the guy who's closer to you than anybody else."

He flinched from her. Everything but his eyes. Those he kept fixed and steady, not even blinking, as if she'd become some harpy and laid a hex on him. It freaked *her* too. Her arm froze, hand still upright, fingers trembling.

Something passed over his face.

Heat. And determination.

Frantically, she dropped her arm.

Too late.

He caught it, snapping fingers around her wrist. Hauled her against him so hard, she winced from the brutal surprise—

For a second.

Until he submerged the sound with the crush of his lips. The invasion of his tongue. The heat between his thighs... spreading through the space between hers.

Brynn struggled. Then didn't. First, there was the whole issue about futility. He wasn't accepting *supposed-to*s from her in this either. But more extremely, why? What use would it be to fight him, when her senses had craved this all day? What good would it be to struggle, when she'd wondered if he'd feel this good without seat belts in the way...when she questioned her memories of his sinful mouth, his dominant grip, his commanding body? And now, even his bold growls as she molded tighter against him, twining her hands around his neck...all the things that made him a collection of Cajun hotness she wanted igniting her blood again and again and again...

But as swiftly as he'd started the clinch, he cut it short.

Set her away from him, letting her stumble back with balance swaying, hormones careening.

Before he slashed a hand across his lips.

Never in her life had words completely evaded her—until now. In hindsight, the asshole probably should have been grateful for that. Instead, he repeated with even deeper clarity, "I'll radio in from the road." Then, over his shoulder, while turning from her for the final time, "Tell Double-Oh to be ready. We have to run this thing true as scripture."

★ ★ ★ ★ ★

True as scripture.

A little under an hour later, she still wasn't sure she'd heard that little tidbit correctly—from the mouth of the asshole who'd given her mixed signals of—it really did apply—biblical proportion. The kisses of an archangel followed by the stare of a demon. A heaven of arousal, ruined by one motion that dipped her into hell.

Excuse the hell out of me for tainting your mouth with my taste, Monsieur *Jerkwad.*

She barely tamed a grimace as the moment filled her mind again. If he'd been testing out his version of the ice bucket challenge, she'd vouch for him. It worked. His disdain had turned her from fire to ice in no more than three seconds. She'd have said that to the bastard's beautiful face too—had he not sprinted for the car like a rocket was jammed up his ass. There was *another* item for her pile of pissed-off.

Which, as Karma would oh-so-poetically dictate, fired back at her with vengeance now.

She could barely believe what she witnessed, looking on from the doorway of the office, as the guys ran through their comm check. It wasn't *what* they said—the alpha-soldier protocol and crazy acronyms were actually as hot as foreplay to her—but *how* they said it, that ratcheted her tension. Their exchanges were smooth and easy, sometimes bordering on banter, reminding her of the buddies who'd been synched with each other last night instead of the adversaries who'd slunk and snarled around here all afternoon.

By the time they ran the final diagnostic on the mouse cam and agreed Rebel would click back in two hours for intel support on getting the device inside the Verge building, her composure approached prickly status—discernibly so, if Rhett's narrowed gaze was a clear alert system. The Viking didn't waste any words addressing the issue either. Damn it.

"Well, peaches, I'd cut to the compliments about your mission gear choice"—he waved at the shorts and *Dance Your Ass Off* sweatshirt she'd changed into—"if you didn't already look like we'd failed the damn thing."

Her face flamed. "Sorry. I didn't mean to imply that. I'm just wondering how the hell..." She averted her gaze and pursed her lips, acknowledging what she was about to say and feeling three inches high for it. "Forget it."

Rhett spun the chair around and rose from it. He didn't stop there, flowing right into the three steps it took to get closer to her. When only a foot separated them, he folded his arms and charged, "You're kidding, right? You really want to 'forget it,' knowing how a guy like me will respond to shit like that?"

She shifted a little. *Shifted?* Who was she kidding? He made her completely squirm, edging closer with those hard ropes of forearm, slicing her deeper with his steel-toned stare. She vacillated between backing up or simply bowing her head.

Idiot.

You don't do submissive, Brynn Monet—not even for a chest that broad, a focus that sexy, a stance that daunting. Your heart isn't a play toy for any *man anymore. Not even "a guy like him."*

The thought did the trick. Flipped the switch on her fortitude, yanking her chin up. "I'm not asking you to *respond* at all. That's the point."

Tiny creases cinched the corners of his eyes. He hadn't expected her lip, that much was clear. But the follow-up *she* expected—the disappointment, the disgruntlement, perhaps both—never arrived. Instead, a slow, knowing smile took over his lips.

Damn it.

"Got it." He murmured it softly but reinforced his posture sharply. Like he *needed* the extra inch of height? "And now that it's clear, you'll have no trouble spilling."

He dipped the end of it in enough of a growl for her to squirm again—in much different ways. Now it was really time to move back. She did so by a step. Another. Neither diluted the force of what he did to her now...of the deep place inside that his snarl reached.

The place that was afraid of him.

The exact same spot that had been afraid of Rebel.

The corner of her psyche that liked it.

God. Good thing she wanted to be a shrink, because she was going to need the peer discount.

Mask the mess, Brynna. Now.

Regrettably, the fastest way to do that was divulging the truth he'd demanded. "I was just wondering about your whole buddy-buddy on the radio with Sergeant Sasquatch."

He spurted a chuckle. "Sasquatch? That's new. And damn good. Mind if I borrow it sometime?"

Now close enough to do so, Brynn leaned against the wall. "Sure—though I don't imagine it'll be soon, now that you two have kissed and made up."

His laugh vanished. Taut lines took over in its place, a blatant expression that hid a thousand messages. "I wouldn't kiss that ape if you paid me, sweetheart—and don't mistake *any* of that radio chatter for *making up*." He unfolded his arms, not erasing an inch of his imprint on the air with the move. But maybe she just thought so because he paced closer again, filling more of her vision with every inch covered. "Finding Zoe is still the first priority on this playing field. Pissing contests and bitch-slap fests belong deep on the sidelines. Reb and I both know that. I promise you that we'll continue to as well." He stepped fully into her personal space, lifting a hand to the side of her neck...sending instant waves of warmth down her arm and through the nearest breast. "We're going to find her, Brynn. I promise."

She swallowed hard. Battled to ignore the eager puckering of her nipple. Much easier said than done, especially when her other breast decided it didn't want to be neglected. *Shit, shit,*

shit. There was nowhere to move, either. He was so close, so hard, so overpowering—exactly how his "buddy" had made her feel on the plane.

Oh, God. What did this say about *her*? One day, two men, a thousand tingling nerve endings...all reacting with the exact same sentiment.

Don't stop touching me. Please don't stop.

Safe subject. She needed a *much* safer subject.

"I... It's... Well, I appreciate it." She rasped it as he trailed his knuckles along her collarbone. *Wonderful.* It felt so damn wonderful. "I-I mean, the fact that you two can behave like grown-ups. I have to admit, I wasn't optimistic by the time Sasquatch stormed out of here." She fought to lift her gaze, despite wanting to cease at the base of his corded neck. Yearning to trace that special bunch of muscles where it blended into the top of his shoulder. Wondering if it was as solid and powerful as she imagined...

"Sasquatch." He laughed again after repeating it. "Well, if he's that hairy bastard, I'm a damn Manticore. Takes an ogre to provoke one properly, yeah?"

For a moment, his words didn't register. She was preoccupied with how the night wind kicked through the room, lifting the red-gold strands from his broad forehead. Even more fascinating were the sweat-dampened spots beneath, reminding her he was truly a man, not some Greek demigod come to life just to taunt her in every tantalizing sense of the word.

And God, was she tantalized. The word was blessing *and* curse through the next moment...and then the next. She needed him to back the hell off. She longed for him to stay. To slide in even closer...to let her inhale him, absorb him, touch him...

She needed a new tactic. *Now.*

Humor? Oh, hell. She sucked at the stuff, especially when her nerves were jangled like stones in a soda can. But options were dwindling. Fast.

"So...this is a common occurrence? You two skulking around, threatening the forest creatures, promising to tear each other's heads off?"

He didn't laugh. Imagine *that*. But she hadn't expected more tension to flood over him again—until realizing that this shit was different than before. It was restless and sensual, brought to life by the churning seas in his eyes, the defined friction of his lips, the confident loom of his body.

Go away.

Oh, God...closer.

"No," he murmured. "Not common at all." His eyes gained heavy hoods as those stormy blues slid to her lips. "But we've never disagreed over something like this before either."

Air finally got to her throat. Three shaky breaths in, three exiting the same way. "Like...what?"

"You mean like who."

Asking him to fill in *that* blank would've been punching an insult. The intensity of his focus was so potent, like a blowtorch melting iron, that her logic was forced to give way to its truth. But what did she do about its effect on the rest of her body? The sparks in every nerve ending, the lava taking over every bone, the molten need dripping through every inch of her sex? How did she answer those demands? More crucially, how did she reconcile this hot, hurting need with the desire she'd felt for the man's best friend not even twelve hours ago?

She couldn't contain the thought from twisting her own

features. *Boom*. There was Rhett, still so close, reading all of her thoughts inside three seconds. He pressed in closer, both hands curling around her shoulders, forcing her head back...as his gaze scorched farther into her.

Oh...*God*.

It was no different than a dance move. She fought to hold on to the thought. She'd been dipped like this more than a thousand times in her life, posed in the ultimate romantic surrender. She'd actually enjoyed every one of those moments, cradled by the strength of her dance partner, able to let go and allow the music to carry her senses.

She didn't feel free now.

She was trapped. Helpless. A slave to his hold, controlled by the force of his stare...and the pulsing pressure it added to every drop of her bloodstream.

"He liked what he did to you today, Brynna." His voice was low, reinforced by hidden concrete. As her breath rushed harder, he pushed his grip in deeper. "Ssshhh. *Breathe*. He didn't come bragging to me about it. That was how I first knew. To be blunt, he always brags." He tilted his head, adopting that let-me-into-your-head-or-else look. "That also means he's going to try it again."

She obeyed him and inhaled. She also heeded the order he didn't verbalize, continuing to meet his gaze. It wasn't easy. His words brought a storm of conflict. What was she supposed to do with his overture, seemingly well-intentioned—that might've been resentment in disguise? Beneath his "concern," was he just feeling like the weird third wheel and making Rebel the scapegoat? Or was his protectiveness—and his attraction— for real? In which case, she had a much more fragile egg to protect. Feeling like a man cherished her, watched out for her, beyond just tossing his coat over the rain puddle for her...it was her Kryptonite. The golden key to the softest, most vulnerable part of her soul.

It was also a myth. The reason she'd sworn off the tight and cozy with anyone dangling dog tags from their neck—and finally stabilized the keel of her life. At last, she was free from the tears, anguish, and sleepless nights of expecting something she was never going to get...at least not from these kinds of men. She'd finally given the grown-up's response to *once upon a time.*

She'd marked the difference between Enya's life and hers.

"Okay." She began her response to Rhett with a flippant shrug. "So he'll try it again. Are you uncomfortable with that? Is that what the ogres were worked up about this afternoon?"

A heavy gulp vibrated down his throat. "He's not good for you, Brynna."

She jerked her head back. "That's a hell of a thing to say about your best friend."

"Best friend?" He chuffed. "That hardly covers it. He's my brother in arms. I'd die for him. But he's still not good for you."

"And I suppose *you* are?"

He pushed out air through his nose. "Remember all the shit Shay spat at Reb last night? It wasn't empty accusation." An expression took over his face that was either constipation or deep worry. "Rebel's idea of *long-term* is buying a subbie a drink after an extra-long session in the dungeon. He's a firework: intense and pretty and perfect until the show's over." His hand rose back to her face. The other followed, until he palmed both of her cheeks. "He's an amazing man. One of the boldest, bravest, gutsiest heroes I've ever met. And sure, he's damn beautiful to look at..."

"But?" She filled in the blank before he got there.

"But he's screwed up when it comes to relationships. Shittiest thing is, it isn't even his fault." The sorrow behind the words was tangible in the tightened pads of his fingers. "I wish that truth were different, so goddamn badly. I want to see him happy, fulfilled, and simply loved for the man he is—but he can't separate that from the child he was." He shook his head. "When a guy can't even remember his mother and has been raised by the asshole sperm donor who nicknamed him *slut spawn*, a psychological mess isn't a tough leap."

Brynn's head dropped. "Shit." Her rasp resonated with shock, though it wore off fast. Sadly, Rhett's disclosure made a lot of sense when joined to thoughts of the man she'd flown here with. Rebel's cobalt gaze exposed so little...his Cajun drawl seemed to hide so much.

"That's a good way of putting it." He exhaled again, blinking hard, rolling his shoulders as if attempting to shirk a huge weight. The broad slabs remained as taut as before. Not stopping to let logic butt in, Brynn reached for both of them, spreading fingers along the firm muscles, gliding back and forth in hopes of helping him a little.

"You care for him a lot." Her soft words reflected how that truth moved her...to feel it as a potent force on the air, so strong and vibrant, despite the asshole behavior Rebel had dished out this afternoon. It spoke volumes about Rhett's character. It was sexy as hell.

"Yeah." It husked fervently from him. "I do." While his words still focused on Rebel, his eyes came alive with a different energy...feeding directly from hers. He let her see every spark of it too. "But that's because I see *all* of him—even the parts that never grew up."

She continued rubbing his shoulders. He swayed yet closer. She breathed in, filling her nostrils with his rich smell, all sage and wind and man. With every inch he moved in, he consumed more of her vision...captivated more of her attraction.

"You deserve more, sweetheart. So much more."

His shoulders filled her palms. His scent consumed her senses. And the rest of him...

Dear God, the rest of him.

His chest, proud and high, pecs carved into matching planes of steel. His thighs, like a pair of fleshed-out Sequoias, making even her dancer's muscles feel tiny by comparison. And the bulge of flesh that sprung from between them...

Ohhhh, God.

His cock was firm and hot, burning her belly through his clothes and hers, provoking her stunned gasp as he fit their bodies tighter. Rhett's returning growl was so deep it barely ruffled the air, though the tremors through his body spoke a different message. The quivers permeated Brynn, no longer making it possible to ignore the obvious. First, he'd awakened her emotionally, earning the Viking prince title with his integrity to the mission and his loyalty to Rebel. That weakened her resistance to the rest—to admitting a physical desire that hit like a surprise storm...a force she hadn't endured in a long time.

Screw endurance.

And screw her damn dating diet.

For six months, five days, and almost twelve hours, she'd been a good girl. No military hunks. No delicious G men. Barely any *men*, period—certainly not the kind she wanted to twine her arms around, stabbing her fingers through thick red-gold hair on the way, while her leg wrapped around a torso that belonged on a Michelangelo statue in an Italian alcove.

Cheat day, girlfriend.

Go big or go home.

Especially if a man is staring like his sunrise won't come unless you do.

She dragged one hand down his nape, the other through the dark-gold stubble along the bold line of his jaw...and then lifted her face until their lips were just inches apart. Into that tiny space, she whispered the expression of heated need...the acknowledgment of growing desire.

"So what *do* I deserve?"

CHAPTER SIX

Rhett's lungs pumped. His blood burned. Every pore of his skin seemed to pop open at once, flooding with the anticipation that thickened the air like springtime fog over the Thames. Bloody *hell*. He hadn't even kissed her yet. But fuck, how he longed to—

Which was why he purposely dragged away.

Not far. Just enough. Giving himself the space to turn his stare into a caress—and a question of its own too. Did she really want this? Did she really want *him* after the "fun" she'd already had with Rebel today—or was Moon's detached passion the only "connection" she really wanted from a man? If that was the case, backing off was the best choice. Though this might be only a no-strings stress reliever during a high-stress mission, it sure as *hell* wasn't going to be "detached." He didn't play that cavalier game. Ever.

Once more, he blazed his stare over her face. Gave her no mercy with his scrutiny, taking in every detail of her tawny brows, elegant eyes, regal Renaissance nose...and at last, the lush berry sweeps of her lips...

The moment his gaze touched them, they parted a little.

A little more.

Damn.

Just one little move, nothing as intent as the question she'd just blurted. But little moves were the things that made the hugest differences. They moved plates beneath the earth.

Were the difference between first and second place.

Could transform one question into an invitation for so much more.

A more he could no longer resist—and didn't want to. An offer he accepted as every sexual instinct blazed to life, firing into his muscles, sweeping his mouth down to claim hers with brutal force.

Fuck. Yes.

She was honey sweet and butter smooth, instantly opening up, letting him plunge and stab, sample and savor, taste and drink every drop of her mewling surrender. As he spread her jaw wider, a gorgeous yelp jumped up her throat. Quite possibly, it was the hottest sound he'd ever heard, the hurricane that ripped the moorings off his self-control. If she still harbored any longings for Rebel, he was pretty damn sure he didn't care.

No. He *did* care—about imprinting so much of himself on her, she'd wonder who the hell Rebel Stafford *was*, let alone what he'd done to her during the plane ride.

He pulled back to let her get some air. Probably a good idea, since he needed a few hundred inhalations too. As their chests heaved together, he reveled in the feel of her breasts against his sternum and barely repressed a groan when imagining how they'd feel without clothes, the peaks pebbled and hot against his skin while he slid in and out of her...

That was enough of break time.

Rhett slid his hands away from her face and through her hair before searching for purchase against the wall. Once he'd planted a firm grip on either side of her head, he lowered his own again—and claimed her mouth with deeper force.

She exploded like fruit on his tongue, tangy and juicy,

giving away her rising arousal. He growled low, communicating how thoroughly that pleased him, before wedging his crotch against hers and grinding with purpose.

"Oh!" Her high cry shattered the air. If he had to give up kissing her, that sound made the sacrifice worthwhile. He kicked up one side of his mouth while sliding his bulge along her cleft once more, delighting in the perfect circle of her lips as a result. "Rhett," she exclaimed. "Oh, God...please!"

Did she know what that begging did to his dick? She sure as hell did now. There was no way to disguise how every vein in his shaft pumped with new blood, reacting to the sweet submission in her voice. Still, he was a smart guy. He was damn sure he had her added up, though the equation of her sexuality certainly wasn't two and two made four. She was a goddamn algebra challenge—a submissive who didn't want to be one, a lioness still seeking her lion but looking in all the wrong jungles.

For now, it was a good option to let her call the shots. He proved it by teasing a chaste little kiss across her forehead before responding, "Please...what? Tell me, sweet peach. What can I do for you? Are you hungry, perhaps? Should we order a pizza?"

She grabbed the back of his head, yanking him down for another kiss. Rhett kept true to his pledge, letting her control every passionate second of it, enduring the extra torture on his cock. "*No* pizza." Her eyes matched the growl, wildcat bright with lust. She bared her teeth in a gorgeous snarl. Her other hand stabbed between their bodies, reaching for the snap on his pants.

That was enough of that.

He grabbed her wrist. "Don't think so, sweetheart."

Her brows knitted. "Huh? But—"

"You've had your fun. Now it's my turn to take the wheel on this op."

Just as fast, those tawny brows jumped. "That so, soldier? And what if—"

She cut herself off with her own shriek—as he leveraged his hold to hoist her off her feet. When he continued folding her all the way over his shoulder, a second scream followed.

"What. The. Hell?"

Rhett marched toward the wing with the bedrooms. "If this is happening, then it's happening right."

The ranch's master bedroom was at the end of the hall, accessed through double dark-wood doors in a dramatic stucco archway. Thick rugs overlapped across the polished wood floor, surrounding a high bed formed of walnut and accented with wrought iron. A glass-walled fireplace faced the bedroom on one side, a sunken tub on the other.

Having played techno-geek throughout the ranch after arriving yesterday, Rhett knew the fireplace was activated by a toggle switch located in the room's lighting control panel, just inside the door. On his way to the bed, he flipped that button and no other. As he'd promised, they were going to do this right, and that included the textbook lighting treatment. If this woman's body was half as exquisite as he imagined, shadows and fire flickers were going to be juuuust fine.

He sent a pair of resounding thuds through the room while stepping to the platform that held the plush king bed. He lowered Brynna to the mattress, following her down in the same controlled motion.

He had an initial plan—something about brushing the hair from her eyes, stroking a gentle hand down her body, and gazing patiently into her eyes—that was shot into hell's huge handbasket once she was prone beneath him. Step one was barely finished before he coiled a hand into her hair, fisting the russet strands in order to lift her face, preparing her mouth for his new invasion.

They shared moans as their tongues tangled, each devouring the other as if they'd embraced like this ten years ago instead of minutes. She lifted her arms and wrapped them around his neck with unbridled passion. When they pulled apart, that fire flowed into the depths of her searching gaze.

Rhett forced down a deep breath. Words. This moment needed words. His careening brain only gave him one.

Unnnhh.

Unnnhh.

Fucking great.

He kissed her again, softly this time, hoping it would break the talons on his tongue. Instead, even the caveman babble went silent, leaving him with no other option but awed silence and what had to be a dorky smile.

Crazily—magically—Brynna smiled back. She pulled on the ends of his hair before husking four soft words.

"You are so beautiful."

So *that* was what his brain meant by *unnnhh*.

He dipped his forehead against hers. Drawled with a wicked undertone, "Good thing you're not strolling through my head right now, peach, because my thoughts are far from beautiful."

Her eyes flared. "That sounds intriguing."

"Depends on how you define intriguing." It took supreme willpower not to accent it by glancing at the headboard, with its custom iron inlays in a stars and moon theme—so easily transformed by his mind into bondage-rope rigging points.

"Hmmm." Her kittenish sound was accompanied by a sexy little wriggle. "Try me."

Well, that did it.

He let a dam break. Just one—but that was more than enough. His psyche flooded with desire; his body coursed with white-hot fire. Both sensations were ruthless and perfect, propelling him to roll on top of her, dragging her sweatshirt up as he went. The second he had the garment ripped over her head, he trapped both her wrists in his grip, shoving them into the pillows, twisting his hand in her hair as he went. She winced as the pressure pulled on her scalp, though her eyes instantly sparked once more, lusty gold flashing in those huge chocolate depths.

The sight widened his grin. Ohhh, the little fox, even outrunning herself about the truth. She'd *liked* that slice of pain; her huge hang-up was appearing weak or stupid about begging for it. A hurdle easily handled. He'd simply eliminate the choice for her.

"Take it," he directed, brooking no retreat from his gaze—or the order. "You can." A sharper twist on her hair. "And you will."

Conflict stormed across her face. He was ready for it as well as the harder jerk of her wrists. He held them fast, letting her see his answering expression: all the heat and pressure and desire she gifted to him with her surrender. To make the point completely clear, he bent in and licked the seam of her lips until she opened with a moan, letting in his wet assault.

During the kiss, he pulled her hair harder. Again, she resisted. Again, Rhett held her tight. By the time they ripped apart, her chest was pumping in triple time, her teeth openly bared. He captured her pantings with his lips, studying all the facets of her eyes again. They were captivating before; they were a damn light show now. So stunning. He was a kid at his first fireworks show.

With one noticeable—and at the moment, uncomfortable to the point of pain—exception.

"You are *so* beautiful."

She wasn't amused. Her grimace darkened. "You only able to say that when your sadist is getting fed?" Her gasp punctuated it as his dick pulsed at the juncture of her thighs. He wasn't going to be sorry for it. Wanted her to know what she did to him, *for* him, with this.

"You like my sadist."

For an interminable moment, she didn't answer. When she did, it was on a reluctant rasp. "Maybe. A little. Only because he's kind of cute."

He replied, equally as softly, "So tell me no. This isn't green light red light, sweetheart. You say no, it means no. Tell me you don't like it, to just let go, and I will."

She blinked, looking puzzled. "And then what?"

"Oh, I'm sure my dirty mind can come up with something."

He smirked, committing in full to the cute sadist thing. Her tension still wasn't eased—but maybe that wasn't such a bad thing after all. Her breaths came harder as her fingers curled in, a sublime demonstration of the conflict clearly hammering her. Rhett waited. Had to issue a few silent profanities at his cock to do it, but no way in hell was he going to hurry her through this choice. An hour of pleasure was hers either way, but would they play by her rules or his? Did she swim in the shallow end and keep the ground beneath her or trust him to lead her into the deep end?

"It's not so bad," she finally murmured. "And your hand... against my head...it makes me feel..."

"Safe?" He supplied it when she trailed off, nervously wetting her lips. After she jerked out a nod, he leaned in tighter. "And...desired? And...sexy?"

He watched her pupils dilate as he drew out each descriptor, lightly licking the corners of her berry-sweet mouth after each seductive pass.

"Yes." She lifted her chin, silently pleading for fuller contact with his lips. "*Yes.*"

He used her hair to yank her back down. A sensual whine trembled out of her, and he caught every note of it with the new invasion of his mouth. He rolled and dipped and teased her with it now, spreading her slowly, tasting her thoroughly, angling her fully as he swept into every wet, welcoming corner...

When he was done, he slipped his hand off her head. Freed her wrists from his clutch.

"No!"

She blinked fast, her own outburst clearly a surprise, before plummeting her head back into the pillows. Her stare popped wider when falling to her chest, where her nipples had turned the cups of her T-shirt bra into erotic teepees.

A blush rushed her whole face. It was one of the most incredible sights of Rhett's life.

"Ohhhh, little peach." His growled endearment fit so perfectly now. The color suffusing her skin, combined with washes of the firelight, transformed her dancer's figure into smooth, light-pink curves that made him want to sink his teeth deep...

Hell if *that* wasn't the one thought that led to another.

Longing became craving. Desire became lust. And

seduction was sure as fuck going to become action.

Another rumble started low in his throat, generated from the depths of his gut. He watched it curl through her too, a proper enough warning for the hand he twisted over the button on her shorts. After that came free, he made short work of rasping down the zipper. Brynn sighed and arched against him, widening the *V* in the denim—and exposing the lace band of the panties beneath.

It was agony to shift away from her and rock back on his haunches, but years of crouching in bunkers and sleeping in the dirt made him no stranger to suffering. Those situations didn't promise this delicious reward, either.

Soon, man. So soon now...

He snagged her gaze with his before nodding toward her sweet juncture. "I need to see more. Take them off, sweetheart."

A fresh look of conflict skated across her face though never entered her eyes. Those lush brown depths affirmed the conclusion that rooted stronger in him by the minute. Given the right guidance with the proper affection, this little fox yearned for domestication as strongly as any submissive he'd met.

But now wasn't the time for theorization.

Definitely not.

As his blood turned to magma, his stare narrowed to the perfect pink flesh she uncovered. Before she was done toeing off the shorts, the moisture evaporated from his mouth. He swallowed hard and then uttered lowly, "Damn."

Brynn's lips twitched, hinting at hope and insecurity at once. "Dance costumes are unforgiving. I have to keep things... clean."

He pushed forward again, stroking fingers up and down

her totally bare sex. "There's nothing clean about what I want to do with this."

A little gasp stuttered from her. "So you don't mind?"

"Mind what? That I can see every gorgeous inch of you? That as I turn you on, every drop of your juice will be exposed for me? That I'll know exactly how ready your pussy is to be filled with my cock?"

She lifted her hands, scratching at his back to bring him closer. Her mouth parted, all but pleading for a deep kiss, but he gave her only the tip of his tongue, making her reach up with her own to meet his taunting stabs.

"Ahhhh." she finally cried. "*Rhett*. I'm... I'm going crazy. Please!"

He pulled back up, indulging a moment of just gazing at her. Holy *fuck*. With her hair splayed on the pillows, her eyes hooded and horny, and her body restlessly writhing, she was a sight he could have watched for hours. A fantasy he didn't even know he had.

A lover who sure as hell didn't fit into the one-night-fun file anymore.

A challenge to be confronted later. *Much* later. If this woman was going to take him down, body *and* spirit, then he was sure as fuck going to enjoy the ride.

"Please what?" Ribbing her was more than a pleasure. It was like splitting a diamond open, exposing fascinating new facets of her. As she arched her neck, glaring at him with a mix of outrage and arousal, he dropped his voice to a whisper. "What do you want, Brynna Monet? I can deny you nothing, creature of my dreams. Should I caress you? Taste you?" He looked deeply into her eyes, purposely drawing out a pause. "Fuck you?"

She wet her lips and gulped. "Is there an all-of-the-above box?"

He chuckled. Adorable little fox. He wondered if she'd have answered the same had he included everything he wanted on that list. Didn't matter. He was ready and willing to give her everything she'd asked for.

"For you, peach, there absolutely is. And oh, look...here's a pair of perfect tits, just begging to be first for the fun."

A quiver claimed her as he tugged her bra straps down to her elbows. He used them to trap her arms at her sides, thereby exposing her erect tips to his heated gaze. "They—I—don't do begging," she snapped.

Rhett didn't miss a stroke as he sucked at her right peak. "Oh, sweetheart...yes you do." He licked and nipped his way over her skin, set on attending the other nipple, already standing at full readiness for him. "In this case, times two."

She wrestled against the straps. "Ohhh, no. We're not going there, soldier. Your little figurative freedoms aren't going to— *Ohhhhh!*"

Biting a woman's nipple had never felt so fucking good.

Her scream was only the beginning. It jolted the air before squeezing his cock, making her taste all the sweeter as he flattened his tongue against her engorged nipple. He primed her other tip for the same feast, pinching the stiff red bud between his thumb and forefinger and then twisting just enough to make her shriek again.

"Ahhh! *Bastard!*"

"Oh, peach. Flattery will get you everywhere."

He scraped his teeth down the side of her breast, cherishing the feel of her flesh against his mouth. He alternated between long licks and little bites, yearning to mark her even harder, pledging to take it slow...at least this first time.

First time? You mean the only time? Yeah, get that through your goddamn head, asshole—the big one and the little one. She may not be a flighty club submissive, but she's also not the kind of woman who wants to ride off into the kinky sunset with you. She deserves a man who can give her stable and strong and normal, not a guy who grew up as a transatlantic chess piece, who learned relationships from magazines and eavesdropping on the flight attendants' conversations...

The discomfort of the memories was eclipsed by the magic of Brynn's thighs.

He moaned while gliding both hands along that flesh, like fine silk stretched over her solid dancer's muscles, while tracing his tongue between her ribs and into the valley of her navel. He stopped there, exhaling hard, forcing control over the cock now threatening a full revolt if not set free soon. The wet spot on the inside of his pants only added fuel to that fucking fire.

Dear God, he couldn't wait to taste her.

Clenching his jaw helped tether his erection, at least for a few more minutes. After that victory, he dipped his head lower. Pushed her legs wider. Inhaled the rich, heady ambrosia of her soaked, pouting pussy.

"*Fuck.*"

"Rhett!"

He pressed in with his nose. Took another long breath. "You smell so goddamn good. Really like peaches...only with a lot of other things added." He slid his tongue out, venturing a tentative taste. "So many *good* things..."

Her intimate lips, engorged by arousal, quivered against his mouth. He licked in, moaning deep as drops of her juice flowed along his tongue. There was no sweeter nectar in the world. When he looked up to see her neck arched back, her breasts thrust up, and her hands curled into the pillows, the sampling tasted even better.

But he didn't just want to sample.

Wrapping his hands around her legs, he angled deeper into her core. Drank from her openly, savoring her pulse beneath him, her folds around his tongue, her desire totally at his mercy. She let out a high moan as he widened his mouth, lunging and then retreating, sucking and then laving, always teasing the slick membranes that led to her body's most secret sanctuary. As badly as his cock begged for its time there, he wasn't going to rush any moment of taking her this high. And higher still...

"Rhett!" It was pitched high with need, finished off on a frantic gasp. "Oh...*damn*...I'm... I'm going to... I won't be able to stop..."

A perfect segue to the moment that he did.

"No!" she yelped again. "Oh, no! What I meant was—"

"Oh, I know what you meant, peach." He leaned back, enduring the cock-to-fly persecution again, praying that Blake was half the slapper the press said he was and liked hanging with the ladies when he was here. If that was the case, there was a good chance the man kept a stash of rubbers—

Yessss.

Sometimes, the treasure really was right where expected. There in the nightstand drawer, neatly layered in one section of an organizational tray, were the square packets he sought. The other compartments of the organizer held a tube of water-based lube, a pink anal plug imprinted with *Just For Her*, a long-tubed vibrator, and a sizable cock ring.

Well, hell. Forget the notorious playboy. Dax Blake was a

man after his own heart.

A sexy-as-fuck whimper trickled from Brynna as he withdrew one of the condoms. "Oh, thank God," she blurted, closing her legs a little and gyrating her hips a lot. "Hurry. Please!"

Imagine that. It was the very thought ruling his brain—until she started her little bump-and-grind with the mattress. With his zipper only halfway down, Rhett stopped. Nailed her with the stare he saved for subbies trying to pull brat moves with him. She wasn't anywhere near a brat, but she also wasn't getting away with *that* sneaky shit.

"You want *me* to hurry, or are you interested in doing the job yourself?"

She froze too. For a second. "You're the one who left me like this!"

He felt a brow arch. Half a grin inch up. "I haven't gone anywhere, peach."

She huffed. "Really? Are you doing semantics *now*? Can we dither *later*? Please?"

The other side of his smile formed. Ohhhh, he just couldn't help it—nor the words that flowed out, easy as the birds that glided over the lake outside. "Little peach pie, are you *begging* me?"

He braced for her profanity. Probably another huff, reinforced with a tormented girl growl.

Instead...she laughed.

It wasn't a huge sound or necessarily a pleased one—but the pure honesty of the sound was like nothing he'd ever witnessed, nor would soon forget. Against his better judgment, he felt his smirk widen. Joining her humor, letting her know how easily she could get under his skin, was against every Dom code that had to exist. But that was freeing. He didn't expect the perfect little subbie thing from her, meaning she didn't expect the flawless big-bad-Dom from him.

Her husky retort was the perfect break-in to his thoughts. "Well, I won't tell anybody the begging thing happened if you don't. How's that?"

He went ahead and added a laugh. Dear fuck, was she really this cheeky little negotiating machine all the time? He wagered the answer was yes—in which case, it became clear how she and Dan Colton, Sir Dark and Dirty the First, were doomed from the start.

Bad news for Colton.

Even worse news for Rhett Lange.

He was a goddamn sucker for sassy negotiators—especially this one. By proposing her little deal, she challenged his brain. By challenging his brain, she revved his imagination. And God help the woman who cranked the throttle on his imagination.

"Deal," he told her, prowling back down the bed. *Enjoy the reprieve, foxy.* As he positioned himself near her feet, he deftly added, "As long as you do it again for me."

Her smile faded. "Do...what again?"

He didn't answer until flattening his hands to the insides of her knees—and again spreading them wide.

"Beg."

He didn't stop there. With fingers skimming the insides of her legs, he moved back between them like human liquid, rolling his shoulders with every new inch covered, flooding her in his unmistakable intent. Giggles aside, she was going to come hard for him. That meant letting him tease at the door of her submissiveness. Just a few light taps...in all the right places...

"I-I'm not comfortable—" She interrupted herself with a hiss as he closed both thumbs over her pussy. "I told you, I can't just be ordered to do it—"

"Not an order." He paused when reaching the outer edges of her feminine triangle. "Only a suggested clause in our negotiation. Isn't that how negotiations work? I give something, you give something."

At first her reply was just shallow, sharp breaths. They intensified, quivering through her whole body, as Rhett pressed in a little more. The action pushed her intimate lips together, indirectly stroking her clit in the process. "Oh!" she finally exclaimed. "God! Oh!"

"Hmmm." He pressed in one more time before dragging his fingers away, scraping toward her stomach. "Nice try, but my name's Rhett, sweetheart."

Her legs fell open a little wider. Such a guileless move... She had no damn idea what kind of heaven *and* hell she opened for him, exposing more of her perfect paradise to his hungry stare. He wondered if she still tasted like creamed honey. *Idiot*; of course she did. What he longed to know now was the perfection of her tight sheath around his cock, taking him deeper with every thrust, until they detonated together.

But not until she gave up her end of the deal.

Not happening. Not yet. Though a stressed sheen coated her face and her muscles visibly shook, her lips thinned and her jaw jutted, hanging on to her defiance.

Rhett wavered between cursing and grinning. Her boldness was a thrill ride he hadn't experienced in years. On the other hand, the shit might just be his undoing. At least he'd enjoy the crap out of the descent.

He chose the grin. It grew, slow and subtle, as he rose higher over her, positioning his thighs between hers—opening his pants enough that she felt the wet cotton of his briefs and the hump of the shaft beneath.

They hissed in unison. He finished his in a rough rasp. "You feel that, sweet peach? That's my cock, wanting you. Needing to be inside your beautiful cunt. Craving to fuck you, fulfill you..."

Her eyes flashed open. Her lips parted, abandoning her resistant scowl. "Yes..."

Gone was his grin as well. How could he concentrate on his goddamn face when hers was one of the most captivating sights he'd ever beheld? He'd been lucky to see many world treasures in his travels across the globe, and now one more—this moment with her endless eyes, yearning lips, and shimmering skin—was added to his list.

"Not exactly the words I was hoping for, sweetheart."

A heartbeat of silence. Followed by the next, exploding with her growl. "Aggghhh!"

He cocked his head. Arched a brow. "Nope. Still not right."

"Are you freaking kidding—"

A tight moan eclipsed the words as he again slid his throbbing length along her pussy.

"Beg, Brynna."

"Screw you."

That's the idea, little fox.

No need to state the obvious. He'd just show her.

Two shoves sent his pants and briefs to his thighs. With equal thrift, he tore open the condom packet and then rolled the latex over his crown and down his shaft. There'd be no need to add any of Dax's quality lube to this picture. Every layer between Brynn's thighs was shiny with the dew of her arousal, jerking his erection tighter every time he stared at that perfect pink bloom.

Like now.

With teeth clenched against the pressure that now consumed every thought in his head and beat of his heart, he eased just his tip into her folds. Instant heat. Perfect tremors. Soft temptation. Fuck. *Fuck.*

The same word exploded off her lips. Rhett angled in, capturing the syllable with a wet but fast kiss. She sounded just as delectable with the breathy follow-up. "Shit. *Shit!* Ohhhh!"

He ground off another layer of tooth enamel but managed a controlled reply. "It's yours, peach pie. Just ask for it."

Her head kicked back again. She scratched up his spine, burning his skin with the tracks. "Oh, my God. It feels so good!"

He teethed the side of her neck. "Still not right."

"Damn it!"

"Beg."

She bit fully into his. "Give it to me."

"*Beg.*"

He pushed in by another fraction. Managed—barely—to keep his groan contained. Sweet *fuck*, he never thought he'd be battling his own lust like this. His body seemed a foreign thing, a gleeful executioner set on killing him in the most excruciating way possible. His balls screamed. His thighs shook. But he wasn't so far-gone not to notice how his control, of himself *and* her, was taking her pussy from a simmer of arousal to an oven of need. Beneath her riotous glare, she was relishing this as much as him.

"Damn!" Her legs hiked up, gripping his waist. "Oh, *damn!*"

He teased his cock into her by half an inch more. "Just one word, sweetheart. Give it to me."

She gritted out a gasp. One more. Then finally cried, "Please. *Please*. Does that make you happy, damn it? *Please*, Rhett. I need it—now. I need *you*."

He tilted his head in, releasing a grateful growl against her ear. "Oh, my little peach." *Not nearly as much as I need you.*

One slide, and his sex was buried completely inside hers.

One sigh, and she clenched him even tighter.

One moment—that wrenched them both from passion to oblivion.

Hands greedy and urgent. Mouths open and hungry. Muscles straining and seeking.

Instincts commanding.

Gazes twining.

Spirits joining.

"Oh...God." Brynna's face distorted, as if his cock had turned into a spear. The clench of her sex told him that was far from the case. That her wince was more the protest of her psyche, reached as it never had been before. And how was he so damn sure? Could've had something to do with the mirrors he now beheld in her eyes, reflecting only one thing back at him.

His own soul.

He'd experienced mortar attacks that were less unnerving than the recognition. It damn near terrified him as he watched her head twisting back, struggling to hide her face in the pillows.

"*No*." He followed the harsh husk by hurling the cushion across the room. Just as fiercely, he yanked her face back toward him. "Now *I'm* begging." He plunged deeper, driving to mark as much of her inside as well as out. "Don't look away.

Stay with me, Brynna. Take all this from me, as deeply as you take my cock. See how beautiful you are to me. See everything you do to me."

She didn't utter a word. She didn't have to. She simply reached out as he had, framing the side of his face too...his mirror.

And she obeyed him. Beautifully. Oh, God...so perfectly.

She barely blinked as he lunged harder, filling more of her, fucking until the slaps of their bodies resonated against the walls. Rhett watched her just as intently, taking in the rhythm of her breaths, the little furrows beneath her eyebrows, the hardness of her nipples—

Until he knew it was time.

One dip of his hand against the very center of her pussy. One more.

On the third, she was completely his.

"Holy— *Rhett!*"

He let his senses drown in her scream. Let his cock rejoice in her climax. Finally surrendered to the whorl of his own lust.

The world turned to fuzz. His balls surged with heat. His vision turned blinding white as the climax roared through his dick. He came in bursting torrents, each yanking him deeper beneath the undertow. He wondered if standing upright would even be possible in a few minutes...making him realize he didn't even care.

Sure enough, the sentiment became prophecy.

Aside from a reluctant pull from her body and then a lunge to lob the condom at the waste can, he was *not* interested in moving from this bed—or anywhere less than a few inches from this woman's delectable nudity. He leaned his head on an elbow while wrapping an arm over her waist, letting his thoughts stay just as tangled. There would be more than enough time to yank the shit apart later...to berate himself for once again pouring too much of himself into a "relationship" that was nothing more than an episode of fantastic sex.

And damn...

It had been *fantastic*.

Couldn't be any harm in addressing the obvious. "I'm wondering how a guy expresses thanks to the power of a million."

Her kiss-stung lips inched up. "Damn it. You stole my line."

He chuckled. She giggled. After a moment, he sobered. Brynn followed suit again. "What?" she prompted, eyes narrowing.

He shook his head. Cocked another smirk. "Nothing. It just feels good to hear you laughing."

"Why?"

"Truth? I was a little worried about an elephant in the room. A big, black-haired Cajun one."

He wasn't sure how she'd react to that. The way she firmed her face, along with tucking a pillow to raise herself a little closer to him, was encouraging. "I'm a grown woman, Rhett. I harbored no illusions about what Rebel and I shared during the plane ride this morning—or what *this* was, between you and me." Her lips quirked. "Let's face it. You're both damn delicious heroes, and my weakness for military sugar is legendary. All circumstances considered, my willpower is zilch right now. Zoe herself would tell me I'm allowed a stress-induced cheat day, especially with two such cooperative...treats."

Though she ended it with a more pronounced giggle, he didn't miss how her lips faltered when mentioning her friend.

On top of his post-sex high, she struck him with a fresh jolt of awe. She was pretty fucking astounding, having left everything behind to help save Zoe. As a soldier, it was his job to do this all the time: his life got dropped, often with just a few hours of notice, for the sake of missions. But she was a civilian, with a job, a home, and college classes, perhaps even a pet and family nearby. *Damn.*

Against every protest of his logic, he adored her a little deeper. Sealed the deal by leaning back over her, dipping his lips to hers in a long, wet, lingering kiss that had them both breathing hard by the time they pulled apart. "You're a pretty juicy lollipop yourself, Miss Monet," he drawled. "And damn if I don't want another lick already."

"Mmmm." She lazed back with a come-hither smile. "Don't think I wouldn't take you up on that offer, Sergeant—if we didn't have a teammate to support in another hour."

He couldn't ignore issuing the obvious comeback. "You think it would take an *hour*?"

Her eyebrows arched. "I wouldn't put it past you, Rhett Lange." A new giggle spilled out as soon as he puffed out his chest. "*Now* do you feel better about the big Cajun elephant?"

He rolled her to the side, just enough to retaliate by soundly smacking one of her delectable ass cheeks. Brynn squealed and scrambled away, making it easy to counter with a laugh—all perfect disguises for the actual answer to her charge.

He didn't feel better about the Cajun at all.

And the fresh twitches in his cock weren't about to let him forget.

CHAPTER SEVEN

He's fucked her.

Rebel was certain of the fact almost the second he walked back into Dax's house, wearily plunking his pack onto the entrance foyer's terra-cotta tiles.

It had started as a tickle in his ear during the mission, niggling him in the Rhett Lange subtext he knew better than anyone else. Unlike the overplayed Brit slang that had defined their earlier comm check, Double-Oh checked in with him for the op itself with a tone that was all talk-show-host congeniality, even when relaying the "fun" little tidbit that the Verge complex had sprouted a pair of guard dogs for the night. Thank fuck for the animal tranq syringes they'd added to the just-in-case pocket of the mission pack. A pair of well-aimed shots ensured the pooches napped during the rest of the time it took for him to disable the three yard cameras, hotwire the loading dock security panel, and set the camera inside the main building.

He'd barely broken a sweat—until that moment.

Right after Rhett's all-clear for the camera, confirming the device was powered and working correctly, alarms honked all over the complex. Somebody inside hadn't been happy about him murdering the yard cameras and quickly informed fifty of his dearest buddies. A smoke canister had already been at Rebel's fingertips. While setting it off provided the diversion he needed, it also sent the guards running toward the hole he'd carefully snipped in the back fence in order to get *into* the place. He'd groaned softly and then barked at Rhett to punch the proper buttons in order to make Plan B happen.

Plan B. *Fuck.*

He hadn't expected it to be a shred of fun. And damn it if he hadn't learned to peg most of his life expectations just about right.

As he straightened from dropping the pack, the verification of his accuracy bled from him—literally. The second Rhett doused the power grid the Verge complex belonged to, he'd handed Reb a ticking time clock. Only thirty seconds until the backup generators revved to life. Half a minute to sprint for another section of the fence and hurl all the way over—between the lines of vertical barbed wire at the top.

"Oh, thank God. You made it!" Brynn rushed across the living room, arms stretched toward him. Like the wrung-out idiot he was, Reb stuck up both thumbs—deterring her from fully embracing him. That seemed just fine by her.

Surprise, surprise.

"Welcome back, partner." Rhett drawled it in an awful twang as he moved up behind her, though his gaze conveyed genuine affection. Could that have had *anything* to do with the hand he pressed to the small of Brynna's back, the dude's version of draping a letterman's jacket over her shoulders? Of course, Double-Oh hadn't worn anything other than Gucci or Burberry before he'd accepted his commission—not that Brynn wouldn't be content with those either. She accepted his contact without a flinch, settling in with ease, as if knowing she'd be thoroughly cherished in that embrace.

Surprise fucking *surprise.*

The words resounded through him, their echoes stained

in bitterness. He didn't like any of this—what Rhett had pulled *or* his reaction—and showed it with a dark scowl that matched the twelves places he was really bleeding.

He had no right to the anger. More importantly, *it* had no right to *him*. If Saul Stafford had taught him anything in life, it was the pitfalls of attachment, devotion, and caring too much. They all led to nowhere but life with a hooch bottle for a best friend, gazing at a swamp full of gators with a heart full of heartbreak. Hadn't this afternoon's *misere* in the kitchen proved as much? He'd tried, damn it. For the first time in a *very* long time, he'd ventured out on a cliff of risk and invited Rhett to join him, to fly from the ledge together. And he'd expected something other than the bastard's shut-down...why?

That answer didn't matter.

The truth was...he hadn't expected this.

Despite his fight, more frustration flew in. Anger joined it. They settled on his shoulders and camped there like a pair of cemetery crows.

Fine, assholes. You want to hang out? Be my guests.

The beady fuckers turned into his best *amis* as he fixed a dismal stare on Rhett. "Good to be back, *partner*." He glanced lazily at Double-Oh's possessive hand, now winding around Brynn's waist. "Anything...interesting happen while I was gone?"

At least he could look forward to Rhett's squirm. Even if it was just for a few seconds, he'd revel in it like—

It never happened.

"Holy *crap*." Brynn lunged forward, yanking on both his arms. "That shit on the fence didn't just slice apart your clothes!"

This wasn't helping. God*damn*, no. She wasn't supposed

to be affecting him like this, simply with the concern in her touch. And the anxiety in her eyes. And the frenzy of her cute little tongue, all over her berry-dark lips.

Lips significantly more swollen between this afternoon and now.

He jerked back. Clenched his hands at his sides. "It was barbed wire, Brynna. I'm fine. They're surface scratches."

"Scratches?" she retorted. "You're bleeding!"

"It happens." Or so he'd heard. Since he was the guy called to light or defuse the fireworks, he usually strutted in after perimeters had been cleared and barbed wire chopped. That didn't make him a stranger to his own blood; the shit just usually wasn't painting zig-zag doodles down his arms and legs.

"Yeah? Well, infections happen too." She snapped it while grabbing him by a wrist and hauling him around the corner, into the kitchen. He didn't—well, couldn't—say a word as she planted him in the middle of the floor, using her other hand to retrieve a bowl and fill it from the faucet. As she started riffling through cabinets, she pointed a finger, sweeping from his head to his toes, ordering, "Off. All of it. Now."

He frowned. "All of what?"

"Clothes," she clarified. "Anything that'll get in the way of my cleaning and treating those cuts—which means you probably get to keep the briefs. Unless you're commando?"

"Unless I'm—" He could only blame shock for why it came out as a scandalized splutter. But a swamp rat from the land of voodoo and Mardi Gras usually wasn't stunned for long, especially when a beautiful redhead wanted him to strip.

Especially when an equally beautiful man hovered in the doorway, looking on with a heated, hooded stare.

"Well." Reb quirked one side of his mouth. "Whatever I can do to make your job...easier."

Brynna rolled her eyes while plopping a big first aid kit on the chopping block. "Behave, raunch dog." She smacked the surface next to the kit. "But if you really want to help, park your ass up here. I can get to you better that way."

"Getting to me. Yeah, that's important." He chuckled despite her smack to his chest—though never let the mirth climb to his stare. He reserved that for the evidence of what this moment was really doing to him...of the weight in his blood, the electricity in his skin, and the crackle in his senses—his body unable to mask its reaction to being near-naked in front of the two people with whom he yearned to be *more* bare. Ironically, the clinical setting didn't help. All the kitchen's pristine surfaces only gave him ideas of accessibility lines for licking and sucking, of perfect angles for bending...and fucking.

He stuffed the thoughts away. The heavy silence that descended over the air didn't help. He considered humming, but all the songs that came to mind were from the soundtrack he'd played in the car on his way back in from Austin: Creole tunes in husky French, most evoking images of the nastiness he struggled to silence.

Damn it.

As Brynna started dabbing at the final cut on his right arm, he couldn't help at least one teasing murmur. "That's the way, *cher*. Get me allll clean."

As he'd hoped, she spurted a little laugh. As he'd expected, still no reaction from the brooder in the doorway.

"Allllll clean?" Brynn's teasing echo carried mystery laced with warmth. The woman should've really considered screwing the psych degree and just setting up shop in a tent with some tarot cards. "You realize, Sergeant, that's like a leopard asking for stripes?"

He smirked. This time, he did let the humor reach his eyes. "Would you expect any less, *minette*?"

She soaked some fresh gauze in alcohol and bent over his leg. "If you shut up now, I won't make this hurt—much."

True to her word, she dabbed at his thigh with gentle care. As Reb stared at the top of her head, it was impossible to fight off the new erotic images, heartless with their invasion. Fantasies about how she'd look in just about that position... taking his cock into her mouth. And damn, he'd make her take it deep. And hard. Maybe he'd even make her gag, but an irrevocable instinct told him she'd like that too...a certainty he hadn't even had this afternoon. No, this was a new revelation about her. A new element exposed *in* her.

A part of her that Rhett had awakened.

Well, that sealed the deal. The bastard had fucked her, all right. And yeah, that still rankled, in its eerie way...just not as much when he imagined himself in the picture too. *Fuck*. What would happen if he and Double-Oh ever shared a woman? No, not just any woman. It'd have to be *this* woman. Would Brynn let them command her like that? If he saw Rhett naked with her, would he be able to keep his hands, let alone his thoughts, in all the "right" places? What if Rhett restrained her, spanked her?

What if he already had?

"So do you always talk about pain with a smile, *cher*?"

Her head jerked up, eyes popping as if he'd asked if she bit the heads off chickens. Astonishment and bewilderment, then rage and repulsion, flashed across her face. "Do *you*?"

He thought about apologizing but wasn't sure what for.

He chose to hold his stare steady, keeping hers locked to it. "Depends on who's asking. And exactly what's...hurting." He drifted his regard downward with the last of it.

She set down the gauze and alcohol with careful control. The same caution now defined her quiet glare. "Well, I don't do 'hurting.'"

He inched his lips up a little more. Her mien didn't change by an inch—and it was sexy as fuck. He'd always wanted to play frosty nurse and bad boy patient. "Oh, I think you do, lady. Maybe you should just...take your temperature, and find out."

She answered by stepping completely away. Her face tightened and pinched, as if she distilled her emotions into one terse vial of emotion.

"I think I'm done here. You can clean the rest up yourself, Sergeant."

Her retreating steps sounded across the living room, toward the office. During the minute it took for the angry thumps to fade, he felt Rhett's scrutiny on him. A look up, twining his gaze with his friend's, told him what he already knew. The double meaning of her words hadn't been lost on the guy—not a single accusing drop.

Hell.

He normally laughed this crap off. Wasn't like Rhett had never given him that glare before. Christ, if he had a buck for every time the man *had* dragged out that combination of sadness, indictment, and confusion, he'd have enough flow for a mansion in the Garden District. He made it easier on them both by rowing his boat right on by, enjoying the scenery on his way to easier waters, letting Rhett wallow in his muck of holier-than-thou.

He didn't feel like rowing right now. Didn't feel like

pretending that Rhett's walls were just as high and ugly as his, just because the *fils de putain* chose not to escape his emptiness in diving for pussy.

Only this time, that was exactly what he'd done.

Because Rhett hadn't been escaping the emptiness.

Rhett had been escaping *him*.

The moments in the kitchen had shaken him so deeply, he'd coped by getting his dick into a female as soon as possible. Trouble was, she wasn't just any female. She was Brynna Monet. Sexy, funny, whip-smart, open-hearted Brynna—a woman who deserved honesty and openness in return, not mooning stares and hints at "forever" when they all knew damn well that this was the craziest set of circumstances from which to expect a forever.

Nope. No rowing by this time. Rhett had sure as hell not played fair, and neither would he.

Nothing like that to lend the resolve to lean back, hands braced behind him, displaying his spread-out body for the attention of anyone who cared to look. And yeah, Rhett looked. And looked some more.

Reb smiled. Leisurely. Knowingly. If Rhett wasn't going to acknowledge the electricity between them, he'd sure as hell handle it for them both.

"I still need cleaning up, Double-Oh."

The man didn't move. Just filled the doorway with that hard tension on his lips, that palpable need in his presence...

That was suddenly too much for the narrow space of the arch.

His energy spilled through the room, hitting Rebel with its full force of fury—and lust.

Immediately, Reb hissed from the impact.

Instantly, his cock punched against his briefs.

Violently, Rhett stumbled backward. From his new position, he hurled a glare back into the kitchen, stabbing the air like spears of ice. "You heard what the lady said. Do it yourself."

CHAPTER EIGHT

Brynn zoomed from fast asleep to wide awake in three seconds. After silencing the alarm on her phone, she ran a hand through her hair and blinked in confusion. Where was she, and why had she set her alarm for the middle of the night?

A gasp took over as the answers surged in. She was in one of the guest bedrooms at Dax Blake's ranch, and it wasn't the middle of the night. It was five thirty a.m., the beginning of the day. In half an hour, she'd join Rhett and Rebel for a check-in with Shay and El and then start her shift at the mouse cam console. Already she prayed it wouldn't be another six hours of looking at nothing but live feeds of halls, doors, and feet. Lots and lots of feet.

She, Rhett, and Rebel had followed those feet everywhere inside that damn building—for three days now. Breaking up the days and nights into rotating shifts of six hours each, none of them had left the mouse cam alone for a second. Rhett had trained Rebel and her on the basic maneuvering techniques for the device, but if they encountered a special circumstance like stairs, elevators, or ramps, the protocol was to fetch him for help. Because of that, Rhett slept on the pull-out futon in the small den next to the office. In a strange display of solidarity, especially in light of the continued friction between the two, Rebel also slept close by, making his bed out of a couple of blankets and a pillow on the living room couch.

Whatever.

She hated—*hated*—being cavalier about it, but it seemed her only safe path to some semblance of emotional stability. "Semblance" was the right word for it too, because their tense blood with each other hadn't stopped either of them from warming more of hers—and endearing themselves deeper on just about every level.

Just as disconcerting? On most of those occasions, the gorgeous bastards weren't even trying. Like the morning she'd spied on Rebel as he tackled the parkour run in Dax's gym, providing his own sportscaster commentary—landing himself in first place, of course. And the night she'd overheard Rhett in the shower, belting every perfectly memorized word of "Welcome to the Jungle." Then there was Rebel's laughter, given with all of himself, at her stupidest jokes—and Rhett's "innocent" grin when he'd pranked her gullible side.

Those events were easier to write off than the purposeful ones, like the way Rhett drove ten miles to find a store that carried her beloved hazelnut coffee creamer and the afternoon Rebel had brought handpicked wildflowers to ease her grief that they hadn't found Zoe on the camera feed yet.

Zoe.

There was her hugest reason to keep the distance from the guys. Good news: she wasn't about to forget it, not with the endless ache in her stomach and the constant tear at her soul. Didn't stop her from being damn glad the guys were bunking across the house. The few hours of sleep she allowed herself each night were the key to staying alert during her shift in front of the monitors.

Now, it was time to get to work again.

That meant shutting off the swoony recollections of Sergeants Stafford and Lange and focusing her mind completely on what mattered.

Please, God...grant me insight about this. The right *kind this time.*

So many times, she was sure they'd found Royce or Adler themselves—as if evil geniuses had a certain "walk" and she'd surely recognized it by now—but the urgent strides had always belonged to a scared minion or determined perimeter guard on their way to some computer room or post. She, Rhett, and Rebel still hadn't found the one location in the place they needed to learn about: the exact location where those assholes were hiding Zoe.

While washing her face in the en suite bathroom, she grimaced into her hands. Gulped away tears. *Stupid, stupid, stupid.* She had no right to this frustration and sorrow when Zoe was living on a diet of the stuff, alone and terrified somewhere in that building, wondering if she'd ever be free—or alive—again.

Hang on, Zo. Please hang on

She hitched up the pink T-shirt she'd worn to bed long enough to throw on a bra and apply fresh deodorant, not bothering to change out of her pajama bottoms. She'd showered before bed, knowing that right now, all she'd want to do was return to the office—though the fact that Rhett hadn't woken her up yet wasn't encouraging at all. If he'd found something, he'd have called her cell from the office. After brushing her hair into a fast ponytail—now was no time for vanity—it was time to get the update on what the mouse had discovered in the last five hours.

Progress. Please, God, just one more favor... Let it be some kind of progress.

She wasn't surprised to enter the living room and see only

Rebel's mussed bedding on the couch. The pirate had started to stir when she went off to bed, having logged only two hours of sleep himself. By now, that wasn't a surprise. Despite their charming moments, the vibe from both men this week had been, in a word, restless. Perhaps even hyper. It wasn't normal for them. She knew it was silly to be so certain of it, but she was. The truth was emblazoned across both their faces, a far different thing than the tinkles they attempted as remnants of their earlier pissing match. This was something...strange. And different. For them both.

Could she be off the mark? Possible but not probable. Though she'd spent only sparse time with both of them before now, there was also a reason the field of psychology was a perfect fit for her. The gut instincts she relied on for everything from dancing to cooking were especially accurate when it came to people.

So why was this mission weirding them both out?

Part of that replay was obvious. They usually didn't have to deal with a mission tagalong, especially one who'd redefined "break the ice" with them both inside the first twenty-four hours of the op. But her intuition insisted there was more. Something about their dynamic had little to do with her or the demands of the mission and everything to do with the demands of their relationship.

If that was even what it was...

Was *that* what was going on? And had her..."fun"...with them become a fly in their ointment?

The questions were jarring. Certainly not because she had an issue with them as a couple—they were actually damn stunning together—but if they'd lied to her about their significance to each other, especially in light of the passion, intimacy, and orgasms she'd given to both...well, now they all had a problem.

Though it sounded like the guys had just hunted up a fresh one of those for themselves.

She stopped as the F-word was bellowed so loud it made the hallway's glass walls tremble. Should she proceed? She felt like one of those too-stupid-to-live ingénues in a horror movie, investigating the bump in the darkest part of the woods.

As she neared the office, another snarl erupted on the air. Fortunately, this one didn't sound like King Kong with a tack in his paw. The words added on to it pegged the speaker as Rhett.

"Moon, you've got to calm the hell down."

A bunch of pounding steps. More animalistic breaths. "That's easy for you to say, isn't it? You're not the one who just blew this mission."

Her brows slammed together. *What the hell?* The mission was blown? Why? How?

"Okay, *chill*. We have no idea what happened. You know there are probably a thousand explanations why –"

"Why what?" She made the demand from the doorway. Spying from the hallway wasn't going to cut it anymore. The pain in Reb's voice wrenched her as much as what he'd said. But now that both the guys spun toward her, she wasn't sure that was the right call either. Aside from their tight black T-shirts and low-slung sweats, they looked like hell. No, worse. Like they'd been to hell, tried to climb out, and then kept getting tossed back in to give Satan his jollies.

Rhett released the first resigned breath. Past a steeled jaw, he gritted, "The mouse cam went dark."

She drummed her fingers against her thighs. Sent back a look of bewilderment, though her heart thudded an equally urgent tattoo. "So what does that mean?"

Rebel swung an arm toward the live feed monitors, both now black. "See for yourself. It means we're fucking blind is what it means."

Brynn shook her head. Wondered why she wasn't throwing herself over into the same hell pit as them. "So we just reboot it or something...right?"

"Tried," Rhett supplied. "And failed."

"Which means what?"

"Any number of things. Perhaps Adler's boys finally detected the unit somehow and then sneaked up and disabled it."

"Highly unlikely, since the last piece of footage would have shown the unit being picked up and examined." Rebel sagged against the wall and clawed a hand through his hair. "Even if those goons figured out the unit was there, they'd have to fish around for a power switch."

"Theoretically." Brynn hated saying it, but the premise made sense. "When El's nieces come over to play, I have trouble finding the power buttons on their toys, and I can *see* those." Five minutes with one's thumb up Twilight Sparkle's butt wasn't an experience easily forgotten.

Rebel rammed his head all the way back against the wall. "Which leads us back to the only possible explanation."

"Which is what?" She didn't like saying that, either. Revision: she hated it. Felt like she'd been drafted to the Spanish Inquisition and been told to drill a steel peg through his leg. Same difference, judging from the pain on his face.

"Primary battery life on the thing is three days," he muttered. "You have to program the thing to activate the backup battery—a *manual* procedure after the unit is turned on."

She absorbed that with careful silence. "And you're not sure if you did that."

His face contorted like that was the second steel peg. "Fucking. Idiot."

"Shut. Up." Rhett wheeled back fully toward his partner. "You perform surgery on bombs, Stafford, not cameras. You're used to being given space, silence, and longer lead times for your work instead of guards, alarms, and deadlines breathing down your business. Cut yourself some fucking slack, and let's move on with a new plan."

A new plan. Brynna darted a glance outside and wondered if Rhett had done the same. It was almost six o'clock. Dawn was already here; daybreak wouldn't be far behind. If "a new plan" included the safer cloak of night, they were screwed for about thirteen hours.

Rebel's barking laugh conveyed his understanding of that fact, so she bit her thoughts into silence as he confronted Rhett with a narrow glare. "I'd state the obvious, but clearly, Sergeant Lange, you're into ignoring the obvious lately."

The corners of Rhett's eyes tightened. Other than that, he hardly moved. "I'm well aware of our present challenges. I just choose to look at them differently." He nodded toward the patio. "This gives us a window to gather intel and form strategy."

Brynn released a resigned breath. "He's right. We can whine about the setback or embrace the opportunity."

"How very Zen of him." Rebel snorted softly before parting his lips, revealing a clenched smile. "On the other hand, who can't be Mr. Zen when they're pumping a load into the world's most perfect redhead every night?"

And there went her dilemma about remaining polite and silent. "Excuse the *hell* out of me?" Followed, weirdly and wildly, by the world's most inappropriate follow-up thought. *The world's most perfect redhead? He really thinks that?*

Now was *not* the time for giddy and stupid—unless they were discussing Rebel's idiocy. Rhett was all over it. He lunged two steps forward and snarled, "You want to reconsider that, Sir Douchebag, before I beat that three tons of bullshit out of you?"

Rebel shoved away from the wall. His chest ended up an inch from Rhett's. Brynna winced, instantly recognizing the irony. In any other situation, the sight of them like that, matched nearly muscle-for-muscle, would have her squirming and wet. Right now, she didn't know whether to scream or bawl.

"You want to tell me it's not true?" Rebel slung back.

"It's not true!" But her outcry might have been a damn dog whistle. Neither of them heeded it, despite reminding her of a Doberman and a Pitbull in a growl-off.

"You want to tell me you didn't jump on her during the plane ride, just to tick me off by getting there first?"

"You want to tell me I didn't?"

"Oh, my God," Brynn blurted.

Rhett pushed forward. Rammed Rebel hard enough to make him stumble back. He began to follow but stopped as if an invisible rope caught him short. His balled fists were yanked back; his heaving chest was thrust up. "You disgust me," he seethed. "She's a woman, not a pawn in your twisted game with *me!*"

Rebel straightened. Smacked his hands together in mocking claps. "Nice, man. Real nice. Pretty speech. Now do you understand all of it? She *is* a woman. A *woman*—not an angel in human form, not a goddess without a pedestal, certainly not the hole-filler for all the shit your parents didn't get right." He stopped too. Leaned over, dipping one shoulder and arching both brows. "How does *that* play on your little chessboard?"

Rhett blew out air like a bull about to charge. "You really going there with the Freudian baggage, asshole? Oh, wait. They don't know what luggage is in the swamp, do they? Hold for a mike while I find that sack on your stick."

Rebel, already poised to pounce, took two seconds to twist his hand into Rhett's shirt. Shockingly—or maybe not—Rhett leaned in to the hold. The pair snarled at each other, though almost seemed to smile about it, leaving Brynna's bloodstream to fend on its own in a mix of fear and fascination. There was no denying the effects of the charged testosterone on the air. As horrified as her mind might be, her pussy was a pure zing of heat.

What the hell is wrong with you?

What the hell is wrong with them?

"Ha fucking ha. I'm so offended now, *couillon*. You going to make a joke about the voodoo priestess who popped my cherry now too? I have a thousand chicken sacrifice jokes that'll go well with that."

"Imagine that," Rhett rebutted. "Jokes. From you. Best coping mechanism there is—especially if anyone starts to mention real feelings. And you wonder why I keep my distance?"

Rebel colored. At least she thought he did. His skin, perpetually tanned, turned the shade of coffee beans. "Your 'distance' has nothing to do with my jokes."

"But everything to do with what I deserve." He jerked his head toward Brynna. "And what she deserves too. Which is better than your damn jokes."

"And *you're* the better, is that it? She's better off with your glass tower over my swamp and sack?"

"Enough!" Brynn's throat hurt from the violence of it. The effort was worth it. She stunned the hulks so thoroughly, she was able to push between them. Both only budged back by a step, but it was a start. "First, *she* is right here, you baboons." She ziplined her glare back and forth between them. A much-needed moment of levity came from imagining them both with bare red asses, chomping on fleas from their own fur. "Secondly, *she* isn't anyone's damn playing piece!"

Rebel's skin darkened again. Thank God she was more pissed at than attracted to him at the moment, because the richer mocha brew beneath his skin was a finer-than-fine compliment to his thick black hair, full pirate lips, and delicious cinnamon scent. "I didn't mean—"

"Shut up. I don't care what you meant. This is about what *I* meant." She curled a hand into his shirt, feeling a little heady when his pupils dilated, his forehead clenched, and his nostrils flared. "I appreciated what you did for me on the plane, but don't think I bought your lame little excuse of *distracting* me from the takeoff. I've faced scarier shit than that flight in the last year of my life alone, Moonstormer." Dear God, how he fulfilled that call-sign so perfectly—at some times more than others. Like now. His gaze was a thousand shades, all of them as deep as ocean waters under moon-drenched skies. "I wanted you as badly as you wanted me." She tugged him closer. "*Wanted,* not *needed.* Got that?"

His focus dropped to her mouth. His stubbled jaw gained

new angles of tension. "Yes...ma'am."

They stared at each other through long seconds, marked only by her pulse in her ears, perfectly synched to the thrums in her feminine flesh. Oh *God*, how swiftly he could make her wet...

She breathed hard, fully expecting Rhett's snicker to cut in anytime. He was still back there; she could feel him. Hovering? Waiting? No way would he let this chance for a gloat pass by, especially after all the venom the two of them had spat.

Finally, her curiosity relentless, she released Rebel's shirt and turned around.

Double-Oh hadn't moved. Or, it seemed, blinked. Immediately, she was enthralled by *his* thrall, his stare taking in Rebel and her like a newb in his first strip club. And yeah, she knew what she was talking about. A dancer in Vegas, even employed by the shows that required her to cover up, had been to a few skin joints in her time. Dumbstruck was as irresistible on him as the blush was on Moonstormer. His normal shit's-all-together scowl was replaced by a lost boy parting of his sinfully full lips.

A pout she couldn't help kissing.

Just a short buss but more than enough to charge the air all over again with his essence, sage and sea and all man, that was solely his. God, she'd missed that smell.

"For the record, and just in case you've forgotten"—she stabbed a censuring look at Rebel over her shoulder—"and because *nothing's* happened since, what went down between you and me was just as consensual." She set him free and then moved back, making sure her vision could include them both. "Let's get something straight, gentlemen. There are no *pawns* or *playing pieces* here. As you've both astutely noted, I'm a woman—but not one of the submissive things you usually like playing with, so I'll cut you some slack for not getting a clue before now. That being said, listen carefully." She angled up her chin and cocked a hand to a hip. "I know how to identify what I want and with whom I want it. I also possess the full capacity to understand the expectations—or not—that are involved in that choice. I enjoyed the times I spent with *both* of you, got it?"

The demand opened the pause she needed for regaining composure. *Enjoyed* was a damn huge understatement of how both these men had deep-fried her blood, fondue-dipped her heart, and hot-wired her libido. Only four days with them, and she almost couldn't imagine life without them. And no, it wasn't because they'd both opened this whole rodeo with their unique versions of warrior sex. Correction: unique and *incredible* warrior sex. That hadn't hurt, but it wasn't everything. Not by far.

That truth shone even brighter as she looked at both of them again. *Damn*, what a sight. How did the room physically contain them both? Her Viking and her pirate. Her North Sea and Caribbean Sea. Her golden-haired god, her black-haired demon. They were two halves of one very perfect bond. Inseparable. Balanced.

Until...they weren't.

Because she'd entered the picture.

Which means they can't ever really be yours.

Which meant the sooner they found Zo and disbanded this triangle peg in a round hole, the better.

She just wished the guys appeared more on board with that plan.

Jamming hands in his front pockets, again practically

pouting about it, Rhett mumbled, "Yeah. Got it."

He joined her in pinning expectant stares at Rebel. Who wasn't pouting. Or mumbling. Or stabbing his hands anywhere near his pockets.

Instead, he stepped over and wrapped both of them around her nape. Curled his fingertips into her hair, yanking her head back—so he could kiss her with blatant, consuming intent.

"Sorry. I don't 'got it.' I need to be reminded of how much you 'enjoyed' everything."

He dictated the last of it against her lips, somehow opening them at the same time. As soon as the words were done, his tongue got busy. *Real* busy. Plunging, taking, swirling, so wet and strong and dominant...

Holy.

Shit.

It was one of those moments she'd always read in books but wrote off to pure fiction: of shock so thorough, nothing but numbness reigned for several seconds. She couldn't take a breath, make a sound, think of a movement. When she finally could, the sensible answer checked in at once.

Slap him.

But oh God...she didn't want to slap him.

She wanted to sigh and melt and open for him more, to acquiesce completely, to make the desperation and frustration of the last three days go away, if only for a little while longer. *Oh, please...just a few moments more...*

Like that was going to be possible, with Rhett all but breathing down her neck too.

Rhett.

Hell! She was all but sucking face with Rebel, while

Rhett—

Made all of it even better.

Ohhhhh...*wow*.

He really *had* been breathing down her neck—as she learned when he did it even harder, pushing in to get a better view of every stab Rebel thrusted down her throat. For several seconds, she fell into numbness again. Could she trust the feedback her senses were sending? Were those really Rhett's growls against her ear, growing with arousal? Was that really his cock, swelling and insistent, against her waist? Was the new scent in the air, all turned-on spiced musk, really swirling from *her* sex?

Was she okay with this? Were *they*?

Those answers were still a blank space—but wouldn't be for long.

Rhett emitted a louder snarl, punctuated by lifting his hand to Brynn's neck. Chafed her by pushing beneath Rebel's hold and taking charge of her head with brutal force—twisting her around for his tongue's ferocious assault.

The abrasions were worth it. The inability to think beneath his mouth's possessive claim, also worth it. But the best reward of all came with the fresh force in his eyes, sheened with lust but strong as steel, as he jerked away and spoke *his* filler for the blank space.

"Maybe you need to remind us both, sweetheart. Right now. Together."

CHAPTER NINE

Rhett watched the *yes* fire up her eyes before it lifted her lips. The light, piercing as dawn through autumn leaves, mesmerized him just as thoroughly—until she turned to give its magic to Reb—

Who was just as worthy of the words.

Mesmerizing. Magical.

Christ. He'd never seen Moon look like this. The man illuminated rooms no matter where they went, but his luminosity always copied the celestial satellite he was nicknamed after, borrowing the glow from something else. Now, for the first time in their friendship, the joy on Rebel's face was an inner thing, inspired by something that was purely his...

Magnified as they locked eyes once more.

The guy's happiness ricocheted at Rhett like a rocket, decimating his chest with its intensity. Rebel had gotten it— thank God. Had understood everything Rhett was trying to communicate with this proposition. Though he couldn't give Reb that extra step in their relationship—fuck, *regular* friendship still wasn't something he knew how do correctly— this was his way of trying. A bridge, in the form of this beautiful, passionate woman, to at least connect them halfway. And God only knew, all *three* of them needed reconnection right now. No guilt. No strings. Just heat, desire, bonding, fulfillment. Just this. Just now. It was a win-win-win.

He really liked those odds.

"Rebel?"

Brynna's query reminded him that Moon hadn't verbally weighed in on things yet. *Psshh.* A formality, really. Rhett almost bellowed the *hell, yes* on behalf of his friend.

Damn good thing he didn't.

Whoa. Rebel really had become a different person. The usual Moonstormer would have been jumping on this invite like it was engraved in gold from the Playboy Mansion. A let's-get-naked playdate, with Brynna *and* him, no regrets or rearviews attached? Why the idiot wasn't dropping trou this second, instead of taking a step back from them both, was a deepening mystery.

"Reb?" Rhett issued his own cautious prompt. "You down or not?" And did he really have to voice it?

Rebel looked up—exposing the bright blue flashes in his gaze. "Oh, I'm down." He moved back in, slipping one hand over Brynna's before spreading her fingers over his crotch. The swell beneath his track pants visibly jumped, stretching a cock-shaped silhouette into the black cotton.

Rhett barely stopped himself from swaying.

God*damn*, that was a stunning sight.

A gulp pounded down his throat. How the hell had this happened? He'd always been an open-minded guy, but as a whole, cock did nothing for him. In prep schools since the age of ten and cross-country at RIT, he'd been in enough group showers to know it as a sure thing. Pussy was definitely more his thing. Soft. Supple. Tender. Tasty.

But the cock in those pants wasn't just any cock. It belonged to the guy who knew him better than anyone else. The man who'd seen enough ugliness in his life not to be bothered about the strange journey of his. The guy who understood what it was like to take life in chunks of *now* instead of pining for the past or stressing about the future, because none of it mattered if a bomb blew your face away. The man who was more his family than the people with whom he shared DNA. His brother in arms, his friend in all times of need—and in so many ways, his soul mate.

Who'd understand, more than anyone, his need to deal with this shit by making light of it. "Looks like you're *up* for it too, dude."

Rebel didn't laugh. Or react in much of any other way. The fucker was still an enigma, his face a taut mask as he caught Brynna's other wrist in his hold. He pulled her hands between their chests with a low growl. "Let's be very clear. I want to do this with you as badly as Rhett does, little *cher*..."

"But?" She supplied the implied word.

"But this time, I won't be able to control myself as much as I did on the airplane. I won't be able to hide so many of my...special preferences." One side of his mouth kicked up – *finally*—when his revelation goose-bumped her flesh. "You're a very bright girl, aren't you? You've already figured out what they are. Maybe even thought about all the...creative ways...I could play with you." His thumbs stroked her inner wrists. "Control you. Then pleasure you."

Rhett palmed the shaft now pushing at his own pants. "And I won't be able to hide what that does to me."

Rebel nailed him with a hot glance. "I sure as hell hope not."

Well, that made things official. Track pants really could be torture devices.

Brynna pushed out a cute huff—*very* cute, considering

how tightly Reb still gripped her wrists. "Are you proposing a negotiation with me, Sir Moonstormer?" The little fox actually smirked. "Though there's not likely a dungeon for miles, nor a submissive's contract on the printer?"

He and Rebel exchanged another glance. His buddy's black brows arched, an ideal expression of the surprise they shared. "Those are some very kinky terms for a *minette* who claims she wants no part of the big, bad lifestyle."

"How do you think I came by that decision?" She tilted her head. "By hitting some Tumblr pages and reading a few novels?"

Rebel smirked. "Novels aren't a bad idea."

Rhett mirrored his look. "I've assigned a few well-researched romances as homework from time to time."

She huffed. "Is this the book club meeting now? If so, it's time to let me go, cowboy."

As she ramped the sass up, Rebel caught Rhett's eye again. Jerked his head imperceptibly toward the rolling workbox next to the desk. If Rhett wasn't so fucking aroused, he would've been a little scared by how thoroughly he deduced the request.

He reached the box, retrieved the bag of zip ties in the top drawer, and offered one to his friend. Inside three seconds, Reb had the strip secured around Brynna's wrists. While he did that, Rhett moved to the corner near the sliding doors, removing a hanging plant from its overhead hook. Looping more of the zip ties together, he formed a chain that dangled from the hook, stopping when he reached a height that seemed right for Brynn standing there, wrists raised over her head.

Rebel commended him with an approving growl. Didn't waste any time guiding Brynna over. After letting Rhett take over by securing her in position with another tie, he stood back, arms folded across his chest, a sensual smirk on his lips. "How does that feel, *mon chou*? Nothing too tight or painful?"

"I..." She pursed her lips as Rhett scooted back, joining his buddy to admire how their creativity paid off with the perfect showcase for every luscious curve of her body. "It's not *un*comfortable, if that's what you mean."

Rebel nodded. It wasn't just a surface move. Rhett knew the many different ways the guy already assessed her statement, weighing the nuances in her voice and the signals her body surrendered, even fully clothed. Rebel might be notorious for his now-you-see-him-now-you-don'ts with submissives, but watching the man actually interact with a subbie was like beholding a champion tight rope act. Instincts ruled, but mistakes had to be miniscule, and the end result was always incredible.

Now, he was an actual part of it too.

And it was just as awesome as he'd imagined.

The air crackled, alive with sexual promise. If only Brynna had gotten that memo. Her feelings were written on her face, betraying her uncertainty about what predicament her blind trust had gotten her into. But if Rhett had discovered anything about the woman during their first time between the sheets, it was her psyche's odd relationship with fear. She kicked and screamed and protested about staring the bastard down but moaned and sighed and climaxed once she'd let it do its worst. As if she didn't believe she could come out on the other side alive...or the same.

Was that how she looked at Dominants, too?

And if so, why?

More importantly, was this the start of helping her heal from that...what...Domphobia? Of helping her see that the pussy hustler—probably hustl*ers*—of her past didn't have to define the pleasure she could have now. That her submission was a treasure not just to her Dominants but *herself*...a revival of her heart, body, and mind?

Could they really bring that truth to her now?

He couldn't wait to try.

He took his turn to press close to her, framing her face with his hand, one thumb beneath her chin. "Comfortable is a good start, peach, but we want to know more. *A lot* more."

She inhaled sharply. Closed her eyes.

He and Rebel hissed softly. Fuck, this was going to be good. She had to be just a couple of years younger than them, but she really was what she declared. A woman. Not some starry-eyed sub gazing up from the club floor, so desperate to please that half their brainpower was sucked up attempting to get the *right* answer instead of just giving the *real* answer.

Downside? The moment he demanded "a lot more," she knew exactly what it meant. They weren't after the surface weather report now. They didn't want "not uncomfortable." They wanted everything beneath that. Truth. Honesty. Revelation.

The hard shit.

Her eyes, huge and unblinking, along with her breaths, short and thready, betrayed her acknowledgment of it—and the anxiety that resulted. That energy poured over Rhett, causing his nerves to green-light a race he'd never been to before. What a revelation she was. A submissive who fought surrender, even when every inch of her body screamed for it. The woman took "mind over matter" to a new level.

Rebel stepped forward again. Rhett didn't blame him. Clearly the guy's fascination with her was also piqued. They were like a couple of kids with a cool new toy. After years of dungeons and latex and high protocol, this shaky girl, in her T-shirt and pajama bottoms, was like Hot Wheels with booster rockets.

Rebel braced the other side of her face, also pressing a thumb beneath her chin. "Talk to us, *cher.*" His demanding husk gave her no quarter. "We need to know everything. There's no right or wrong here, no fantasy that's forbidden or off-limits." He dipped his face closer, nipping at the corner of her lips, giving Rhett a perfect view of the desire tightening his jaw, heating his gaze. "The more you give us, the more we can give you. And perhaps"—he lifted his stare toward Rhett—"we'll even push you a little. But all you have to do is communicate, to say no. Here, with us, that's exactly what the word means."

Air left Brynna in rickety bursts. Still, she flicked her gaze at both of them and rasped, "I don't want to say no. Not yet."

Rebel pressed in a fuller kiss. "I'm glad to hear that. I'm sure Rhett is too."

Rhett nodded. Sort of. He was unable to rip his gaze away from watching them tease each other's mouths. Hard against soft. The dusk of Reb's stubble against the peach dawn of Brynn's cheeks. The Dominant adoring the submissive.

His dick swelled to the point of pain.

Focus on something else, moron.

"You haven't answered our question yet, sweet peach." How he uttered it without his voice cracking, he'd likely never know. "How do you feel?"

Rebel pulled away a little, clearly sharing Rhett's expectation that she'd attempt an evasion. Instead, Brynn's expression reminded him of a philosopher, perhaps a poet, selecting her next words with ultimate care.

"Exposed."

Even with the beautiful honesty with which she spoke, she blinked rapidly, fighting to control her fear. Witnessing her push at that barrier was one hell of a turn-on. Rebel's lusty bayou smile conveyed how thoroughly he agreed—and how merciless he was going to be about pushing it.

"Beautiful," he told her before turning in, filling her personal space, and capturing her mouth in a full, deep kiss. Brynn moaned and arched toward him, so perfect for how he fisted her T-shirt and dragged it up her body. Once the fabric was bunched at her neck, Reb shoved it higher, stretching the neckline over her face until she was blindfolded by the folds of cotton. He pushed the sleeves to the same level, turning them into pink cotton cuffs around her upstretched arms.

Breathtaking.

"Oh!" Her muscles stood out as she wriggled, testing the bonds. "Oh...*my*."

"Doing okay?" Reb inquired.

"Y-Yes." She sighed. "I'm okay."

Rebel glanced to Rhett, who nodded approval at his handiwork. "Make use of what's around, man." Well, imagine that. One of the battalion's most common mottos had some interesting secondary applications.

Reb swung his head down a little. "Front-clasp bra."

Rhett laughed out a growl. "Halle-fucking-lujah."

"That's got your name written on it, man."

He needed no further prompting. Sliding in to take Reb's place in front of Brynn, he twisted open the clasp between her breasts, setting those two perfect globes free of their cupped constraints. Behind him, Rebel let out a praising rumble. He didn't blame the guy. Her breasts were like a masterpiece on canvas in the Louvre, full and ripe and perfect, begging to be shown off and worshipped. And a few other treatments he could absolutely get on board with...

"How do you feel now, little peach?" He asked it while scraping hands along her ribcage, letting the heat of his breath fall over her nipples. As deeply as he craved to taste both of them again, he held back. Neither Rebel nor he had definitive knowledge of what her path in kink had been so far, though his instincts screamed that her "research" didn't equate to experience. Even more proof of that came in the form of a shudder that claimed her whole body, making more tiny bumps stand out on her peach pearl skin. But was it a good shiver or a get-me-out-of-here shiver?

"I feel..." More breaths slashed in and out of her, serrating her confession. "Vul...nerable."

He softly kissed her forehead. "Vulnerable is okay."

"Wh-What about a little scared?"

He frowned. "Just a little?"

Her dreamy smile dialed his stress back. "Mmm-hmm."

"In that case..." He slid his lips to her cheek, nuzzling her with more erotic intent. "A little is okay."

"What else?" Rebel grated it while sliding up behind her, circling hands around her waist, skimming fingers beneath the waistband of her pajamas.

She trembled again. Pulled in air through her teeth. "Oooohhh. Ummmm..."

Rebel pressed in tighter—then caught Rhett's attention with a sneaky leer over her shoulder. No. Not sneaky. Slutty. Why the *hell* did that cause an erection surge? "Focus, *ma minette.* Tell us everything." His head dipped, lips flat to her skin, indicating he'd gone for a full bite somewhere on her nape.

Brynn stiffened and groaned, confirming the assumption. "We can't do anything better if you don't tell us."

She lolled her head to the side, baring more of her neck. "Well, *that* felt pretty damn good."

Rebel laughed softly. Licked the spot he'd just abused. "What else?"

She twisted once more, only this struggle was different. Her body rolled with the bondage instead of fighting against it...as if she needed to know it was still there. That she was truly helpless to protest anything they asked of her...

"Electric," she finally responded. "Everything...tingles. I'm so...alive."

"Yes." Rebel didn't transform it into a tease or a seduction. Rhett watched in awe—and arousal—as the man focused completely on her, stowing his inner Lothario for the privilege of nipping more at her heated skin. "I know the feeling."

Rhett gave in to a growl. "God*damn*." And then the hunger for her sweet tits beneath his mouth. "Roger that," he finished, dropping his lips to the nipples that now appeared like shiny bits of hard candy. *Fuck*...such treats. Rebel's snack time on her neck had made them taut, red, delectable. He swirled and licked, nibbled and bit, alternating his mouth between both mounds until they resembled scoops of creamy ice cream with dark-red gum drops on top.

"*Merde.*" Rebel stared over her shoulder at what Rhett was up to. "*Les doudones...c'est trés belle, mon chou. Je bande plus grand pour toi.*"

"Exactly what he said." Rhett gazed up at them both and grinned. "You have the most stunning set of breasts it's been my pleasure to taste, sweetheart."

Rebel worked his head forward a little more, sucking on

the curve of her ear. It didn't escape Rhett's attention that he also tucked a hand deeper beneath her pajamas, working his way to the cleft between her legs. As Brynn emitted a high-pitched moan, the spice of her arousal knitted through the air.

"Suck on her again, Double-Oh." Reb's voice was sandpaper. He began rolling over her pussy, fingers sensual and sure. As soon as Rhett complied, he demanded, "Now bite them. Hard."

"*Bite* them?" Brynn gasped and bucked—but the effort was more for show, a half-assed effort to prove she *still* wasn't going to just hand them her submission on a platter. "But—"

Rebel shoved down her pajamas—and landed a hard smack on her ass. "Hush, *ma petite*. You're going to scream for us. And you're going to love it."

"The hell I—aaahhhh!"

She definitely screamed—as Rhett closed his teeth around her nipple. Once more as he performed the same on the other breast. The way her tips stood straight up for him, bursting from their areolas, tempted his mouth down again. He soothed the peaks with long, warm licks this time, unable to hold back a satisfied moan from the feel of her proud erections against the flat of his tongue.

"Fuck. Your tips are hard as diamonds, sweetheart."

"And your cunt is wet as a rain-drenched flower." Reb continued working the folds of her sex in languorous rolls, sliding in his middle finger every third or fourth stroke, snarling in pleasure as she mewled in need. "Spread your legs. Open the bloom for me, Brynna."

With a strangled sigh, she obeyed.

The scent of her pussy permeated the air even more. Rhett breathed it in, swearing again. His lips fell away from her flesh, just to keep his lungs supplied with what they needed as he gazed at Rebel's fingers, incessantly pumping into her flesh.

"Christ, Brynna," he blurted. "You always smell so fucking good."

She frantically licked her lips, a perfect match to the T-shirt still keeping her in sensual darkness. She moaned softly as Rebel pulled out his hand, fingers glistening with the cream from her channel, and then spread the arousal up and down her bare pussy lips, now swollen with arousal. "I'll bet she tastes even better," he stated.

"Oh, she does." Rhett couldn't help his been-there-done-that smirk.

Rebel chuckled softly. "Yeah?"

It was probably the easiest damn question he'd get to answer all year—but when he opened his mouth, only silence seemed appropriate. Rebel's inner glow had intensified, turning into a sexual force he'd never seen the guy exude—and certainly never felt for himself... Not like this, like a thrumming from inside his blood, growing stronger by the minute. If the man kept up this tall, dark, and irresistible shit, Rhett would have to call Seattle before they flew home—more specifically, to Max Brickham, owner of Bastille, the BDSM club they were both members of. No submissive in the place would be safe once Reb walked back through the doors.

Damn. *Damn.*

"Yeah."

He finally got it out, though couldn't manage another grin to go along—likely because of what needed to happen next. *Needed* to happen.

"But you shouldn't take my word for it."

Rebel's dark brows cocked up—though aside from that, he

didn't break stride in the new bites he trailed along Brynna's right shoulder. When her breasts rose and fell from the fresh acceleration of her lungs, Rhett knew she'd caught on as well.

"Is that so?" It was a drawl though far from lazy. Only adding to the impression that he'd swallowed a stick of dynamite, Rebel sizzled the air with every movement, circling to stand in front of Brynna again. Without speaking, he delved a hand into her hair, angling her head back for another thorough kiss.

Watching the man explore her mouth, suck on her tongue, and plunge into her throat had Rhett gritting against a fresh rise of his cock. The idea of freeing himself now was so fucking tempting, but it felt lame when Rebel was still keeping shit under wraps. But standing here like a voyeur perv felt equally lame—irony of ironies, since Rebel Stafford had to be the biggest pervert in the army, if not all the armed forces.

That was because pervy had nothing to do with this. The truth? He was being as clingy as a fourteen-year-old girl. Simply put, he had to be closer—to both of them. Yeah, yeah; so his overattachment thing was as concerning as Reb's slut-from-Mars thing, but this wasn't a time for the therapy couch. This was a time for feeling good.

It was ideal inspiration.

He stepped over, sliding into Reb's old spot behind Brynn. Like a key in a lock, his body fit flawlessly against hers. His thighs cradled her hips. His dick nudged her ass.

It was...good.

Yeah.

So good.

Who the hell was he kidding? It *wasn't* good. It was fucking agony.

Just getting to gaze at her from this angle, hands bound overhead, every naked inch of her body exposed...

Staring at Rebel's bite marks on her neck and then imagining how his own would look next to them...

Taking in the perfection of her skin and envisioning its tingles as he brushed a flogger across it...

Christ.

At this rate, no fucking way was he going to make it to the good parts of this thing. The ordeal only continued as he stared at the perfection of her spine. The column, bowed just a little and stretched so all her muscles were emphasized too, was just as erotic as her breasts—*how was that even possible?*—a torture worsened because it ended at the sweet rosette of her anus. If he made it past all the fantasies that attacked because of *that*, no way would he withstand thinking of what came next: the tender folds between her thighs, soon to be quivering beneath Rebel's expert mouth.

Fuck. *Fuck.*

As if reading Rhett's thoughts exactly, Rebel cast a single glance over Brynn's shoulder. Rhett groaned at once from the impact. The man's eyes, shimmering like Excalibur itself, sliced in and ripped him open—but instead of spilled guts, he released pure energy. An erotic freedom that was stupefying, dizzying. The force of it was so potent, even Brynn was affected. Her head jerked, twisting at her T-shirt bondage. Her lungs pumped, bouncing her breasts in hypnotic rhythm. Her hips jerked as if Reb's beautiful blade really had run her through.

Lust fired Rhett's blood. He yanked Brynn tighter against him, forcing the roll of her hips to match his. She succumbed at once, trembling mewls emanating from her stretched throat. He greedily sucked that creamy column, at once recognizing the earthy scent of the man who'd been there first...as he vowed to add his own claim there too.

They rocked harder together. Harder. Their tempo was urgent, pounding, primal—but not for long. They slowed as Rebel curled his hands over her from the front, dragging over her with possessive force: down her breasts, along her ribs, to the V at the center of her body. Once there, he dropped to his knees, muttering something filthy in French as he buried his nose in her pussy. He switched to English for his next hard growl. "More." Backed it up by reaching up and wrapping his hands around her ass—

Which pressed his fingertips against the sides of Rhett's cock.

"*Fuck.*"

All three of them shouted it at once.

Rhett finished his bellow with a groan. Brynn added a shuddering sigh.

Rebel—goddamn bastard—unfurled a wicked laugh.

"I'm going to eat you now, *mon chou.*" His stare was still a sword—that had been honed in a forge of dominant sexuality. "I'm going to spread this blossom wide and drink every drop of its juicy nectar. Then I'm going to drill my tongue into your perfect cunt until you come hard against my mouth."

Brynn moaned. Shivered all over. Rhett knew it as a certainty because every last one of those quakes zinged through him too.

Rebel dug into her ass, his hold becoming demand. Rhett clenched his teeth and almost swore. *Don't do that again, asshole. Please do that again, asshole.*

"*Ma chatte?*" There was no sensual tease to it now. "Tell me you understand and that you'll accept the pleasure I'm ready to give. You know the words to use."

"Oh, God!" Brynn moaned it as he extended his tongue, swiping into her sex with slow deliberation. "Ohhhh...shit... please!"

"Not the words. Should I tell Rhett to spank you again, perhaps as a reminder?"

"No, Sir."

No, Sir?

Rhett didn't hide his bafflement. Even with the small bombshell reference to the spanking, those were the last words he'd expected from her. Well, almost. Her breathing was more shallow and her limbs more tense, conveying her fresh conflict. Did that mean she'd hated the words...or loved them and hated *that* fact?

"I-I mean yes, Sir," she suddenly added. "I mean that I understand. And...I'm ready to accept it. All of your pleasure. Please!"

That sure as hell answered things. In all the right ways.

A smile hooked at Rhett's lips. He looked down to Rebel—who sent out the same message with the warmth in his eyes, considering how his mouth was full with the sweetest pussy on the planet.

"Fuck." Rhett issued it while burying his face in her thick strawberry hair, though throwing his gaze directly into Rebel's. "This is going to be so damn good."

As if he needed any more affirmation, the ten fingers against his cock squeezed again...another invitation down a path where secrets were safe and the rules were damned.

CHAPTER TEN

Who the hell are you? What the hell are you doing? What the hell have you become?

The demands slashed from the edges of Brynn's psyche, puncturing her mists of arousal, desperate attempts to remind her that a week ago, she'd vowed never to be a bound, begging thing at the end of a tether, all but asking a man's permission to draw her next breath.

Hypocrite.

Where's your conviction now, Brynna? Where's the woman who vowed she'd make no man her religion? Where's the person who swore her life would be bigger than what Mom promised... better than what Enya settled for?

She was still here, damn it.

She just wanted a break.

Needed a break.

Oh, God...just this once, just for this razor's edge in time, she needed to dance on that dangerous blade, to court every nasty, naughty creature of her desires to twirl there with her... to bleed from the cuts of her own salacious fantasies...

To give up. Give in. Give over.

To trust.

Just

for

one

moment...

Funny things, those moments.

In one, a person could be wrestling with themselves but still be halfway sane. In the very next, the world was a different place, blinding and brilliant, centered on a tiny bundle of nerves at the center of their body, being touched so exquisitely that concepts like gravity, time, and linear thought were total farces.

The morning sun beamed into the office, warming her skin—and emulating the recognition that blazed into her soul. There was no way to fight it, to deny it, to ignore it. She belonged to them. Right here, right now, on this edge of existence, she was at the complete mercy of these two men: these mavericks who'd shattered her, broken her, exposed her...and adored her for all of it. More than that, were actually determined to reward her for it. In *such* incredible ways...

"Ahhhh!"

Maybe not so incredible.

She twisted her head, trying to glare down at Rebel. Hilarious concept, considering her scope of vision had turned bubble gum pink. "Did you—"

"Bite your gorgeous clit?" He responded as if inquiring if she wanted ketchup with her fries. "Why yes, *ma chatte*. I did. And it was delicious. Thank you. I liked it so much, I may just take another taste."

"No!"

"Excellent idea." Though Rhett's voice was a drawl, he cupped the side of her face with opposite intent, forcing it up toward him. "And this time, I'm going to watch every effect it has on our darling girl."

His promise short-circuited her logic. Rebel's teeth, closing in on her *there*, truly wasn't the most pleasant sensation—but getting to hear more of that rasp in Rhett's tone, coarse and sexy with arousal...what would she do for that?

Like she had a choice in the matter.

"Ohhhh!"

Which, clearly, she did not.

Rebel chuckled as he dug in again, gently teething the flesh along one side of her pussy and then the other, before trailing inward with shorter, sharper bites. Brynn's buttocks clenched, trying to fight the strange combination of stimulation and pain, but the man commanded her to compliance by grabbing her cheeks harder, followed by a reprimanding grunt.

Rhett backed up his friend's intent, pulling the T-shirt from her eyes so she confronted the rebuke in his eyes. "Hold still, sweetheart." He twisted his fingertips into her hair.

She blinked, vision distorted by the sudden light. "I'm trying!"

He softly kissed her lips...but then gritted against them, "Not enough."

"Damn it!"

"*Brynna.*" He coiled her hair tighter. "Why are you fighting it so much? Fighting us?"

She didn't know what to say. His query alone tossed up her logic worse than a first-night bartender mixing a perfect Manhattan. His tone, snowdrift gentle, was accompanied by the scorch of his torque on her scalp—a conflict that should've been troubling at the least. But it wasn't. Not at all. In actuality, the confinement made her feel...safe. Even a little...treasured. Which had her sympathizing with the damn bartender all over again.

"I—" Okay, it was a start. But his expectant scowl repeated his message. *Not enough.* "Because I'm confused," she finally confessed. And did they have to be taking this up *now*, with Rebel continuing to nip at her in so many amazing places down *there*?

Until...he didn't. And started the biting thing again.

The biting thing.

That was going to be followed by the sucking thing. Then the licking thing.

Which now, didn't make the biting thing so bad anymore.

Oh *God*, she was so mixed up.

"Why?" Rhett asked it with his North Sea eyes, roaming them across her face as if the fate of freaking nations awaited in her answer—as Rebel continued to spiral the incredible heat in her sex. This was so unreal, she almost couldn't believe it was happening.

A new pinch from Rebel's teeth reminded her that really wasn't the case.

A new, *harder* pinch.

"Aaahhhh!" She exploded the air with the scream but concentrated on controlling her struggles through it. But why? *Why* the hell was she struggling so much to please them, when she didn't want all this? When she should've been ordering them to cut her down, set her free, and stop digging their teeth into the most tender tissues of her body? Confusion. Yep. That pretty much pegged it. "Be-Because he's hurting me, okay?"

One side of Rhett's mouth turned up—another "reward" that wasn't supposed to feel so damn good. "That's honest," he praised. "Thank you."

"And that does *not* help me." It was cranky, probably dancing near some Dom line of his, but she didn't care. Not that he let her know at all, continuing to regard her with Perry Mason calm.

"Because you're still confused?"

Brilliant deduction, counselor. "Because it's *pain*. And pain shouldn't also feel so..."

"Feel so...what?"

She huffed. Like that was going to get her out of this. Averting her eyes, or even trying to, was out of the question. Rhett vised her chin between two fingers, ensuring she knew that as one really unalterable fact. *Demon Viking.* Rebel was the man's evil accomplice, spreading tingles down her whole left leg thanks to his savoring growl against her inner thigh.

"So...good," she finally rasped.

Rebel gave her another growl. This time, the right leg got some sugar.

Rhett relaxed his hold and widened his grin. It was the opening she'd needed to jerk away, but God, did he have to tilt his head into the sunlight that way, firing the rays through the tips of his hair, turning his eyes into azure crystals? She couldn't look away if Moses himself appeared to part the waters of the lake.

"That was also honest," he said. "And really stunning, sweetheart."

His approval, piled on top of his beauty, was the undoing she didn't want to disguise. "Thank you," she murmured.

"Now what else?" he urged. "How else does it feel? Tell us about now. What do you feel right *now*?"

Her lungs filled with a long breath. What did she *feel*? Okay, so interpreting feelings was what she did for a living—even kinky ones from time to time—but she wasn't on the clock right now, damn it. Weren't they all just here for, as the man himself would say in that half-and-half accent, a little snog and shag? An escapist fuck?

She tensed again, resisting the harder push at her composure.

But as Rebel eased his tongue in, soothing his abuse of her clit with soft, wet strokes interspersed with teasing, masterful flicks, her muscles softened. Her defenses dropped. Heat suffused her once more, though the flood was really different than the first. This heat had energy. Urgency.

"It's warm," she finally rasped. "*Really* warm. Like how everything feels after I've had a tough rehearsal, only..."

"Better?"

At that moment, Rebel shifted his tongue again...tucking just beneath her hood.

"Yes!" She choked it out as her womb convulsed and new arousal sluiced through every inch of her sex. "Ohhhh...yes." Oh, *God*. Again, he hit the spot that sent shockwaves clear down to her knees. "B-Better," she stammered. "*Better.*"

"That's our good girl." Rhett crooned it before devouring her mouth in a deep, hard kiss. At the same time, Rebel greedily sucked the fresh juices from her trembling tunnel. Her senses spun. Her mind whirled. The only way she recognized "up" was due to the zip tie chain over her head.

How life could change when all the rules were shattered.

How amazing one body could feel when all its boundaries were stripped.

And holy hell, they weren't even done. Her confession revved their attention to new realms of intensity, turning their moans into sounds of savagery, transforming their tongues into living creatures in their own right. Both men licked and sucked and adored her, Rebel at her clit and Rhett at her neck, until the sounds crawling from her own throat were just as harsh, hungry, needy—

Until those moans broke into screams.

In the moments when the duo locked gazes, traded grins, and sank their teeth into her...together.

Moments like now.

"*Aaahhhh!* Ohhh, shit!"

Rhett's sensual snarl curled into her ear as he rubbed a thumb across the nipple he'd just pulled taut between his teeth. "Enjoying the ride, peach?"

She forced a hard swallow, wetting her dry throat. "You two are driving me crazy, if that's what you mean."

"Hmmm." Rebel planted a kiss to her mound while lifting a shit-eating smirk. "Yeah. That's what we mean."

He gave her no room for a comeback, gliding his lips back down into the tender flesh that now all but screamed for his touch. Perfectly synched, Rhett scooted around and circled her nipples with languorous licks.

Crazy. She suddenly recognized it as a huge misnomer on her part. It fell pitifully short of the tempest they'd really unleashed in her blood, across her skin, inside the deepest corners of her sex. She was debilitated by their bondage, drugged by their lust...but at the same time, never more awake, alert, *alive.*

No. Not *crazy* at all.

It was magic. And fire. And need. The furnace in her sex intensified. The flames in her blood turned white-hot. Her body trembled from scalp to soles, tripling the torment of remaining still for them—especially as Rhett cupped both her breasts, pulling out her aching, taut nipples and declaring, "Look at this, Moon. Look how hard you've made our little girl's tits."

After a heated glance up, followed by a rough, approving

groan, Reb stabbed his tongue higher against her sex.

"Ohhhh, God!" she moaned.

"Hell, *yes*," Rhett growled. "Give it to her, Moon. Fuck her with your tongue, man."

Rebel didn't waste a second on hesitation. A small scream, then a bigger one, erupted from Brynna as her walls clamped down on his probing tongue. She wanted more. Needed more. Contracted her pelvic muscles to make her pussy pull him deeper inside. *Deeper.*

As her knees turned to mush, she sagged. Rhett supported her from behind, one arm around her waist, his other hand sliding forward, gripping her inner thigh.

"Spread wider for him, sweetheart. I want to see the cunt you're offering my friend. Is it worthy of his kisses? Is it worthy of an orgasm for him?"

"For *you*." The words sprang up, feeling so natural, so good—because, she suddenly realized, they came from a place deeper than just the places that throbbed physically for them. "For both of you...Sirs." She let her head fall back, searching for his gaze with her own. "Please. Yes?"

His generous mouth curled up in a proud smile—lighting that same place in her spirit with its brilliance. He didn't falter the expression as he directed, "Shove it in deep, Reb. Make her explode."

He finished it by plunging his tongue into her mouth—coinciding with the first complete stab of Rebel's tongue. Holy *hell*. She thought the man had been licking her as deep as possible before but now conceded that lashing as a warmup before the real assault. His teeth ground into her clit. His lips damn near broke skin on her mound. His nose was so deep, he inhaled nothing but the trembling tissues at the top of her pussy. Rhett didn't relent either. Her mouth was prisoner to his, stretched wide by his relentless drive, her sighs tangling with his eager groans.

It was so much. *So much.* Their scents in her nose. Their tongues in her holes. Their hands on her...*everywhere.* Yet she craved more. Mewled and moaned for it. Writhed and strained for it. Soaked up every drop of their consuming, conquering desire, reveling in its power through her veins and its command in her spirit, until her resistance gave way, giving over in ultimate, exquisite surrender.

She came on a tidal wave of blinding heat and thoughtless rapture, her body seizing as her mind left the building completely. The surge turned into a tsunami, consuming the shores of her thoughts, her logic, even her sense of which way was up. She didn't care. Didn't feel a damn thing beyond the pulses in her sex, the throbs beneath her breasts, the thorough surrender to the strength and heat of her two incredible lovers, keeping her safe as she drowned, over and over and over again...

Wow.

Fucking...wow.

Rhett kept kissing her, seeming to know she needed the release for returning slowly to herself. It was a blessing and a curse. Huge parts of her longed to pull away as an overwhelming sting burned the backs of her eyes. She could *not* cry on them—not after she'd been the one declaring she knew what big-girl panties were as well as how to wear them.

After a few seconds to breathe deep and regroup, she was fine—

Until she wasn't.

The tremors took over every inch of her body, annihilating her from the inside out. Damn, damn, *damn.* She'd managed not to cry but lost it over everything else in her nervous system: uncontrollable shakes that made no sense at all. She wasn't even cold. What the hell?

"Shit." Rebel shot to his feet, yanked the twist ties off the hook, and then curled her arms against his chest. "Scissors?"

"Roger." Rhett's reply overlapped. It took him three seconds to slide the shears in and snip the plastic loose. Rebel braced his legs wider, absorbing her sagging weight in full.

"Brynna," he reproved. "*Ma belle.* Why didn't you tell us about the issue with your circulation?"

She lifted her head, unable to hold back a seductive grin. *Buh-bye, irksome shivers. Hello, pirate stud.* "What issue?" Oh hell, he was so much better to gaze at from this close, with that stubbled jaw and stressed-out gaze. And God, his chest... Despite concealment by the dark T-shirt, it seemed broader, harder, more grip-worthy now than it'd been on the plane, but she hadn't been able to truly explore him then. Now, that opportunity waited to be grabbed by the proverbial horns— with both hands. In light of how *he'd* just fondled *her*, this was damn near her right.

He was so perfect. Truly built like a pirate who'd been hoisting sails and slinging rope. His pecs were like slabs of rock. His tattoo-covered arms visibly rippled beneath her caresses. Best of all, he felt like he'd just walked in from the Caribbean sun. So wonderfully warm...

"Wow." She couldn't help blurting it though managed to dial back the syllable from a roar to a rasp. *His* circulation was certainly working fine. Her arms finally free, she formed her body tighter against his. Everything else was working just fine too. *Better* than fine.

And just like that, another shiver claimed her.

The one that made all the difference in the world.

God, she wanted him. Yes, right now. Yes, stroking at her clit and her pussy before filling every inch of her clenching channel. And yes...doing the same thing with his cock this time.

"Sweetheart." Rhett's admonishment was stricter—not that she had a problem with that. She'd just had his breath in her ear and his cock at her ass, priming her libido for him in about a dozen ways. So yeah, she wanted him too. With all the same nasty, naked abandon she craved from Rebel.

"You can't blow this off by feeling Moon up," he continued. "As nice as that possibility feels, your silence about this isn't acceptable."

"To either of us," Rebel adjoined.

Rhett pulled at her fingertips, holding one of her arms up. "Look at these deep indents from the ties. If you were cinched too tight—"

"*Pssshhh.*" She yanked her hand back. "I'm the girl who did the research, remember? The one who looked at *a lot* of pictures while deciding if BDSM was the thing for her?" She rolled her eyes while joining their survey of her wrists. "Calm down, mama hens. I loved every second of that. And the skin's not even broken."

The hen line had Rebel jerking back like one, folding his arms and cocking his brows. "You see me laying an egg, *cher*?" he charged. "No. But I can tell you what *I* saw. *You*, shaking like a goddamn feather in the wind." He stepped back again, practically posing with his puffed chest. "We're open-minded men. Enlighten us, *minette*. If that wasn't a fucking circulation issue, then what—"

"It *wasn't* a circulation issue." She almost regretted the outburst but stood by her words when both of them refused to shuck their inner ogres, unwavering in their growly vigilance. She just wished they'd lean more toward the warty, smelly end of the ogre spectrum, not the hulking, stares-like-pure-sin side. "Unless head-to-toe horny is considered a circulatory thing these days?"

Rebel lowered his arms. Well, there was a shocker. He didn't vibe overbearing giant all over her any longer. As a matter of fact, he looked...stunned. Rhett's mien matched.

She'd astonished them?

And at the moment, did it matter? Not when the pause on the air thickened with breaths, hers and theirs, racing each other in new lust. Her stare accepted the heat of theirs, burning it in, fusing it to her senses.

Lust flared between all of them like a Stratocaster plugged to a wall of amps.

Thank God. Maybe *now* they'd gotten the message. But could they really give her pleasure like that and not expect she'd want more? Not know she'd crave to give them the same thing in return?

The huge, hard ridges between their thighs gave her hope. Lots and lots of hope.

Now, guys, just start thinking with your little *heads, okay?*

So, there really was a first time for everything in life. She just happened to be experiencing a few in a row today. If fate was really on her side, that list would soon be growing by one more.

CHAPTER ELEVEN

What the hell was going on in that beautiful brain of hers?

It was the wrong question, and Rebel knew it. More accurately, it was just the question that didn't need to be asked because it had already answered itself. He knew damn well what intent ruled her right now—exchanging a glance with Double-Oh confirmed he wasn't the only one. He just didn't know how to process the recognition as reality. Doing that meant confronting the *actual* mystery on his mind.

Was this woman going to be his dream or his destruction?

And at the moment, did the answer matter?

His cock issued a resounding *no*—and he wasn't complaining. *Damn.* She was five and a half feet of everything he could have conjured from a fantasy. The sensual focus of her huge brown eyes. The stiff tips jutting from her dusky areolas. The fresh dew gleaming between her creamy thighs.

Jesus. So perfect.

Maybe she simply *was* a hallucination...

But when he reached to stroke her shoulder with a knuckle, she didn't disappear. Her reaction was the exact opposite. So responsive, her flesh pimpling beneath his touch. So open, her full lips parting. Then so real, her voice rasping the air between them, reaching for him like a touch all its own... but zapping his senses as something more. A caress he felt to the core of his being. Electricity. Lust. But more. Needing so much more.

"Issues? Yes, I guess I have a few, Sergeant." Lifting her chin, she edged closer. Closer. Letting him see her quiver anew as he skimmed his hand down, brushing the pucker of her breast. "And now I *am* speaking up for help." She slid her hips in too, rocking her pussy against his hand. Her sparse whisper mingled with the sound. "Help."

Fuck.

His dream?

His destruction?

Now, the answer felt even more important. *She* felt important. But why? *Why?* And what was that...*thing*...her voice kept triggering in his brain, like a damn bullet she'd shot there, tearing so many things apart as it ripped inside? Painful things. But...significant things too.

Why did this *all* feel so damn significant?

And why the fuck was he dwelling on it, when this amazing, *naked* woman all but climbed him like the tree of life? And Rhett, the glorious asshole, had become her accomplice, cheering her on with hums intending to arouse...

And goddamnit, they were working.

His cock, damn near bursting before, threatened complete combustion. His desire grew into a long snarl as he snapped an arm around her, locking her close, forcing her to ride his thigh. Brynna's legs convulsed. Her eyes turned heavy. Her lips popped open on a gasp.

"Ohhhh!"

Rhett released a lusty rumble. "Fuck *me*, that's a beautiful sight." A rough rasp of fabric followed. Reb glanced in time to watch the guy free a beautiful erection and then palm the broad red shaft and begin to pump.

The veins in his own cock pumped double time.

He turned back to Brynn. Loomed his face just inches over hers, letting his stare fall to the berry-sweet welcome of her lips. Beneath his study, her mouth opened more. He didn't give her the kiss for which she pleaded. Instead, with eyes still fixed on her face, he reached with his free hand—

To Rhett.

Their palms hit hard. Rhett's fingers curled tight.

Reb moaned, devastated by wonder, gratitude—

Completion.

It hit him harder than he'd imagined. He likely had the Brynna bullet to thank—or blame—for part of that...but not all. The rest was Rhett. The huge step he'd taken. The precious gift, even if that was all this would ever be, that he'd given. While Brynna sent him soaring, his tether to earth was centered in that hand, twined with his. The one person who brought him sanity in all the *in*sanity that was his life.

"Is your futon still set up?" Though he charged it to the man at his side, he didn't stop studying the woman in his arms. He *really* needed to make sure she was still all-in for this plan.

"Of course," Rhett responded.

"And you have...supplies?"

His friend chuckled. "I have the basics, but I also know where Dax keeps his accessories."

"Of course you do."

"Would you like some?"

"Roger the fuck out of that."

"Handled. Be right back."

Brynna frowned as Double-Oh left. Her bafflement wasn't surprising, considering the lusty glaze in her eyes. If shit like auras were real, hers would be throbbing with the kinkiest colors in the spectrum. He only hoped she was still capable of a few words.

"Wh-Where's Viking stud going?"

Well, that was a few words. Unexpected ones, but he'd roll—even did so with a laugh. "Viking stud, huh?"

She rolled her head toward the door. "Viking stud." Then back at him. "Pirate hunk."

He chuckled softly. "You're really sticking to that, eh?"

She bit her lip, suddenly sheepish. "Unless you don't like it?"

"Oh, I fucking love it." He unfurled half a smile, ensuring it met the endearment's licentious promise. "Just making sure *you're* positive, *ma petite*. Do you know what us pirates like to do with our...treasures?"

Her eyes flared. A heated breath escaped. "Things involving rope, pistols, and daggers?"

He framed her jaw in his free hand. Jerked her face upward. "Now you're bringing rope into this, Miss I-don't-do-submissiveness? Because that boundary doesn't get crossed until a hell of a lot more talking takes place—and right now, I sure as fuck don't feel like talking."

She dipped her face until her lips collided into his forefinger—where she pulled on it with her teeth. "Neither do I."

He hissed. The pain wasn't brutal but was sharp enough to spike his heartrate, shooting fresh blood to the places that did *not* need it right now.

"Such a talented little mouth," he growled. "Perhaps you'll show me what other things it can do...and other ways it likes to play."

She gazed up at him through her lashes. "It'll be my pleasure."

He sucked air back in. "Well, Miss Not-Submissive, you've grasped the hang of *that* one pretty well."

"Thank you, Mr. Stafford."

He shifted his hand to the side of her face. Dug his grip in, fingers forming to the curve of her jaw. "You're going to say that again, just as pretty, when my dick's deep inside you. Then again every time I make you come."

It was a bit of work to hide his smug smile at her flush of arousal. God, he loved how his nasty ways stunned her—and fascinated her. She was like a blank book embedded with secret ink. Every time a page was turned and stroked the right way, a unique design appeared, delighting him all over again. He couldn't wait to paint her newest pages with his most illicit intent.

"Tell me you understand, *mon chou.*"

She wetted her lips and swallowed hard. "I-I understand."

He issued approval with a curt nod. Slipped his hand away from her face. "Now go wait for me in the center of Rhett's futon. Reach back with your arms and grab the cushion over your head. And spread your legs, knees bent up, exposing your pussy for me. Is all of *that* understood?"

"Very, *very* much...Sir."

She turned and sashayed away, letting the impact of that snatch his mind *and* cock in all the best ways. It was the work of his staunchest self-control not to smack her pert little ass, working in glorious harmony with her dance-toned thighs.

He couldn't get naked fast enough.

His own movements probably looked like a wasted ape in comparison to hers—not that he was bucking for the grace-under-pressure trophy any time soon. The day job had maxed out his points on that scoreboard anyhow—and the only priority at this point was freeing his cock from his track pants without breaking the damn thing off. It was stiff as a poker but felt fragile as ash.

He'd finally kicked the fuckers free just as Rhett walked back in. In one of his hands, he toted a bottle of lube and a pretty little anal plug. In his other were nipple clamps on a chain and a finger-held vibrator.

"Dude. She calls me the pirate, but *you* hit the bounty."

Rhett's gaze flicked down as if tractor-beamed to Reb's erection. Though his face suffused with color, he murmured, "Guess I did." Inside a second, he retracted to all-business mode. "Pirate?"

"Subject for later." He pulled on the same gruff mantle. If not, he'd end up making a move Double-Oh clearly wasn't ready for yet. Better to take things back to the setting that worked...the new portals of communication Brynna had unlocked between them simply with the light of her presence and the openness of her spirit. In his book, there was absolutely nothing wrong with that choice either. Just thinking of her on the futon, arranging herself as he'd instructed... "Come on. I think you'll enjoy the view in here just as much, man."

"Yeah?" Rhett smirked, another step in the right direction. Though Brynna was still in another room, he was able to relax without her. Maybe he'd begun to see that Reb didn't want to change what was *them*...only enhance it.

Another subject for much later.

Especially after they walked into the adjoining room— and halted together at the sight awaiting them on the futon.

"Fuck," Reb uttered.

"Me," Rhett finished.

She dropped his jaw. Seared his blood. And moved his

spirit.

Yeah, there was the physical resplendence, undeniable and endless. She was something out of a sappy classic hair band ballad, all Godiva hair, endless legs, and honeyed skin, with those high puckered breasts and her pussy pink and glistening. But that wasn't her perfection by half. The reason his breath still clutched and his cock still surged had everything to do with the rest. The sincere glow in her eyes. The tentative pout of her lips. The eager strain of her arms as she gripped the cushion not only out of obedience to his wishes but a necessary restraint of herself, especially as she took a visual drink of his nudity for the very first time—an experience that actually made him as nervous.

"I'd try to be witty and say that's my line," she finally told them, "but I don't want to be witty right now."

Her admission moved him as deeply as her stare. With both, she openly adored him, uncaring that he wasn't some smooth, flawless thing from a magazine ad. Both his arms were full of the ink that told his life's story, some of it good, some of it pretty damn ugly. As bodies went, he supposed the rest of his wasn't bad, covered in swarthy skin a lot of women found hot, if they didn't mind the nicks and scars that served as fun little souvenirs of the skirmishes he'd survived—just as many before his army career as after. But now, she saw it all and openly accepted it.

No. More than that.

She craved it.

"You want to be mine."

Cocky? Yes. Accurate? If her soft, thankful smile was any indication—*hell, yes*.

Damn. *Damn.* She was so incredible in her earnestness

about all of this...about her blatant need to please Rhett and him. Soon—very soon—he vowed to sit the woman down, pick apart where and why she'd learned to pair *submissive* with *weak*—and then set her straight about the truth, specifically as it applied to the passionate, perfect depths of her heart.

But the woman clearly didn't want her *heart* plunged right now.

Which his cock received as the greatest fucking news in the world.

"Astute observation, my friend." Rhett said it in such a conversational tone, he actually became a distraction from Brynn—a pretty nice one. Reb was damn glad his hard-on was uninhibited now. Clothes would've been a problem once being dunked in the fathomless waters of his friend's gaze. *Christ*. It was a baptism of pure erogeny for his body—and another bullet in his brain. *That man's fucking eyes.* They hit things so deep, he couldn't even identify it all—a recognition almost driving him to look away. Almost.

"She wants to be yours, Moon." The man finished it by inching up one side of his mouth—another gesture so sinister but sexy, Reb's composure was jarred again. Hell. Between this bastard and Brynn, he'd been off his game more times today alone than the last three years combined. It was fucking awesome.

He recovered enough to square his chin, settle hands on his hips, and mock, "What would you like me to do about that, *Sir*?"

Well, hell.

It was the craziest way he'd ever gotten back in the game. Exactly what game at this point, he wasn't sure. If he was with a subbie in a dungeon, it'd clearly be cat and mouse—but this sure as hell wasn't a dungeon and Rhett sure as fuck wasn't a cute little subbie, demonstrating as much by closing the space between them with a single, steady step. He stopped about a foot away, letting the gray-blue intensity of his gaze travel down, down, down...and then back up again. Remained still while Reb stared ruthlessly in return.

Goddamnit, the man was beautiful. The bold slashes of his forceful jaw. The stark desire in his eyes. The taut planes of his abs. And just below that, the stiff shaft forming a huge tent in his pants...

He abstained from licking his lips but indulged a heavy gulp. If this was all he'd ever get from Rhett in the way of acknowledging their connection, he'd be happy—especially if Brynn got to remain in the picture. If the guy had to keep a toy on the field to distract the crowd from what was really happening, then fuck *yes*, please let the toy be her.

The same thoughts appeared to be stomping through Rhett's mind. "Well?" he prompted, nodding toward the spectacular woman on the bed. "Give her exactly what she wants, man. Climb up there and put that hot cock inside her. Bury yourself in her—and make it good, because I'll be watching."

Rebel curled a come-hither grin. "Promise?"

It was a jibe too many. The Atlantic-dark stare turned black. "Shut up and fuck her."

It sure as hell wasn't a request. For a second, bravado and resistance were tempting—but why? So he and Rhett could get in a pissy little turf battle over...what? He'd already won. He was getting to screw the girl—while Rhett watched. In what book didn't that triumph compute?

Still, the awareness of *those eyes* as he turned and crawled up onto the futon, raking over his back and ass, watching his thighs coil as he slunk closer to Brynn...

Those eyes, staring as her breath quickened and her thighs quivered...

Those eyes, watching his hands slide over her knees and then inward, toward the sweet, shiny folds of her cunt...

Those eyes, knowing his exact intent once his shoulders squeezed and his head dipped...

"Ohhhhh!"

Could those eyes see now too? Did they watch her pussy transform to a rich coral hue as her blood rushed to meet Rebel's eager licks? Did they see his tongue against her flesh, serving her in the most intimate way a man could, moistening her tunnel for his penetration?

Well, goddamnit, he'd make sure they did.

He pulled back a little. Ordered from between his teeth, "Wider."

Brynna's breath clutched. "I— What?"

"I said spread your legs wider." *He has to see. He has to know exactly what I'm doing to you. How I'm already claiming you, inch by delicious inch.*

When she did, Rhett's harsh grunt stabbed the air.

Oh, yeah. You do see, don't you? Just remember, you demanded to watch. So watch, goddamnit—and imagine how good this tongue could feel on you, Rhett. Imagine how good it could be, if you'd just let go...

"Rebel!"

Brynna's cry didn't just pull his sights back around. It honed him in on the heat he'd started to crank for her too. The sweet ridge of *her* erection, juicy and hard beneath his lips, was just as much a turn-on as Rhett's lust. Her tight whimpers and piqued sighs were an ego feed like no other, especially when she responded to every lick, suck, and nip as if it were the very first time he'd laid his mouth on her.

"I'm here." He kissed the word into her mound, just above her pouting slit, before sliding lower, savoring the taste of every fresh dewdrop on her folds. "Right here, *ma chatte*. Holy Christ, how sensitive you are...how ready for me..."

"Mmmmm. Aaaahhh!" Her hips lifted. "It...it feels so— Oh, my *God*..."

She undulated, harder and faster, until he gripped her upper thighs like a trainer taming a tiger, squeezing with an unmistakable message.

"Be still, *mon chou*."

"But—"

"Brynna." The unbridgeable baritone, booming from the man behind him, ignited even Rebel's nerve endings. "He's right. And right now, he is also your master."

The word hovered, suspended above them like a knife thrown into the netting over the tigers' cage. Holding his breath, Rebel lifted a little. How the hell would she respond? Would she let the blade tear through and down, maybe just for this moment, taking a chance on the beautiful wound of her submissiveness? Or would she reach for the hilt of that knife and drive it back at Rhett, ensuring their show was officially finished now?

Above him, a conflicted mewl trickled out.

He had to help. Make this a safe place for her soul, even if her mind and body still duked it out for jurisdiction.

He raised up more. Kissed his way up from her navel until his face rested between her breasts. Freely, he tangled his gaze with hers. Fearlessly, he smiled. Ferociously, he ordered the shadows beneath her lashes to stand the hell down.

"There's no wrong choice, *minette*." He could afford the generosity, thanks to the man who'd commanded him up here with her. When Rhett became the dictator, he made it possible for Reb to take over as Prince of Understanding, fading the possibility that she'd feel two-upped. "It's still *your* free will, *your* safe word to call if you're over the edge. But know this"—he reached for one of her nipples, smiling a little as Rhett's hiss sliced behind him—"you *will* go to the edge. And it will be my deep pleasure to take you there...because that's exactly what that beautiful man back there wants me to do."

A longer silence.

Rhett didn't make a sound—at least not any Reb could hear over Brynn's urgent breaths. Her breasts jabbed even higher, corresponding with her rhythmic kneads of the cushions next to her head. Her stare searched into his again. Darted up at Rhett.

Before she jammed her eyes shut and whispered, "Yes, Sir."

Rebel let out an approving growl. Gently suckled one of her breasts and then the other. "Thank you, *ma cher*."

A cute little growl sprinted through her chest too. "Gee, kids, just giving it my best."

He really wanted to chuckle. Kept it subdued to a lazy smile as he bit her nipple, sharply enough to turn it into discipline. "Then that means no more sarcasm. You'll communicate, but it'll be with honesty and openness. Understood?"

She pulled in a deep breath—letting it out in a hiss as he sucked the nipple again, this time drawing in as much of it as he could. He devoured her flesh with deep, hard passion. "Ahhh!" she yelped. "Y-Y-Yes, Sir!"

She noticeably squirmed as he slid over to the other breast, circling her stiff peak with his tongue, preparing it for the same brutal kiss. "Ssshhhh," he admonished. "Breathe, *ma fille.*"

"Trying!" she gritted back—until he added another new element to their play. She was so stressed about where his mouth was headed that she never comprehended how he sneaked his free hand between their bodies, probing into her most secret tunnel. "Oh!" She stiffened at his first determined lunge. Trembled as he added another finger, just as he bit into her breast. Then, as he released the pressure of both, went soft as a buttered noodle. "Ohhhh...*my.*"

"Damn. So hot."

Rhett's rough rasp came as a surprise only because of its proximity. As satisfying as Brynn's arousal was his buddy's new boldness, for the guy had moved close enough to scoot a knee up on the bed and then peel off his shirt. Fuck, his chest was impressive. While Rebel had to hit the gym hard for definition, Double-Oh had the God-given cuts of a linebacker—hilarious, since his job required the elegance of a quarterback.

Brynn obviously agreed. She sighed and writhed while reaching an admiring hand toward Rhett...captivating Rebel all over again. He wondered when he'd last seen a more incredible look on a woman's face. With her neck arched, eyes hooded, and a sheen of sweat on her brow, she was an image of raw arousal and authentic need. No practiced pouts or coy stares she "thought" they'd like. No being demure out of respect for protocol or preventing herself from crying out until she "obtained permission." When she swung the look toward Reb, his chest nearly caved in. Her awe and wonder mirrored his own. Everything had gone from zero to eighty in the last hour, overwhelming even for a slut monkey like him. But he hadn't felt so alive in a long time.

A *long* damn time.

He had to have more of her. Now.

Transferring his weight to one knee, he crawled higher up her body, suckling her neck as he went. He rounded the curve of her chin, fitted their mouths, and then plunged into her without hesitating, scooping her tongue against his, devouring her with deep, primeval need. Beneath him, she moaned with answering need. Her lungs pumped, her nipples tightened, her body undulated.

"Damn," Rhett repeated. "*Damn.*"

It was all the inspiration he needed to push his fingers back up inside her, making her gasp against his mouth as her hips came off the mattress.

"Twist them." Rhett's teeth were locked now. Reb had never heard such a brutal tone from him before, though he'd been to two dozen countries and nearly as many dungeons with the man. "Both your fingers," he growled to clarify. "Twist them while you push into her pussy. Yeah. That's...fucking nice."

"Not bad from where I'm at, either." He leaned over, pressing kisses to Brynn's cheek and forehead. "How about you, *minette*? You still with me?"

She'd closed her eyes but nodded frantically. "Yes. *Yes.*"

"Good, baby girl. That's so good."

None of them spoke again for the next few minutes. Just enjoyed the sound of him finger-fucking her, wet and slick and rough, as their lust filled the air, musky and heady and spicy. For a guy who relied on breath control to disarm bombs at the perfect moment, Rebel had trouble remembering what his breath even was. Wrapping his mind around this awesome reality, pleasuring a woman while his best friend directed down to the kinky details, was outrageous—and incredible.

And damn near unbelievable—as Rhett leaned in bearing another special gift.

In his fingers was the anal plug, its pink crystal surface already drenched with the lube. Rebel didn't remember even hearing the bottle top pop but wasn't that stunned considering the alternative for his attention.

He sat up. Twined his gaze again with Rhett's, whose eyes gleamed with feral anticipation. Below them, the reason why: the magnificence of this woman's surrender, symbolized by her spread, soaked sex.

"Put it in," Rhett directed. "And screw her with it."

Brynn let out a soft keen, mixed of dread and arousal. "Oh, my God."

Rebel regarded her steadily. "Sounds like you're a little familiar with this sight, *cher.*"

She huffed. "Not intimately. And not lately."

"And that's not clear enough." Though he issued the reproach mildly, he took the plug from Rhett and displayed it to her like a holy artifact. "This is an anal plug, Brynna. You clearly know what it is—so you also know that Rhett is ordering me to work it into your asshole and then fuck you there with it."

She gulped. "Well, we're pretty clear *now.*"

"No. *I'm* clear now. You still aren't." He dropped his head, angling his stare more directly at her. "'Yes, Sir' or 'no, Sir,' *mon chou.* What will it be?"

She hesitated another moment. It was all the opening Rhett needed. With a resolute growl, he lunged in, grabbing Brynn by the neck, forcing her mouth to his.

"Fuck," Rebel groaned, watching the man mesh their mouths, inhale her scent, and drain a lot of the tension from her arms. Women had a special term for kisses like that. Bone-melting. Rebel could understand the point though didn't sympathize. He wasn't melted. He was galvanized. And he hoped like hell that the moment Double-Oh released her from that kiss, she let her lips part on only two words.

"Yes, Sir."

Sometimes prayers *were* answered.

Rhett softly kissed her again—but instead of drawing all the way back up, he kept his face hovered inches over hers. Without looking away from her, he told Reb, "Do it. Now."

She whimpered. Rhett hushed her with a sound that came from deep in his chest: gentle layered with pure animal. He breathed it into her parted lips. She sucked in its energy, transforming it into a high sigh that blew back into Rhett with visible force. His shoulders shook, his body trembled.

Power Exchange—in its purest, best form.

And Rebel was about to help them paint it even more vividly.

Fuck, this was going to be good.

Swinging around and seating himself between her legs once more, he crouched in, parting her pussy on the way to stimulating her clit. Her arousal would ease the plug's penetration. Besides that, it looked damn beautiful from this vantage point.

"Mmmmm." Her sensitive button shivered beneath his finger—which he soon joined with more. Rebel echoed her hum, deeper and gruffer, as Rhett's three middle fingers webbed with his. They twined and writhed their digits, rolling like two bodies against the world's softest, wettest pillows. As

Rhett danced his tongue against Brynn's, he set a matching pace with their fingers, until Brynn's gasps forewarned of her encroaching climax.

He pulled off. Yanked Reb's hand away too.

"No!" she screamed. "Oh hell, please! I'm so close!"

Whatever she had left to say, Rhett stole with another kiss. "You'll be close when we say you're close, sweetheart."

Rebel had to grin. He'd never seen Rhett as a bad boy wolf. He enjoyed the fuck out of it. His cock probably had a few deeper sentiments, but there wasn't time for phallic therapy right now.

Not when he'd reached the sweet aperture of her anus.

Not when he'd stretched it a little wider, watched it fight his invasion with an adamant pucker, only to force it open again. And then again.

Not when he trickled lube down and watched it disappear into the tight darkness of that forbidden dark hole. Preparing her...

"Deep breath, *minette*. Relax."

For this.

"Oh! *Oh!*"

He'd pushed in just the plug's tip before she struggled.

Rhett easily caught her by one leg, hiking it high to help Rebel keep her spread. "Easy, little peach. *Easy*. Don't fight it. Don't close up."

"I... That's easy for *you* to—"

"Make it easy for *you*." Rebel borrowed a page out of his buddy's book, though he barked it to snag her attention. He persisted, "Have we given you anything you can't handle? Anything that hasn't been amazing in the end?"

She fumed, body still tense. Her knuckles were white

against the cushions. Even her toes were coiled tightly against the sheet. But she finally mumbled, "No. Not yet."

He growled a kiss into the center of her pussy. "Well then, relax, *bébé*, and trust that we'll do the same now."

She wetted her lips. "Yes, Sir."

"*Bien*," Rebel soothed. "*Trés bien, ma belle*."

Rhett layered in an approving growl. "Breathtaking woman. You have no idea how much you please us already. Ssshhh, sweetheart"—he urged it as Rebel twisted in again on the plug—"almost there. Push out to open yourself up. Take it in, girl. Take it in."

Brynna squirmed again. The cream from her pussy tremored down, blending with the shimmery drops of the lube, sliding into her ass along with the plug. Though Rebel clenched his jaw, precome spurted at the tip of his cock. Like he could be blamed, with this as a view?

"I-I can't!" she cried.

Rhett leaned in. Bit her lower lip. "You can."

"So tight. So full..."

"That's the idea, peach."

"I don't know—"

"Yes, you do. Take it, Brynna. For me. For Reb. You please us so much with your trust."

"Oh, God!"

"In." Rebel declared it as the base of the plug fell flush against her body, the pink acrylic so captivating beneath the blush of her pussy. "You did it, *cher*. Damn. It's so beautiful."

Her relieved laugh blended into a tight wince. "Still tight. But...better. Kind of nice."

"That's honest." Rebel pressed kisses to the insides of her thighs. "And equally as beautiful."

Above him, Rhett played his lips over hers with just as much meaning. "Don't hold it back, sweetheart. We want to see all of it. Know exactly what you're thinking. Feeling. There's no right or wrong. There's only your sensations. Your pains...and your pleasures."

As he drew out the last of it, Rebel withdrew the plug well past the taper, letting it almost escaped her body before sliding it all the way back in. No stopping this time.

A longer scream from their girl.

"First item covered," she finally spat. "Can we get to number two now? That little thing called my pleas—"

Rhett chuckled, watching the effect of his thumb in her pussy take hold. "Now what were you saying, sweetheart?" he queried as her voice fizzled. "Something about...your pleasure?"

"Crap," she gasped. Reb almost joined her, since he got to watch how her back hole convulsed on the plug with new vigor.

"God*damn*," he grated. "That's it, *ma chatte*. Show me how much you want it."

"Her cunt is dripping too." Rhett's voice was hoarse with awe. "You can just keep her lubed with this cream."

"Great minds." He grinned while dragging some of that gorgeous juice down, rolling it around the base of the plug.

"Fuck. Brynna Monet, you are one *hell* of an incredible sight."

Her response was a groan in breathy, sexy spurts—as Reb withdrew and then pushed in again. And again. And again.

"That's good." Rhett started pumping a hand along the hump between his thighs. "Really, really good."

"Certainly is." Rebel cast over a glance to clarify he wasn't just referencing her now.

"Good." Brynn echoed it in a high-pitched sob. "Mmmmm. Yeah."

Rhett swung his gaze over to her. "Then why do you sound like somebody just ate your last piece of cake, sweetheart?"

A little grimace dug into her forehead. "Because I—" She flung her head to one side. "I need— Ohhh, I don't know what I need!"

Rhett leaned in, grabbing her scalp to realign her gaze up. "I know, little peach. I know." Without any other assurance, he swiveled back toward Rebel. "That's it. No more of that teasy-taunting-mamby-pamby bullshit. *Fuck her* with it, Moon. Ram her like you want to with your cock."

"Shit." Brynna gritted her teeth and rocked her head back. "Oh, *shit.*"

A slow grin lifted his lips. "What Double-Oh wants..."

On his first thrust in, she screamed.

On his second, she moaned.

On his third, she gasped. Snapped her head back up, gaping at them both, as Reb continued stuffing in the pink plaything, over and over, learning quickly what angle dilated her eyes the most, made her pussy seep the wettest, made her dig her heels deeper into the mattress.

And made her swear the filthiest.

Yeah...that was the best part of all.

"Fuck! Ohhhh, fuck me. So good...it's so deep and so, so *good.* Rebel. Rebel. *Rebel!* Do it to me again. Please. *Please!*"

"Do what?" Wait. Rhett's murmur, like a drill officer crossed with a Zen master...*that* was the best part. "You know what we need, peach. Total communication. Tell him exactly what you want him to do, beautiful."

"I— I want him to keep fucking me like this."

"Like what?"

"Like *this*, damn it. Putting that plug into my ass, just like that. Oh, crap, just...like...ohhhh! Please, don't stop. Don't stop!"

Rebel grinned. "Sounds like a *very* good plan to me."

Rhett added his smile. "You're perfect, sweetheart. Open so wide like this for us...giving everything you have to us."

Despite the steady thrusts Reb kept giving, she blinked up at Rhett as if emerging from a thick fog. "Amazing," she rasped. "I've never felt this good before...so deep inside."

Rhett angled back toward her. Brushed strands of hair off her gleaming forehead before penetrating a deep gaze into her eyes. "Welcome to learning the wonders of deep anal, sweetheart."

Her lips turned up like a kid who'd tasted candy for the first time. "So *this* is what all the fuss is about."

Rhett laughed softly. Rebel probably should've joined him, but the grin splitting his face wouldn't acquiesce by an inch. Without faltering his pace, he stared long and hard at her. Vowed to seal the memory of her face, just like this, on his mind forever. He needed to remember the gift she'd given him, far beyond her submission. The gift of her awe. Her wonder. Her total focus on the moment itself. In her awkwardness, she was dazzling. In her openness, she exploded *his* mind. Her newness had let him experience it all as brand-new.

But in many ways, hadn't it felt like this on the plane ride too?

Would it always be this way with her?

No. There's no always *here, man. You don't know even know how to do second dates, let alone* always.

In a nutshell, he had to treasure every last moment of this.

With fucking gusto.

Harder and harder he pumped the plug. Tighter and tighter her body closed around it. Her whimpers began again in earnest as her body pitched and rolled beneath him.

"God*damn*," he gritted.

"No shit." Rhett's teeth were locked just as tight.

"*Tu me rends fou, ma belle.* You're so close, aren't you? You need to come for me, don't you?"

She panted hard. Licked her lips in frantic swipes. "Yes. Oh yes, I need to— I want to...but...*God*... It's gripping me from the inside, and I don't know how to process—"

"Ssshhh." Rhett kissed her hard, quelling her sudden and obvious distress, but that didn't stop the tears it loosened. He dragged up, looking once more to Reb. Good fucking chance their stares were mirrors, filled with the same conclusion. Brynn didn't know how to process the next step. And why should she? Prior to a minute ago, anal had probably been good but not awesome for her, a necessity to be tolerated, not a pleasure to be celebrated.

It was going to be damn fun to open her mind.

He openly questioned Rhett with his gaze while sliding the plug deep in her ass again. Didn't mind lingering over the view, either. He and Rhett Lorimer Lange had traveled across the world and back with each other, but the last hour had taken them further than all those miles combined. This... was a different galaxy. They'd landed in such a different place than what he'd imagined or expected, especially after their bitter fight in the kitchen and the setback of this morning. Yet here they were, in a connection despite dysfunction, a bond so twisted and strange and weird, making as much sense as borrowing steak knives from Edward Scissorhands. But did it matter? Their cuts were theirs and no one else's. Who cared who'd plunged the hilt or dealt the pain? He'd eagerly bleed for this man.

The pledge deepened his dedication to the next task.

"Leave the plug right there. Then take your cock and give her the orgasm she's worked so hard for."

He extended a rubber fresh from the packet—again, seemingly from thin air, and again, nothing Reb cared to question—which got rolled on fast, despite fingers that burned beneath the heat of the man's stare. This was crazy. How many times had they been bare-assed together, in locker rooms and barracks and even tanks, boats, and planes? But nude wasn't naked. Right now, for the very first time, he was truly naked for Rhett Lange.

And never wanted to be covered up again.

And sure as hell refused to be ashamed about it anymore.

The resolution lifted him off his haunches. Reb widened the brace of his knees on the mattress, lending his posture even more power—forcing Rhett to get naked too. He didn't give a crap if the guy kept every stitch of his clothes on, but damn it, Rhett was going to bare his spiritual nads, even if it had to happen thread by thread.

Bleed with me, Double-Oh. Goddamnit...please.

"Oh...wow." The assertion burst from the gorgeous redhead sprawled beneath him. With honeyed heat in her eyes, Brynn added, "Dear God, Rebel. You're—"

"Beautiful." The interjection was a fusion of misery and ecstasy from Rhett's throat. And it should have been enough. But if Rebel was the kind to settle for enough, he'd still be sitting on that rotting porch between Father and the hooch, staring at the gators slicing through the swamp slime. So he went for it. Pushed his fucking luck.

Fisted the base of his shaft, making it leap like a thing alive.

Touch me.

Rhett hissed softly. Swallowed deeply.

*Damn you, Lange. Just do it. Just once. Please...*please. *Touch me.*

For an instant, the risk was worth it. For that one perfect moment, the man cast off the shutters on his gaze—and let Reb see his truth. His desire. His blood.

Before he slammed the shutters back down, as vehemently as possible. "Get on with it." More words torn from the depths of his throat, this time skipping any pleasantry. Rebel went for impulse too, spreading a cocky grin, hoping the fucker held until he could extract the boot he'd lodged up his own ass.

Fine. You strained the boundaries and got bounced. Those were *the odds, asshole. You knew that going in. Why the fuck did you expect anything different? Time to stow it, soldier—and give your cock to someone who's going to appreciate it.*

His smile kicked a little higher. He regarded Rhett for a long, heated moment. Finally started working a hand over his dick, pausing every few minutes to squeeze over the crown. "Get to it?" He clutched in, pinching precome into the condom, letting the man see every inch of arousal across his face. "With. Extreme. Pleasure."

You want to admire from afar, Mr. Lange? Then admire this.

He shoved his thighs apart to widen her some more while nudging his throbbing crown against her pouting slit. He knew damn well what this was going to look like from Rhett's point of view. Knew that the bastard would see his cock stretching her entrance, his balls pounding the pink toy in her ass. He hoped to God that every second was torture for the man too.

"You ready, *minette*?"

Brynna shivered. "Yes. God, yes!"

"Then hold on tight. This is going to be a rough ride."

She lifted her legs a little higher, securing them around his waist. "Promise?"

The laugh she induced was the perfect warmth to reconnect him with his lust. He was already as hard as a piston thinking about this command performance for Rhett, but her passion was the right jab of lightning in this amazing erotic storm. "I promise." He snarled it into her ear, inducing her legs tighter, her hips higher. "Fuck," he rasped. "*Oui. Oh, oui, ma cher. Tu miaou est vraiment étroi.*"

She sighed. "If you just told me I taste like chicken, forget about the translation."

He chuckled. Teased his tongue along her neck, his dick deeper into her passage. "It means you have a magnificent cunt."

She arched her torso up. "It's yours to fill. To fuck. Please!"

"Keep up with *that* poetic license, and I can't guarantee I'll try to be Mr. Gentle Minstrel about this."

"Minstrels are boring." She dug her heels into his spine, running them up and down the vertebrae, causing her pussy lips to give his stalk the hottest massage he'd ever experienced. "I prefer pirates."

"Well...aye." He reveled in the spellbinding copper candle glow of her irises. "And what a fine, sexy little galley wench ye are for it, too."

A giggle tumbled from her. She cut into it with a high gasp as he pushed his luck again—ramming all the way inside her with one decisive lunge.

"Holy...*crap!*"

Sometimes, pounding at the boundaries worked. In all the best, breath-robbing ways.

His invasion jacked her head back more. Pumped her carotid against the taut column of her neck. Rushed new blood into the hard berries that tipped her breasts, straining higher and higher toward him.

"Crap," she repeated. "Ohhhh, it—"

"Hurts?" Rebel supplied.

Her forehead creased. "Yeah."

He suckled the edge of her jaw. Ground his cock in deeper. "You were the one who wanted to be filled, *cher.*"

"Shut. Up."

He felt Rhett before he saw him, moving back in like a sensual wraith. But he halted at the edge of their peripherals, silently hovering, steadily breathing, dancing on the edge of completely creepy with his behavior—if it wasn't for the raw sexual force he zapped into every molecule of the air. The effect was so potent, it was like a fourth person in the room. Rebel sure as hell wasn't one to turn down a good orgy.

And hell...was this *good.*

"You'll take him, Brynna." Oh yeah...*so damn good.* No, better than that. Rhett was someone more than their voyeur, more than their lover, more than their Dom. He was a spirit, infusing them with more of his unique sexual power. "You'll take him," he dictated once more. "*All* of him. And you'll take the plug as well. You'll keep being filled and fucked and used, until we say you're finished—just because it pleases us."

Rebel bent in, smashing her lips in open sexual need. "You bet your sweet, sore ass it does."

She moaned, seemingly in protest, but didn't fool either of them. Her vagina and ass responded to their filthy praise like vises, heatedly milking everything stuffed into them. *Everything.* Rebel grunted hard, clenching his thighs and ass, ordering his cock to keep the climax bottled, at least for a few more minutes.

Not...yet...

His shaft thrummed with pressure. His balls bobbed heavily, pounding with fresh heat every time they slid against the stem of the plug, reminding him of how deep he filled her with every hard stroke. More than anything, he craved to let it all go and pump everything into her, but he needed every incredible memory he could soak out of this moment. She looked too amazing beneath him, arms spread, hair fanned, cheeks flushed, lips swollen...a pinup girl, only better. A fuckable fantasy come true.

"So perfect. Yeah, so pleasing." While the words were tender and praising, Rhett shifted away, to the edge of the futon once more. Rebel couldn't help a dark scowl. *Wrong direction, damn it.*

The payoff was worth it. Finally—thank *fuck*—the man rasped the air by dropping his pants.

Rebel jerked his head around. No way was he keeping his eyes to himself now.

Brynna clearly concurred. She, too, looked over with an eager whimper. The sound intensified as she roamed her stare over Rhett's hulking nudity. *Hell, yes.* She was a lioness in heat, unfurling the sound like a ravenous growl until letting it erupt into a throaty snarl—

Just as Rhett took his erection in hand.

"Yesssss," she whispered.

"God*damn*," Rhett gritted.

"Holy fuck," Rebel uttered.

Rhett stroked himself from balls to crown. Then again... and again. Rebel joined Brynn in being hypnotized by the sight, honing on the stunning contrast of those broad, powerful fingers against the rigid purple flesh. He couldn't help smiling when realizing Rhett timed his rhythm to every thrust *he* gave Brynn.

Damn. *Damn.* This really *was* happening. All of it. Both of them. Brynn, with that stare and those tits and her tight paradise of a pussy. Rhett, with *his* stare and those abs and that broad, magnificent cock. But beyond that, the wonderment across both their faces too—knowing they'd been hit by the same jolt of amazement and surge of arousal.

He was going to remember this fuck for a very long time.

"It feels so good." Brynn's murmur, hoarse with awe, betrayed how much she agreed with that. "Here, with both of you... Yeah, so damn good. I really want to please you both. I-I really...need to."

She winced while faltering over the last of it. Her confusion was adorable—and understandable. Rebel leaned over, pressing a palm to her cheek, compelled to reassure her. She'd carved a special little place inside him before today. It wasn't so little anymore. And a hell of a lot more special.

"*Ma petite chatte.*" The entendre was a grate, vibrating the air between their mouths. "How you amaze me. How you please *both* of us..." He slid his thumb over, pushing in to make her jaw open for him. "So much."

Her high sigh pulled him down, sealing their mouths once more. God, *yes*... She was so soft, so giving, full of such passionate surrender. He had to have even more, and he took it: conquered her tongue with long rolls, passionate sucks, and hard stabs, drinking in her desire as his own raced through his blood, thundered up his cock.

Deeper.

Hotter.

Faster.

More. He needed even more.

Especially as he felt Rhett's need for the same. Heard it in the man's rougher masturbation. Inhaled it as his friend's wild musk blended with the nectar of Brynn's sex.

The cloud of his lust thickened. In less than a minute, it damn near choked him and sure as hell possessed him. Still, he needed more. He twisted his hips harder, gaining deeper impact on the velvety depths of her body. Brynn flung back screams of ecstasy, trying to intersperse with words but babbling half syllables instead. Her head flailed against the cushion, turning her hair into gorgeous tangles. Her breasts quivered for him, their tips erect and flawless. Her arms began to shake. Inch by inch, her grip slipped on the cushion. *Fuck, yeah.* He was screwing the strength right out of her—and in its place, filling her with the pliant, passive joy of letting her Dom take complete control.

Rebel's gratitude was boundless. He kissed it into her mouth. Fucked it into her cunt. And locked it over her limbs. *One, two.* It was so easy—and so damn perfect—to reach and pin her wrists beneath his hands. She agreed and let him know so, releasing a long moan against his lips.

"That's it," he growled, his mind surrendering to blinding heat of its own. "Let it all go, *cher.* Let me do the driving now. You're such a good little girl. So fucking perfect. Let it all go."

Her sigh fanned his mouth, remnants of toothpaste

mingling with the hot salt of her desire. "Yes, Sir."

He rewarded her with a smile just before biting her jawline. When he got to the sensitive skin beneath her ear, he sank his teeth in harder. "This is exactly what he wants, Brynna. To see my cock driving into you, pushing at all your walls. Listen to him, jerking himself off. He's watching everything I do to you and getting harder from it. Can you hear him rubbing his cock? Can you feel the pleasure your exquisite body is giving both of us?"

"Oh, God." It was a sparse choke, strangled by the force of her lust. Rebel wasn't surprised. Her walls squeezed around him, agonized in the wait for their final release. "Oh, damn," she rasped. "Yes. *Yes*, I can hear him."

"Me, too. It turns me way the hell on, *bébé*." He secured their gazes. Her classic features were sheened in sweat and alive with passion. If this was even half of how gorgeous Helen of Troy was, no wonder men sacrificed armies for her. "It's going to make him even happier to see you milk my cock with your orgasm."

"Yes." She gasped. "Oh, yes, please!"

Rebel yanked her arms forward, securing them to the mattress at her sides so he could rear up, allowing her to watch his dick each time he slid it into her pussy. It wasn't the only benefit of the new position. Amazing, what shifting a little weight could do to the penetration of an anal plug. Her head jolted up. Her mouth popped open all the way. Her pussy visibly shuddered.

"Fuck. Me. Ohhhhh!"

Rebel chuckled lowly. "It's good, *oui*?"

Her face crunched as she tried to laugh past a wince. "Full," she finally stammered. "So full...so tight..."

"And so good," he crooned. "*Vous êtes si belle, ma minette.* Being fucked like this...all your holes filled..."

"Not all of them."

The interjection overjoyed as much as shocked—though he opted for focusing on the former for now. He watched, savoring the view of sinew and strength, as Rhett climbed back onto the bed and leaned close to Brynn's head. One of the man's huge hands glided over her face and then back into her hair. She mewled as Rhett pulled on the strands, the sound intensifying as he coiled them tighter. Rebel wove a gritted moan into the mix. Every time Rhett torqued on her hair, her sex clutched harder at his cock. Sensing Rhett's next move, he shifted his hands inward, bracing her hip with one and thumbing her clit with the other.

The moment he made contact, her mouth dropped open again. She began a gasp—but never finished.

Her breath was cut short by the invasion of Rhett's cock.

Rebel grunted hard.

Brynna groaned deep.

Rhett rumbled in satisfaction. "*Now* her holes are filled."

Rebel's ass clenched. He closed his eyes for a moment, hoping the blackness behind his lids would lend a moment of control for his cock, but it was no use. The scene of erotic perfection called him back, consumed his vision. The pink plug still stuffed in Brynna's ass. His iron-hard shaft, parting her swollen pussy. And now Rhett's sex too, using her mouth for its carnal fulfillment.

He wasn't going to last long. Brynn sobbed deep in her throat, betraying the precarious hold on her sanity. If that wasn't confirmation enough, her walls tremored violently around every inch of his throbbing length.

"She's close." He tossed a glance to Rhett. Just a glance, lest he lose his shit there and then. The man had never looked so fucking hot. One knee was slotted to the curve of Brynn's shoulder, the other was hitched over the back of the futon. The tree trunk he called a cock hung nearly straight down into Brynn's mouth, stabbing her lips with an unrelenting pace. "And damn it, so am I."

Rhett looked up too.

Rebel groaned. So much for fleeting glances now. Even if he'd wanted to look away, he couldn't have—as Rhett ripped his hand free from Brynn's hair and drove it into his instead.

His scalp ignited with fire. His balls flamed like rocket boosters. Imagine that—they felt damn similar to the flames in the depths of Rhett's eyes.

"Do it." Rhett's command was as merciless as his grip, setting a pounding pace for Reb's body. "Do. It."

The fires engulfed him more.

Rebel didn't blink.

Lust crashed through his blood.

Rebel didn't falter.

The come surged up his cock.

Rebel didn't breathe.

Rhett yanked harder on his head. "Look at me." His nostrils flared, his chest lurched. "Give it to her, but look at me. Show it *all* to me."

The cataclysm hit.

Every scalding drop of come exploded from Rebel's cock, draining him, shaking him, consuming him. He pumped and pumped, his mind spinning, his chest thundering—but as soon as he slowed, Rhett burst with a vicious snarl, pulling on him even harder.

"Uh-uh. More, Moonstormer. You have more."

"Rhett." He attempted a similar growl, but his throat was parched. Humping a ruck forty miles would have drained him less.

"Please. *More.*"

Brynna's desperate moan was a bittersweet endorsement for the point. Reb sure as hell never intended to leave her unfulfilled, but the new clenches of her body were unmistakable in their siren song, coaxing something strange and hot and shocking from deep inside his body. Just as he'd commanded Brynn to do, he let the feeling in. Groaned as it pumped up his dick again, forcing heat back to his throbbing head. Though he had only a few more drops left, the intensity in his cock was surreal. He lunged harder than ever into Brynna, giving her every last drive of his hardness, every last roll of his hips.

"Holy...fuck." He grated the words between labored huffs.

"That's it." The words thrummed from Rhett, hot and heavy and seductive, as he curled fingers tighter, driving the pace with his hold on Reb's hair. "Fuck into her. Deeper. *Deeper.* Give her every drop."

Rebel lifted his head. Impaled his stare right back into those breathtaking blues. "You too. *Do it*, goddamnit." He leaned in, sliding fingers down both sides of Brynn's cheeks, until his hand framed the bottom of her jaw. "Open up, *mon chou*. Rhett's going to come in your mouth...as you come all over my cock."

His declaration unlocked the last reserves for them both.

Brynn screamed around Rhett's flesh. He, in turn, moaned hard, his hand slipping away from Rebel's head. His balls drew in. His cock swelled. His seed spilled down into her, answered by her erotic cry. Her throat convulsed as she swallowed his come deep.

The sight was so incredible, it damn near hurt to look, but Rebel forced his gaze to stay fixed and his thoughts to remain lucid. He needed to remember this. Every amazing moment of it.

Rhett slipped free from Brynna and dropped back against the cushion, still breathing like *he'd* humped the ruck for forty. Rebel took the opening to slant back in and kiss her, nobility only half his motivation. He needed to taste Rhett's essence in her mouth—not that Brynn hadn't figured it out already, clearly proven by her sweet smile as she opened her lips and offered her tongue to him.

He kissed her gently.

Then not so gently.

His mouth filled with a mixture as complex as a fine wine. Sexy and musky, a little spicy...and a lot intimate. He hoped his gratitude flowed through his stare, because he wasn't sure he had words to touch it. Could she see all of it? Did she comprehend the scope of what she'd just given to Rhett and him...the walls she'd helped them crumble? Barricades that might have taken years to breach, if ever. She'd done that by letting them see *her* courage—by looking at her submissiveness, despite how it terrified her, and coming through on the other side with new parts of her soul uncovered.

She inspired him.

Moved him.

Humbled him.

And tore him apart from the inside out as she rolled away and burst into tears.

CHAPTER TWELVE

"*Cher.*" He murmured it into her hair while pressing to her from the back as Rhett slid in to cover from the front. To his massive relief, she didn't resist their crowding—and for the moment, that was all he needed to know. "It's all right," he reassured. "Let it out. As much as you need. As long as you need to."

She eagerly took him up on that. As she sobbed harder into Rhett's chest, the guy cast a grateful glance over her shoulder. Clearly he was in equally strange territory as Brynn—tempting Reb to the brink of a laugh. Sometimes being a man-slut had its advantages. Being best friends with one's cock made it easier to figure out how others connected with theirs—not that Mr. Manners here was too difficult a case. Rhett liked his D/s dynamic so formal, it edged on the same pompous protocols as the royal court of his mother's land. But while the guy declared it all added "meaning," it was really just a way of keeping distance. *Meaning* meant *messy*—and since everything they'd just done had decimated *Rebel's* psyche, he could only guess at the storm damage in Double-Oh's brain.

And Brynn's reaction? Probably the healthiest he'd ever seen. He continued telling her as much, repeating his praise in different forms. He stroked her body in long, reassuring caresses, saving the strength of his gaze for the man who still looked like he stood in Times Square with his pants down. And wouldn't *that* be a wonderful sight to see—except for the part about sharing the magnificence of the man's cock with twenty thousand tourists. Though he had no right, Reb was feeling bizarrely possessive about that cock right now—and took no measures to hide that particular sentiment either.

Rhett averted his eyes. Fast.

With a weeping woman on his chest, he didn't have to look too far. Instantly, his face suffused with tenderness. "Our sweet little peach." He brushed a hand to Brynn's cheek. "You all right?"

She sniffled. "I...don't know. I'm really upside down."

"Upside down is okay." Reb purposely picked the nuts and bolts tone. It wasn't as pretty as Rhett's hearts and flowers but just as necessary. Maybe more so. The truth would sink in better if delivered straight. "And totally normal too," he added.

Rhett quirked a brow but didn't say anything. He didn't have to. Brynn launched into the dirty work, returning to her back, lobbing up a laugh of pure indictment. "Normal, hmm? Because you've run some Rebel Stafford *test studies* on this shit?"

He was ready for the stab. Still didn't mean he had to like it—or the fact that he'd earned it. "I know what it's like to come down from an intense session, yes."

"An 'intense session'?" Her features wobbled, struggling for a thread of humor in the words but just unlatching her composure for more tears. "Oh, sheez. That's exactly what it was, wasn't it? A 'session'."

"*Minette—*"

"Don't. Please don't with the *minette* right now." She backhanded her forehead, balling her hand into a fist. "I still have to wrap my head around 'session' without wondering how many other sub—" Her lips parted, revealing clenched teeth.

"How many others you've used that one on."

"None." He snubbed Rhett's scoff—also fully justified—while pushing upright. "Fine. Have I lied to you—either of you—about what I've done and what beds I've done it in before this week? Even now, as shitty as it is to admit, I won't hide the truth from you. I may be a slut, but I'm not a liar. Ponder that when you hear *this*: I've never experienced *anything* like the last hour of my life. I won't fry and sugar this like a goddamn beignet. You two just devoured me, body and soul, like a couple of *rougarous* from the Mancharac."

Rhett raised a wry brow. "Fun. I always did want to be a half-wolf zombie."

He ignored that as well. Simply hoping he could conjure the right mix of strong and sympathetic, he looked back down at Brynn. "It's my clumsy way of saying that I get it. If you need a good long cry, you go right ahead."

She'd already beat him to the punch, more shiny streams cascading down her cheeks. Now they were interrupted by a real laugh. He joined Rhett in observing her with open bewilderment—and enchantment.

"Clumsy," she finally clarified, "and then you, in the same sentence. Doesn't add up, Sergeant Stafford."

Rhett snorted. "You've never seen him in a blast suit when he has to take a leak."

Her eyes clouded as the image took hold. Then burst back to full intensity, brilliant copper and gold, as she succumbed to a new laugh.

Rhett shot a stare dunked in deeper confusion. Rebel tried to urge continued calm in return, but how did he explain a subbie's emotional overload and endorphin drop in the space of a glance, especially when it was only being half heeded?

Already Rhett attempted to fold Brynn against him again, but she was a goner, consumed by her brain's new chemical dump. And yeah, he was pretty damn certain about that—since it was stamped across her face as she rolled over, seeking *his* embrace.

He sent his friend an apologetic look—not that it was noticed. As usual, most of Rhett's "big head" was now officially tied into the urges of his little one, slamming him into a world-class fume. Wasn't anything to be done about that. She'd sought safe shelter as her catharsis continued, galloping out of her in hiccupping sobs. No way was Reb going to refuse her, not after all the passion she'd given them with such heart-stopping openness. If Rhett wanted in on the comfort jamboree, he could get his ass over here. Rebel would never refuse him on the giving *or* taking.

They passed the next few minutes focused solely on the woman between them. As she continued crying against Rebel, Rhett pushed past his shit long enough to scoot close once more. Gently, he ran a hand through the tresses of her hair that wrapped against her back.

She finally huffed hard. Sniffed harder. Pulled away, shaking her head. "I'm a horrible person." She punched the heels of her palms against her swollen eyes. "And a hypocrite."

Rebel yanked up—and openly glowered. "Excuse the fuck out of me?"

"I— This—" Fresh tears brimmed. "This isn't me. None of this...is me."

"Not you?" He let her see his wry smile. "Hmmm. Not you. Which part might you be referring to? The 'not you' who dropped her whole life in order to help two near-strangers search for her kidnapped friend? Or the 'not you' who's been rotating shifts in that office with the same strangers, who've been doing this kind of shit for years? Or the 'not you' who managed to tame those same *imbeciles* with an hour they won't forget for the rest of their lives?"

She pierced him with a gaze that gleamed like morning sun. "And I won't forget it, either."

He kissed the tip of her nose. "Good."

Weirdly enough, Rhett appeared the somber one now. "But you refuse to feel good about any of it."

Rebel dipped his head, adding his silent support of the query. The insight couldn't have been more spot-on.

Brynna drew in air through her nose. Let it out on a long sigh. "Because I'm right. You guys see that, yeah? Here I am, cup running over with warm and gooey because of the best sex I've ever had in my *life*, while my friend—my *best* friend—is still wondering if anyone will be coming for her—"

"Whoa." Rhett tugged on her shoulder, urging her back around. "Right there. Just whoa." As she scooted back up against the cushion, jabbing the sheet into her armpits, he persisted, "Do you really think Zoe has given up on us searching for her? Does that woman think, for even one second, that her husband will let that happen?"

Her lips pursed. "That doesn't excuse what happened. What I *allowed* to happen."

Rebel propped an elbow up on a knee, narrowing his gaze again. "Right. And neither of us had anything to say about it."

Rhett jogged his head in open sarcasm. "I know *I* had plenty to say about it."

Rebel smirked. "You sure as hell did."

The guy chuffed. "You had some good shit to chime in too."

Brynn tucked her arms in, staring at the tops of her own

knees. Though her gaze warmed a little, the rest of her face maintained resolute lines. Humor was clearly not the key past her tension—once more, not a surprise. Even without a missing friend in the mix, many submissives threw themselves onto pyres of guilt, using it as a coping mechanism to help deal with the freaky flag they'd just let fly. As a Dom, it was often hard to combat, since no argument but the obvious made sense: that sexual pleasure wasn't created for shame or guilt or remorse.

But this, at least, was an argument he could deal with. All it took was getting pragmatic to the point of tough and turning it into a resolute stare at her adorable frown. "Listen to me. We're both just as desperate to find Zoe as you, but in doing it with the best tools, with the right timing. This morning's snag was just that: a snag. I'm sorry that this didn't happen twelve hours from now, but at this moment, we've got no choice. We'll formulate a new approach into the building and then hang back until nightfall for execution." He let darker emotions drag his head down. "Nobody—*nobody*—wishes that wasn't the case more than I do. As the guy who fucked this all to hell in the first place—"

"You don't know that."

Rhett tacked on a significant glower—which weirdly warmed Reb's chest. The sex hadn't affected the guy's views on the mission, thank fuck—including his support about the mouse cam's failure. Nonetheless, Reb muttered, "Well, you don't *not* know it."

Rhett glowered. "Really, shithead? Weren't we right here an hour ago?"

Nothing was the same as it was an hour ago.

Rhett illustrated the point by caressing a hand along Brynn's calf. The move, given in lazy reassurance, pulled Reb right back into the unnatural thrall the man had over him. Damn it. He could stare at those powerful, graceful hands for an hour...or ten. In this instance, he wasn't alone. Nobody in the battalion had escaped being captivated at some point by Double-Oh's magic with a recon intel screen, a GPS box, or even fixing kids' toys in third-world villages across the globe.

But witnessing the reverence Double-Oh emanated over the skin of a woman...

Fuck.

Yeah. An hour. Or ten.

Brynna herself cut that dream short. She jerked up her head like the world's sexiest CEO about to conduct a board meeting. "I just want to focus on what we do *now*. Sitting here in a stupid funk isn't...going to..." Her voice cracked on fresh tears. "Damn it! This is the most ridiculous... Why am I still doing this?"

As if moving with one mind—and maybe they were—Rebel swept up with Rhett, surrounding her once more. Crisscrossing their arms over her chest and tucking their heads against her shoulders, they each captured the wet streams of her desperation with their lips. Rebel prepared for her resistance, perhaps even for her total flight, but the woman only tensed for half a heartbeat before urging them closer and then weeping even harder.

They stayed like that, in a three-way cocoon, as Brynn's sobs mingled with the morning songs of the birds outside. Minutes went by, as if he even cared. Vaguely—maybe not so vaguely—Rebel considered the concept of heaven on earth. If there was one for everybody, his may just have just been revealed.

Like every law-abiding heaven, it was over all too fast.

Brynn brought her hands in, swiping again at her puffy eye sockets. "Thank you." She gazed from one to the other of them though clearly struggled for focus. "Thank you both... for...well..."

Rhett pressed a thumb across her lips. "We know. And you're welcome."

"This still isn't me," she rasped. "I don't know *who* this is, but it's sure as hell not—"

"The woman who told us she *doesn't do submissive*?" Rebel filled in.

Her gaze had been melting to a gorgeous milk chocolate shade. It rehardened inside of two seconds. "What does that have to do with any—"

"It has to do with everything." He didn't let her go, securing her wrist as she dug in her heels, trying to push away. "Especially because it was part of what just happened."

"I'm not going to discuss this." Her tone was rebellious but her stare pleading, especially as she lifted it to Rhett. The move earned her only a pair of raised brows and a nod toward Reb.

"Sorry, peach. I don't have a golden Dom patch, but even I can see he's right—with a pretty huge *R*."

She squirmed. Rebel held tight. He felt like a complete shit for it, but her waterworks flooded back on, confirming just how big his *R* really was. "Easy, *mon chou*. Easy. It's only us. And just to refresh your memory, we both really enjoyed it." He dropped his gaze along with his voice, making sure she felt just how much he meant the words. *Enjoyed* was the hugest understatement for what she'd given him with her submission, but this was going to require baby steps. Lots of them.

Rhett leaned in with the same message taking over his

face. Though his lips were firm, the oceans in his eyes swelled with sensual waves. "You enjoyed it too...right?"

She flung a glare. "I appreciate your respect for my interpretive acting work—but I'm not *that* good."

Rebel pulled her wrist against his lips. "Actually, you're still enjoying it." He nuzzled her skin with his nose. "Your heartbeat. Racing and ready. You like the fact that we're even talking about it—"

"The hell I do."

"As well as every moment you gave in to it."

Rhett performed the same treatment on her other wrist. "Gave in to *us*."

"The *hell* I did." She wrested both arms free. Jabbed them close to her torso and then under the sheet, like a kid hiding a stolen candy bar. "I'm *not* going to talk about this."

Rebel rested back on his haunches. "Well. That's completely your prerogative, Miss Monet."

She huffed. "Oh, it's 'Miss Monet' now? Turning on the ice water so I'll coerce you to heat it back up by baring my soul?" Her eyes rolled. "You want to try something that I didn't ace a psych exam on two years ago?"

He teeter-tottered his head before quickly nodding it. "Fair enough. But at least I cared enough to try, considering you've tied my hands against using the method that'll really work here." He settled back a little more, folding his arms. "But that's exactly how you want it, isn't it?"

She wasn't so snappy with her next retort. With hands still rustling beneath the sheet, she pressed, "Fine. I'll bite. What method would that be, Sergeant Stafford?" Slinging the payback on the formality had her preening a little, proud of herself—

Until Reb issued his rebuttal.

"Brynna Cosette Monet...you need to be spanked."

"Pardon the hell out of me?"

"Nothing to pardon." He shrugged, ignoring her stiff spine and plummeting brows. "The lines have clearly been redrawn, so there's no need."

"Lines?" she demanded. "Redrawn? For what?"

"For whatever you now want them to be. That's right, isn't it?"

"I—" If she were on a stage in rehearsal, she'd be the one begging for script help. "I don't know what—"

"But if, hypothetically, I was still acting as your Dom, you'd probably be flat on this mattress now, taking my hand on your ass. *A lot* of times."

The sheet rustled. Her lips twisted. Oh, he'd gotten her attention, all right—and likely a little more. And the woman *still* wanted to deny her attraction to sexual surrender? It made no sense. He checked in with a glance toward Rhett, whose face reflected the same incredulity.

Brynn scowled deeply, though her voice was an unsure rasp. "Wh-Why?"

It wasn't hard to preface the answer with a soft smile. "Number one, because you'd like it. Number two, to establish a connection between us of energy and trust so you'd feel better about opening up to me. And number three, because you'd really, *really* like it."

Her face tightened again. But more importantly, her legs squirmed beneath the sheet. Little minx. She was clearly hot, bothered, and on her way to being wet again—but there wasn't a damn thing he could do about it except watch. Because, for whatever insane reason, Brynna Monet *still* "didn't do submission."

"So I like a little bite to my passion every now and then. It doesn't mean I'm a damn submissive."

Rhett reentered the fray with a wry smirk. "With all due respect to every gorgeous inch of you, peach, I've been naked and horizontal with you twice in the last week. Between those two occasions, I've had the fun of pulling your hair, biting your nipples, sucking your clit, zip-tying your wrists, and fucking you senseless, among other pretty good highlights. You know when I've seen that lovely pussy the wettest?" As he asked it, he leaned in, making sure their gazes were level for his whispered answer. "When you begged me for more, sweetheart. When I *made* you beg me for more."

"When you had to let it all go," Rebel confirmed.

"When you submitted to us."

Her eyes slammed shut. Her body balled up. Rebel had expected the withdrawal, but this was extreme. Her face contorted as if they'd both punched her in the gut.

"I don't care." She huddled tighter. "I *can't* care."

Rebel bit back a number of Creole words that perfectly fit his fury. God*damn*. If they could only lay her out and redden her ass...

Good thing Rhett was up in her grill right now and not him. The guy's composure was nothing short of astounding as he gently prodded, "Why?" He ran a soothing hand over her head, not caring about her little flinch. "Why can't you care, Brynna?"

She lifted her head. Leaned a little toward his touch, giving in to a moment of its strength and safety. Rebel was envious. *That man and his hands...*

Without opening her eyes, she rasped, "Because Enya

cared."

Rhett didn't falter his caresses by a beat. "Who's Enya?"

She ducked her head from him. "Enya cared. Now she doesn't."

"But why?" He reached again, but she jerked away. "Sweet peach...you can tell us. You can *trust* us. It's just Rebel and me."

She snapped her head up. Glared at both of them, the scared kitten instantly grown into a terrified cat. They both watched, bemused, as she whipped the sheet fully around herself. Through every second, Rebel never remotely anticipated her next move.

"I won't do this. I *can't* do this."

With an acrobatic move only possible for an accomplished dancer, she flipped backward and then twisted, escaping over the back of the futon—leaving Rhett and him to gawk at each other in shock more naked than their dicks.

CHAPTER THIRTEEN

Two hours later, Rhett paced into the office with refilled water bottles in his hands and a tight scowl on his face. He was showered and changed, his faded BDU bottoms topped by a black T-shirt emblazoned with yellow lettering: *Actually, it* is *rocket science.* Rebel looked up from one of the two chairs now parked in front of the computer desk, arching a wary brow—which he decided to ignore.

"She's still sleeping."

Reb chucked a pencil at the desk. Rocked back in the chair. "Because, of course, you decided to check again."

He banged one of the water bottles down. Dropped into the empty chair just as bearishly. "Beats sitting here looking at you."

The shithead leaned back a little more. "Hmm. You sure about that?" He laced fingers in classic criminal mastermind style, a shout-out to every superhero movie they'd seen together—which meant nearly all of them. Trouble was, no Joker or Loki or Luthor looked good enough to jump just sitting in a workout tank and shorts.

Damn it.

Rebel. Him. *Them.* He couldn't treat it like a bothersome summer cold anymore, could he? It wasn't going to "just go away" on its own. Every moment of this morning's adventure had sure as hell changed that.

Adventure. Okay, that was a good way of looking at it.

Like all great adventures, it had been exhilarating and new, an adrenaline rush not soon to be forgotten. At least not by him. But was that where everything stopped?

The waters in which he still swam—at a desperate pace—said no.

Treacherous waters.

Where his fucking feelings had turned into boulders.

"Yeah, I'm sure," he finally grunted, peering through the water at the monitors. A little plastic, a little H2O, and the world was suddenly a different place. Only...it wasn't. Only his view had changed. "Damn sure."

It was time to see things clearly again. To push the boulders back into the stream.

He took another long pull of the water. This time, pushed it away after setting it down. "So...you think she's all right?"

"As opposed to the ninety-eight other times you asked me, Mother Hubbard?" Reb came out of the Magneto pose to balance the opposite way, elbows propped on the desk, tiptoeing the base of the chair. But by the time he looked up at the monitors, his snark dissipated. "You know what? I think she's exhausted. First, we weren't exactly about hearts, candles, and Air Supply with her this morning. On top of that, after the details we've uncovered here..."

Rhett grimaced. "No shit."

Two lamer words had never been spoken—in light of the information relayed by the two screens. Rebel pointed at a picture from the Facebook page of a woman named Enya Sabine Monet, dated a little over two years ago. "This has to be the Enya she was referring to."

"Who clearly has to be her younger sister." The photo served as the *no duh* for that. The shot, which looked like it was taken at a club or party, displayed Brynna and Enya along with another woman, only referred to as Nadine. They all wore black cocktail dresses, though Enya and Nadine had finished theirs off with fishnets and pleaser boots that wouldn't have left any dude at that party guessing about their end game. Brynn, with those incredible gazelle legs, didn't need any enhancements but the sleek black heels on her feet. As it was, Rhett shifted to readjust his fresh boner. Just imagining her in that dress, with those legs circling his waist and those heels digging into his back...

Focus, you wanker.

Beyond the erotic fantasy value, the picture was a revelation. Though Brynn and Enya stood on opposite sides of their friend, their resemblance was too striking to be ignored. Duplicate kitten eyes. The same high, defined cheeks. Their chins tapering to matching heart-shaped points.

"Beautiful girl." Rebel stated it as if rattling off mission intel, peering analytically at the monitor. "Looks happy, healthy, fulfilled. Lived about ten minutes from Brynna and had friends as well as an active social life. According to her tax records, worked a good job as a special events manager at The Wynn—"

Rhett interjected with a low whistle. "Niiiice."

"But apparently she was lying to a lot of people."

Rhett took that as his cue to click open another window. A page from a new social media site appeared, which incorporated elements of the popular standard social sites but with kinkier twists. Photos of Enya Monet also filled the screen—only it wasn't her name at the top of the page. *Hestia Hyacinth* was a different creature entirely: a woman who wore latex minis, training corsets, and leather accessories with D-rings for bondage hooks. Her blond hair was hidden beneath wigs of various colors and styles. Her face was coated in glittering makeup and swirled decals that turned her into everything from a half-naked butterfly to an erotic zombie to a naughty schoolgirl and everything in between.

"At the risk of being redundant," Rhett inserted, "no shit."

Rebel scooted in, a fascinated stare taking over his face. "Check out the dates. Her posts to Facebook faded as her entries on this kink site ramped up."

"Definitely fits." Rhett clicked another tab, opening up a detailed credit card purchase history. "Check out the other records I was able to yank."

Rebel leaned in again. "She went to a lot of the lighter D/s play clubs in town..."

"Until she didn't."

The guy's gaze flared. "Wait a second. Brick and Bondage Corp. Isn't that—"

"Max Brickham's company." Rhett offered the name of the Seattle-based Dom who owned Bastille, the kink club they frequented when they were back at base. Last year, Max had opened a second location in a subterranean bunker beneath the Nevada desert, halfway between Vegas and Henderson. Catacomb wasn't advertised or promoted anywhere in town— partly because it was successful without the fuss; mostly because it was known for the most hardcore BDSM play in the valley.

Rebel scooped up the pencil again. Tapped it on the desk in a fervent staccato. Rhett tried not to stare but failed. It was almost as fascinating to watch the guy think as it was to watch him fuck. "So she heard about Catacomb. And got in."

"Looks like it." Rhett scowled. "But we can only go by the

receipt trail. Max is, as we both know, paranoid about security. His firewalls can be cracked, but it would take me three days minimum to do it."

"Don't bother." Rebel started scrolling deeper into the pages of "Hestia's" kink account. "I think we'll find what we need right here."

Scroll. Scroll. Scroll.

Rebel kept going, though some of the shots made him stop and zoom in before shaking his head, looking as stumped as a *Jeopardy* contestant who had no clue how to answer the Daily Double. Rhett had to admit, his friend's confusion was oddly reassuring. Rhett had seen a lot of the world, and that included BDSM dungeons from the tame to the bizarre, but even to a jaded guy like himself, the pictorial chronicle of Hestia's submissive journey was intense. The images depicted the woman in increasingly extreme D/s situations, including fire cupping, public whippings, and even a needle and thread session where the sides of her spine were pierced with eyelets and then "laced up" like a corset.

The captions on the photos declared it was all for her Master Peter, a guy who looked like the love child of Billy Corgan and a Harajuku Girl and did his part for the Vegas BDSM community by ensuring the camera loved him in all the right ways. From his rock-star pout and shit-kicker boots to his kohl-lined eyes and multipierced ears, Peter baby was all about projecting the brooding rebel guy mystique. He apparently played that way too. Rhett lost track of how many red flags he set off, all of them overlaid with one resonating word.

User.

His instinct wasn't soothed as Rebel continued scrolling. The pictures of Enya and her Dom were clearly all captioned by her, in language that made more alarms go off.

He is my sun, my moon, my stars.

I am his to rule forever.

His happiness is mine.

Next to him Rebel grunted. "His happiness?" he scoffed. "Does that guy understand what happiness is, beyond a popular Instagram account?"

The answer came with hardly any notice. Between one mouse click and the next, Hestia Hyacinth's profile relayed a dramatically different story. Gone was the cute and curious little subbie as well as the lovestruck woman devoted to the will of her Dom. Gone were photos of the *woman* at all. Haunting images took over her feed, some borrowed from other sources, others taken with her cell. Moody landscapes. Pining poems. Shots of things like tumbleweeds, cloud-filled skies, lone swans on foggy ponds.

The captions to the images were just as desolate. Rambling and grief-stricken, the texts were filled with pleas and questions, begging Master Peter for an explanation of what offense she'd committed to turn him from her so suddenly. From the looks of things, diva-boy Dom had left her to hang, despite how she begged him for a phone call, a text...a chance.

Rhett pounded down more water. "Why do I suddenly wish this was vodka?"

Rebel cocked back his head, closing his eyes. "Asshole saved all the pretty for the camera."

"A lot more makes sense now. About what Brynn said."

"Truth." Reb straightened, taking in the images with newly scrutinizing eyes. "So what happened after that? These last pictures are dated nearly a year ago."

Rhett clicked open the window with his original search

results for Enya's name. "I had more hits here... Let me see if anything turns..."

"Whoa." Rebel voiced the polite version of *what the fuck* as the monitor was filled with a certificate bearing the state's seal—then three words in ornate script.

Power of Attorney

It was easy enough to skim the legal mumbo-jumbo and locate the names of the key people on the doc.

"Enya gave Brynna her power of attorney?" Rhett frowned.

"And not to a parent?" Rebel countered. "Are their mom and dad around?"

Frustration seared Rhett's chest. He'd shared sexual ecstasy with the woman now embedded into his bone marrow but barely knew a thing about her life, especially her family. While the connection of this week was hardly going to transfer back to their real lives, the incongruity still felt wrong. "Wait." A memory blasted in. "Wasn't Brynn's mom at Shay and Zoe's wedding? The funny little thing who sat on the hay bale all night?"

Rebel's head jerked up. "Yeah," he said slowly. "Right. She was the overgrown garden gnome crossed with Kathy Bates, circa *Misery*."

"Only she thought that corner was her little pulpit after a while. I think she quoted every apostle in Jesus's posse, along with Paul and a few guest stars from the Old Testament too."

"Right." Reb snickered for a second. "Thank fuck Zoe wasn't showing with the *bebette* yet."

"Well, that clarifies Enya's choice. A little."

"A *little*." Rebel used the emphasis to drive in the opposite. There was still a lot they didn't know about all this. "What the hell isn't adding up?" He dragged a hand through his hair and turned his gaze out the window, as if the towering cypress and oaks would magically give up the answer. "What are we missing?"

"Or, more accurately, what can't we find?"

Suddenly, Rebel swiveled his head back around. His eyes were as brilliant as cut stones. "You mean what can't we find... legally."

Rhett returned the stare with rising comprehension. "Things like health records...or sealed court documents." He tapped knuckles against his chin, thinking deeper. "Or...a restraining order?"

"Perhaps." Rhett hedged. "But filed by whom? Look at Enya's posts again. Her desperation adds the detail. She lists everything about her time with Peter except goddamn bathroom breaks. There's length of their play sessions, depth and intensity of the guy's discipline—"

"Toy types." Rhett's brows jabbed up. "Positions. Climax counts. Christ. This shit is juicy."

"And just as abundant after their breakup, only the information is different. The little Jane Austen can spin the angst with the best of them."

"Roger that." The material would've been a little comical had the heartache beneath not been so palpable. "'*Breathe in, breathe out, but I only swallow glass...top of the world, but I'm sitting in trash...*'"

"Wonder if she ever thought of selling to Nashville. Girl could stir herself up a pile of gold." He held up both hands at Rhett's censuring glance. "Just sayin', *podna*."

Rhett reveled in warmth from the man's casual endearment—for a moment. He shoved it aside just as quickly to focus again on the monitors. "So if Peter didn't file it, and *she* didn't—"

"We're still looking in the wrong place." Reb started the pencil drumbeat again.

"But still seeking something protected by the court."

The drumming stopped. As if drawn to the very lightbulb that seemed to blaze to life inside it, Reb lifted his head. "Like psychiatric care?"

Rhett pivoted in his chair. *Bam.* There was his lightbulb too. "A fifty-one fifty psych hold?" The words even felt right to say. "Or something else? Or both?"

"Not sure it matters. But it sure as hell slides some things into place." Rebel rose, braced hands to his hips, and then paced toward the doorway leading to the other den, where the rumpled blankets on the futon were a blatant reminder of what had gone down this morning for all three of them. "*A lot* of things."

Rhett nodded. The circuits in his brain kept snapping into place, gears hitting at high speed. "That was the reason for her meltdown, wasn't it? It wasn't all just about Zoe."

It wasn't a shocker to him—nor to Rebel, judging by the guy's unchanged posture. After a long moment, the sinews of his shoulders twined and shifted as he reached for the doorframe, noticeably clenching the dark wood. "Taking on that kind of responsibility...especially if her sister had a significant breakdown..."

"Because of a Dom who took *wham, bam, thank you, subbie* to a whole new level of asswad." Rhett leaned forward, meshing his hands and dropping his head. "Unbelievable."

"No wonder she's fighting so violently against her submissiveness." Reb's hands glided downward, almost caressing the wood. "Though I've never met a woman more perfectly created for it." He rocked back and forth in the portal, embodying the rate at which both their brains now churned. It all started to fit. The memories of what she'd said, together with the facts they'd just learned, added to some damn confident inferences on both their parts.

Rhett tilted his head up again. "Damn. A natural submissive who refuses to submit."

"Unless her brain is forcibly locked out of the situation."

Rhett chuffed. Another unarguable point from the "Look what we learned in bed this morning" folder. The things Brynna had agreed to...the heights they'd taken her desire, once she'd just given up, given in, and surrendered to their full control...

"A situation we managed once." The argument needed to be voiced aloud. "Fat bloody chance she'll allow it to happen again. In that gorgeous head of hers, losing control doesn't just mean surrendering her body. It's a matter of losing *herself*."

Rebel turned around, lifting his hold to the doorway's upper jamb in the process. "Just like her sister did."

Damn. Talk about losing oneself. Moon's stretched, burnished muscles were an eyeful that made Rhett forget his own name for a second. He readjusted his position in the chair, silently cursing the events of this morning—for the thousandth time. And, for the thousandth time, taking them back. The revelations they'd known and all the new things he'd seen in this man... He'd never forget any of it and knew that in time, when the recollections melded into the places of his mind reserved for the most special moments of his life, that an image of Rebel's passion-drenched face would be there too.

In the end, he'd be damn glad it all happened.

He wasn't sure Brynn would be joining him in that boat.

Once more, he decided to finish his musing aloud. "But her tenacity about the control...it's like clutching greased rope. The tighter she holds on, the more her grip slips."

"Which we witnessed in full, sobbing Technicolor."

Rhett stood now too. Stuffed both hands into his pockets while battling the urge to reach out and just run his hands beneath Reb's tank. It wouldn't be for any sexual thrill this time, though. He felt the visceral need to put an outward display on the new things he felt for the man. No, not even for the man. This was just about...the *person*. The connection to him. The acceptance by him, for him. The better ways they could already read each other, know each other. Their synchronicity on missions, already legendary, was going to be off the fucking charts now.

But it wasn't possible. Couldn't be. If he touched just one place, he'd want more. Then Reb would want more. Then a touch wouldn't be enough, maybe not even a kiss. And it would be amazing. Conflagrating. A bonfire for the ages.

A passion he'd never be able to recover from.

Working side-by-side with the man wouldn't be synchronicity anymore. It would be hell.

And then there was the matter of the beautiful redhead sleeping across the house. The way he saw her haunting Rebel's eyes, the same way she dogged so many of his own thoughts and longings. There was so much more to uncover about her... and so few bricks remaining that could be loosened from her walls, if at all. The woman who'd tumbled away from them this morning had been spurred by one motivation alone. Fear. Her remaining barriers would take patience and strategy and time, lots of it, to scale.

Time they didn't have.

He said as much to Rebel by widening his stance and squaring his jaw. Added a twist of his lips before venturing, "So what do we tell her we know?"

Translation: *How pissed do we risk the woman being, about prying into her sister's personal shit and using it to analyze her issues about submissiveness?*

Rebel started with the human metronome thing in the doorway again. Pretty much expected.

"All of it," the guy gritted.

Okay, *not* expected. At all.

"All of... Wait... Whoa... Moon?" But he could've been stammering stanzas of *Three Little Pigs*, since his friend wasn't listening. Clearly, the decision had been made—for what reason he couldn't fathom, but Reb blowing a gasket of common sense seemed like a damn good option right now—especially now that Reb squeaked the floor from his bare-footed turn and then started toward the bedroom wing with determined steps.

"All of it," he repeated along the way. "This girl needs to learn she can trust us—with everything."

Rhett felt himself cut loose a grin. "Well, damn. That actually makes sense."

Rebel chuckled. "You sound surprised."

"I am. I didn't think either one of us was thinking straight about her right now."

"Still not quite sure I am, brother." Reb paused at the door to the guest bedroom she was using. "But putting *her* needs first seems like a good place to start."

Temptation or not, Rhett refused to let that go unanswered. He reached over, delivering a sturdy clap to his friend's shoulder. "I agree, man."

Just like that, thank fuck, it was over. He'd gotten through it without wanting to go too much further with the affection.

Too much further...

Stow it, asshole. Deep.

Rhett twisted the doorknob and then quietly swung in the bedroom's door. "Sweet peach?" he called softly. "You awake?"

Rebel rolled his eyes while striding past him. Once the guy got to the bed, he hitched up on it, curling one knee in. "Brynna." He tenderized the charge at once. "*Minette*, Rhett and I would like to speak with you."

There was no response from the woman beneath the covers.

Low blow though it was, Rhett let a chuckle fly.

"Brynna? *Mon chou?*"

Still not a move. Not a groan, a sigh, or a rustle.

Rhett moved to the foot of the bed, laughing a little harder.

With a glare over his shoulder, Rebel slid farther up the mattress. Rolled over and curled around Brynn, completing the sensual spoon by slinking his arms around her waist.

Before his whole body seized and jerked.

"Moon?" Rhett scowled. "What the—"

Shock choked back the rest. As Rebel swept the coverlet high and then hurled it off the bed—exposing the pillows mounded together to create the effect of a slumbering body. On the pillow where Brynna's head should have been, there was a note scrawled on the back of a crumpled rehearsal schedule, probably yanked from her purse—which, along with her cosmetics and hair products, was also gone.

She wasted no time getting to the point—escalating Reb's low growl to an enraged bellow.

She's my best friend.

I had to do something.

I'm sorry.

Rhett added his own snarl to that—but did it while whirling out the door and back down the hall to the office. He plummeted back into a chair and jammed on his headset before issuing a furious vow beneath his breath. "She has no idea what sorry is yet."

By the time Rebel joined him again, he'd hailed El, who answered from Vegas like a fairy flying on ecstasy. "Howdy, Texas! What's up?"

"Cut the crap, El." Rebel glowered at the note in his hand that might as well have been the thorn in his paw. "She did this with your help, damn it. Unless you want to consider two best friends chained in Adler's magic lab of wonders, you'll spill."

A long pause. El's pissy huff. "She told me you'd do this. That you'd be impossible bullies and try to intimidate me into—"

"*Everything*, El. *Now.*"

CHAPTER FOURTEEN

Brynn's cell buzzed on the SUV's passenger seat. Again.

It was El. Again.

She ignored it. Again.

She jolted as the air vibrated with a heavy *thwop-thwop-thwop*. Forced herself to breathe deep, telling herself it was only another media helicopter, not Rhett and Rebel about to fast-rope from a Blackhawk and torch through the rental car's roof. But the fact that the scenario was in the realm of possibility for those two? Another shiver was fully justified— as well as a glance up at the sky, just to confirm the media chopper theory.

She'd just tucked her head back inside the car when the phone buzzed again. Cockroach-crawled across the cushion at her. A new shudder. Damn if she didn't wish for the thing to just turn into a real roach.

Did she want to know what the auto redialing was about?

Rhetorical question. The way things were going today, she wouldn't flinch if El was calling about a flash flood on the river or even a swarm of locusts on its way to munch down on Austin. But not answering meant the thing was going to buzz through every mile between here and the old Verge building.

With a dreading huff, she scooped up the phone. "What?"

El whooshed out a breath. "Damn it. You picked up."

"Excuse me? You've been calling like Crazy Cory."

Surely that would loosen El a little. Cory had been a

charming fan who'd talked El into a few fun dates, only to turn semistalker and earn his name on a restraining order. Their Crazy Cory jokes had stuck even after the guy decided to move to Florida, suddenly switching his obsession to a new Latina pop star who lived there.

But El's tension only notched higher. "Where are you? Damn it. You can't be done yet—unless Adler and Royce didn't buy your act and left you out at the gate."

"Not in these hose, they won't." She ran a hand up her calves, just to be sure the seams still extended up the back, to the point where they clipped into garters against her thighs. When packing this "nice girl with the secret naughty side" outfit back at home, she'd gone for the garters and stockings out of ruthless instinct, thinking only about what might capture Adler's attention if she had to resort to this tactic. Now that push had come to shove, she wished the demure stockings had gone in too. She felt obscenely exposed, despite the boy short panties still covering every inch of her privates beneath her pinstriped pencil skirt. Maybe that had something to do with her white button-front shirt, open down to the fourth button, giving an ample peek at the white lace of her cami-bra beneath—and the flesh filling it out.

"What does that mean?" El pressed. "And where the hell *are* you?"

She lifted her head and looked around, almost laughing from bemusement. "Just leaving the motel."

"*What?*"

She yanked the phone away from her ear. "El, I get enough screeching from your cat."

The line filled with a girl growl that was just as bad. "How are you still there? *Why* are you still there?"

"Well, I wasn't sitting here redoing my nails." She couldn't help the defensive burst. "The traffic was bumper-to-bumper on the road for at least an hour after I checked in." Then transformed into the slinky-heeled, va-va-voom-haired vixen who was going to charm anything she wanted from Homer Adler—including access to the room where he was keeping her best friend. "I think I heard someone say that they're screening the new Tarantino film this afternoon."

"The new—" A sharp *smack* cracked through the line, confirming her friend still excelled at the fine art of face-palming. "I can't freaking believe this."

"The next time Zo gets herself kidnapped, I'll just ask her to steer clear of the SXSW dates, okay?" Out of convenience, she used the acronym for South by Southwest, the monster-sized alternative film and cultural festival that took over Austin every March. Her view across the motel parking lot alone included a pink mohawked woman walking a trio of similarly-coifed wolfhounds, a guy dressed as Dracula on top and Wolfman on the bottom, and a dreadlocked couple toting a pair of mobile keyboards, singing "Wrecking Ball" in perfect harmony.

"Just confirm you're able to get out of there now. As in, *right* now." At first, El's tone just seemed irritable. But after three major dance show tours with the woman, Brynn knew the nuances of irritation in her friend. This wasn't one of them.

She trembled again. Hard. Then finally muttered, "Shit."

"Ummm, yep. That about hits the nail on the head."

"So they just found out?" She cut to the chase. The particulars of how Rhett and Rebel had grilled El didn't matter. She hadn't even asked her friend to keep any confidences, knowing the guys would use any means they could—probably even a threat to El's screechy cat—to make her spill about Brynn's logistics. Putting El in that position wasn't fair. She'd only asked El to buy her some time by scrambling the tracking chips on her phone and the SUV. Her mistake had been misjudging how much time that would take, figuring the guys would've let her "sleep" for at least three hours before bothering her in the guest room.

"That's the million-dollar question." El's confession wasn't the thumbs-up Brynn was looking for. "Especially because I don't really know the answer."

Brynn frowned while powering up the car. "What do you mean?"

"I mean that those men are devious sonofabitches."

Tell me something I don't know. Only by yanking a page out of that very book had she'd been able to get out of that ranch without them knowing: a stunt she'd regretted *and* validated as soon as concocting it. Did she like sneaking off to pour herself into this getup, knowing she would walk into the lion's den by herself in it? Had she enjoyed deceiving the men who'd been brave enough to show her *their* truth, despite the terrifying new ground it had been for them? And had she wanted to slip out that door, away from them—and the place where they'd made her feel so good, so right, so complete about herself?

No. No. And *hell, no.*

But as they said in Mother's world, traitors only got one kiss goodbye. Brynn had pressed hers into a note, laid atop a mound of pillows, in a bed she'd left as cold as the ache in her heart. She'd left it there with a prayer too—a plea that Rhett and Rebel might, by some sliver of possibility, understand that she'd done this for them as much as Zoe. That if she'd stayed, she would have pulled unfair shit on them, begging them to take her to bed again. To open her up again. To lead them on into giving her just one more hit of that amazing shit called submissiveness...

Wasn't going to happen.

She was still in control, damn it. She wasn't like Enya. She sure as *hell* wasn't like Mom. She wasn't going to run away from her life by giving it over to men, whether they wielded whips or Bibles...or just the power of their kisses and touches. She was going to make something of her life. Make it matter. Make it connected. And yes, that meant making hard decisions. It meant walking out the door, getting in a car, making a good plan, and sticking to it—especially when that plan involved saving the friend who meant so damn much to her.

At the moment, it also meant finding a way out of the motel's parking lot.

Though San Jacinto Boulevard was moving again, it was still a snail crawl. The backup into the motel's lot was five cars deep. She pulled out of line, praying this place had a back way out. On the way toward the rear of the property, she maneuvered around a ninja banjo player, as well as a couple who wouldn't stop making out, while urging more details out of El.

"I'm all ears," she told her friend. "Though I'm not sure I want to be."

El whooshed out a breath. "Why do you have to be so smart?"

Her lips quirked. "And why do you always know exactly what I need to hear?"

"What the hell are you talking about?"

"Just...thanks." All the reflection about life, purpose, and friendship made her suddenly mushy. It had *nothing* to do with having her soul bared as naked as her body less than half a day ago. "Thanks," she repeated with more conviction. "For being you. For being there. Even right now."

El filled the line with a curt *pssshh*. "You feeling okay?"

She pushed out a quick snort of her own. "So give me the rest. What did the devious duo do?"

Her friend was done scoffing. El's pause could only be described as anxious. "They slipped me an electronic ruffie," she finally mumbled. "At least I'm pretty damn sure they did."

Brynn's hands tightened around the steering wheel—and not just because of the confession. There was no viable back exit to this place, except fifty yards of off-road action over really chunky terrain, followed by a hop off a sizable curb. Some drivers in four-wheel-drives were tackling it with no problem. She was in a rental SUV. Damn it.

"What happened?" She swung the car back toward the front of the motel.

El expelled another breath. "Well, as you warned me, they got on the comm line as soon as they figured out you were gone. That was...about half an hour ago."

"*Half an hour?*"

El's whimper carried an implied apology. "Soooo, you still glad I'm here? Maybe a little?"

"Of course," she reassured. "I just don't get why you waited so long to call after that."

"I didn't."

"Huh?"

"Remember that roofie I mentioned?"

She nudged the car back into the exit line. Drummed an impatient hand on the wheel. Not only was the queue now eight cars long, something about El's account wove an additional thread of anxiety through her gut. Suddenly, getting out of here felt more important than ever.

"I just got off the line with them, Brynn. It was only then that they weren't firing questions at me so fast, making it impossible for me to think of anything but answering them, that I could chill enough to focus on *their* side of the exchange— and the sounds I heard during it."

Another schism of tension shot through Brynn's belly. "What kinds of questions?"

"Don't you want to know about the sounds?"

"The questions first. What did they ask you?"

El growled again. Brynn almost didn't hear it. The sound was her thing, like her personal stress ball. "Well first, they wanted to know if you normally pull shit like this."

"And you said what?"

"Aside from telling them it was a lame question?" El's snort was so rough, it sounded like she sat on the phone instead. "Do you *normally* pull shit like this? Are they serious? What the hell about this situation is normal for any of us?"

Strangely, Brynn smiled. Sounded like the guys were in ogre mode, which conveyed one clear truth. The bigger they puffed up the ogres, the deeper they actually cared. Warmth tickled her veins. It felt...nice. Damn nice. She'd inspired ogre status. And God, how she wanted to just dive back under their bridge with them now...

No more ogres. No more bridges. Focus on getting Zo and then getting back to what your life is meant to be. Predictable. Settled. Safe.

"What did they ask about after that?"

El's sigh was a verbalized shrug. "They were all over the place. They made no pretenses about not being on to what your plan is, so I didn't either. They wanted to know all the logistical stuff, like if they had to step in and save you, what was going to be relevant."

"If they have to step in—" She sliced out a cynical snicker. "Guess they still don't realize that I've been saving *myself* for quite a while now."

There was a pause equivalent to an eye roll. "Testosterone. Isn't it a wonderful thing?"

Brynn winced. This morning, it had been a *damn* wonderful thing.

No more ogres. No more bridges.

She forced neutrality back to her tone. "Just tell me what else they said."

"Let's see... First, they asked if you could run in those heels if you had to. Also wanted to know if you planned on taking your phone with you and if you're carrying."

"Carrying what?" Only after El's burst of a laugh did that one click. "Like a *gun*? Are they crazy?"

No. They were soldiers—who were thinking like soldiers.

Which meant they *might* know a few things more than she about how to do all this undercover/subterfuge/charm-the-bad-guy shit.

Which also meant they might have been making an intelligent point about waiting to make another move on this thing—

Which meant Zoe would be in that madman's captivity even longer.

Not an option.

Sometimes the most dangerous decision just had to be the right one.

She pushed on the gas, edging the car forward. Seven

more cars between her and the highway.

"Then they asked a bunch of questions about Zoe and the pregnancy," El went on. "Like exactly how far along she is, whether there have been complications, what doctor's orders she's on, how her overall health is."

"Understood." Six more cars now. "So they're going straight to the Verge building."

"As the soldier boys would say," El responded, "roger that."

She could mark that part down in ink. She just couldn't fathom what *their* plan possibly was. They'd been adamant about waiting for nightfall to go back, though her move had forced them into a new strategy: a twist they were *not* fond of, if her gut was telling her true. She could feel their displeasure as if they'd made it into a fifty-mile-long lasso and already cinched it around her neck. Regardless of the choices they'd granted her during sex, Rhett and Rebel had been damn clear about who called the shots on the mission plans.

But damn it, their caution had come at a cost. They'd avoided one of the most obvious assets they had—*her*—and for what? She'd volunteered to come here with them so she could be of more use than gawking at a computer monitor for three days! No way in hell was she buying any lines about their "protective instincts" bubbling to the surface, either. Maybe, *maybe*, it would have floated as a viable—if thin—excuse after what they'd shared this morning, but it bought them no allowances for the two days before now.

The inner throwdown couldn't have been better timed. Her shoulders straightened and her jaw firmed. "That'll have to be fine, then, won't it?" she rejoined to El. "It's a free country. Those men can go wherever they want, the same way I can."

Four more cars. Three. She was almost out of here and the guys hadn't even hit the interchange to 71, just outside Marble Falls. "I'll simply have to beat them to the party. If the cake's gone by the time they get there, it's not my fault."

Should've taken El a couple of seconds to punch out a conspiratorial snicker. No such sound came. "You may want to hold up on defrosting that ice cream, party girl."

Shit.

"Why?" She didn't pull the doomsday demand from it.

"Well...when the guys first radioed, I assumed they did so from the comm station at the Blake ranch."

"Of course." She would've thought the same thing. "But now you think that wasn't the case?"

"Oh, I'm past the point of thinking it." El tossed out a darker, and slightly apologetic, girl growl. "I'm pretty damn certain they took the call wireless nearly from the moment we started, purposely muting their end of the line so I couldn't detect any traffic noises and be wise to their little cahoots. A truck blared into the middle of one of Rebel's questions. They cut the connection faster than Zoe tearing after a fruit roll."

All the stress in the world couldn't have held back both their spitting laughs. Zo's adoration for fruit rolls was legendary, no matter what show they were in or where in the world they traveled. During rehearsals that had redefined grueling and painful, the fruit roll jokes pulled all three of them through, literally and figuratively. Whether it was Zoe using the whole roll as a director's baton or El using scraps of the sticky stuff as makeshift pasties, they'd never failed to shift Brynn out of her pity party and back to work.

And right now, in the middle of what had to be the most bizarre day of her life, she needed the exact same kick in the tush.

She could've done without the nostalgic waterworks though. "Damn it, El." No use trying to hide her teary wobble. When El snickered again, she snapped, "Ruthless bitch."

"Weepy wench."

"Camel toe queen."

"Sleep drool diva."

The tears dissolved into more laughter. "Okay, okay. I give up."

"Wise move, darling." El's preen was evident even over the miles. "Though I must admit to being glad that we stopped that wheel on the wedge of drool."

"Oh, no." She attempted another laugh. "I don't dare ask why, do I?"

It was almost a rhetorical question. El filled the next pause with the smallest of hums—the kind always responsible for the hugest rips in Brynn's gut.

Well...*hell*.

"Because if I'd been Facetiming with those boys instead of just yakking, I would've seen drool stains on their chests... wouldn't I?"

Brynna never thought she'd be so happy to see red and blue flashing lights in the rearview mirror. "El...um...I..."

"Am avoiding the question? Uh-uh, missie. I need at least the Twitter tease about this. Those guys were more into my answers about you than a couple of bachelorettes at *Thunder From Down Under*. A hundred and forty characters or less. Now."

"I have to pull over."

"Not necessary. We can hash out more later. Just strip to the basics—especially if that's what you did with *them*."

She couldn't figure out what qualified as more insane right now: Eleanor Cordelia Browning's I-know-the-nasty-you-just-did ESP or the driver of the state highway cruiser that had slid in behind her. The officer behind the wheel jabbed his hand out, ordering her to hitch a sharp left back into the motel's parking lot with all the subtlety of Genghis Khan.

"No, El. I'm really being pulled over. This guy has the highway patrol disco lights on and everything. Son of a—"

"Oh, gawd. Now *I* give. You always could act circles around the rest of us."

"I really have to go."

"Yeah, yeah. Okay, okay. You don't want to talk about stripping for the soldiers."

"El—"

"The subject is tabled, Monet, *not* dismissed."

"*El!*"

"Byeeeee!"

She disconnected the line while pulling into a parking space near the room she'd paid for under the name Peach La Couer. She'd used it an hour ago to change into the sexy pharma rep persona but hung on to the reservation in case Zoe needed a place to rest after they sneaked out of Adler's hellhole. It wasn't going to be easy, though she counted on the Taser and pepper spray she'd sneaked from Rebel's mission pack to be helpful little elves for their cause.

A sexy disguise. A Taser gun. Helpful elves.

She was a long way from the girl who just wanted to open her own counseling office, settle down with a banker, and be happy with a life dictated by routine.

"Shit!" She didn't hold back the violence from it, even causing the ninja banjo player to jump as he passed by.

Other than him, the festival-goers didn't blink an eye at her predicament. "Okay, Brynn," she muttered. "Breathe in, breathe out—and be sweet. The faster you cooperate, the faster they'll let you go."

It wasn't like she'd broken any major laws. The rental probably had a burned-out tail light. Maybe she'd rolled too fast through one of the stop signs in the motel's back lot. Spewing profanities and attitude wasn't going to speed up this process by a single second.

"You can do this," she whispered. "Just be nice. Be helpful. Be"—she quickly wetted her lips—"sexy." Hell, this could even be a dress rehearsal for the cute-and-coy she had to pull on Adler later.

Just not too much later...God, please.

She concluded the prayer by checking the dashboard clock. "There's still time." Her whisper was desperate but reassuring, so she repeated it. "There's still some time." Okay, not hours and hours of the stuff but enough to keep her plan still fully railed. She just had to play this right, accept her ticket, and get the hell out of here in the next ten to fifteen minutes.

Even with their thirty-minute lead out of Marble Falls, Rhett and Rebel had some major real estate to cover. Once they reached Austin, they had to drive across town to get to Verge's gates. That still gave her the logistical advantage. She wasn't turning cartwheels of joy about it—they'd let her come along and now *she'd* cut *them* out of the picture—but something had to happen, damn it. In the end, when everything turned out all right, they'd eat their proverbial hats, forced to admit the exact same thing to her.

But right now, speaking of fancy hats...

Showtime.

"Officer." She looked up, all blinking innocence and pursed lips, at the patrolman who strode to the lowered driver's-side window. He slowly peeled off his sunglasses as a second cop joined him. In her peripheral, the two backseat doors of the cruiser swung open, sprouting two more sets of long male legs. Shit. Out of all the Texas Highway Patrol teams to pull her over, she had to get the clown car division. She managed a demure smile while venturing, "Um...is there a problem?"

Clown Number One tucked his glasses into a shirt pocket, never taking his eyes off her. He had nice eyes, actually. In other circumstances, she could imagine those whiskey-colored irises filling with light as he laughed. Even with his stern expression, there were dimples in his cheeks and laugh lines bracketing his mouth. "License and registration, ma'am?"

She pulled her Nevada license from her purse and handed it over. "I'm sure the registration's in the glove compartment or something. It's a rental." Cue the oh-aren't-I-the-cutest giggle. "Like you aren't used to that one by now, right?" When he scrutinized her license like it had turned into a thousand-dollar bill, she tried babbling through the silence. "How is the festival going? Bet it's been a crazy week. I can only imagine—"

"Please step out of the car, ma'am."

She smiled tightly. "Is that necessary? I mean, what's this all ab—"

"Just step out of the car, please."

Be sweet. Be cooperative. He just has to do his job. Make it easier and faster for him, and it'll be easier and faster for you. Besides, she could test how scintillating her legs looked in this skirt. She was completely fine working the sexy leggy thing in a sequined leotard and matching go-go boots, but the skirt and blouse were an impulse buy from three months ago, in anticipation that she'd start needing "real life" clothes for the next stage of her life. She never dreamed she'd have to rely on the sex-freak-in-nerd's-clothing bit, least of all in the middle of a motel parking lot at high noon during the SXSW festival. *Keep Austin Weird.* She was sure doing her part.

"Like...this?" After opening the car door, she slunk both legs out and slid them provocatively along each other. The move earned her an impatient cough but little else. When she finally stood, she could look both officers straight in the eyes. She did just that, going for another disarming smile. No more coughs this time. No more nothing. Both cops were practically statues.

Well...hell.

Did she suck *that* bad at nerdy sex freak?

Wait. There was still hope. Dimples gave her a once-over—a *fast* one—before bolting his gaze to her face once more and querying, "So are you staying at this property, Miss Monet?"

That's more like it.

Perhaps.

Had she just dug herself into a really deep rabbit hole? She was going for alluring, not let-me-fuck-my-way-out-of-a-traffic ticket. A bogus one, at that. What the hell *had* she done wrong?

"Yes." Did no harm to relent at least that. It validated her presence here, so they couldn't trump up some bullshit like trespassing. Or practically fornicating in the middle of the parking lot.

"What room?"

Shit.

"I don't see how that's relevant. And why aren't you guys

out on the highway? Doesn't this qualify as the jurisdiction of Austin City Police instead?"

"What room number, Miss Monet?"

She huffed. Rolled her eyes. Finally mumbled, "One twelve."

Clown Number Two, whose rugged face and stark lips said he *didn't* do a lot of laughing during his downtime—pressed a shoulder-mounted radio and repeated the number. Didn't take a rocket scientist to determine their intention from there. Frankly, if time wasn't such an issue, she wouldn't have cared if they turned her room upside down. If they were after some expensive hair product and a brand-new case of MAC cosmetics, they were going to be thrilled. Otherwise, they clearly had mistaken her for someone else and were now wasting precious minutes to discover it.

The rabbit hole was getting too freaking deep. And damn it, she didn't have time to play any more with Tweedledee and Tweedledum.

Which meant a new plan. And a huge new risk. Huge, as in the possibility of Rhett and Rebel plastering her face on their target practice silhouettes from now on—if they chose to acknowledge her presence in the world at all.

Her eyes stung. Her throat thudded. And her frustration raged.

Like they were going to acknowledge your presence after all this anyway?

The three of them owed each other nothing. They'd come together for this mission only—learning ways to help each other through the stress that were, admittedly, off-the-charts amazing—but thinking of it as anything more was only digging herself farther down the hole.

It was time to take care of business, no matter how rough the decisions to accomplish that.

She dumped the seductive stance. Lifted her shoulders, firmed her chin. "Okay, listen. I'm going to be straight-up with you guys now—because I really need your help." She nervously wet her lips. "This is going to sound insane, but I swear it's the truth. I have to get to the old Verge Pharma building, and soon. I'm... I'm undercover." She tacked on in a rush, "*Deeply* undercover."

No-Nonsense crunched his brows. "With what entity?"

"I-I can't tell you that, either. Uh...way above your pay grade." And if he swallowed that, she was going to take El's advice and really start an acting career. "But there are men on their way who want to stop me, and if I don't get to the Verge building before them, my whole op could be blown. There are things happening in that building that nobody knows about—"

Whiskey Eyes stopped her with a raised hand. "We're aware, Miss Monet."

The thud in her throat took over her chest. "Wait. *What?*"

He tilted his head. "You...*are* referring to Doctor Royce, aren't you?"

Her whole body trembled. "You know about him already?"

The second cop shot a skeptical look. "Only that the work he's doing has to be kept super secure because it has the potential to help so many. If any of our country's enemies got wind of his scientific advances, we'd have an international incident occurring on native soil—right under our watch."

"Are you kidding—" But they weren't. That much was clear. "Royce," she blurted. He was the face of Adler's operation now and had the cops buried so far under his snow job, a hundred blowers weren't going to clear the shit. "That's all you know, huh? You guys aren't even aware of Homer Adler, are you?"

"You mean the nutwing who used to run the freak show at Verge's back door?" The cop gave her a patient smile. "He's long gone, we promise. On the run now. Likely overseas somewhere—"

"No." Brynn surged forward but yanked herself back. All she needed was to look like a fruit-loop herself now. "No, he's not. That's what I'm trying to tell you. Adler's got you all drinking the same Kool-Aid. He's let Royce be the public face of this thing, only he's running the exact same game out of that building—and now my best friend is one of his freaks. He had her kidnapped five days ago, out of Las Vegas. Get on your smart pads and confirm it. Her name is Zoe Bommer."

She stopped, forcing in a breath. *Stay calm. Losing your shit isn't going to convince them of anything.*

The clowns actually looked ready to believe her—until Whiskey Eyes shook his head in obvious bafflement. "Why weren't we notified about any of this?"

"Because Adler's that dangerous!" She threw up her hands. "It makes the most sense, I guess. I've been down here, at a place in Marble Falls, helping out my...errrr...a couple of friends—at least I thought so, until—"

Hole. Deeper. Damn it. *Damn it.*

But sometimes, as any performer knew, committing to the mistake was better than struggling through a cover-up.

"Okay, so they're Special Forces but have been working off-grid because Adler and Royce are monitoring everyone—I mean *everyone*, you guys included. Alerting you all would've instantly alerted them as well."

"Them? You mean Royce."

"And Adler."

"Right." Clearly, neither of them bought her account by even a penny. "Adler."

Commit to it. "I begged to be allowed to help. Zoe's my best friend, and Adler has this kinky thing for redheads—"

"Of course he does."

"But nothing was happening," she pushed on. "For *three days*, we monitored and monitored, and now...well...Zoe is still in danger, and—"

"Whoa." The contrast of No-Nonsense's calm hands, countering her wild-waving ones, wasn't lost on her. She'd committed, all right—and look where it had gotten her. "Okay, whoa now, sugar. Back it up and chill it out."

Wise words. And yet, no. All the logic that had made sense in her head just half a minute ago was lost on them. She'd wasted the time for nothing. Brynn bit back a sob as desperation bit in with freshly sharpened teeth.

"'Chill it out'?" It was a snarl, and she didn't care. "Respectfully speaking, that's all I've been doing for four damn days now. Officer, I'm really done with *chilling it out*. And I'm really done with all of this too. So unless you're going to ticket me..."

"Ticket you?" Whiskey Eyes let his partner join in his soft laugh before concluding, "Miss Monet, we're wondering whether or not to *arrest* you."

She flashed a glare between the two of them. Their stares were as steady as Tibetan yogis. "Arrest me? What the hell for?"

"Stolen vehicle."

The response had her gawking at them again in confusion... Because neither of them had issued it.

The drums in her chest froze to silence—as her ears

connected to her brain, finally registering who had. That voice...resonating with the dark command that had teased at her memories and haunted her blood for four days, since its seduction had first mingled with a Piper plane's engines and forever changed how she thought of the words *mile high*...

That voice.

Impossible.

But she pivoted her head to find her sights sucked toward the towering, glowering pirate of a man, suddenly manifested from thin air, about ten feet away. What other explanation could there be for how he was suddenly *here*, long legs braced, inked arms folded, cobalt eyes drilling into her? And oh, yeah... there was the whole turning her blood to lava thing too. As if she needed any more proof that this hallucination was actually real.

"How—" She stopped herself. For some reason, time still felt of the essence, and wasting it on worthless questions wasn't an option. She had to focus on the subject at hand. What the *hell* had he just said? "Stolen vehicle?" She fired it back as an accusation of her own. "Excuse me? In what universe does this qualify—?"

"In the universe that your name is listed nowhere on the rental agreements in that car, *cher*." A breeze kicked up, smelling weirdly of magnolia blossoms crossed with french fries, lifting his glossy black waves off his proud forehead. "And the one in my wallet, which is still in the glove compartment, which adds to your list of stolen goods. On top of that, these fine men can probably run one of their fancy checks on that speedometer, to discover you were likely in breach of the state's posted highway speed limits on your way down here." He scooted a finger up, tapping it thoughtfully at his lips. "Hold on. I'm sure I've missed a few."

"Probably." Dimples the clown cop hooked thumbs into his front belt loops. "That list doesn't sound nearly as complete as it should."

Rebel smiled at the guy. "*Beaucoup* kind of you to offer, Jake—but I couldn't impose any further."

The whiskey in Jake's eyes caught some light. "You're starting to piss me off, Stafford. For the hundredth time, escorting you and Lange into town was a privilege, not an imposition."

Brynna barely kept her jaw from hitting the pavement. Well, that explained Reb's "teleportation" trick. He and Rhett had been "escorted" into Austin by the highway patrol, likely with lights blazing, sirens blaring, and pedals to the proverbial metal. It did nothing to explain Rhett's absence now, but she had bigger—*much* bigger—fish to worry about skinning.

Skinning quite a few creatures around here was suddenly a damn nice idea.

"As I recall, somebody insisted on using the SUV for a frozen yogurt run last night," she retaliated. "So whose fault is it that said person's wallet is still in the damn car?"

Jake swiveled back around, re-arching a tawny brow. "Our concern isn't about last night, Miss Monet—only what was reported about the car today. According to Sergeants Stafford and Lange, this SUV disappeared from the driveway of the ranch where they're enjoying a well-deserved spring vacation with a sweet little lady friend."

She swung a venomous glance at Rebel. "Oh, I'll show them *sweet*."

"It was their opinion that the perpetrator of this crime was headed this way, apparently to cause some havoc at Nyles

Royce's building." Gone was the ribbing he'd shared with Rebel. He gazed at her with all the earnestness of a male lead in a Zeferelli film. "With all due respect, Miss Monet, everything you've just stated—"

"Walked me right into that trap." Brynn seethed through her locked teeth. "Didn't it?"

Jake and his partner, who went by *H. Osten* according to the name badge he finally turned her way, shared a weighted glance. "Traps aren't always what they seem," Osten finally stated. "Depends on how you look at them."

The man clearly spoke from the standpoint of been-there-done-that—which would have intrigued the hell out of her under normal circumstances. But nothing about her life had been normal since taking Rebel Stafford's hand and climbing into a Piper airplane four days ago.

Where was he going to take her this time?

And where the hell was Rhett?

And why did the possibilities of both answers make her shiver with anticipation as much as rage?

"Is that so, Officer Osten?" She made the mistake of emphasizing that by glancing back at the infuriating pirate. Reb was ready for her glare, rocking back on his heels, muscles pushing in all the right places at his jeans and T-shirt. *Damn it.* If he had to be so smug, couldn't he be less stunning about it? "How I look at it, hmmm? And let me take a wild-ass guess about who's holding my rose-colored glasses."

Osten held up both hands. "Nobody's holding the reins but you, little lady. Choice is totally yours."

She snorted. "And that choice would be...?"

"Fairly simple." Rebel flashed a smirk that made her yearn to slap him and climb him at once. "Turn over the car keys—and yourself—right now to the guy who *is* listed on the rental agreement."

He braced to both legs now, his stance matching the strength of his jaw and the audacity of his eyes. Brynna pivoted, feeling like a dorky David up against a bold, breathtaking Goliath. She cocked her head, openly accusing. "Oh, is that all?"

"Yep. That's all."

"So walk away with you—or them?"

"Technically, you'd ride away with us," Jake inserted. "I've been told that the cruiser's back seat is comfy, all factors considered."

Osten nodded. "Me too. And the women's holding cell should be fun for you, at least. We always have at least a few characters in there during festival days."

"Did we release Madame Curie yet?" Jake threw a sardonic look to Rebel. "You know how hard it is to locate family for a scientist who's been dead for eighty years?"

"Not yet," Osten replied. "Though Davis told me she'd changed her mind. Today, she's Susan B. Anthony. Made for a colorful exchange with the three lovelies in black latex bikinis brought in by second shift."

Jake laughed. "I'll bet it did."

There was more where that came from, Brynna was positive of it—and she was damn tempted to let them string out the performance, even at her expense—but in the end, she recognized a deck of stacked cards when she saw one. It was time to throw up her hands, jog up her chin, and capitulate while she still had some dignity left.

"Fine. You win." She shot a glare at the gallingly serene man across the pavement. "You *win*, asshole. Happy?"

She braced herself for Rebel's gloat. Instead, with unfaltering composure, the man strode forward and hooked a hand around her elbow. "Not by a longshot, *minette petite*."

His snarl was menacing and low. His grip closed in, painful and tight. But before taking another step, he stopped to address the two uniformed men now behind them—for all intents and purposes, the bastard's partners in crime.

"Gentlemen, it's been a supreme pleasure. I'm certain Double-Oh agrees. Thank you again for the help with the interesting...errrmm...predicament today."

Both officers shot back more loaded laughs. "Moonstormer, when have your predicaments not been interesting?" Osten drawled.

"Just happy that this time, he has his pants on," Jake rejoined.

"For the time being." Osten retrieved the keys from the SUV, pushed the lock button on the fob, and then tossed the whole set to Rebel.

The pair chuckled harder, enjoying the air sliced by Rebel's raised middle finger. Seeming to forget his parting shot as rapidly as he'd dealt it, the man dug the full force of his deep blues back down into Brynna. He'd left his cocky smirk behind too—leaving her with a bunch of residual wrath and not a shred of courage with which to hurl it at him. No action felt right except the lead brick of a gulp now thudding down her throat, while she endured more of the storm that had invaded his face.

He leaned tighter over her. Lowered his mouth next to her ear. She swallowed again, breathing hard from the fresh firefall that tumbled through her body. Against even her strongest will, her head fell back—*more, please more!*—until he snapped it back up, using only an unfaltering grip on her nape.

"March." His mandate was as hard and rough as his hold. "And don't stop until we get to your room. One hesitation or word of backtalk, and you'll be looking at the world from over my shoulder. Understood?" After a long moment, he dug his fingers into her scalp. "I don't think I heard you, *mon chou.*"

"*Yes,*" Brynn finally retorted. "Yes, I understand you." Then in a bitter mutter, "Asshole."

Tension poured off him, making her tense in expectation of being thrown over his shoulder. He only pushed harder at her neck, guiding her to the little room at the back of the main building's bottom floor, located across from an old icemaker and soda machine. Brynn wasn't surprised to find the door already opened by a crack, kept open by the safety latch from inside, undoubtedly the result of more fancy Rebel Stafford string pulling.

Through the opening, she smelled dusty air-conditioning tinged by the Shalimar perfume she'd reluctantly dabbed on before leaving. She was shocked by how much the stuff permeated the air, but what the hell did she know about fancy perfume? She liked light body spray that kept as close to *her* as possible; as it was, the Shalimar had spent years in her bathroom cabinet before she tossed it into her bag as a last-minute "what if" essential for this trip.

That list of "what ifs" had been a long one.

It had never included a contingency for this.

Especially because she wasn't even sure what *this* was.

Strangely, she wasn't sure she wanted to.

Between one step and the next, almost like a time warp effect in a movie, everything...changed. The focus of her world was completely different. The breeze on her face, nonexistent.

The echoes of their steps on the concrete hall, now muted. The creak of the door as Rebel pushed it open, nearly silent.

But her heartbeat...pure thunder.

The potency of Rebel's form behind her...painful.

The throb of his breath against her neck...excruciating.

The answering pulse from deep in her pussy...torment.

The atmosphere thickened as soon as Rebel ushered her in—to face the man already waiting for them inside. With his Viking chest already shirtless and his denim-covered legs braced, he sucked out her breath even as frantic air pumped her lungs in and out. As he regarded her from head to toe, his North Sea eyes were as tumultuous as Rebel's. He raked her over with them again. Then again.

"Shit." She finally got it out, though the thudding ache between her breasts didn't relent. But she sure as hell didn't have a lot of options. There he was, less than five feet ahead, while the man behind her formed another wall with the magnitude of his stance.

"Afternoon, peach."

Rhett hooked both thumbs into the belt loops of his jeans. Cocked his head at her as if striking up a water cooler conversation...if said cooler happened to be filled with ice.

"Hi." She managed it but in a rasp that nearly squeaked. *Good God.* Maybe she really *could* make this day into a stranger circus than it already was. She should be pissed as hell right now. They'd chased her here, calling in favors on a scale *so* outside the lines that unorthodox didn't begin to touch it, and then had gotten into her room using God knew what kind of line on the pierced punk rocker at the front desk...

For what?

What the hell were they going to do now?

She needed to be more furious about that answer too.

And scared. Really scared.

She fought the thought, jerking her head higher. "Well. Bravo, boys. You found Waldo. Am I—what?—in trouble now?"

Rhett's scrutiny didn't falter until she injected the mocking tone. Only then did his head tilt a little, making her think of a warden contemplating a sassy prisoner. Trouble was, she felt like that captive too.

"Do *you* think you're in trouble, sweetheart?"

She almost thanked him for the line. It brought a laugh she *really* needed right now. "Oh-ho. Taste of my own head shrinker medicine, hmmm?"

"No." There wasn't a single note of celebration in Rebel's comeback, growled into her ear from behind. "He was asking a simple question—which you *will* answer, while I contemplate a prayer to the porcelain god from being so fucking sick about finding you."

For a long second, she couldn't speak. She blinked hard, feeling punched in the gut—which apparently wasn't as rough as what his stomach had been through.

He'd been worried *sick* about her? Why?

A fresh look at Rhett socked her with the same feeling. He didn't seethe it like Rebel, but the emotions tugged at the rugged beauty of his face just the same.

"Oh, my God." She dropped her head, chastened and moved but still a little pissed and afraid—and other things too. Things like wishing she wasn't here but not imagining herself anyplace else. Things like craving how they looked at her, even with their censuring eyes and their tight lips, because all that anger was ignited by something deeper. So *much* deeper. Their fear.

She'd scared the crap out of them.

So much more than they'd ever terrified her.

Until maybe now.

Whatever was going on now, between them and then arced out to her, was like a thousand live electrical wires on the air—currents that fried the ends off every nerve ending she had in her body, replacing it with a buzzing awareness of them... only them. Every harsh breath they took, tiny move they made, drop of sweat they shed, hit her conscience like another burst of light that opened her, shattered her...

Moved her.

As she started to tremble, Rhett released a long exhalation. His face shifted like he'd scrubbed it with his hand, though he still barely moved from gazing so hard at her. She had no idea how to read the look—but knew she hated being the source of it.

"I'm sorry." The backs of her eyes heated. The liquid fallout coursed down her face. "I didn't want to... I didn't mean to... I'm really, really sorry."

She couldn't remember meaning an apology more.

As she rasped it out, he drew in another breath. When he let it out, he lowered himself to the bed just behind him. Spread both hands to his thighs and then pushed them out toward his knees. He stopped just before getting to the caps—then patted them both. Just twice.

But that was enough.

"Come here, Brynna. Lie across my lap. Grab my calf for support...and lift your ass high."

The lead brick clunked down her throat again. Her heartbeat screamed. Her bloodstream raced. Her senses roared with conflict.

No. No! Okay, you're sorry—but you don't show it like this. Think. Think. *Give them other options. You don't do things like this. You're not submissive!*

But as she took a step toward Rhett and then another and another, her lips parted, dry with fear...and arousal. Finally, they forced out two hoarse words.

"Ohhhh...*shit*."

CHAPTER FIFTEEN

Well...damn.

As usual, Brynna Monet was fucking up all their plans—in the most incredible, beautiful ways she possibly could.

Rebel shot his stare to Rhett, not shocked to find the same sentiment stamped on his friend's formidable features. They'd gone through a vision of how this confrontation would go down—extensively. Even with the high-speed escort into Austin, they'd had time to outline exactly what they were going to do with this infuriating little wildcat, if her crazy stunt didn't get her raped or killed first. Some of the decisions had been easy—like deciding she wouldn't leave this room with the ability to think about sitting down for three days. Other calls weren't so cut and dry—like admitting that while her execution sucked major ass, her idea about getting in past Adler's security was actually the best option they had right now.

Shit.

He refused to think about that at this moment.

But thinking was exactly what he had to do. Calmly. Ruthlessly. Preferably with a shit ton of anger along for more clarity, but fuck him if she hadn't blown that to hell as well, her sincere apology and her honest tears cleansing the air yet clinging to it, like a sudden spring rainstorm. Only better. And worse.

In this case, so much worse.

When had the thinking part become so fucking hard—

especially about Brynna Monet? She was an addition to the mission, brought along exactly for this purpose: so they could throw her adorable little ass—and right now, with it swaying in front of him, he could really attest to the adorable factor—into the mix of options for rescuing Zoe from Adler's place? When had thinking about this woman become next to impossible?

The answer bit in. Drew blood.

He'd stopped *thinking* about Brynna Monet...when he'd started *feeling* for her.

From their first kiss, a kneejerk thing that'd soared his senses to the skies they were traveling in—to the days after, where he'd discovered her humor, her laughter, her grace, her grit, her courage, her tears, and yes, her passion—to the magic of this morning, when her passion had saved Rhett and him from tearing each other apart...

She hadn't just made everything okay. She'd made everything magic.

Because she didn't step in as their wedge. She'd built herself in as their bridge.

Now she was doing it again.

Though the floor beneath their feet was covered in cheap no-pile carpet, every step she took toward Rhett was a boom in Reb's soul, loud as the gongs of Notre Dame itself. If that made him Quasimodo, so be it. He gazed at the new tension in her back, evident even through her prim business blouse, and relished it. He reveled in her grace and poise, even while doing something as foreign to her as bending over Rhett's thighs, and was awed to his fucking toenails by it. And yes, he savored the resplendence of the man who welcomed her to his lap: the approving hum in Rhett's throat, his strong caresses along her spine, the way he parted his legs a little more, imparting stability to her pose...and giving Rebel a glimpse of the growing ridge beneath his zipper...

A bulge he let Brynn experience firsthand as he secured her body tighter against his.

"Oh!" She gasped and then wriggled. Well, tried to. The muscles of Rhett's forearm were impressive ropes of sinew against her waist, keeping her firmly in place on his lap. "Ohhhh, my God."

Rhett lifted his other arm...and cupped a hand around one of her firm ass cheeks. But he did nothing more. Instead, he raised his head, seeking out Rebel with a dark, inquiring gaze.

For a long moment, Rebel didn't do anything either. Didn't want to. He communicated as much by curving up a steady smile, paying unabashed reverence to the sight before him. *Fuck*. Few things in life got more perfect than this: the two people more beautiful to him than any others on the planet, bodies fitted as if sculpted by a master artist, too stunning to be real. He was awestruck. Mesmerized. Caught in a reverse trance. Instead of everything in his body running numb, he was a network of humming nerves and electrified awareness, amped like he would be for a mission, only sporting a boner that grew larger by the minute. Wow. Was this what people felt like when in the presence of true masterpieces? He'd never been a "museum guy" but started to appreciate the allure of the places, in ways he'd never imagined.

"Damn." Imagine that. Quasimodo *could* speak. It wasn't eloquent, but who needed to be when the artwork spoke for him? "Damn...*yes*."

The praise wasn't lost on Rhett—or so Reb guessed. He couldn't be certain, when the man's return smile should've earned him a place on the wall next to the *Mona Lisa*. What was with the cryptic intention—and did it really matter? God only knew, if their positions were reversed and Reb sat there with that stunning woman wriggling on his knees, primal instincts would've crawled their way through his brain faster than a caveman bearing the world's first fire. Clarity would definitely not be a priority—especially if he had someone standing nearby to pick up the rational-thought slack.

Rebel was all too happy to be that someone for Rhett. They'd played reverse roles this morning, with Rhett calling all the shots—and fuck, it had been *good*. Nothing like an ideal opportunity for payback on the best scale possible...

He let his body do the talking about that conclusion first.

On measured steps, he approached the bed. With calculated intent, widened his stance. With even deeper resolve, let a weighted silence pass. The room's stillness was unique, as if suddenly sealed off from the party of the world outside the door. The only sound on the air was the soft scraping of Rhett's fingertips along Brynna's spine.

Rebel turned. Leaned in. Ran his own fingers along skin, choosing the stretch from Rhett's elbow to wrists, before meshing his fingers between the long, firm digits that caressed over Brynn's back. Like his, Rhett's fingers were seasoned by years of military duty. Their nicks, callouses, and bruises said hello to each other while the marked difference in their heritage still separated who was who. Nordic snow against Cajun pepper. Marble next to dark gold. The contrast captivated him in entirely new ways.

Hot, blood-hammering ways.

Would their bodies look this good, twined with each other...buried in each other?

Brynn's moan yanked him back to the moment—though

with no less seduction. Holy fuck, she was entrancing, her body responding to every touch they delivered, arching and dipping in response to the direction of their hands, up and down her spine.

Her face gave him a different story.

He crouched down to look at her fully, though reluctantly ended his handclasp with Rhett to do so. But he was damn glad he had. This was all uncharted territory for her, and the torment on her face confirmed it with solidarity. Her lips were twisted, and clearly she'd not stopped crying. The rest of her features were contorted as if they'd clamped her nipples and clit at the same time. While the idea was beyond appealing, it was also beyond impossible, at least for a submissive like her: a submissive still violently opposed to even the word itself.

A submissive so conflicted about her journey, she didn't even know what to do with herself after lying across her Dom's knees.

"Oh, *minette*." He whispered it while brushing the hair from her eyes, thumbing the wetness from her cheeks. "Our sweet, sassy little Brynna."

Her face screwed tighter. "Don't call me sweet," she sobbed. "I'm not sweet!"

He made sure she watched him smirk. "As a man who's tasted all the best parts of you, I strongly beg to differ."

Reb held her fast, despite her struggle to wrench back again. "I don't want you to 'beg to differ,' either. Just—"

More tears welled and spilled down her face. Rebel dropped to both knees, pushing closer to her.

"Just...what?"

"Just...be *mad*, okay?" Her gaze blazed, pure fire against pine, before she closed it once more. "Be what I thought you were going to be. Stop *worrying* about me."

He pushed his thumbs against her hairline, and was two seconds away from delving them farther and then seizing her scalp as hard as he could, demanding the full revelation behind those words. She would've been fine with their rage but not their apprehension? She was totally okay with the consequences of pissing them off but not the emotions from stirring theirs?

This shit went beyond the dynamics of denying her submissiveness. It was tied directly into her whole sense of self—and the worth of that self.

Or, in her case, the total lack of that worth.

No fucking way was he letting her listen to *that* playlist anymore. He'd grown up as the king of those self-hatred mix tapes. Hell, he still wore the crown. The filthy hoard of them was right there, stacked at the back of his mind, guarded by a historian who made Jabba the Hut seem like Snow White. He knew the steep price of keeping up the self-hatred collection— and he'd be damned to see her pay it too. *Not Brynna.*

A sharp jab at his shoulder commanded his head up...

To where Rhett waited, steely gaze and set jaw—with a new tape to jam into his deck. The one that had all *his* crap filtered out of the song, letting him hear just Brynn's again. The one that told him she wasn't listening to anything right now but her confusion and chaos—and that they needed to slice through that crap before she could hear anything else.

The one that dictated they were the perfect men for the job.

The revelations cascaded, one on top of another, as Rhett looked on, smirk rising higher and higher. The beautiful bastard had known every shred of this already. It was why he'd ordered Brynn across his lap in the first place.

Rebel grinned. Then, with one definite glance downward, told his buddy it was time to hang on to her a little tighter.

Rhett grinned back—and complied at once.

As that happened, Reb bent his head again, realigning his gaze with Brynna's.

"I'm not going to lie to you, *minette*. We *were* worried. But *mierde*, we were also mad." He cupped her chin in one hand, ordering her gaze to remain locked in his. As he felt a storm brewing in his eyes, a growl formed in his voice. "Damn near out of our minds, Brynna—from both. Do you understand that? Do you truly get it?"

Her eyes were dry now, but her lips trembled. Perhaps she sensed they were getting on to the part she dreaded but needed. Perhaps even craved. "I get what it's like to be so concerned for someone, especially because of shit they brought on themselves, that your stress becomes fury." She swallowed hard and grimaced. "It...sucks," she stammered. "Real bad."

Rebel released a long breath through his nostrils. Yearned desperately to kiss her but held back. She didn't need tenderness right now. Nor did she even want it. Still, his voice was a grate as he affirmed, "Yeah. It does suck." He dipped his head. Adjusted his weight against his haunches. He was going to be here a while. "And yeah, you *do* know all about it, don't you?"

He almost felt like shit for that one. Almost. She wasn't stupid, meaning it was easy enough for her to fill in his inferences, to know they'd done some research about the shit she'd blurted this morning. God, was that only this morning? They'd come so far since those tangled, crazy moments on the futon. Now...they were about to go further. Goddamn, at least he hoped.

She didn't respond to his probe. For long moments, he wasn't sure if she would. Her shallow breaths told him nothing. Her continued tears told him nothing.

But her new grimace, trapped by claws so vicious they almost made *him* wince, told him everything.

"I'm...sorry. I am." The sobbing echoes vibrated with grief, confirming his original conviction. All of this—her breakdown back at the ranch, her secret escape and solo crusade for Zoe, even the way she'd flipped from ferocious in the parking lot to this teary mess now—was wrapped into shit that twined deeper inside her.

Much deeper.

Shit they were never going to get to unless her remorse was cleared out of the way. Until she felt like the debt had been paid, the scales righted.

"Ssshhh." Now, he did kiss her—a quick tap, on the tip of her nose, before assuring, "We know you are, *cher.* We know."

She didn't look reassured at all. "You know but you don't forgive."

He palmed her cheek. "Our forgiveness was yours from the moment you uttered your first apology." He filtered his fingertips into her hair. "But that makes no difference in the end. Forgiving *yourself* is what matters and where the changes take place." He let a long moment—and those words—settle over her. "You haven't forgiven yourself for anything in a long time, have you, Brynna?"

The start of a sharp *pssshhh* burst from her—until he jerked her chin once more. As the sound cut short, so did the protest in her eyes. Even so, she gritted, "That's a little easier said than done, Sergeant."

Rebel gripped her a little tighter. Angled his gaze closer. "Sometimes more than a little, *minette*." He didn't blink, letting her see the emphasis behind every word he uttered—that nobody knew the truth of it all better than him. "And sometimes, you just need extra help to get that done." He dropped his voice to a whisper. "Do you understand?"

She swallowed. The breath behind it never left her. Rebel held his own breath—and his grip on her. Tighter. A little bit tighter. She finally exhaled—on a whimpering sigh. *Fuck.* Doing this—to her, with Rhett—felt so damn good. So damn right. He treasured every passing second, knowing it might be the last he felt it. That any moment, she'd choose to pull another acrobatic escape, leaving the two of them with libidos clamoring and nuts hanging. At least this time, the latter wouldn't be so literal.

"Yes."

It was his turn for the boulder gulp. He'd been so prepared to let her go, her consent strangled the center of his throat.

And the roots of his balls.

And damn, the girl dared to smile as if she didn't know that. As if his hold alone had already sent her halfway to subspace and all she craved was more of the next step he'd all but promised.

He couldn't believe it. He almost didn't dare. The ideas must have reflected in the fierce sweep of his gaze, because she repeated, adding deeper conviction, "Yes. I understand. I need this...Sir."

Her utterance, so purposely soft and submissive, harmonized his low groan to Rhett's taut growl. He looked up again at his friend. One second was all it took for confirmation: they were fixed on the same perfect goal. Brynna's ass. Bare and red. Beneath Double-Oh's palm.

He lowered his stare to her once again. God*damn*, she was so lovely. So much of her spirit was already exposed...her desperate need for their passionate discipline.

"Very well, then." The words sliced from him like cut timber, smooth on the surface but edged by ruthless angles. He loved watching what the tone did to her—and to Rhett. Those eloquent hands constricted against her waist and hips, causing a quiver to consume her body. "If you need this, then we'll give it to you—but this time, there are going to be some rules."

"Yes, Sir," she murmured dutifully.

He gave her an approving smile. "It's incredible to hear you say that, *ma cher*, but from now on, it won't be necessary unless requested of you. Same goes for any unrequested outbursts, backtalk, or commentary. No focusing on what your next witty one-liner is going to be. No worrying about whether you're entertaining us or not. All that crazy chatter in your head is turned off now. It belongs to us now. *You* belong to us now." He squeezed in a little more on her chin, waiting until she concentrated harder on him. "Do you understand that fully? Do you trust us to know what you need from us and to give it to you as fully as you surrender yourself to us? Do you trust that we're going to take care of you, *all* of you, and honor all of you as the amazing gift that you are?"

She swallowed again. A new sheen appeared in her eyes. But her lips lifted as she rasped, "Yes, Sir. Completely."

Rebel brushed a thumb across those gorgeous strawberry pillows. "That wasn't easy for you, was it?"

She sighed against his finger. "N-No, Sir."

Damn it. He couldn't help it. He had to kiss her—and he did. The brush of his mouth over hers was threaded with the same silken reverence as his caress. "Thank you."

When he pulled away, it was to have Rhett filling his vision, nuzzling his full mouth against her gorgeous neck. "Gratitude is always best when shared," he murmured. "Thank you, our wonderful peach."

As he rose back up, Rebel couldn't help but follow with his eyes, still mesmerized. The fluid power of the man's muscles... It was scenery he'd seen hundreds of times, but now it was even more breathtaking. More meaningful.

And it made him itch—unbearably—to get just as partially naked.

In one motion, he peeled his T-shirt up from the bottom and then tossed it to the room's other bed. Rhett didn't cloak his full stare of appreciation. Neither did Brynn. He flashed a smartass smirk at both of them but kept the look pinned to Brynn while drawling, "The look of the hour is skin, *minette*— and you're woefully down in the tally. Maybe you should fix that, Double-Oh."

One savoring growl later, Rhett returned, "Copy that, buddy. Loud and—"

He snapped into silence the moment he slipped her skirt higher. Rebel picked up the slack, choking loud enough for them both, before scrabbling to rediscover his voice.

"Fuck. Me."

Okay, the rasp wasn't really a voice either. At the moment, he didn't care. Not much made sense beyond the roaring blood in his ears and the pounding weight in his cock as Rhett tugged the garment, higher, higher...revealing the black lace garter set and thigh-high stockings she wore beneath. And the centerpiece of the whole delectable paradise? Not a skimpy little thong or even a pair of bikini panties. The smooth, muscled mounds of her unforgettable ass were hugged by lace-trimmed boy shorts, the look that officially dared a man to turn not-so-naughty into not-so-nice...

Game. On.

"God*damn*." Rhett slid two fingers beneath the edge of that adorable underwear. He didn't stop until reaching the center panel, between her thighs. "The prim pinstripes kit came with a devil-in-disguise option, eh?"

Brynn, clearly recognizing the question as rhetorical, only responded with a whimper—a composure she could only keep to her mouth. Her body handled the situation much differently. Beneath Rhett's exploring fingers, her ass was a feverish undulation. Rebel's point of view afforded a perfect view of her breasts, nipples nearly stabbing through her bra to get free. His mouth actually watered as he leaned in to assist them—never let anyone say he wasn't a giver—by twisting the shirt's buttons free and then shoving aside the lace-lined cups.

"Let's get this moving." He ordered it at Rhett in a snarl. "She's ready, man. This beauty's tits do *not* lie."

Rhett sent back a savoring rumble. "Gigantic roger on that." He curled his hand over the satin waistband of the shorts—before jerking them down to her knees in a masterful sweep.

Mouthwatering. *Now* Rebel really knew what it meant.

Her ass, poised high and completely nude, was a landscape of cream perfection, tinted with just enough of the peaches that had earned her Rhett's special nickname. As if she could feel the weight of their stares, Brynn tensed a little. All the muscles flexed beneath her flawless skin, giving them one hell of an evocative preview for how she'd react to each of Rhett's smacks.

"Holy fuck." Rhett gritted it while sweeping his fingers across the perfect globes. On the second pass, he scraped his nails too...just enough to leave discernible marks.

"Well said." Rebel traced a finger along one of the scratches. "And so beautiful." He didn't stop there. Continued his caress along the back of Rhett's hand. "The canvas...and the brush."

Without saying more, he bent again to Brynna. Studied her features closely. A sheen to her eyes but not because of any more tears. A growing flush to her cheeks. Tongue sneaking out, restlessly licking her lips. He almost laughed. The woman looked like a drug addict awaiting her fix. No matter how this all washed in the end between the three of them, one thing *would* happen before they said goodbye to her again. A long, *long* conversation about the submissiveness she could no longer ignore.

"A quick review, *ma chatte*." He cupped her chin once more, angling her face a little higher. "You know why you're here like this, right?"

Her anticipating glow sobered. Her mouth tensed. "Because I sneaked out of the ranch without telling either of you."

"And...?"

"And planned to flirt my way into Adler's good graces as a pharmaceutical rep with a closet sex maniac side."

He shared a stunned choke with Rhett.

"Well...all right. You've certainly given new dimension to brutal honesty."

Her brows quirked up. "What? Did you think I'd captivate him with my witty personality alone?"

With an I-got-this nod, Rhett lowered a fast slap to one

of her ass cheeks. It was enough to make her yelp, followed by a self-castigating bite to her lower lip. "What did we say about your words, little peach?"

Brynn dropped her gaze, so damn magnificent in her meekness, before replying, "That they belong to both of you."

Rebel lowered a tender kiss to her forehead. "Good girl."

She sighed. "Thank you, Sir."

He only acknowledged her words with a polite nod. She wasn't acquiescing to this because she wanted hearts, flowers, and sonnets. She'd given them her straight-up honesty because she craved the same: voices that would intervene with the screams in her head, leaders who could calm the confusion that'd driven her actions in the first place. It felt damn good to comprehend that—and to know Rhett did too. Disciplining her for it was another twine in the rope that bound them closer. He hoped like hell it led to more—but if it didn't, this was *beaucoup de bien* for the memory books.

With that in mind, he nudged her chin up again. "Let's be completely clear. None of *this* honesty earns you a free excuse from the *dis*honesty that's already gone down." He read the retort that sparked into her eyes, quickly reined into silence. "Oh, don't worry, *minette*. I saw where you went with that. And yes, running away from us was just as devious as boldface lying to us. Perhaps worse." He made sure she could take in every inch of his face again, now defined by the memories of the panic when realizing he'd climbed into bed with nothing but a mound of pillows. "You ran from us, Brynna. After we all shared ourselves like that—bared so much, stripped away so much more than our clothes—you bolted from our bed and then fled the ranch itself, not even giving us a chance to help you process the emotional fallout. I think there's a word for it in *your* vernacular. Something like *unhealthy*?"

This one would earn him her wrath. And there it was, blasting away the haze in her eyes, pushing through her locked teeth as she seethed, "That's not— *Ow!*"

Rhett's hand against her butt, smacking down twice as hard as before, prompted her outcry.

"It's not...what?" Rebel countered. "Not correct? Not fair?" He paused, making sure she saw the anger fire up his eyes too. "Because...why? You thought we wouldn't listen? Wouldn't understand? That we wouldn't get it, about that war in your mind? That we wouldn't know what it's like to look for the path between your head and your heart? Between the duty and the danger?"

He'd clearly hammered another nerve. Her fury gave way to grief, tightening her body, making her yank in his hold. Rebel stretched to secure her by the nape, forcing her gaze to remain on him. "You have to hear it, Brynna. What you did was dangerous. Very, *very* dangerous. You—and Zoe and her unborn child—could have easily been killed."

Her face crumpled. "No!"

Rhett didn't discipline her for the outburst. Reb didn't blame him. Her own agony was punishment enough.

"We know that wasn't your intention." He rubbed her neck, pressing his fingers as firmly as his words. "And we know you're sorry. But now...you're going to prove it to us as well." He let her drag in a long breath and then let it out on a rickety sigh. "Do you still understand me?"

She nodded, shaky and teary. "Y-Yes, Sir."

"Good."

He slipped his hand back to her jaw...unable not to notice how her lungs heaved harder, pushing out her nipples, now erect as two perfect rubies. The only thing that would make those breasts more stunning would indeed be a pair of clamps, maybe attached with a glittering chain, turning her chest into a sparkling masterpiece...

"Rhett's going to spank you now." He descended into an authoritative tone. He liked the voice best for scenes. Not only did it help keep his cock in check—definitely a plus, considering where the damn thing clamored to be right now—but purifying everything into strict business mode also separated emotions from actions, meaning he could fill in the gap with as much naughty dirt as he wanted.

In the case of this extraordinary woman...he *wanted*.

Without even looking back up at Rhett, he knew the sentiment was shared.

Fuck, yes.

"Eighteen," he intoned then. "That's the number you're getting, *cher*. One for every ten minutes of the hours you decided to run from us instead of trusting us."

As he spoke, Rhett massaged her ass again—though the strokes were tougher this time, kneading and pinching. As he dug in harder, Brynn let out a high-pitched mewl.

"Ssshhh, little peach. Take it in. Breathe. I'm warming you up. Bringing the blood to the surface of your skin so you're well-prepared...for what's ahead."

She struggled to obey, but the wicked lilt he laid over his promise was a steel hook down her throat, snagging her breath. And damn it, the woman wore uncertainty like most others wore silk robes. So fucking alluring.

Rebel couldn't wait to strip it from her.

He showed her so by tangling a hand in her hair and pulling her head to the side. Slanted his mouth over the exposed column of her neck, which looked and felt like the silk he'd evoked. "The warmup, *minette*... It's like foreplay, only better."

She tasted so good. He licked, sucked, and nipped at her, reveling in her wild pulse against his tongue, as he sneaked a hand into what little was left of her cleavage, fingers seeking a pert nipple to toy with. She gasped as he made contact. Her areola crumpled against his fingertips. Her nipple was hot and hard, swelling tighter as he rolled and then tugged on it. Before he even touched the other, a harsh cry broke from deep in her throat. As he actually pulled at her nipple, she sobbed.

Rebel captured the sound with a deep sweep of his lips. "Better?" he asked after dragging up from her.

"Yes, Sir." Her gaze radiated over his face, full of wonder and arousal—

Smack.

Then pain.

"Ahhhh!"

"One."

Her lips twisted and her throat convulsed, clearly debating the legitimacy of Rhett's placid claim. In her mind, they should've been at eight or nine already. The guy hadn't pulled the blow by a single fraction—a move for which Rebel issued approval with a quick glance. Rhett replied with a sexier-than-shit smirk while raising his hand back up...

Smack.

"Two."

To Rebel's shock, she responded with nothing but a stubborn grunt—and a newly tense body. Rhett's face tightened, taking notice of the same thing. Rebel dipped in at once, hoping to help the situation. Though she relaxed a little as he trailed the flat of his tongue from her earlobe to collarbone, she tensed the moment Rhett lifted his hand again.

Smack.

"Ohhhh!"

"Three."

"Damn it!"

Rhett gave her four and five without a reprieve.

"Mother*fucker*."

Six. Seven. Eight.

Harder. Harder. Harder.

"Crraaaap. *Really?*"

Rhett grunted hard. Pinched both her cheeks just as brutally. "Any more creativity on that little tongue of yours, peach? Because that just earned you another swat. I'd *love* to make it a nice, even twenty, just for symmetry's sake."

"God*damn*." Rebel couldn't restrain it—not when the vibrations of the spanks still rang on the air and the bloom over her backside filled his greedy vision. "So would I." He chuckled, not a little sheepishly, as she shot him a who's-side-are-*you*-on glare. "*Trés désolé, ma belle fille*...but if any woman's ass was made to be thrashed like this, it is *most* certainly yours."

Rhett rumbled with baritone agreement. "She's so hot already." He flattened his hand, smoothing the perfect humps now. "Fuck. *So hot*."

Rebel fought the urge to raise his hand and test that theory—but his mind already created the scenario that would follow. The heat of Rhett's hands, fusing into his own. The craving to have more. The need for those long, powerful fingers against *his* flesh...around his balls...

Never to be.

The boxes of Rhett's life were clear—and made of steel.

While Rebel had danced along their edges, even teased the man to peek out a little, he'd never even hoped for the chance to gain more. Then Brynna had come along—magical, sensual Brynna—stirring a sexual freedom in Rhett that surpassed anything Reb dared to imagine, much less desire. When she was finally gone, the man's box would slam shut again.

That meant focusing fully on everything they could have together now. Basking in the beauty of her soft shoulders and lolled head, feeling the force of what she gave back to them, right here and now. Of how incredibly she processed the power Rhett had infused to her body and then refilled so much of the air with it. The power of her submission made his senses swim...and set his libido ablaze.

"Fuck."

He breathed the word, robbed of its volume by his pure gratitude. Thank fuck for the counterweight of lust, helping him push out the rest of it.

"Make it hotter."

He didn't miss how his command made Brynn shiver—or the tighter puckers at the tips of her tits. She was scared—but damn, did she like it.

"Do it, man," he emphasized to Rhett. "More. Make her ass hotter. Eleven more swats." He grinned a little at Brynn's taut little moan. "We can do a lot with that, can't we?"

To his pleasure—more than he could admit—one side of the guy's mouth kicked up in a devil's smirk. But to his surprise, Rhett didn't lift his hand again. He kept taunting the two fleshy hills, squeezing more color into them by the second.

Finally, Rhett murmured, "How *much* hotter?"

Rebel grinned. "You have something special in mind?"

"The bag we brought from Dax's...the special one on the

nightstand. Open it up."

The moment Rebel complied, his smile widened—before he pulled out the compact leather spanker atop of the other accessories they'd "borrowed" from what Rhett referred to as "Dax's drawer of wonders."

"Well, well, well," he crooned, twirling the base of the toy in the palm of his hand. "My friend Dax has some mighty interesting 'splainin' to do the next time we go bourbon tasting in the Quarter."

"No shit." The light played off the red tints in Rhett's wagging eyebrows. "Found *that* one in a cabinet near the futon. Quality craftsmanship. Leather's formed over the wood real well." He issued the praise while accepting the paddle from Reb. At once he rubbed it over their subbie's ass in rhythmic little circles.

As he lengthened the caresses, Brynna shifted restlessly. Rebel had anticipated as much. He gazed carefully at her once more and then checked her pulse through her wrist. He also surveyed the color across the rest of her body. They didn't have her bound, but her unusual position made him extra diligent, especially because the woman looked well and truly on her way to the happy land of subspace. If that happened— and that was a big *if*, considering the level they were about to take her to—then diligence would have to be his middle name. Her complete welfare would be in his care. He was used to the responsibility, of course; every Dom had to be ready for it in any scene...

But never in his journey into the world of kink had he been honored by it.

Before now.

"*Minette?*" He brushed fingertips over her cheek. "Are

you still able to understand me?"

Her eyes were open but thickly glazed. She blinked at him with surprising focus, though her lips pressed as if she struggled for words. "Y-Yes...Sir."

Rebel pushed his fingertips in, silently praising, though he kept his voice timbered with authority. She needed his strength more than ever. "Same rules apply now," he stated. "No speaking unless spoken to, unless it's to call for a stop or a slowdown." He contemplated giving her a tiered safe-word system, even if it was just the basic green light, yellow light, red light, but even tap-dancing at the subject sparked new trepidation into her eyes. "No means no," he told her instead, framing fingers to the back of her jaw for emphasis. "Is that completely understood?"

"Yes, Sir." This time, she gave it without hesitation.

"Good girl." He continued his grip back against her scalp and then tilted her head all the way back. Her upturned profile almost stole his breath again. He couldn't resist dropping his mouth and pressing it to hers, though he didn't delve past her parted lips. With their breaths still mingled, he directed Rhett, "Start again, Double-Oh. Make her really red for me."

Without a word of comeback, Rhett drew back—and whapped her ass with the full force of the paddle.

Rebel sucked every note of her scream into his mouth.

The next one too.

And the one after that.

By the time Rhett delivered smack twelve, the outcries stopped—and her quivers began. Only tiny tremors at first, starting as soon as he pulled the paddle from her flesh, but grew to full shivers by the time he reached the top of his sweep, ready to crack the leather back upon her naked flesh. Once the blow connected, her tension was detonated, broken into splinters of energy through her body, only to be pulled back to her core, repeating the intense sensual cycle.

Thirteen. Fourteen. Fifteen.

Rhett's spanks intensified.

Brynna's ass bloomed brighter red.

Rebel's cock pushed harder at his fly.

Still, he didn't let her go. Couldn't. Not when every blow shot that heat harder through her, flowing out until it seemed to burst through her pores, making him hurt and writhe and shiver with her—

Then melt. And float. And fly.

"Damn."

It was barely a whisper but resonated with his shock. Holy *shit*, what was this?

As the sixteenth blow reverberated through her, he couldn't even manage a voice. She panted against his mouth, silent but desperate. Her eyes were closed, seeping once more with magnificent tears.

He needed more.

He rose up, pressing her face against his chest, twining her hair around his fist. As his heart thundered harder, he looked down over the luscious curve of her body, her naked ass and thighs still fitted so beautifully against Rhett's lap.

This couldn't be real.

It was so good. *Too* good.

It was no exaggeration. He wondered if he was simply living a dream, a "conscious unconsciousness" of some kind. He was only a few feet off the floor, but his senses soared as if he were a mile high again, viewing the world from a strange advantage. From that view, he didn't see three separate bodies in a motel room. They were one being, bound by desire and elevated by passion and then ensconced in a whole new level of existence. There wasn't any past that haunted or future that loomed. No baggage to drag or labels to apply. No limits to watch or lines to color in...

There was only need and its fulfillment. Energy and its response. Power and its return.

Dominance...and deliverance.

Only why was *he* the one who felt transformed? Why did the dip of her head against his chest make his mind blast to the moon? Why did her hand, now lifting to his waist, make his dick lurch anew, the tip moistened with precome? Why did his blood sing and his nerves throb, thudding in anticipation of the last three spanks still left...but completely dreading them too?

He wasn't the one who was supposed to feel this...any of it. He wasn't the one here to learn a lesson. He knew all the lessons, damn it. Once upon a time, he'd possessed hope that BDSM could mean more for him than a hot fuck and a raging orgasm—but "once upon a time" was for things like fairy tales, not a real-life guy who'd worked his way out of the swamp, only to travel across the world and slog through more swamps. These days, D/s was a formatted way for him to keep all the demons happy...the "fun" little memories that crawled into his head, fed with something as wild and ravenous as they were. But it would never kill them completely. Nothing ever would.

Or so he'd believed...

Until now.

Brynna's quivers started again. She panted harder into his chest. Her hand tightened on him. But her eyes flared with pure erotic light, betraying her own love/hate conflict about the paddle Rhett hoisted up.

He smiled down at her.

She smiled back up.

And might as well have lobbed a brick along with it.

There wasn't just light in her eyes anymore. There was understanding. Connection. Commiseration. *She gets it. Somehow...she just does.*

"Fucking perfect." Rhett's murmur couldn't have been better timed—or worded. With the paddle still aloft in one hand, he swirled over her ass with the other, tracing the dark-pink-and-red patterns forming one hell of a sensual masterpiece. "Moon is right. I've rarely seen an ass more ideal for this. Look at these colors...all this beauty." He rubbed a little harder, making Brynn moan into Reb's chest. "And just listen to *that*."

Rebel dipped his lips to her hairline. "You please us so much. *Je t'adore. Tu est mon petit éclair crémeuse.*"

He almost expected her to giggle at the endearment—and wouldn't have minded if she did—but she embodied it instead, sliding closer, silken and soft as cream, her hair flowing across his nipples. Rebel bit back a hiss. Holy *shit*, that felt good. But right now, he was sure the woman could rise up, bite off his nose, and he'd thank her for the pleasure.

"*Fuck.*"

No other exclamation seemed to fit, not alongside the epiphany that slammed behind that vision.

This...craving...to make her happy, fulfilled...

Was this what submission felt like?

Or was it real Domination?

He twisted her hair tighter, pressing her in closer. All of it felt like a Band-Aid on a chest wound. His.

"What the hell?" he grated. "What the *hell* are you doing

to me, Brynna?"

But while he pleaded it into her hair...he angled his gaze directly at the man still poised with the paddle. Who suddenly let the thing fall backward, onto the bed. Who then curled forward, also wrapping himself around her, before rasping, "And me. Fuck. And me too."

A shaky whimper unfurled from Brynn. Rebel felt the conflict through her body. He slackened his hold, letting her turn toward Rhett, damn near encouraging it. Watching that man's mouth on her neck and lips, taking in the sure strokes of his hand down her body, did things to Reb's system that did nothing to calm the whirl of his confusion.

Right now, he didn't even want them to.

He let Rhett pull her all the way up, mesmerized with the play of muscle in the man's arms while fitting her chest against his, before drawing her in for a wet, hungry kiss. Rebel rose higher on his knees as Brynn locked her arms around Rhett's neck, sighing into him, using her lips in the only way they'd allowed her to communicate. Rhett answered her with a harsh groan, taking advantage of the chance to tangle hands in her hair, commanding her head to one side so he could deepen his penetration into her mouth.

A strange knife of frustration stabbed at Rebel. At once he recognized the problem. He couldn't see enough. Had to watch absolutely everything they did to each other...for each other. With a couple of impatient jerks, he peeled Brynn's shirt all the way off her shoulders. Buttons ripped free as he did, pinging against Rhett's jaw and then across the room. Reb scooted behind her, anxiously unclasping her bra. Once it was detached, he had to draw her arms free from Rhett's neck...

Pushing her wrists together at the bottom of her back.

A dark, savoring snarl escaped. "Dear fuck." He grabbed her tighter, deciding to use the bra's straps to bind her like that. "This has got to be one of the best sights of my life." He twisted the straps a few times, arranging the bra so the lacy cups finally dangled down between her fingers. "You're more gorgeous than the Taj Mahal, *cher.*"

Rhett added a new growl to the mix—just before hiking one of her legs up and over so she fully straddled him now. "How about now?"

Rebel froze. Choked. Finally uttered, "Christ."

Rhett chuckled. "Not a bad view from here, either."

Brynn only made everything better with a longing sigh... as her shoulders dropped and her head bowed. Still, not another word tumbled from her lips. Rhett rewarded her for the obedience by cupping her face and then kissing her again, gentler now, not stopping until a needy keen vibrated through her throat.

"Goddamn." Rhett pushed it out between heavy breaths. "So beautiful. Such a perfect little girl, aren't you?"

"She is." Rebel issued the agreement while rising fully to his feet. "But also one who hasn't fulfilled her punishment."

Rhett lifted a rogue's grin. "So true. And we know how this good little girl wants to do things right."

Rebel nodded, enjoying how his new pose kept the guy's stare engaged. It certainly wasn't the first time Rhett had gazed at him with feet braced, legs firm, and torso high, but it felt fucking great to see the man finally enjoy the sight. Beneath Rhett's hot scrutiny, his skin warmed, his nipples turned to rocks, and his cock hardened to the texture of a dynamite stick. With the same urgency to explode...

"I'm going to do it." He hoped to relieve at least a little

tension with the command, but no joy on that endeavor. Instead, his dick clamored harder at his jeans, the juice at the tip soaking through his briefs, starting in on the denim. "Give me the paddle, Double-Oh. The last three swats are mine."

Rhett's smile cracked wider beneath his tawny stubble. He leaned back to retrieve the paddle. "Won't this be fun."

"Stay there," Rebel ordered. *Fun.* Such an objective word. Oh, they were definitely going to have some...just maybe not in the conventional sense—or anything that they'd want to submit to Webster's in the end. This was one for his personal records, to be remembered and treasured for the rest of his days. "Now lie back, Rhett. All the way. Take her with you. Keep her safe for me."

Rhett's new growl carried an approving hum. "Well," he finally murmured, once he and Brynn were settled into the position Reb had dictated. "Yes, *Sir.*"

Rebel couldn't help an answering chuckle...though he made sure the sound carried a hum as well—a darker sound than Rhett's emission. "Ah...so eager," he said with matching intent. He gazed steadily down at his friend—while pushing Brynn's thighs wider. That done, he leaned over them both. "Can I count on that attitude from you...even now?"

He illuminated the point of the question by reaching in and unzipping Rhett's fly.

As his friend's eyes popped wide, he grabbed the throbbing stalk of flesh from inside.

As his friend's mouth dropped open, he pulled out the hot balls too.

As his friend groaned and writhed, he stroked that perfect cock to full erection.

"Still eager to please, Sergeant Lange?" His voice was

coarse—but he was stunned he still had a voice. Admiring this dick from afar dimmed vastly from the magic of getting to touch it himself. To feel the power surging beneath it...

"Fuck!" Rhett's hands dug into Brynn's back. Against the edges of Reb's fingers, his powerful thighs quaked. "Fuck, Reb. That's so...damn... *Christ.*"

Rebel rumbled in satisfaction, running his thumb over the slit atop of that pulsing shaft. "You're so goddamn beautiful." He curved a savoring smile, relishing Rhett's violent jerks and moans. "Both of you."

"Thank you, Sir." Brynn smiled softly.

"Fuck you, Sir." Rhett gritted his teeth, clearly battling the urge to blow into the cage of Rebel's fingers.

"You're getting the right idea, man. Kind of." By the time Rhett's brows leapt in curiosity, Rebel had reached into the magic toy bag on the nightstand, quickly locating one of the packets of latex fun. With economy that came from tons of practice, he had the rubber out and ready in about ten seconds. But he deliberately slowed down for the next phase of the plan, teasing the sheath over the tip of the man's broad shaft.

"Damn," Rhett gritted. "*Damn*, even that's good."

"Looks good too, brother." As he stroked two fingers over the veins of Rhett's hardness, he slipped his other hand between Brynn's buttocks...and parted the intimate lips at her core. "It's going to look even better when it's driving into this girl's sweet cunt."

Brynn voiced her version of an approval to that plan. As her high-pitched sigh stabbed the air, the walls of her tunnel clamped over his fingers. *Fuck.* That was so good. He might be the perv getting the nastiest floorshow in town today, but Rhett was the lucky sonofabitch starring in the performance.

This hot, tight sheath was going to give his dick one hell of a fine workout...

"Fuuuuuck."

Rhett's groan, hoarse and guttural, emanated from the throat that strained as his head rocked back—and his cock pushed the limits of the condom. Rebel marveled at the feel of it, running his hand over the taut latex while silently ordering Rhett to stay in place by gripping his balls with the other hand. Took his time about the torment too, rolling the cream he'd collected from Brynn's pussy over the sack that throbbed and jerked, aching to punch that magnificent dick deep into her body.

Finally, he let go. The moment he did, Rhett let out a longer groan—and then worked his shaft to the cleft Reb had prepared so perfectly. "Ride me, sweetheart." The harsh, almost hurting growl rasped the air. "Ride my cock hard."

Brynn's cry twisted with Rhett's groan as he slammed her body down over his.

It was one of the best fucks Rebel had ever witnessed.

He didn't want to think about the true significance of that statement. So he didn't. He focused on the pure perfection of the moment in front of him: the two bodies blended in a dance so perfect and right, not even live music could've made the scene better. Peach skin against alabaster muscle. Smooth nectar against sculpted brawn. Soft submission wrapped by dominant power. An energy so pure and perfect and right, it almost pained him to think of interrupting...

Almost.

As he stepped back in, he reached for the sight that drew him the strongest: the paths of pink bruises along the fleshiest planes of her delectable ass. He didn't even clutch her roughly at first, simply held out a hand and basked in the force of Rhett's thrusts throughout her body, but soon, the craving to caress called too strongly. To rub in deeper, searching for the heat that still danced across her skin, exploring the welts Rhett had formed with his harder smacks.

When he brushed those, she shrieked the loudest. "Perfect," he murmured in response, even dipping his lips to kiss a few of the raised, hot ridges. "Fucking perfect." He scooped up the paddle from where Rhett had left it on the coverlet. "I'm going to add three more to your collection now, *minette.*"

He doubted Brynn was aware of how her wobbly little sigh acted as a giant honeycomb of temptation to the lusty black bear prowling his bloodstream. Rhett only concurred with a short grunt instead of a full growl, but he planted his thighs a little farther and began pumping his cock harder, giving full rein to the beast stalking his instincts too.

It was an incredible view—but Reb couldn't wait to add the imprint from his own discipline to the mix. He twirled the paddle in his hand a few times, testing the weight of the wood and the breadth of the handle, before swirling the blade across her ass, assessing how sensitive she possibly was after fifteen blows from Rhett already. As he expected, she flinched a little. As he also expected, Rhett was giving her a damn fine distraction with every masterful lunge into her weeping pussy. Every time his balls smacked her body, a tiny, high cry escaped her. Reb caught glimpses of her breasts too—still tight and erect, evoking the damn watering mouth again.

It was so time to do this.

And he did.

Whomp.

She screamed once more. Rhett, dedicated to keeping her physically balanced while continuing to screw her hard, didn't think of absorbing the sound in the same way Rebel had. That freed her outburst in full on the air, flying through the room like a soprano's aria, piercing and heartbreaking and agonized—and soaring and stunning and transforming.

Rebel swayed, rocked to his core. The sound filled his marrow, fired his muscles, turned even the hairs down his arms and legs into strands of electricity. It scorched him. Terrified him.

And fuck, he wanted more.

He sucked the feeling in, yearning to hoard its magnificence while damn near sure it would splinter him apart. Somehow, he balled up the energy enough to funnel it down his arm, into the fist still wrapped around the paddle...

Then swinging down with all the force of that passion.

Whack.

"Ohhhh, my God!"

Music, inundating his soul.

Power, infusing his spirit.

Submission, slamming his cock.

"Fuck," he rasped.

"Fuck!" Rhett growled. His balls turned a deeper red, flooded with the pressure of new blood. "Beautiful. Little. Peach. So tight...so good." His fingers clawed down her back, digging in as if intending to rip her open. With every new swipe her head rocked to the side and a keen of desire spilled off her lips.

Rebel spread his free hand along her delectable ass cheeks, ensuring the heat from his blows remained memorable in her skin. "Pain is a *trés belle* look for her."

Rhett curled his fingers into the ends of her hair, forcing her head back. "Couldn't agree more."

"Of course you couldn't." He was waiting, arrogant smirk in place, when Rhett cocked his head out for a what-the-fuck glance. A little reminder, silently delivered. *We're not done— which means I'm still very much in charge.*

Brynn added her own contribution to the exchange: a sigh that conveyed desperate need with exquisite pitch. The sound stuck Rebel in his most visceral centers, thundering through his heart, pounding up his cock. Thank fuck Rhett had kept his head out a moment longer, allowing him to catch his friend's in-the-same-boat-buddy stare.

Holy God. They were both in trouble.

A thought he couldn't explore any deeper right now— not when she drew him closer, compelling his senses like the magic of a symphony, violins and horns and flutes replaced by the concerto of her breaths, sighs, and cries, until he was a creature enraptured...

And convinced the final stroke of her punishment had to be something just as special. Something imprinted on the inside of her body as well as outside...

He tossed the paddle to the floor. At the same time, stepped the other way, toward the nightstand—as he made short of releasing his erection from his jeans. Once he got to the toy bag, he pulled out two items. The first, a repeat of the little package he'd retrieved for Rhett, got quickly yanked open and used. His dick jerked in protest as he stretched the condom on. With a determined grunt, he secured it down to his balls and then squeezed both in order to keep his lust in control.

With his libido tamed, at least for now, he turned his attention to the second item. One push of his thumb popped the lid on the water-based lube. A drop of the shiny liquid burst out, as if voicing its eagerness to get on with the wicked plan at hand.

Brynn didn't make anything easier with a new little sound, an inquisitive cry that had her wriggling against Rhett—and proving that as stunning as her bondage was, it wouldn't serve cohesively for what Reb intended to do to her next.

Reluctantly, he loosened the bra straps from her wrists. Not so reluctantly, he pressed himself over her, his chest formed to her back as he rubbed the slight abrasions to her shell-colored skin and then meshed his fingers between hers. It gave him the ideal angle for suckling into her ear before whispering, "Something remarkable for your final punishment, little one. *Oui*?" He slid his hands back up her arms, fanning them in and across her breasts, before raking them back down to reclasp their fingers. "You feel this? Is this good?"

She smiled so hugely, he felt it against his jaw. "Y-Yes, Sir."

"Good. Because this is how I'm going to hold you when my cock's buried in your ass."

Her smile dropped as her hips bucked.

She stilled upon discovering the movement only pushed her globes higher against his erection. Too little, too late. Rebel's shaft fell deeper into the cleft of her ass, meaning she only squeezed him tighter while making the correction. He didn't hold back an appreciative groan, letting the sound fill her ear, gripping her hands tighter, grinding his hips harder.

Beneath him, she shivered from top to bottom. A sound unfurled from her, half aroused whimper but half frightened moan, that tugged to the core of Reb's balls. Wasn't too far off the mark for Rhett either, gauging by the guy's quivering thighs.

"Sir?" she finally squeaked. "I-I'm not sure that I can—"

"Oh, yeah." Rhett beat him to the interruption. "You *can*, sweetheart. And you will." He tugged her head down, locking his gaze into hers. "For us."

"*With* us." Fewer words had felt more the right thing at the right time—especially as Rebel slipped a hand free and lowered it to Rhett's jaw. He fanned fingers along those bold lines, showing Rhett that the communication, connection, and friendship they'd always had was still here, right now, only deeper. Better. And nothing to be afraid of.

A message they both needed.

Especially as he brought the lube inward and began to work it into the valley of Brynna's buttocks. A little more, warming the liquid as he glided it deeper in, seeking the puckered hole of her most forbidden entrance...

"Ohhhh!"

"Ssshhhh, *petite*. Breathe. Now again. Relax."

"I can't—"

"You *will*." He emphasized the order by turning his head, gently sinking his teeth into her ear. "You're still being punished—and this is how it pleases me to administer the last strike of your discipline. We'll get there, *minette*, I promise you. I'll be fucking this ass soon...and you'll be thanking me for it."

CHAPTER SIXTEEN

Brynna barely held herself back from spewing a sarcastic laugh at the man. Correction: the bastard who'd become all ruthless pirate, poised there with his lube and his fingers and his invasion into her body like she didn't already have the world's hugest cock stretching her to the fullest, making her unsure whether she wanted to scream in ultimate pleasure, bawl in ultimate pain—or both.

And damn it, there was the rub. Literally as well as figuratively.

Pain is a trés belle *look for her*.

Did the damn pirate have to be so right?

Fine. She felt *trés belle*, all right. But that wasn't all of it. Not nearly. The pain...it had become...a release. A tangible, logical reason to her to feel things like insecurity, fear, and trepidation—that allowed all her *il*logical reasons to tag along for the ride. For the first time in over a year, she had permission to feel...everything.

And she did.

And it was...better than *belle*.

It was freedom.

So despite every hot, heavy drop of quivering hesitation, she inhaled deeper and obeyed Rebel as best as she could. Daring to believe him. Gambling on trusting him.

Breaking every single one of her own damn rules.

And hating her body for answering with wave upon wave

of rebellious tingles...

As Rebel Stafford probed her asshole deeper.

She decided to focus on what he'd instructed. Worked to push her muscles against his fingers, to open her passage wider for him. She was shocked by the results—not because it physically worked but because of how...*nice* it felt. She actually had nerve endings back there...membranes that began to warm and spark from his contact, soon spreading across the throbbing tissues of her pussy too.

He worked himself in deeper...and it felt even nicer. Even inside other places. Even against the hot, tight walls of her womb...

She wasn't the only one who knew it.

"Christ." Rhett's teeth openly gritted on the word. "I can feel you, Moon. Your dick...I can feel it against mine."

"Oh, God!" Brynn cried.

"Oh, *yeah*." Rebel growled. "God*damn*, Rhett. You're... big."

Brynn spurted an adorable chuff. "No shit."

Rhett grinned, though a sound curled up his throat that was feral, fierce, and savoring. "So deep. Oh, little girl, you're taking both of us so damn deep."

"*Trés bien, ma chatte. Merci...merci.*"

"Yeah. What he said. That's pretty damn...*fuck*."

Rebel's chuckle tickled Brynn's nape. "So, is that the head of your dick, Lange, or are you just happy to see me'?"

"Is this your pervy attempt at a hand job, Stafford, or are *you* just happy to see *me*?"

"I'm always happy to see you."

Suddenly, there wasn't a note of sarcasm in the man's tone. Gone, too, was the easy sexuality Rebel always seemed to have at the tip of his fingers and the surface of his thoughts. Oh, there *was* that edge to the words; it just wasn't easy this time...a truth displayed in every stark angle of Rebel's profile as he sank in tighter over Brynn...tighter still...

And clutched Rhett's jaw again.

And sealed their mouths in a burst of inescapable passion.

As he pushed open the entrance to her ass a little wider... making room for the conquest of his cock.

If her screams had shaken the walls before, they threatened the foundations of the ceiling now. Like she cared. Oh, it hurt. Rebel wasn't a small man, nor was his erection. As he inched in a little more, she cried out even louder...

Only to have the sound yanked again from her mouth.

In a way that startled her so much, she temporarily forgot about the incursion in her ass.

It wasn't Rebel's mouth that absorbed her scream. Nor was it Rhett's. Instead of stopping their kiss to get her through the pain, they simply shifted it...expanded it. They invited her into their passion...and shared every incredible drop of it with her. Her lips were devoured by two mouths, not one. Inside those mouths were tongues that demanded everything from her. They danced and coaxed. Sucked and commanded. Moaned and growled. In return, she mewled, whimpered, and screamed, abandoning all restraint, embracing every hot, incredible moment.

They stuffed her, filled her, overwhelmed her—and it definitely wasn't the only place. Both their cocks were embedded deep, taking her completely in their pleasure... and pleasure it certainly was, if their passionate grunts and deep groans could be interpreted right. If Rebel's aim was punishment, this was definitely it. Rhett's girth alone was a lot for her pussy to handle; the added pressure of Rebel's cock in her ass was assurance that she'd think twice before skipping off on the two of them again.

There's not going to be an "again."

The thought slammed her like such a huge locomotive, all her discomfort was suddenly a small pea beneath a huge mattress. She wouldn't ever know this again? Be with them like this again? Wouldn't ever fly with the spiritual freedom only they'd been able to give her?

The tears tumbled before she could even check them. As soon as the guys detected the wetness, they slowed their thrusts and pulled back their mouths.

"Little peach." Rhett tightened his grip on her hip. "What is it? Too much? Do you need us to stop?"

His concern shattered her inner dams even more. She sobbed, watching her tears rain on his face, adoring him for simply letting them. "Y-Yes," she stammered. "It *is* too much. But if either of you stop, I'll find both your Bosse Jacks and slice off your nipples with them."

"Holy shit." Rhett chuckled. "I've just met my dream woman."

"Copied and echoed." Rebel's cock swelled against the walls inside her ass. "Talk about knives like that some more, *cher,* and I may just build an altar to your name in Jackson Square."

She jabbed a glare over her shoulder. "Respectfully speaking, Sir, are you going to talk or fuck?"

"Just in case you're confused, Moon, the answer is B."

Rebel dipped his face again, his grin sensual and his eyes soft. "Thanks for the enlightenment."

The next moment, he was gone. All right, not gone—but

shifted. Brynn moaned as he rose up, scraping both hands down her back as he went, until he was nearly upright behind her. She battled not to think about how illicit the whole movement felt, with his denim-covered hips abrading the insides of her thighs, but the effort was as useless as a rowboat against his massive pirate ship.

He resecured his hold atop the two hills of her ass, digging his thumbs into the flesh next to the entrance he filled, spreading her even wider. He capped the action with a grizzly dark groan.

"*Mon dieu, minette.* This is good. So fucking good. Hang on, now. We're almost there."

Almost there?

Before she could process the shock, Rebel sank all the way into her ass.

Pain. Pressure. Heat.

Fullness. Sinfulness. Nakedness.

Acquiescence. Acceptance. Surrender.

So many sensations layered on each other, like fine silks blowing in a gale wind, elusive and uncatchable. The gale wind of Rebel...grounded by the solid mountain that was Rhett. His body was like granite, his cock like the tree she held in the storm, keeping her safe so she could reach and embrace every electric particle brought by the wind. She could fly without falling. Jump without shattering.

Fall apart...in the arms of the men she completely trusted.

Rhett, seeming to read that thought, beamed a smile that honored the Viking gods from whom he'd surely descended. "Oh, little girl. You're so close, aren't you? So fucking close. It's written in every one of those stars in your eyes."

His appraisal coerced Rebel to lower again. By now, he

drove his cock in and out as feverishly as Rhett. His body was sweat-slicked, his breaths heavy sluices against her neck. It all only added to the erotic spell he wove with every brutal thrust. *So deep.* He was so deep inside the forbidden realms of her body.

"You've taken your punishment well, darling *fille.* Now it's time to accept your reward." He bit into the space just behind her ear. "Come for us, Brynna Cosette. Come for us hard."

She wanted to. Oh God, she wanted to climax for them more than taking her next damn breath...

But no.

"Not yet." She looked again over her shoulder at the pirate. Just as quickly, she swung her stare back to the Viking. Because they both already locked on her, their gazes naturally tracked to each other. A sweaty smile broke out across her face, but she said nothing else, desperately hoping they'd connect the dots from there.

Rhett mirrored her grin first.

Just before Rebel erased it from his face by plunging in, fusing their mouths together.

"Ohhhh, yes." She sighed. "You *did* get it."

"So did you." It spilled from Rhett on a growl as he ramped his thrusts into her pussy. "That really made you wetter, didn't it?"

For a long moment, his treatment made it impossible to speak. "Yes...Sir," she finally got out. "Oh, God. That's *so* good... Sir!"

Rebel added another animalistic sound. The gritty snarl vibrated along the top of her shoulder. "Somebody has a very naughty cunt. And an even naughtier ass. And likes to have them filled by two dirty Doms with hard, pounding cocks."

"Who adore her so much, they'll even make out for her."

"Oh yeah." Rebel dropped in again, though not all the way. His tongue snaked out, laving along Rhett's bottom lip. "There's that."

A new energy flashed between the men. Rhett's eyes glowed, silver lights against the deep blue, as if Rebel had beckoned him to an arm wrestling match instead of another kiss. The competitive spark was sure as hell unexpected—or was it? And did Brynn really care? Her body was the willing recipient of the fringe bennies, fucked with greater vigor by the dueling owners of both those beautiful cocks.

Rhett lifted his head off the mattress, biting out at Rebel. "Come on. *Come on.*" But when Rebel lowered, he still played coy, dodging his tongue, nipping at Reb's chin. Watching their sensual sparring had Brynn panting hard, whimpering in need.

"Take him." She blurted it, not sure if her intent was a plea or a command—as if it really mattered. Her body throbbed so desperately. Her clit pulsed so fast. "So close," she whispered. "So...close. Pussy...needs to...just take him. *Take him.*"

Rebel stabbed her with eyes full of pure cobalt sex.

While ramming his tongue down Rhett's throat.

And growling deep as she screamed out, blasted by the explosion of her orgasm.

The shockwaves went on, wave after wave of heat and bliss, tearing her apart before bringing her back to herself, only to sweep her back into a sea of fire and fury from which she never wanted to be rescued. That was all before Rhett and Reb started pumping harder, faster, longer, transforming from wind and mountain into hurricane and earthquake, groans layering as their climaxes struck damn near in tandem.

It was one of the most incredible moments of her life.

Followed by one of the most devastating.

How would they move on from this? How would *she*? How would she get up from this bed, cover herself, and even step outside the door again, when everything in her soul was still stripped naked, exposed as never before?

And why did she never want to cover it back up again?

So much that she'd never dreamed of or hoped for.

So much of exactly what she'd feared.

Ecstasy. Vulnerability. Pain. Pleasure.

Weakness.

The guys fell into equally thick silence. She could almost hear the thoughts in their heads, hopping on the same dismal track as hers. This was all never meant to be more than simple stress relief, enjoyed by three mature adults who needed the shit in light of the grim circumstances that had brought them together.

But something happened on the way to rescuing Zoe. Now, Brynna wondered if *she* needed the liberation—only from what, she still didn't know or understand. And wasn't sure she wanted to.

It was a disgusting, confusing tangle—in a love life that seemed doomed to possess them. And like the idiot she always was, she kept attacking the thing with an emotional comb, hoping that if she looked at it from another angle or tore into it with more resolve, the strands would work themselves out.

Because *that* had worked before?

She pushed out a determined breath. This was different. *They* were different. Still pressed between their huge bodies, feeling the cadence of their hearts and warmth of their embraces, she was certain of it in every cell of her body—and was damn sure they were too.

Right. Okay. So the three of you will live happily ever after now? Maybe buy some cute little Craftsman in the Seattle suburbs, settle down into your routine jobs, and enjoy your routine life? The showgirl, the bomb guy, and the top-level security specialist, just one big happy, normal family?

"Sweetheart?" Rhett's murmur made her painfully aware of the tiny sob she'd let out, despite battling otherwise. "You okay?"

"Fine." It was too hasty to fool either of them, but she gritted a smile at their scowls anyway. "I'm...better than fine. God, that was..."

"Yeah." Rhett didn't bother with the phony ease. "Yeah, it was."

Silence crawled between the three of them again. It wouldn't last long. She waited, along with Rhett, for the filthy Cajun one-liner that would snap them all back to normal, at least for a little while.

Wasn't happening.

Instead, without a word, Rebel carefully slipped out of her and then disposed of his condom. As Rhett did the same, Reb walked to the little vanity in the corner and dampened a washcloth. He returned bearing that, along with a larger towel off the rack. Nodded toward the center of the bed. "*Reste là, s'il vous plait, minette.*"

It wasn't a command but resonated with so much solemnity, she obeyed it like one. After scooting in obedience, she watched him walk back over and lower to one side of the bed. Rhett circled around and positioned himself on the other side. He looked on as Rebel dipped a soft kiss to her lips.

"What a gift you are, Brynna Monet." He gently ran the damp cloth between her legs and over her thighs, which were still coated in the sweat all three of them had shed. "*Merci, ma belle.*"

She attempted a flippant laugh. The formality of his tone, teamed with the intimacy of his care, was like psychoanalyzing a priest and a hooker at the same time. Maybe humor would diffuse the discomfort. "It *was* a team effort."

She didn't expect huge guffaws—but nor did she anticipate them looking like she'd just referenced crawling over glass instead of three mind-on-the-moon orgasms. Of course, glass seemed to be in abundance already—since the two of them also erected an invisible pane of it between themselves. They damn near pretended they didn't know each other, much less had been devouring each other's tongues fifteen minutes ago.

Not. Acceptable.

Even if the three of them would never be a possibility, at least *they* could continue on with each other—or try to. The strength they gave each other, and the connection they shared...it was good; damn good—too rare and awesome to be ignored, even for a day. As early as next week, they could be airlifted to a battle zone from which one or both of them would never return...

There was a heartening thought for the moment.

"So...you're all for the team effort now, huh?"

She shot her narrowed stare toward Rhett. "You still want to make cracks about that, *Sir*? I've got a throbbing ass that states I've just learned my lesson about that point. Can we move on?"

"Okay, okay." Rebel's placation came along with his hand on her knee, gentle but quelling. "Everyone dial it back."

Brynn squirmed. The message was right but the messenger was wrong. Rhett, with urbanity in his veins and the

North Sea in his eyes, was always their calm under pressure. Rebel was the Caribbean savage, as willing to tread hot coals as he was to deactivate an IED. Had they swapped more than spit during those kisses?

"Double-Oh's trying to make a point." Rebel patted her dry, taking extra care with the tissues that were sensitive from use in the last twenty-four hours. "He's just not making it very well."

Rhett snorted. "Thanks for the encouragement."

Rebel side-eyed him. "Because you planned on throwing *me* any?"

"Hello?" She grabbed enough of the towel to whack out at him. "Dialing it back? Remember?" She gave herself an inner five, at least for staying on message. Wasn't the easiest task, considering neither of them had opted to tuck themselves back into their jeans. On any two other men, the whole drained cock/unzipped jeans look would've been justification for the squeebs—but damn it if these two men didn't have a pair of the most incredible penises on the planet. Her blessing—and curse.

"She's right." Rhett tossed a look that ventured toward an apology. "We have to bury the awkward—for now."

His shot clearly addressed some kind of elephant in the room for them. Part of Brynn ached for them, yearning to jump on the pachyderm's back, help them wrestle it down, and then get the damn thing digested, bite by painful bite. The other half was pissed at them both. Fate had given them something remarkable, and they were choosing to throw the treasure back like it was rotten fish.

She'd show them rotten fish. His name was Master Peter, and he'd broken her sister's heart into a thousand pieces.

Rebel straightened. Set the washcloth on the far nightstand before dropping a decisive nod. "Double-Oh brought up the teamwork thing because...on the way here, we had the chance to discuss your game plan." He let out a breath through flared nostrils. "Given better logistics, it might be the best option we've got. I *said*, given better logistics." His addendum shot out in response to her gloating grin.

Rhett dipped his head, underlining the command in Reb's tone. "We're going to talk this through before making another move on it, Brynna. You're not even going to sneeze inside that complex without us giving you clearance first." His shoulders squared as he settled on both haunches. As he raised his hands back to his hips, a dry swallow grabbed at Brynn's throat. He looked just as foreboding as the moment she'd first walked in here—except for the unzipped jeans and the exposed cock part.

"This isn't us trying to be dickwads," Rebel adjoined. "This is us, acting as the eyes and ears you won't have." He turned toward Rhett. "Did you connect with El yet?"

Rhett nodded. "While you were outside." He really could've been a Viking fighter, with the afternoon sun streaming through a crack in the paisley curtains, painting patterns of forest green and coral pink over his corded shoulders. "She's standing by for our go in a couple of hours."

"A couple of hours?" Brynn jackknifed up so fast, her breasts wiggled a little—but her joy was so consuming, she didn't even mind the guys' roaming eyes. "Seriously?"

Rebel grumbled a few sentences in gutter French before rolling off the bed and gawking into her overnight bag. "This is a damn good time for everyone to rethink wardrobe choices." After tossing her a pair of shorts and a baggy T-shirt imprinted with the Braneff Brothers logo, he palmed the shaft that wasn't so soft at the V of his crotch and forced it beneath his briefs. With a matching wince, Rhett did the same.

They all sat back down on the bed—cross-legged this time, a triangle-shaped powwow. Brynn's pulse raced with excitement while her heart sang in hope—a mood *not* matched by the men on either side of her, their faces stamped with grim resignation. Well, shit. She hadn't seen this kind of tension from them in nearly a week, since they'd stood in the Bommers' living room ruling out the horrible possibilities of what could've happened to Zoe. No. This was even worse. Deeper. Perhaps she needed to understand that too. None of this was conjecture anymore. They were formulating a real plan, going down with real logistics, in two hours. For some reason, it felt even more dangerous than before, when she was flying solo.

Perhaps because you were flying totally blind?

So there was something to be said for the blind thing. While she'd been racing around with the *Save Zoe* banner, shields thrown up and rose-colored glasses on, there was no possibility of confronting the truth: that Adler and his gang were very real, very dangerous, shoot-to-kill sons of bitches. She stared at Rhett and Rebel now as they pulled out a smart pad with the schematic to the Verge building, and all the Rambo gung-ho and Beetlejuice sarcasm had been ditched in favor of just one element overriding all others.

Respect.

It spoke more volumes to her than anything else. The men might've hated the bastard with every drop of blood in their bodies, but they still respected the living shit out of him—a lesson she had to soak up as fast as she could and remember with every step she took into that complex as his cute, redheaded bait.

Because God help her—and Zoe—if she took just one wrong step in front of that man.

CHAPTER SEVENTEEN

Rebel scowled. "You think she's okay in there?"

Rhett shrugged, going for a vibe of half-asleep nonchalance. Who the fuck did the ass think he was kidding? Rebel would've called him on the act with a boot in the side of his chiseled jaw, but battling the lust to kiss him again was proving a huger challenge at the moment.

Damn. Those kisses.

Those kisses with that man.

Few things had ever felt so fucking right to Rebel, in a life where so much had gone so piss-poor wrong. He fought the urge to let his eyes slide shut, to let those perfect moments consume his memory again. Those full, forceful lips beneath his. The heat of the mouth beneath. The power that burst in that wet, hard tongue, meeting every thrust he delivered, as if they both knew it was the closest thing to a real fuck they'd ever get.

Now who the hell was he kidding? He didn't have to shut his eyes. The torture was just as vivid with his eyes wide open, glaring across the bustling parking lot of a typical suburban Texas strip mall.

He grunted hard. Groaned low. Readjusted himself in the driver's seat of the SUV. Even the hot little MILF walking by, so cute in a flowery top, tight capris, and come-fuck-me heels that should've been on a porn goddess instead, didn't detract from the erection that again swelled for the man just three feet away from him.

Rhett rolled his head from right to left against the passenger-side headrest. Didn't bother to drop his Oakleys, though Rebel detected the eye roll under them. As he'd just catalogued in silent but excruciating detail, the man's mouth alone was very expressive.

"You need to relax." *Now* Rhett let the sunglasses drop— just by a fraction, so he could lock a visual on the we-sell-everything fashion store they'd found for Brynna to run into. If she appeared at the front gate of the Verge building in her clothes from earlier, Adler's goons would be taking bets on how many pharma offices she'd fucked her way through already. The woman herself had forced them to recognize the fact, something along the lines of Homer Adler preferring to think his dick would be the first inside a woman for the day. After he and Rhett had choked back enough nausea to speak again, they'd reluctantly agreed.

"Relax?" he countered. "So *that's* the right call for the moment. Sorry. Guess I was incapable of figuring that out on my own. Should've observed your stellar example, pal."

Rhett didn't say anything. Just pushed his lips together— an action that, obviously, immediately reminded him of how kiss-stung they still were. Though he released the pressure right away, the damage was already dealt to Rebel's dick. He grunted and shifted again.

"Goddamnit, Moon. What's your problem?"

"Nothing." He thrust out a pout. Complete pussy move— but did he care? Just as he'd known that Rhett would rise to his wanker-ific best and find the biggest carpet under which to shove this afternoon's magic, the ass should've expected the finest quality Cajun brood from him. "Not a damn thing.

Everything tidy and clear now? Good. Let's just drop the mic while things are good."

"Just drop the mic?" Stunningly, the guy actually punched a snarl beneath the echo—*and whoa, kids, alert the press*—whipped off his sunglasses all the way. The blade of his steel-dark glare impaled Reb's chest with an implacable chill. "That's how you want to handle whatever bullshit this is, when we're about to send Brynna into the lion's den?"

Insult to injury flashed instantly to mind and stuck there. Was the douche actually going there? The king of head-in-the-sand about everything that had happened this week...was now attacking *him* about trying to move on?

Fucker.

Still, he tried for the diplomatic route. He still felt too damn good from this afternoon to give it up now. "Can you trust that I *am* handling it?" He answered the accusation in Rhett's gaze with a lift of his head. "When have I ever not brought my A game to an op, man?"

Double-Oh jutted his jaw. Arched his brows. "You've never been on an op like this one."

"And you have?"

"There's a lot at stake here, Rebel." He looked toward the store's entrance again. His profile tightened as if expecting the sliding doors to part for a royal princess. "More than what we're used to."

"Yeah." He paused for a long second, seizing the chance to openly stare at the man's bold forehead, noble nose, and high-cut cheeks. "Now we *can* agree. A hell of a lot."

With vision edged by a fog that thundered with his heart, he reached out. Farther.

Curved his fingers around the hard meat of Rhett's

shoulder.

Waited for the flinch. The profane, pissed-off utterance. The spell shattered.

Instead, he gazed in awe...as the man's gold-tipped lashes slammed down. Listened as a harsh sigh spilled off those strong lips.

"Fucking hell, Rebel."

There was the profanity, at least. The rest of this—the conflict gripping his beautiful face, the tension conquering those broad shoulders—came so unexpectedly, especially after they'd damn near Ozzy Osbourne'd each other's head, that Reb froze, dumbfounded. *Him*, dumbfounded.

"Yeah." The dull razor of his voice matched the moment so perfectly. He hated every rasp of it. "You're probably right about that too. Fucking *hell*."

Rhett's head, following the lead of his lashes, dropped nearly all the way to his chest. But at the same time, his hand lifted. His fingers—just the trembling tips—meshed between Rebel's. Twisted like a drowning man on a life ring. An equally tortured breath stuttered out of him.

"I didn't ask for this, damn it."

Rebel let a growl tear out. "Neither did I."

"I know, man. I know."

Shock still flooded his senses. His brain dog-paddled to keep up. At least that was the excuse he went with for what spilled out of him next. "I guess fate doesn't need clearance orders."

Rhett clearly debated a laugh—but lost to the resignation sneaking over his eyes. He dropped his hand back down to his lap. "Fate or not...you know we can't do this anymore."

Rebel slid away. Parked himself into the corner created by

the seat and the car's door. "You mean you won't."

"Fuck." It was little more than a grate—followed by a burst from the other side of the communication spectrum. "Okay, asshole, so tell me how *you'd* do this. If you were me, would you be banking on Rhett and Rebel Airlines to even clear the goddamn runway, let alone hit the mighty blue for fireworks and champagne?"

Rebel let that fun little idea roll around in his head for a second—before pounding the steering wheel and letting his own profanities fly. In the filthiest French he could remember.

The Prince Charming wannabe and the hopeless man-slut. Yeah, *that* was an idyllic vision.

No wonder Rhett glowered through the windshield and only saw a rock and a hard place outside the car.

No wonder Reb looked the same direction...and saw the same thing.

He gripped the steering wheel as hard as he could...wishing the thing was his own neck. Why the hell not? His throat was so dry and tight, he truly should've gone for it.

"Lange?" He didn't look away from the parking lot.

"Yeah?" Rhett didn't either.

"For what it's worth"—and he knew, coming from him and his alley cat dick, it wasn't much—"I've never felt this way before. About a woman *or* a man."

Rhett didn't speak through a moment of burlap-thick silence. Another. Finally, he cleared his throat. Shifted in his seat like a linebacker being stuffed into a bumper car. "Yeah, well...stop it."

Rebel didn't respond. Weren't a lot of options, since he pretty much deserved it. He'd demanded that Rhett pull up the rug and expose the dirt and received exactly that. But he'd brought the wrong cleanup crew. The filth wasn't what he'd expected. Rhett had freely clasped hands with him, totally unafraid of openly acknowledging their connection. He had no more issues about being publicly affectionate than Rebel did.

So the man's steel box...didn't exist.

The filth...was him. His casual sex. His disposable submissives. His "Rebel's Roadhouse" of an apartment—he had no idea what the word *home* even meant, much less how to create one—complete with a spare bedroom so his partners could "enjoy their space" after he was done with them. More accurately, so *he* could enjoy the space...

He saw the whole truth with glaring clarity now. And let his head plummet back to the steering wheel from the disgusting sludge of it. He was dragged lower by an albatross so heavy, a dozen bricks must be attached it. Bricks wrapped in more of that sludge.

Shame he'd never be able to escape or change.

So this was what they meant when they talked about the weight of loneliness.

A breath pushed out of him. Another. He lost himself to their cadence, so consumed that he gained air off the seat when something suddenly pounded the window next to him.

Not something.

Someone.

A beaming brown-eyed girl, still clad only in her Braneff Brothers T-shirt and those cute short-shorts, bouncing on her toes and beaming like a kid at a carnival.

Brynn giggled, obviously realizing she'd pulled off the impossible and startled him, while her lingerie-less breasts bobbed to distraction beneath the tee. Reb didn't even try to avoid the view, and the reflection off the window showed him

Rhett had hopped on that bandwagon too.

"Hey." She yanked open the door and moved into the little crevice she'd just formed. "Are you two out here slacking?"

If she meant learning that that there really wouldn't ever be a chance for him with Rhett, then yes, he'd absolutely been slacking. He didn't bother masking his *bah, humbug* scowl because of it either. Yeah, yeah, so it was the middle of May. *Bah fucking humbug.*

Though the next moment, fate really set out to test him on that one—to the power of four.

Brynna hopped up and down a little more, only now with a hand gesturing forward, over the hood of the SUV. "Look what I found!" she exclaimed. "Hot damn. Can I shop, or what?"

"Hot damn" wouldn't have been Reb's first expression when lifting his sights to the five familiar figures standing shoulder-to-shoulder in front of the car, each dressed in camo BDUs and carrying a sizable mission go-bag. Looked like El had been a busy little bird since their radio conversation—and earned herself a night of thank-you beers from Rhett and him in the doing. He'd never been happier to lay eyes on Garrett, Zeke, and Kellan again—the latter now accompanied by the man who was the usual surgical attachment to his side. Tait Bommer, clearly having finished his top-secret training, now stood between Kell and his little brother.

Thank fuck *someone* had stepped up for the duty.

Even clothed in head-to-toe black, Shay Bommer was an intimidating sight—especially with his face set in a glower that matched his fatigues. His older brother's arrival hadn't soothed the raging giant at all. Shay's eyes were bloodshot, his cheeks skeletal, his dark-gold beard unshaven. A couple of passersby eyed him as if wondering what crazy lunatic the military boys were being so kind to. Little did they know that before anyone blinked, Shay could overturn their cars with a few flips and then take out all three of the mall's security guards.

The guy's arrival dumped a thousand fire ants into Reb's bloodstream. Once they actually found Zoe, Shay was going to be either their greatest asset or their hugest liability—especially if Adler knew his prize stallion was even in the same state. But no way in hell was Rebel going to order the man off the op. A week ago, he might've attempted it. Today, he looked at the agony in Shay's eyes and realized he'd appear close to the same way if Adler had Brynna locked up somewhere.

A look he might be trying on for real if they didn't take care of their girl every way they possibly could.

While he dealt with that not-so-entertaining thought, Rhett let down the passenger-side window with an efficient *snock*. "So where'd you find these bozos in the store, peach? The dollar bin or the platform heels section?"

Kellan's brows instantly jumped. *"Peach?"*

The observance went unnoticed, thanks to Zeke puffing out his Dark Knight chest—while brandishing a new pair of five-inch heels covered in blood red rhinestones. "The heels aisle can be a fun place, man. Rayna's going to thank me prettily when I strap them on her—right before tying her down to our new spanking bench."

Not shockingly, a dark growl tore out of Shay. "Can we move the *fuck* on with all this?"

Rebel swung outward and then up with a foot on the SUV's running board. Spread his arms along the car's roof to ensure everybody stayed where they were. "I sympathize with where you're coming from, I-Man." *More than you know, brother.* "But as you all have likely been informed, this op almost hit the skids once today. Let's square everyone to the same plan before we throw down with these jackholes and their underlings."

"Agreed." Zeke stowed the shoes, snapping back to mission mode.

Garrett copied the move. "You guys have a place we can drill through a powwow?"

Rhett nodded and then asked, "Did you guys bring wheels?"

"Wheels?" Garrett snorted, throwing back an expression he usually saved for his book snob moments. "Well, gerd dang, Mr. Cartwright, we didn't know you wanted *wheels*. Our mules are hitched up around the corner, though..."

Rhett rolled his eyes. "Assmunch."

Shay's jaw locked. His gaze kaboomed like twin grenades hitting at once. Again, Rebel sympathized—more than he wanted to admit. While premission banter was necessary to ensure everyone's nerves, it did nothing for the guy on the team with the most at stake. As the one usually climbing into the blast suit, Rebel knew exactly how it felt to be dealing with a gut razed by nervous fire.

"We're burning daylight." He punctuated the growl by jerking his chin at Garrett. As the young dad in the bunch, Hawkins was now the most alert driver on the team. "Follow us east. We have a motel room. Brynna can change into her... battle gear"—fuck, how he hated saying it, let alone imagining it—"while we discuss staging points and possible exfil."

Everyone bolted their head into the game now. As they all began moving out, Rebel hopped down to open the backseat door for Brynna. He'd just buckled her in and closed the door when Shay skirted the SUV's hood and caught his arm.

The fires in Bommer's stare had settled to restless embers.

His growl resonated with the same barely banked violence. "Stafford. I haven't said it yet...but thank you."

Reb ticked up one side of his mouth. "Not necessary, man."

Shay swung a look toward the back seat of the SUV, his face conveying how valuable the cargo there had come to be for Reb. "*Very* necessary," he murmured. Then, just before he turned away to join the others: "Kiss her goodbye like it's the last time, man. You never know when it will be."

★ ★ ★ ★ ★

A little over an hour later, Reb reflected once more on Bommer's advice—and didn't change his response to it by a single syllable.

"Well, fuck."

It had been close to torture, tasting her so deeply that he sprung a boner worthy of the Longhorn State itself. Then inhaling her with all the force in his lungs, knowing all he'd breathe in for hours would be her wildflower scent. And then, *oh fuck*, watching her tuck a hand down her cleavage until he had to glance away for a long second.

Hell. Did she have to linger about it too?

Well, yeah...since she was doing it to secure the delicate necklace he and Rhett had just given her, with its three golden charms dangling off the chain: a ballet shoe bracketed by two daggers. The gift shop next to the motel had nothing else representing Vikings and pirates, so the daggers had to do. Before tucking the jewelry in, she kissed the charms with tears shimmering on her own lashes—a moment that gutted even Rhett. He'd closed the door to the sporty rental coupe they'd gotten her exclusively for the op, just in case Adler had learned the plates for the two SUV rentals already, and ripped his stinging glare at Rhett, one adamant message searing out. *Don't you dare start too.*

Now, there was no time to even think about slinging razzes at each other. Everything his life had been—the missions, the team, the "roadhouse," and even stupid shit like bills and needing to get new tires for his truck—was all banished behind what his life was now: the demand of being in this moment. The necessity of focusing thoroughly on the video being fed through the palm-sized monitor in Rhett's hands as well as the tinny audio filling his right ear. Both were made possible by a camera El had rigged into a broach and scarf for Brynn's outfit, designed to be worn so the broach hit just the right spot in her gorgeous cleavage. The placement ensured that they received clear feeds—and Adler's unbridled attention. Sure as hell had been the case when Rhett installed the device on her—and Reb had found several convenient ways to "help out."

By the time they'd finished, there'd been more than enough one-liners from every soldier in the motel room to confirm one truth: Shay hadn't kept close to the vest with his observation about the new energy between the three of them. So much the better, as far as Reb was concerned. Now every fucker in the group would be even more on their game about getting Zoe *and* Brynna out of that building alive.

Nothing was more important than that.

Nothing.

Rebel's throat tightened—again—from his devotion to the vow. It was the only thing keeping his breath steady and his body utterly still as he and Rhett waited in the shadows and tall grass beneath a huge oak tree, located about fifty yards from the fence he'd hurdled four nights ago. About the same distance to the left, he knew Garrett and Zeke had belly-crawled their way behind a small storage shed. To the right, somewhere behind a large copse of kidneywood and esperanza, was Kell, possibly saddled with the hardest task of them all: keeping Shay sane—and contained—until Brynna worked her guile on Homer Adler.

The very reason *he* was hating the whole "sane and contained" thing right now.

The red ants in his blood turned to cockroaches of disgust, burrowing deeper every time that vermin dropped his beady eyes to Brynn's breasts. That meant the little fuckers were mighty busy—like right now, as Adler added a greasy smirk to his gawk.

"So," he drawled, "Miss Diamond...where, exactly, did you say you were from?"

"Please." Brynn's sultry voice didn't do anything to calm the roaches. "Call me Valentina." Nor did her insistence on using a porn star name, telling them it would only entice Adler more. She'd been glaringly right, damn it. Men really were pigs. "And I'm originally from Iowa, sir. Just a little farm out in the middle of nowhere, where the corn's as high as an elephant's eye."

"And they grow gorgeous goddesses as well as they grow those fine crops."

Brynna's giggle tinkled through Reb's earpiece. The flirty sound was as fake as the double eyelashes she'd plastered on back at the motel. So far, her act seemed to be working. Thank fuck.

But if it slipped, he was ready.

Put together right, the contents of the pack at his side

were enough to blow up the whole east side of Austin.

"Oh, Mr. Adler. You have *such* a golden tongue."

On the little monitor, Adler scooted out from behind a broad desk. "You have no idea how golden, baby."

"Good girl." Rhett muttered it into his comm link as the image rushed by, indicating she'd scooted free from the man's advance. She was patched into him and everyone else on the team through a tiny audio bud adhered to the inside of her ear. "You're doing good, sweetheart. Keep reeling and releasing. That's it."

"Mmmm." Her tone was laced with double meaning: the concurrence with Rhett and her flirtation with Adler. "Naughty," she went on, answered by a tight scowl from the scientist. "You know the rule, Mr. Adler. Business before pleasure." A jerk of the image—she'd tugged her blouse back into place—before she dipped her tone back into seductive territory. "And you did promise me a tour. I'm not going to let you forget that. I'll be the talk of the office at Peach Pharmaceuticals. A grand tour of Homer Adler's prestigious labs."

Adler leaned on the desk, folding his arms in a smarmy preen. "I had no idea I was so notable."

"*Very* notable," Brynn crooned.

"Goodness." He spread his bony legs a little—then a lot. "I'm sorry I don't have a signed photo or something. A... souvenir of sorts."

Brynna cleared her throat, clearly in place of having to comment on the "souvenir" he referred to. "Maybe we'll find something...interesting...on the tour."

Rebel couldn't tamp a low growl. "A little too convincing, *minette*—which means it was fucking perfect. Now get him out of that damn office before he decides the undersides of those shoes might be more interesting than the top."

"Christ," Rhett grumbled. "Thanks for *that* mental."

"Left." The interjection on the line told them both to shut up at once. Even in hushed tones, Zeke's voice packed one hell of a commanding baritone. "You want to make him go left, Little B." He used the honorary call-sign they'd all come up with for her. "Hawk just completed the close-quarter thermography on the building. There's a room at the end of the hall, bottom floor, with a signature reading a lot like a petite pregnant woman."

Rebel traded an incredulous glare with Rhett, who barked, "How the fuck did you get that reading?"

Garrett's trademark snort burst on the line. "With the help of Mr. Tumbleweed."

"Well, shit." Sure enough, no more than twenty feet from the storage hut, a tumbleweed the size of a baby rhino inched across the dusty ground. The two guards bracketing the loading dock, as well as the goon strolling the yard, actually looked at the thing three times each and never noticed that it slid instead of—well—tumbled. Thank God for the late-afternoon breeze. And Mr. Tumbleweed. "Great job, Hawk. Little B, you copy that intel?"

Brynn's phony sneeze rang in his ear: their established code for a yes.

On the screen in Rhett's palm, Adler turned right.

Damn it.

"Oh, poo." A descending hitch of the camera. The woman was going for broke on the cleavage contingency plan. "We've already been that direction. What's over here?" A swing back to the left—down a long, nondescript hallway—with no discernible door at the end.

"What the fuck?" Rhett rasped.

"No shit," Rebel concurred.

"What's going on?" Shay broke in.

Rebel joined Rhett in gaping at the footage Brynn captured for them, showing the entire length of the hallway. The images showed up as a weird mix of green tones due to the tint from the passage's fluorescent lights, renewing the permit for the acid party churning in Reb's gut.

Finally he said, "You solid on that intel about the room on this hall, Hawk?"

Garrett grunted. "As sure about it as my own nuts."

"*This* hall?"

"For fuck's sake, Stafford."

Rebel shot a long huff. "For fuck's sake yourself. There are no doors to the damn thing."

"*What?*"

"We're looking right at the feed," Rhett rejoined. "There are a couple of bathrooms three-quarters down the corridor and no other portals beyond that. At the end, the hall turns to the left without another interruption."

Rebel cocked his head toward his friend. Rhett's gaze was jolted with the same new comprehension. "Unless...the room is accessed differently."

"Pressurized entrance?"

"Even a hidden panel?"

A thousand shades of blue gave away the rapid shift of Rhett's thoughts. "Wouldn't put anything past the bastard. Your theory makes the most sense, Moon. It's probably operated with a second door inside the first, so the first wall only opens far enough to let a man through."

Rebel's teeth locked. "This is why the mouse cam never

returned anything to us."

"Nothing we could use or see." Rhett returned the feed to the live stream. His face was clamped in tension as he stated, "Try to get as close to that wall as possible, Brynn. Pretend your shoe broke or fake a fall."

Brynna sneezed again before stepping forward.

With every tap of her heels on the tiles, he couldn't get over the intuition that they were sending her to her doom—at the hands of that sick fuck.

Suddenly, the image whipped around again. They caught a glimpse of Brynna's wrist, with Adler's hand clamped around it, before the front of the man's wrinkled shirt filled the view. "There's *nothing* that will interest you down there, Miss Diamond. Now come with me, if you please."

"But—"

"*Now.*"

"I have to pee!" As she readjusted her shirt, Adler punched the air with a rough grunt. A couple of ketchup stains on his shirt looked like congealed blood—or maybe it *was* congealed blood—as she stepped all the way into his personal space. "And perhaps take care of a few...other things."

Adler's growl instantly went all appeased hound dog. "Well, why didn't you say so?"

Rebel was about to question Brynn's punt from the ninety when he saw her clear at least half the hall's length before dashing into the ladies room. He let her hear his complimentary hum. "Very nice move, Little B."

"Yeah?" She disguised the whisper by whapping the stall door closed. "Well, what the hell do I do now? Walk out of the bathroom naked?"

"Don't you fucking dare," Rhett gritted.

"You guys...I'm getting nervous."

Her voice trembled. Her helplessness jerked hard at Rebel, transforming the bile in his stomach into a strange sensation through his whole body. The feeling was so foreign, he had no identifier for it. He was frustrated, furious, and close to dizzy from the agony of containing himself to this hiding place. Uselessness wasn't his goddamn forte, especially when his very bones craved to rush the complex at a full run, guns blazing like a fucking cowboy.

"Stay calm, *minette.*"

"You're doing really great, sweetheart," Rhett added.

"Homer baby's been shooting me some weird looks. The boobs aren't working their magic anymore. Do you think he's figuring something out?"

"Brynna Cosette." Rebel knew if his growl didn't work, the middle name would. "Listen to me, all right? *Breathe.* Keep your eyes open and your thoughts clear. We'll make this work."

"That's right," Zeke concurred. "Stay calm and stay safe. If you think things are hinky, get the fuck out of there. Don't jeopardize yourself for this. We'll just go to Plan B."

"Then Plan C, if we have to," Rhett emphasized.

"Try to get him upstairs." The suggestion came from Garrett. "The scan didn't detect as many heat signatures up there."

"Which might just mean the bodies up there aren't warm." Brynn's soft giggle was sprinkled with enough hysteria to stress the fuck out of Rebel. Well, more than he was. He caught Rhett's new glance, filled with a strident message. *We have to calm her down.* And yeah, if that meant resorting to Dom tones in their voices, then that was what would happen.

"No." Rebel went for it. "That means that more of Adler's

team might follow him there, making it easier for us to get inside the building undetected."

"Okay." Her voice still shook, but the lilt on the second syllable was all confidence. Good. That was damn good—because the orders he had for her next would demand it.

"Brynna, I won't cover this in pixie dust. The second we're in, we might not be so incognito. Make sure that pistol I gave you is at the top of your purse—and be prepared to use it if you have to."

"On his *head*." Rhett leaned over the monitor, as if she'd be able to see the urgent lines on his face, the anxious glints in his eyes. "You put that bullet right between his eyes, peach."

"Yes, Sir," she whispered.

"Just save his balls for me." The slow, furious snarl was Shay's alone. "I'm going to filet them, barbecue them, and then feed them to the coyotes out in Red Rock."

"And Zoe's going to help you." Her heartfelt assurance to the man, even from the middle of a situation where her next steps would take her deeper into danger, tempted Rebel to roll over in the grass, stare up at heaven, and implore the angels, *How did you get it so right with this woman?*

She was, singlehandedly, the most incredible woman he'd ever met.

The woman he'd fallen hopelessly in love with.

Staying motionless in the grass sure as hell wasn't a problem now. The realization struck him like fucking Saul on the road to Damascus, blinding and paralyzing, sucking every molecule of air from his lungs. Thank God Brynn didn't need him on the comm during the thirty seconds it took to act out her bathroom break excuse, flushing the toilet and washing her hands.

And thank fuck all he received from Rhett, once he could lift his head again, was a stare of complete agreement.

He narrowed his own gaze, hoping the guy read his return message. *As soon as this is all over, the three of us are going to talk. About everything.*

Thank God he hadn't squandered the moment.

Because in the next one, coherent thought fled his brain...

Just as all semblance of logic fled his senses.

As terror like he'd never known flamed through his body.

On the monitor, Adler awaited her in the hallway—with a lord's polished posture, a gentleman's sedate smile—and a monster's evil glare. Before he even spoke, one conclusion was horrifyingly clear:

Brynn had been blown.

Her gasp betrayed how thoroughly she understood the reality too—right before Adler made a brief motion with his hand, ordering a pair of men forward who looked recruited right out of the WWE. He still didn't seem to know about the camera. A good thing, since it gave Rebel the precious seconds he needed to reach into his bag for his RPG launcher.

On the monitor, Adler smirked at a now-squirming Brynna. "You know, Miss Diamond, we live in an age of such amazing technology. Even from a hidden security camera, one can generate a high-quality image within seconds and then run it through facial recognition software. And then...*voilà!* One has the naked truth about their seductive little...guest." The man's face darkened again. "Hmmm. No. That's not right either."

Adler motioned again. A loud rip distorted the audio, along with what sounded like Brynn's scream. The monitor was black for a second. When the visual feed returned, their view was a drastically different angle.

They looked at everything from the floor...including the two huge guards dragging a flailing—and nearly nude—Brynna down the hall. Somehow they'd let her keep her panties and stockings. The corridor was strewn with the garments that didn't make the cut.

"Ahhh." Adler's voice was still disgustingly clear on the audio feed. He'd remained behind, chuckling at the destruction he'd ordered. "Now *there's* the naked truth."

Rebel mounted the RPG gun to his shoulder. Squeezed the trigger tighter...tighter...

"You can barbecue the bastard's balls, I-Man. I'm going to spit-roast his dick."

CHAPTER EIGHTEEN

Noise.

Noise, damn it.

Scream, Brynna. You have to scream!

Her mind bellowed it from somewhere beyond her body, almost like a sensei evaluating a student. She'd kicked and screamed and twisted against the meat slabs who'd grabbed her, even landing some blows that had them resorting to language more colorful than their grunts—but that had justified them to pinch and squeeze in very specific places. Locations that didn't require imagination about what Adler had permitted them to do with her.

Oh, God.

What they were going to do with her...

Because of that, she couldn't reconnect. Couldn't reach far enough to grab her mind and shove it back into her body. Maybe she didn't dare. Letting go of her mind... It didn't have to be such an awful thing. She'd learned. She'd been damn stubborn about it, but she'd learned. Rhett and Rebel had been the teachers with the strength, determination, and patience to bring her into the light of that recognition. Caring for her enough to make her really see...to let her really fly...

To give her the beautiful wings of her submission.

A sob spilled from her as the truth finally ripped into her.

Rhett.

Rebel.

They'd called her the gift, but *they'd* been the gifts. Their faces burst across her vision, confirming it to the point of pain. Their lips, infusing her skin with their passion. Their eyes, the dual oceans of their adoration. Their bold jaws, set with the same resolve: to make her scream as she succumbed to everything she felt and everything she was to them...

And she had.

And, with the admission, she knew she'd never feel the same way in her life again. Not with anyone *else* again. Certainly not these two monsters, who hauled her into a room that had weirdly just...appeared. Holy shit. Rhett's theory was right. The room-that-wasn't-a-room was hidden behind a secret panel, concealed behind the hall's real wall. So did that mean—

"Brynn!"

Zoe's scream was as excruciating as being dumped on the room's cement floor. For several seconds, Brynn couldn't respond. As all the wind rushed into her lungs, her brain decided to make a not-so-triumphant comeback to her head. The full horror of this nightmare, until now just feeling like an episode of a graphic HBO show, gripped her like the reality that it was.

Her sob erupted into a scream. She kicked away from the guards, not wasting time being modest about it. Too damn late to play Laura Ingalls when a pair of Neanderthals were clearly thinking behind-the-barn-fun with naughty Nellie Oleson.

She had to keep her shit together. Had to make her brain stay put this time and use it to think clearly. It might be the only way to keep Zoe and herself alive.

Rhett.

Rebel.

Their names ripped into her consciousness again, this time bringing hope. They were here. Somewhere. How much had they seen and heard on the feed? Did they know Adler had exposed her? *Facial recognition software*. Didn't that stuff only exist on TV shows? Again, she fought past the sense that she was just playing out a movie scene—that any second, the director would call "cut" and everyone would break for coffee. The two thugs would help her off the floor before talking about their weekend plans with their wives and kids...

"Brynn. Oh my God!"

Zoe's voice was thick with tears. Brynn's own eyes stung, tears stemming from a mix of joy and horror. *She's here. I've finally found her*. But even turning toward her friend was impossible. Her arms had been pinned against the floor. Her head was locked in place too.

What the hell?

There was a third guard. Of course. The one who'd been keeping watch over Zo already. The asshole had dropped behind her and then clamped her head using his knees. He trapped her wrists beneath his hands. His face, upside down because of the position and that much more disgusting for it, floated over hers with a slow smirk—and breath that smelled like old cheese and stale beer.

"Awwww. A present. You guys really do care."

"For all three of us." She couldn't tell whether Thing One or Thing Two had spoken. Like it mattered. Didn't matter. Her stomach would've churned with as much dread at the sound of their pants unsnapping, their zippers sliding down. "I think she tried to get in to save the duffed-up bitch."

"Well, thank you, darling." His friend knelt in front of her, pushing her knees out wide. "You saved something, all right.

Our very blue balls." He tossed a look back at his friend. "She's all yours, Burt. Just push the lace out of the way, I guess."

Burt chuckled. "Yeah, I'll figure it out." He stroked his rising erection while staring down over her body. "This boy knows his way to the goods."

Zoe's cry pierced the air. "Oh, my God. Brynna."

"Shut up." The brute still holding her right thigh flung a threatening glare. "I can't fuck you, but I sure as hell can smack you."

Brynn bit her lip hard to refrain from hurling an insult of her own. It wouldn't gain her anything and might get Zoe struck. God only knew how many times her friend's spicy temper had earned her such abuse over the last week. Her mind took off with the worst possibilities, since she wasn't able to run an actual visual check. Squeezing her eyes shut only worsened the possibilities, but at least she didn't have to look at the third monster, who dropped to his knees between her legs with an oily growl—

Then burst into a stunned choke as an explosion rocked the building. "What the fuck?"

Brynn's head fell to the floor as the first guard lurched to his feet. "What the hell was that?"

Even through the wall, the alarm peals were ear-shattering. Brynn had never heard better music in her life, and that included all three of her favorite dance music stations. Lurching to her feet and whirling, she found Zoe on a small daybed in the corner, gripping the mattress like it was her life raft. Holy crap, her belly was big. Brynn wondered if Adler had forced her to pad the swell out for ultimate protection, until seeing the dent of her friend's belly button against her cotton maternity tee.

"Zo!"

As she raced to her friend's side, another explosion sounded, closer and louder. Though the boom turned the adrenaline in her system to rocket fuel, it was a secondary boost to hugging Zoe once more. "Finally." She inhaled, treasuring the spicy scent that belonged solely to her friend. At last she yanked back, peering carefully into the eyes that nearly matched the sapphire stud in the woman's nose. "Are you okay?"

"Yeah." Zoe braved a wan smile while picking up a T-shirt off the bed and tossing it at Brynn. The all-white thing draped to the middle of her thighs. Perfect.

"Oh, honey. Your dancing always *was* way better than your acting."

Zoe rolled her eyes. "Fine. They've kept me alive. Let's leave it at that."

"And the baby?"

"Good." She suddenly grabbed her belly. "Ow!" Gritted out a laugh. "*Really* good. Especially today. *Owwww.*"

Brynn watched her friend even more closely, while letting Zoe nearly squeeze her hand off her wrist. "That doesn't look 'good.'"

"No." It was damn near a snarl. "It's fine. I'm fine. She's just...kicking."

"Kicking. For a full minute?"

Another boom. Bellows followed it, male yet indiscernible, orders and countermands that pounded the walls like billiard balls in a drain pipe.

"What's going on?" Zoe gasped out.

"I didn't come alone." *Thank God.* Her Doms had saved her from that very fatal mistake.

Her Doms.

New tears jabbed, welled, and flowed.

Somehow, in some way, those two words had become two of the best syllables in the English language. And if the wrong side was winning in the skirmish outside this room, she'd never have the chance to tell them.

No. She couldn't believe that. She wouldn't.

This time, she chose to believe. To trust. To throw her heart completely into the power of love.

"Rhett Lange and Rebel Stafford came with me." She murmured it close to Zoe's ear so the Neanderthals wouldn't be alerted. "If anyone can get past that door, it'll be them. But keep acting scared."

Zoe hugged her tight again. "*Gracia a Dios*, it won't be that huge an act."

But her friend didn't get a chance to stretch her thespian chops. Before they could release each other, Zoe curled in, emitting a longer cry of pain. "Ohhhh shit!"

Brynna held her as she sank back onto the mattress, clutching her stomach, lost to an agonized grimace. *Ohhhh shit* was right. "Zo. I think you're in labor."

"No!" Her friend moaned it while clutching the meager pillow. "No. Not here. Not now!"

The last of her scream was devoured—by a blast that left the walls shaking and Brynn's ears clanging. She pressed herself over Zoe as smoke billowed into the room, smelling horrible, stinging her throat.

"*Ay!*" Zoe yelled.

Burt the guard fell, downed by a single gunshot.

"Holy crap." Brynn gulped.

The second guard toppled, taken down the same way.

Through the smoke, Brynn watched Garrett and Zeke tackle the third guard. They *thwick*ed him into plastic cuffs before ordering him back onto his knees. Bursting into the room behind them were Kellan, Tait, and Shay, guns brandished, warrior glares blazing.

"Here!" The word fell from Brynn on a desperate shout. She coughed from the effort of drawing air to get it out. "Over here! Shay!"

"Shay?" Zoe jolted up, invigorated now that her baby's "kicking" had abated. With the sheen across her face and breaths whooshing in and out, she wasn't fooling anyone about what was really going on. Maybe she'd listen to her husband, once he—

"Dancer?" He swept her up into his arms, crushing her close, frantically kissing her hair, neck, cheeks. Once his mouth found hers, it was time to cue the swelling Hollywood soundtrack again. Despite the chaos, Brynn swooned a little inside at the epic passion of their kiss.

Until Zoe stiffened. Crumpled. Fell to the bed once more, a taut scream pouring out of her.

"What the fuck?"

So much for Shay buying a clue.

Brynn whipped toward the next-best hope for Bommer brother logic. "She's in labor," she told Tait. "We need to get her out of here. Now!"

Tait's scowl, copied nearly feature-for-feature by Kellan, wasn't the answer she'd hoped for. He glanced at his little brother and Zoe as if hoping Brynn's assertion wasn't true. A hard exhalation left him. "At the moment, that is *much* easier said than done."

Kellan nodded. "Adler's booby-trapped the building. The

second we breached the hallway, steel doors dropped behind us. There's also a set blocking the route to the front door."

Another form materialized from the gloom. Her heart turned over at the sight of a scowling, grit-covered Rhett. Though his eyes nearly matched the smoke as they caught sight of her, nothing else about his face was gentle or reassuring. The next moment, they all learned why. "That's not the worst of it." He swung his gaze back toward the corridor. "If I'm reading the control panel right, he's rigged the whole room to blow in ten minutes."

Brynn blinked. "*This* whole room?"

Shay lurched to his feet, eyes more fierce than one of the animals his blood was spliced with. "Not an option."

Rhett grunted. "Want to tell me something I don't know?"

"So why the fuck aren't you doing something? Christ, Lange! My wife's in labor!"

Tait planted a hand to the center of Shay's chest. "And you're not doing her or your child any good with the melodrama."

Shay snarled. "He's the goddamn tech specialist—"

"And you're not helping him focus!"

Rhett dropped his head but not before Brynn took in every tormented twist of his noble face. He thrived on being a hero the way other people needed air and water. Shay's agony, while justified, was tearing him apart. She yearned to run to Rhett— and confess her love to him. If only nine minutes remained of her life, she wanted to spend every one of them declaring how deeply his and Reb's devotion, passion, and patience had changed her, to the very bindings of her heart.

"It's not a matter of focusing," he finally confessed. "I can't just go into the panel and cut the red wire or the blue wire.

Adler's system is on an auto cut. If the sequence gets started and the box is popped, the explosives will fire right away."

Tait scrubbed a hand over his grimy face. "So we have either nine minutes or thirty seconds."

As he finished the bleak prognosis, all their comm links squawked. The sound echoed in Brynn's ear too, making her jump. In the chaos since she'd exited the bathroom, she'd forgotten about her audio bud. The voice that filled the link, husky and thick with odds-be-damned resolve, seared her belly with dread—and wrenched her heart with love.

"Double-Oh...I've got this."

In front of her, Rhett's head snapped up. His mouth was contorted—and his eyes were wide with terrible knowledge. He scared the living shit out of her even before shouting, "The fuck you do!"

"Tell everyone to get back. *Way* back."

"No! Goddamnit it, Rebel!"

But everyone shot to action anyhow. Tait, Kellan, and Shay helped Zoe, yanking the bed to its side to shield them. Garrett and Zeke towed their prisoner and hunkered against the wall too. Brynn rushed the other way, reaching out.

"Rhett?"

He grabbed her in return, clutching her so close that her breath punched out, shaky and shocked. Just as abruptly, he shoved her away. "Brynna, what the hell? Get down!"

"Why? What's—"

"He's going to try to blow the hall door. But all the explosives he has left... It's all too much fire power." He fell to his knees, jerking her down with him. "He won't have time to try to figure it out. He's just going to use too much and—"

"And what?" She seized his face, forcing him to lock

gazes with her. Though she hated every dark, awful light she confronted in his eyes, she peered deeper—hoping to find a single shred of hope. "And *what*, Rhett?"

Her answer came in the form of a deafening explosion from the hall.

Literally, a deafening explosion.

By the time she pushed through the ringing in her ears and the pounding in her blood, she realized that she was standing. No...walking. Then running. No, that wasn't right either. She was *attempting* to run, urged on by Kellan. Somehow, he'd latched on to her elbow. He was also yelling things at her.

Come on.

Move, Brynn. You have to move.

Run. Run. Run.

But the world was a bowl of Jell-O. A giant, smoke-flavored gelatin, through which she tried to force her feet with terrible, painful steps. *I'm trying.* The words reverberated in her head as if she'd spoken them, but Kell didn't let up on the pressure, just kept pulling her toward—

What?

She finally understood. There was a knife in the gelatin. Kell wanted her to get to the knife. No...

it was...

light.

It penetrated at strange angles, cutting through the dark one way and then the next as different figures crossed the acrid-smelling corridor.

Shadows. There were so many shadows. With her hearing still so jacked up, she couldn't discern which were real and which weren't. In one, she found the tatters of her purse. *Real.* As she jerked Kell to a stop in order to pick it up, her gaze rolled to the next—which held another strange shape.

A head.

Homer Adler's head. Severed...somehow. Blown off by the blast? Hacked away before or after? Did she care?

She screamed. At least her head vibrated as if she did.

Kellan, thank God, jerked her back to her feet, and farther away—

Until another shadow moved. This time, prompting her to throw down her purse, shove away Kellan, and deny anything else existed—even time.

The shadow surrendered a man.

The Viking of a man she loved.

Steps ragged. Dirty face tracked with tears. Arms stretched up and out...carrying the limp body of the other man she loved.

CHAPTER NINETEEN

They were out, thank fuck. Free. Then running as fast as they could, through the fence Rebel had severed with that first grenade launch, into the wide field beyond. With burning legs and raging lungs, Rhett pushed himself faster. Torqued himself to the edge of cardio resistance, in order to get as far away from the next detonation that rocked the twilight air, exploding more birds out of the trees and turning the sky more orange than the sunset toward the west.

Thankfully, the ground dipped a little. The nine of them dropped into the crevice, breathing hard, anxiously eyeing their wake.

"Holy crap," Kellan panted.

"Holy shit," Tait seconded.

"Holy *fuck*!" Zoe screamed.

Shay, having never left her side, murmured words of encouragement that did little to ease the tension in the air. Though emergency truck sirens wailed in the distance, Kellan and Zeke went elbows-up against the berm, sighting the horizon through their guns in case any of Adler's goons decided to play hero and give them pursuit. Tait had joined his brother, attending to Zoe.

That left Garrett and Brynn to join Rhett—at the side of the man he'd laid in the grass as if he were suddenly handling sheer glass.

"Moon." He touched fingers to Rebel's face with the same

hesitant care.

Rebel didn't move.

He pressed in harder.

"*Moon.*"

He lifted his hand, brushing the distinct black waves back from that noble French forehead. They were covered in so much soot, they now looked gray. Shit. The Cajun bastard was going to be just as hot as an old man as he was now.

You will grow old, damn it. Prove it to me now. Prove it, and laugh in my face all you want to about it.

Garrett leaned in. Rhett snarled at him, and at the hand he extended toward Rebel's carotid. "Get away." He glared at Garrett's hand, making it clear he was ready to bite it off if he had to. A little blood and flesh would blend fine to the stew of agony boiling in his gut.

Garrett froze but didn't back off. "Double-Oh. Let me help."

"You can help by backing the *hell* off, Hawk. Are you fucking listening to me?" He lunged out, hovering over Reb like an overprotective wolf, until a soft, quivering hand scraped against his scalp.

"Rhett." Brynn's husky whisper shook as erratically as her fingers. "Let him help. We...we need to know...if..."

Her high gasp sliced it into a hundred shaky slivers. Each one of those blades gashed at him too. He hated his own breath. Hated himself for sitting here, whole and alive, while—

No. Not whole.

He clutched Brynn's hand in, smashing it against his face. He framed Reb's face the same way. "Cold. He's so cold." It tumbled out of him on one of those hated breaths as Garrett checked for vitals...and was ominously silent about what he found. Or hadn't found.

No.

No.

"Why is he so fucking cold?" He blurted it because he refused to hear anything else. Even Zoe's new shriek was a relief. Like the bastard he was, he secretly thanked her for it. Anything was better than the silence of Garrett's readings... than the stillness of his friend's body.

No. Not his friend.

His love.

"Moon." Another damn breath he was taking instead. Another ragged sigh in its wake. Another moment of living on because of what this man had done for him...added to a list that numbered in the thousands. No. To fucking infinity. How was the gift of love quantified? Measured? Marked? It couldn't be.

It could only be symbolized.

With a kiss, soft and pleading. *Why are you still so cold?*

It could only be shown.

With an embrace, pressing a pounding heart to a still chest. *Don't give up.*

It could only be whispered.

With words that emanated from places of truth...deep in the soul.

"Come back, damn it. I love you."

CHAPTER TWENTY

Tears blurring her eyes, Brynna reached again for Rhett.

Garrett slid to let her get closer but, on the way, let her see the dismal truth of what he'd found during his brief check of Rebel's vitals. The sorrow in the man's light-blue eyes was like an ice pick into her heart. Her vision quivered.

Rhett snatched her in tighter. Tighter. Yanked her so hard, her torso was enveloped between his and Rebel's. The heartbeat against her left ear was a raging tattoo of grief. The heartbeat against her right...

Barely there.

But she squeezed her eyes shut and clung to both the beats...for as long as God would allow.

And clung.

And clung.

Even as the night wind kicked higher. Even as the sirens shrilled nearer. And yes, even as Zoe's screams lengthened. Brynn knew, without even doubting, that Zoe understood why she was here and not over there. Her friend wasn't alone. Zo had both Shay and Tait, helping her ride the contractions that would soon bring a new life to the world.

As she and Rhett said goodbye to another.

The tears thickened, welling from chasms in her so deep, she couldn't fathom the bottom. Maybe they had none. It was certainly possible, given how the sobs followed, stealing breath, draining thought, demanding surrender. She had no choice. She set them all free, gladly offering them as sacrifice to the last mortal moments she'd have with these two beautiful, brave, amazing men. And she told them so by giving them the most precious gift she could think of.

"Thank you...for everything. For all of it...my Sirs."

God gave her the best reward for it too. A few more heartbeats. A few more.

Then a sparse rasp from just above her. "You're welcome, little peach."

And then, as if the wind itself brought it. "You're welcome, *ma belle minette.*"

She and Rhett jerked up so sharply, they collided heads. But she knew her lesson now. Pain at the hands of these two was the very best pain of all. "Oh, my God." She swiped impatiently at the tears now, despite the jubilant well they overflowed from. Blurred vision wasn't going to do. She needed to see him clearly—to confirm that the reality wasn't just a trick of her mind or a fluke of the wind.

No trick. As she raised up, soot-covered lashes lifted off her pirate's carved, dirt-covered cheeks. But blazing out from the dirt, orbs the color of Caribbean lagoons shined at her and then Rhett.

"Oh, my *fucking* God." Rhett's burst embellished her words with brutal, joyful force. A smile shining past his tears, he dropped another kiss directly on Rebel's lips. Immediately after, he jerked his head at Brynn, commanding her to do the same. Rebel's mouth moved eagerly beneath hers, tasting smoky and sweaty—and perfect.

Rhett punctuated off their kiss by landing a punch to Rebel's shoulder. "Shit clot," he growled. "Don't you *ever* fucking do that again."

Rebel attempted a laugh but had to stop at a parched cough. "Yeah, yeah," he mumbled. "I love you too."

★ ★ ★ ★ ★

Four months later, she replayed that moment in her mind for at least the millionth time. Cherished its warmth in her heart even as she tugged her thick sweater close, battling the chill that seemed a perpetual resident in her bones now. No matter how hard she tried, her body wasn't accepting the message that it was August first in Las Vegas, Nevada.

Just as her heart hadn't accepted that life had to go on without the two men she loved.

She'd stayed in Austin for another week, switching shifts in the hospital with Rhett, making sure that one of them was at Rebel's side through every minute of his recovery. The Cajun had saved his own life by setting enough of a timer on the explosives that he could dive into the bathroom for cover, resulting in a broken arm, a hell of a lot of bruises, and a whopper of a concussion, the main reason why it was necessary for the doctors to hold him for a few days longer.

That extra time was just what the guys had needed. Brynn had looked on, heart swelling, as their connection and devotion to each other grew by the day. When Rebel was finally discharged, Rhett held his hand all the way to the car.

Neither of them were the wiser to how deeply she'd fallen for them.

It was how things had to remain. How things *would* remain.

They had each other now. They had their team now. She had been nothing more than a pleasant add-on to the package for a while—one Rebel had even fought at first. She could carry no illusions about mattering more than she had or ever would.

And there was the cloud that wouldn't leave the skies of her world. That rained a chill on her even now, as she enviously watched a bunch of women enter the lobby of The Wynn in their skimpiest cocktail finery. Their Louboutins and Jimmy Choos made luxurious taps on the marble floors; their jewelry looked like wearable stars even in the vestibule's muted lighting. They were on the arms of dashing men in designer suits, laughing with seductive smiles. No doubt, they were all heading out for the massive preview party sponsored by the city's newest high-roller resort, The Nytc. The membership-only hotel was opening soon, and besides the gleaming rise of its tower over the skyline, nobody knew much about what it would offer. Grand opening staff members were only allowed to release one public statement: *We'll be the best.*

Fleetingly, she wondered if The Nyte would be casting for an in-house show.

Agonizingly, she realized that she didn't care.

She'd just looked through the UNLV courses being offered for September, confirming that if she bit the bullet and attended school full-time, she'd complete her psychology coursework by Christmas. After that, she'd be ready for her internship. She was both invigorated and terrified—a combination of emotions she could've processed better if she just gave in to her growing craving for a hard spanking—but facing her submissiveness wasn't the same as trusting someone with it. She just wasn't... *there*...yet.

Who the hell was she kidding?

She'd never be *there* with anyone but Rhett and Rebel for a very long time. Perhaps not ever. And she was fine with that.

She had to be.

"Brynna."

She pushed down the tears, plastered a smile to her lips, and looked up. As her gaze hit the handsome face of the man who'd invited her to lunch, it stunned her that the smile wasn't as tough to sustain as she thought.

"Well, Dan Colton, as I live and breathe." She teased it while standing to hug the guy she once thought she'd spend forever with. Dan was a hunk in anyone's book, despite the burn scars down his right cheek that also denoted him as a hero. The rest of his face was all chiseled model perfection, topped by delicious Dijon waves that were cut in the latest masculine trend. And damn, could those broad shoulders fill out a designer suit.

"Wow." Her ex stood back and raked an admiring glance over her trendy romper and knee-high boots. "And you're doing the living and breathing thing quite well."

She rolled her eyes. "You're so full of shit. But I guess that's what it takes to be the world's hottest CEO. What's it really like, on the dark side?"

He took a swing at the eye-rolling thing. "A lot of work." His tone was heavy with that truth. "But hell, it's never a dull day—and Tess is grateful I'm not running through burning buildings and dodging bullets anymore."

"CIA's loss; Colton Steel's gain." She winked to finish off the jibe, knowing that part of him would always pine a little for his days with the agency, feeling like he'd made a real difference in the world. One day, he'd hopefully see that creating jobs in a fair, positive atmosphere was an equally awesome way to give back to his world.

But she wasn't here to play shrink on the man. God knew

she'd already attempted to do that too much already—and had psychoanalyzed all the magic out of their relationship. Or perhaps had tried too hard to inject some *in*...

"First things first. How are Zoe, Shay, and the baby?"

Her smile grew. "Mommy, Daddy, and little Selene are awesome. She's so beautiful. Truly the best baby in the world."

"Says her favorite auntie?"

"Mmmm...perhaps. I can show you pictures at lunch. I think I have a few saved."

"Just a few?" He laughed deeply, showcasing the dimples in his jaw, before tucking her hand beneath his elbow. "I've made a reservation at the Lakeside." He proffered his elbow. "Shall we?"

After they were seated at a table on the patio overlooking the hotel's impressive manmade lake, they each picked an item from the specials of the day as recited by the waiter, making it possible to set aside the menus and refocus on the conversation. That was a good thing. Dan fidgeted like a kid about to face shots at the doctor's office.

"Okay, big guy." Brynn leaned back in her chair a little. "Out with it. What's up?"

Dan loosened his tie. Pulled in a deep breath. "I need to know...that we're okay." He groaned and scrubbed his face. "No. Wait. That sucked. Scratch that. Do-over?"

A giggle spilled out. It was one of their little private jokes, and it brought back some nice memories. Despite the downfall of their romantic relationship, they'd always been rock-solid friends. "Granted," she offered, taking a sip of sparkling water. "Besides, it's kind of fun to watch you squirm."

He scowled. "I deserved that."

She copied the look. "Bullshit."

"I'm sorry. For everything."

Well, that diffused her remaining sarcasm. With a weighted breath of her own, she reached for his hand. "Don't be."

He pressed his other hand atop hers. His gaze darkened to the indigo of the lake's waters. "You put up with a lot of grief from me, Brynn. After the fire, during my rehab, dealing with this"—he lifted his hand to smack at his scars, once an area he'd treated like a patch of leprosy—"I was a messed-up fuck."

Brynn tilted her head. The move accomplished its goal: getting him to look directly at her again. "And I was an advanced-level psych student who should've known that." She lifted a soft smile. "Both of us used the relationship to escape our shit. I guess it beat booze and drugs, yeah?"

Dan flashed a grin that deserved its own trademark. "Sure," he murmured. "I guess."

She shifted back as the food arrived. Dan had ordered pistachio-encrusted salmon, and she was damn glad she'd decided to splurge on an Italian picnic plate, with gourmet cheeses, olives, and bread next to a rustic salad layered with berries and nuts. After the waiter left, Dan angled back toward small talk, questioning, "I've heard that you're opting for full-time school come next month. I couldn't be prouder of you."

She nodded while spearing an olive and then a slice of soft cheese. The salt and cream were perfect together. "I'm finally getting a little bit of state aid for Enya, so financially it's possible."

"She's still struggling?"

She spread some of the cheese onto a slice of bread, glad for the chance to twist her lips in private. "Yeah. She is. But in some ways...this is going to sound weird, but...I think I understand it a little better."

She raised her head, suddenly emboldened. She'd been wanting to talk to someone about all this so badly, and maybe Dan was the perfect person. Who said she had to mention names?

"You see, a...friend of mine...was just involved in a brief D/s thing too. I mean, she's the last person you'd expect to do something like that—and she wasn't *looking* for it or anything—"

"Of course not." Dan returned her stare with one of friendly interest. *Whew.* She was really capable of this—and felt like a genie suddenly freed from a bottle for it.

"Like I said, it just happened." Okay, that part was probably rushed, but Dan still didn't even quirk a brow of suspicion. "She wasn't at a club or *anything* like that."

Dan's lips twitched. "It happens outside clubs all the time, Brynna."

"Right? And she's not somebody who would identify herself as a submissive or anything close to it—except for how these guys affected her, when they were together. It just...felt good. It felt right. It felt..." She frantically fought the sting at the backs of her eyes. "Perfect." The salad at the end of her fork was suddenly as appetizing as cat barf. "And now, nothing feels right or good or perfect at all." She swallowed hard. Gritted her teeth, forcing emotional bleach through the aching heat in her blood. "For my friend, I mean."

Dan's stillness compelled her head back up. She found him with a bite of neglected food on his own fork, training *that* stare on her. The one that never failed to read her mind, even when their relationship had started to falter. "Right." One side of his mouth jerked up. "Your 'friend.'"

As he went for the onehanded air-quote, a blush crawled up her face. "Smartass." She wadded her napkin and threw it at him.

"Yep." He grinned. "That would be me." The expression turned sheepish as he returned the napkin, having gallantly refolded it. "The smartass...who's been thinking about taking some more major steps in his life soon."

She seized the chance to do a little mindreading of her own. "As in...things that involve collars, rings, or both?"

He chewed his salmon with a teasing smirk. "Perhaps."

Brynn let out a little squee. "I'm so happy for you, ya big dork. So *that's* why you're mysteriously in Vegas."

He nodded. "I met with Tess's dad this morning, to ask for her hand and shit."

"And shit." She snorted out a laugh. "You do have a way with poetry, Colton."

"Guess you're glad she's taking me off your hands for good."

Back in her seat, Brynn playfully booted his knee. "She's a lucky lady. I'm sure she knows it too."

"Hopefully." He shrugged. "I fly back tomorrow—but I need to stop at her favorite jewelry boutique in town for a special order."

"She's going to be thrilled."

"She thinks I'm just here schmoozing clients—but she also knows I wanted to meet with you. She's been worried about us clearing the air with each other."

"Well, you can ease her mind now. We're clear." She pushed around the rest of her food, her appetite still not restored. Maybe she'd hit the gym on the way home. She belonged to a barre studio with a busy class schedule, and exhausting her body instead of her mind felt like a great idea, especially now. "And I'm...grateful." She pushed up one last smile. "It took guts to reach out like this, Mr. Colton. Thank you."

It was the prime opportunity for another charming Colton comeback. Didn't happen. Dan seemed to turn her words over carefully before squaring his shoulders and leaning forward in his chair. "Mr. Colton? So formal, after just declaring how *clear* we are?"

She snorted. "You complaining about a little respect now?"

"Just saying it might be better directed elsewhere. Like at them."

She followed the line cast out by his knowing nod.

Until her gaze locked on two figures, poised on the bottom step of the restaurant's sweeping staircase.

A pirate.

A Viking.

Both in attire that perfectly fit the red carpet upon which they stood.

"Holy...shit." She didn't know what stunned her more: seeing both of them here to begin with, or seeing them here in cutaway tuxedoes.

And did it matter?

It didn't.

They were here.

They were here.

She pushed to her feet, yearning to just keep going, to throw herself into their arms and desperately beg them never to let her go again. But their faces were so stark, so tight, so unreadable. Was this just a coincidence? Were they in town for some fancy military awards thing and had just come by to say hello to their buddy before the festivities? Okay, even that sounded beyond weird. If that was the case, why weren't they in the dark blues of mess dress, with medal fruit salads across their chests? And why were they dressed like this in the middle of the damn day?

No algorithm computed this. At all.

She forced her mouth to close. Snapped a disbelieving gawk back at Dan. The handsome hotshot dared to answer with a grin she could only call coy. "Hawk and Z filled me in on the gang's latest off-books adventure—in detailed splendor."

Now the algorithms lined up. "Oh."

"Oh?" The coy disappeared. In its place was the squared stance and folded arms of a man extremely comfortable with his dominant side. "That's all you're going to give me, girl, when I had to move the river to Moses in order to contact them in the field, just to get their blessing to speak to you today? When they moved the damn river *back* in order fly here no more than two hours after returning from that mission?"

A gulp thudded down her throat. *A mission.* They'd been out on a mission for the last four months, likely humping it through the middle of nowhere. Was that the only reason she hadn't heard from them since Austin? And now they'd flown straight here to see her... What the hell did *that* mean?

Wait. Back the wicker basket *way* back up the Nile. Dan had pulled major strings to contact them during that mission... to ask for their "blessing"?

Clearly the three of them needed to talk.

Not a hardship she was complaining about.

She grabbed Dan by the hand again. Smiled up into his face with all the warmth that now filled her heart. As he curled up that movie-idol grin in return, she murmured, "Thank you again. Tess really *is* a lucky woman."

"No more lucky than those bastards waiting on you. Now *go*. I'll settle up here."

After she made it—somehow—to the space in front of Rhett and Rebel, she simply let herself revel in the perfection of them once more. Their scents, sage and cinnamon. Their eyes, North Sea and South Caribbean. Their faces, rugged and chiseled. They would never stop taking her breath away. No matter what happened right now—hell, even if they were here to invite her up the wedding salon to witness them take their vows—there were parts of them both that would always, *always* belong solely to her. Her heart knew it. Her spirit resounded with it.

She finally molded her mouth around a word. "Hi."

Rhett stepped down first. Curled a strand of hair around the back of her ear. "Hey, sweet peach."

Rebel came down and did the same thing. *"Bonjour, ma chatte."*

Their greetings, like cream mixed into Creole coffee, zapped her adrenaline into all the best—and worst—parts of her body. Her nerves sizzled. Her blood tingled. And God, did her sex pulse back to life.

Rhett trailed a hand to the back of her shoulder. Looked around the room like James Bond, checking the corners for shifty enemies. "We need to talk to you."

She didn't hide the shiver his touch sent all the way down past her ass. "Yes, Sir."

"But not here." Rebel did the secret spy glance too— completely not preparing her for his little bombshell of a follow-up. "We have a room. Let's go."

By the time she recovered from the shock that they'd

actually sprung for a room here instead of bunking out at Nellis or in one of the less expensive properties in the city, they were ten floors into a thirty-floor ascent. The lovely string orchestra lilting over the speakers didn't accomplish its goal of Zen tranquility—not in this tiny space, situated between her golden, brawny Viking and her dark, burnished pirate. Not when all she could think about was—

Exactly what they did to her.

"Fuck." Rebel spun around, smashing her body between the car's wall and his demanding form. He locked her head with his hands, holding her in place to receive the heat of his snarled command across her panting mouth. "No more waiting, goddamnit. Not another second more."

And then, thank God, his lips were slanting over hers. Slamming into hers. Possessing her ruthlessly, his tongue stabbing, his teeth invading. His fingers knifed into her hair, pulling until she moaned, long and hard and needy.

Oh *God*, the pain was so good.

She didn't hold back on telling him so. She couldn't. Every minute of her bottled-up need, every second of her restrained lust... It all exploded in wonderful, bountiful new ways. The pressure in her breasts fanned along her arms, making her grab him as violently as he did her. The throbs in her pussy echoed down her thighs, compelling her to lift one and lock it around his ass. She gave in to wanton desire, pulling the core of his body against the aching slit of hers.

Just when she was certain she'd splinter apart from the illicit joy of his embrace, he yanked away, only to look on with heated eyes as Rhett stepped in, claiming her lips and body in much the same way.

He tasted like desire and decadence. He felt like six and a

half feet of raw, raging lust—especially after hiking her ass onto the lift's inner rail, using the extra leverage to slide the bulge in his pants along the crux of her sex. As their kiss deepened, Rebel circled around them, guiding her legs higher around Rhett's waist.

"Fuck, that's good. Yeah...grip him tighter, *mon chou*. Grind your sweet body up against his. Let me see—"

As the elevator dinged, he bit out a string of French profanity.

When the doors slid open, he extended a hand into the opening.

"I'll take care of the door, Double-Oh. Make sure our girl makes it in safe."

Rhett's growl vibrated against her lips. "Roger that, my love. Loud and fucking clear." He dipped his head back toward her, only brushing his mouth over hers this time. "Hang on tight, peach. I'm going to handle this as fast as I possibly can."

She nodded—before clamping her thighs around his broad, hard torso.

Every step to the room was a mix of agony and ecstasy. While she couldn't wait to finally be alone with both of them, she cherished the feeling of being watched over once again... just letting Rhett take every step and think about every move. She tucked her face against his neck and tangled her hands against the back of his head. He moved with effortless grace beneath her, his wide steps eating up the hallway between the elevator and their room.

Finally, they were there.

He set her down on the massive bed in the middle of the room, illuminated only by one bedside lamp and the glow of the city lights, thirty floors below. *A world below.* Up here, ensconced in this space just for them, there was no more traffic or music or dinging, crazy casino sounds. Not the din of a thousand conversations or the blare from a million points of light. All that existed, all that mattered, was the heat of their mingled breaths...the energy of their rising passions.

At least she hoped.

Oh God, please...

She finally gathered up her girl balls and opened her eyes.

There she was, still positioned on the end of the bed—

Now gaping at the two men in tuxedoes, on their knees in front of her.

She didn't know whether to sigh or cry. Maybe both. They were both adorably rumpled now, thanks to how they'd all attacked each other in the elevator. Rebel's bow tie was unraveled. Rhett's shirt had a smudge of her lipstick down the front. While her libido jumped and her heart swelled at observing the marks of her passion on them, she was still cautious, inwardly clutching the keys to her soul.

So they still wanted her...at least physically. She'd be completely down with that. Didn't mean they got to see the keys—or anything in the spaces she kept safe. Keeping it all hidden from *herself* was hard enough as it was, let alone breaking it open and then having to shove it all away once they left again.

And they *would* leave again.

Not just because they had to.

Because Vikings and pirates were meant to explore, to conquer. They didn't have roots or commitments or permanent addresses. That was why these two suited each other...and clearly still saw that for themselves as well. Their connection practically formed visible ropes on the air. She could feel good for helping to make that happen, at least.

After a huge inhalation, Rhett finally spoke. "We've just completed the east Asian jungle tour."

She studied their faces for clues about an appropriate response. "Ummm...congratulations?"

Rebel's face clouded over. "We would've brought you a souvenir, but we suspected you didn't want us to bring back malaria or dysentery."

"You were right." She laughed it out. "Thank you." Then, in a softer murmur, "You brought back the only two things that really matter anyhow."

He reached to take her hand. "It's damn good to hear you say that, *minette*."

Rhett repeated the action with her other hand. "What he's trying to say is, all those miles of bogs, mud, and sludge didn't compare to the hell we knew...without you."

Rebel slid closer. Gazed up at her with eyes that glowed like sapphires in the sun. "We agreed that you needed space. We've tried like hell to let you have it. But Brynna...pieces of us both are missing without you."

Rhett sent a nod at the man full of approval and adoration. Rebel returned the look, seeming to validate an unspoken message between them.

Words Rhett uttered the next moment, in that entrancing blend of New York and London, making her instantly glad she was still sitting down.

"We're in love with you."

Brynna blinked. Then nothing else. She wished one of them would pinch her—or something even better—to confirm she wasn't dreaming.

"Both of us." Rebel let go of her hand to slide his touch up her arm, clenching his jaw as he stopped at her elbow. In his eyes, she saw the desire to go farther. "Nighttime in the jungle means you get a lot of time to talk."

"About *a lot* of things." Rhett wrapped his free hand around her knee, just above her boot. Her whole leg erupted in shivers from his knowing contact. "Like about how amazing it is that we've finally opened our hearts to each other—only to realize that all this extra space is empty."

"Not empty," Rebel asserted. "Simply missing the element that belongs there." He copied Rhett's grip, curling his long fingers around her other knee. "The missing magic."

"The love of our lives."

Rebel nodded as if his partner had sung the final note of a beautiful song. His eyes closed for a long moment. Rhett openly adored the expression before tilting his head back toward her. Brynna simply stared back. She struggled for words, but they never came. They couldn't make it past the glorious, miraculous disbelief flooding her heart.

"Look, we know it sounds crazy, but—"

"No." His declaration finally unlocked her own. "No." The tethers on her tongue finally fell away...as the wings of her heart spread, daring to hope, to believe. She grabbed them both by the nape, letting them see her joyful tears. "I've been trying to talk *myself* out of crazy too. For four damn months..."

Rebel raised his hand to the back of her head. "Meaning...?"

"Meaning I'm in love with you too." She shook her head. "I kept telling myself I was insane, that four days couldn't have possibly been enough time to change my heart, much less my life...but I couldn't shove any of it out of the way." Their gazes, so pure and blue, the oceans that her soul sailed on, encouraged her to continue. "I couldn't forget how much courage you two pulled from yourselves...the shit you confronted for the sake of finally being together. Your bravery inspired the same thing in me. Only, once I realized how I felt, I didn't know what to do with all of it. I figured I'd just been the naughty little fling that turned into the wakeup call for you two."

Rhett chuffed. "You woke us up, all right."

Rebel smirked. "In some damn good ways."

"In some *better* than good ways." Rhett halted, as if craving to say more. His nostrils flared and then again—until a look of pure fuck-it-all crossed his face.

He lunged, taking her mouth again. There wasn't a damn meaning left out this time. He was out to dominate, and Brynna was so ready to let him. She moaned from his raw, relentless conquest, giving in to every blaze he brought to her body, every fire he ignited in her heart.

Nearly the instant he released her, she was jerked the other direction. The dark command of Rebel's face consumed her lust-clouded vision, and her lips parted, preparing for his kiss—

Which didn't come.

"Have you registered for the new school semester yet?"

She blinked, wondering how he could disguise such an ice bucket of a question beneath that hot, sexy stare. "I... What?"

"Answer the question," he growled. "Have you registered—"

"I heard the question." She snapped it, despite his delicious pull on her scalp. Perhaps because of it. "And no. Registration isn't for two more weeks. How does that—"

"Good."

"Good?"

He flicked a quick look to Rhett. Seemed to like what he

saw there, so he nodded and impaled her with his beautiful stare again. "We want you think about finishing your coursework in Washington."

Her eyes popped wider. "In—what?"

"There are at least a dozen outstanding colleges and universities between Kirkland, Seattle, and Tacoma," Rhett added. "They all have extensive graduate and post-graduate psychology programs."

"Meaning there are also some exceptional group homes." Rebel's lips tipped in a soft smile. "If you decide that Enya needs to be moved closer as well."

"Moved?" Her brain latched on to the word and then let her heart pound all over it. "Wait. What? You...you want me to—"

"Move." Rebel pressed the word into her lips. "Yes. To Seattle."

"With us." Rhett turned the kiss into a three-way thing, caressing half his mouth over Reb's, half over hers. "Jungle downtime also means a lot of real-estate dreams."

Rebel's smile took on more meaning. "It means a lot of dreams, period."

"We figured if we looked at a bigger place in the suburbs, we could have a yard. A few spare bedrooms. One of them could be your office..."

"And one of them our bonus room."

Brynn couldn't help but giggle. "But of course. Boys have to have their...bonus stuff."

Rebel nodded solemnly. "Soundproofed. Halo and Call of Duty were made for cranking to level ten."

Rhett dipped his head, teething at one of her breasts through her clothes. "I'm more interested in the other toys that cause level tens."

Brynna let a gasp escape, as much from joy as arousal. She let it spread into a smile while Rebel growled his support of Rhett's assertion. He joined his friend in pushing her all the way back on the bed. As he coaxed her farther up on the mattress, Rhett busied himself with pulling down—on her clothes. More gasps tumbled out as he stripped off the romper in a few deft moves. Rebel nudged his nose beneath her bra, teasing at both her nipples, while Rhett made short work of her panties.

"You two certainly know how to make a case for your cause." She punctuated that on a shiver as Rhett climbed back up her body by way of sliding his fingers through her pussy. Within seconds, she dripped even wetter than before, soaking his fingers enough to leave a trail up her abdomen toward her navel.

"Oh, *minette*." Rebel pushed back the lace cups of her bra, scraping his thumb over her nipples. "We're just getting started."

She arched into his touch. "Does that mean I shouldn't tell you that I'll be packed and ready to go in a few hours?"

"Who says you're going anywhere past this bed for the next few hours?"

As he issued that, Rhett demonstrated the extent of their point. From seemingly nowhere, he pulled out a padded leather cuff and secured it around her right wrist. As he did the same to her left, she instantly felt a tug on the first cuff. They'd brought in some kind of under-the-mattress bondage system before going downstairs to get her. Oh God, she was a lucky girl.

As soon as he was done, Rhett slid over to gently kiss her on the lips. "Be good, and we'll let your legs stay free."

Brynn lifted her head, instantly missing his spicy taste. "And if I'm bad?"

Rebel bit the curve of her shoulder. "Oh, please be bad." A light tap of his fingers on her mound, and she was instantly inspired to rename herself after every bad girl she could think of. *Maleficent...Mata Hari...Bettie Page...*

"He's tempting you to the dark side, peach." Rhett ran a graceful, powerful hand through her hair and then Reb's. He lingered, alternately caressing and pulling, letting her share his captivated stare as Rebel responded with groans of lust and heat.

She traded one moment's worth of a glance with Rhett, knowing his thoughts tracked with hers. To think of how close they'd come to losing Rebel...to being without the free, wild wind upon which both of them could ride to the fulfillment of their fantasies...

She didn't want to think about what life would be like now. But nor could she bear to contemplate it without Rhett: the mountain who gave her his hardness, his strength, his unfaltering foundation so she could lift herself up, arms and heart open, into the wind...

They were everything she needed.

Everything she ever *would* want.

"Brynna?" The whisper came from Rebel as he hovered his face above her own.

"Yes?" She deliberately tugged at her cuffs, making sure the movement brushed her erect nipples right under his own.

"Come to the dark side."

She gasped, sharing breaths with him.

Cleopatra...Madonna...Joan Jett...

"Do it." Rhett's voice, now above them, was thick with lust.

His fingers dropped to her jaw, compressing in, forcing her mouth open. "Let him take you, little girl."

Brynna welcomed Rebel's tongue. Let him stab deeper into the recesses of her throat.

Mystique...Poison Ivy...Bellatrix...

"Now spread your legs for him."

She obeyed without question, her body surrendering, her heart racing, her mind rejoicing. Oh God, this was so much better than she remembered. Far, far better than she'd fantasized. Especially now, as Rhett shifted to the space between her legs, shoving on both her ankles so her knees bent up. The whole time, Rebel continued kissing her, alternating between deep probes and gentle strokes, his breaths getting heavier and faster—

Until Rhett reached between their bodies and yanked down the zipper on Rebel's fly.

"*Fuck.*" It tore from the depths of Reb's throat. His stare sliced into Brynn's, intense as blue glass, as Rhett pushed his pants to his knees, freeing the stiff, full length of his beautiful, swollen cock.

"That's definitely the right idea."

Rhett's voice was edged with wicked sadism. It clenched at Brynn's womb, making her shake with need. She watched, enraptured, as Rhett wrapped an elegant grip around Reb's cock and pulled hard. He did it again and again, growling low as French profanities spilled off Rebel's lips—which were then presented with Rhett's palm, now shining with the moisture Rhett had squeezed off his head.

"You know what to do," Rhett dictated.

Ink-thick lashes closing, Rebel licked the length of Rhett's palm. After a few strokes of that, Rhett curled his fingers in, forcing two and then three of them into Rebel's mouth.

Brynna was damn certain she would climax just from looking at the sight.

Her pussy was so wet. Her nipples were so tight. And God knew how her mouth watered—

A damn good thing, since Rebel paid the favor forward.

She moaned as his fingers slid against her tongue. Sighed as he joined a fourth to them, now fucking her mouth with everything except his thumb. That he used for leverage, ensuring that he impaled her as deep and hard as he could.

After just a few minutes, Rebel yanked his hand away. "Christ. I need to fuck her now, Rhett!"

The Viking rumbled low with agreement, though a needy grunt broke into it. When Brynna darted a curious glance as to why, she was treated to the sight of Rhett's own dropped trousers, his erection free, jutting at damn near a right angle to his body. Her admiration made his cock jump. He rewarded her with an appreciative smile. Brynn's heart did a girlish flip. The lips on that man could tempt a damn nun...

"Seems everyone's in the mood to fuck," he murmured.

"Thank God," Brynna countered.

"Yeah, yeah. *Voulez-vous coucher,*" Rhett grumbled. "Let's go. God*damn*, I need this."

Brynna let out a husky laugh as he positioned himself between her thighs. "And I need you."

"Because you're on the dark, dirty side now." He angled up by just a little, using the space he created to give her pussy a harder smack. Then another. "And dirty girls get hurt. Then fucked."

"So do dirty boys."

She wouldn't have thought it possible, but her sex

clenched tighter, squeezing out more of her creamy arousal, as Rhett knelt directly behind Rebel, a bottle of lube and a pair of condoms in one hand. They groaned in tandem as Rhett flipped the cap and then feverishly rolled the rubbers over both their magnificent lengths.

"Hang on tight, Moon."

"Hang on tight, *minette*."

And then, they were one.

Cocks embedded. Hearts pressed. Breaths mingled. Arousals built.

Higher.

Higher...

Surging. Retreating. Fucking.

Loving.

Nobody closed their eyes or even threw back their head. Brynna gazed up at her two lovers, knowing their thoughts as clearly as her own. All three of them had been alone for so long, wandering paths through life's forest lined by different trees of pain, hardship, and solitary trials. They'd stumbled, feeling lost. Fallen, feeling defeated. But always, *always*, gotten back up and kept going, praying that the other half of their soul was on a similar path, fighting along until their crossroads was reached...

Now, here she was.

And the crossroads was beautiful.

Not two paths converging. Three.

That was the way life rolled when a girl fell in love with a pair of rule breakers.

But the most important view now was the road ahead. The *road*. Wide enough to be traversed by three.

She wasn't delusional. There'd be twists, turns, valleys,

and haunted forests, but now she'd be sharing the journey—
with the two people who'd given her the courage to break her
own rules. Who'd had the guts to break theirs. Who'd believed
so strongly in what the three of them could have together,
they'd invited her to share their life, to walk with them in love.

"Yes." She rasped it at the peak of her passion.

"Yes." She gave it from the depths of her soul.

"Yes." She promised it to the mavericks who had earned
her trust, dominated her body, and mastered her heart...
forever.

Continue the Honor Bound Series with Book Nine

Conquered

Coming Soon
Keep reading for an excerpt!

EXCERPT FROM *CONQUERED*
BOOK NINE IN THE HONOR BOUND SERIES

Of all the days to vie for an Olympic medal in tripping over one's own feet, Jen Thorne had to pick this one.

To be fair, however, maybe the circumstances had picked *her*. Most days, the most exciting thing that happened in and around her little accounting office at Nellis Air Force Base was a freak desert thunderstorm or a UPS delivery. Because the legs on the UPS guy...

She wasn't thinking of the UPS guy right now, though. Or much of anything else, except staying upright as she and Lola, her assistant, headed back inside from their lunch break. In the Las Vegas Valley, wind was a fickle bitch. One second, the air could be eerily still, only to switch up and gust so hard, one expected to see Auntie Em pedaling by with Toto in her bike's basket.

Caught by such a gust, Jen was faced with saving the leftovers of her burrito or the hem of her dress. Normally, the issue would be moot, but the burritos was a Zapata's special, meaning she'd have a decent dinner tonight while working late to close out the pilots' logs for the month. Besides, Lola was too busy trying to see through her own hair, a frizzy mass she'd just had hennaed to a deep purple, to notice Jen was flashing a similar shade in French panty lace—

As the wind rushed in again.

And had her stumbling, one suede-heeled boot over the other, just to maintain *some* semblance of upright balance—

Until a pylon popped up in the middle of the parking lot to help her.

Shit.

"Shit!" Only when Lola's echo hit the air did Jen realize she'd blurted it too—for damn good reason. The pylon wasn't a pylon. No pylon on the planet looked like this, with commanding muscles on a six-foot-plus frame that turned even his plaid shirt and jeans into an outfit worthy of Camelot itself. The guy's stance was worthy of nobility too, with posture that bordered on arrogant and booted feet braced to steady both himself and her. None of that was even the most gulp-worthy part of him, as she learned when jolting her sights up to his face.

Oh, God.

He was worth way more than another gulp. Full-on gawking was now in order—but could she be blamed? Those thick ginger waves. That deep-dimpled grin. Those eyes, wolf gray and just as keen, seeming to take in every detail about her...

Including her exposed underwear.

Ohhhhh. Geez.

And yeah, *that* had spilled out too—in the highest, most horrifying squeak she could imagine. Not true. Nowhere, in any shoot-me-now nightmare she'd ever had, had she let out a sound as obnoxious as that.

Lola, clearly agreeing, didn't help by barking a giggle and snapping her gum.

Neither did Major Skip Tremaine, a man who'd never

matched his call sign better. Cat Five, with his sharp nose and flawless high-and-tight haircut, turned around from his position about fifteen feet ahead of them all, and barked out, "Thorne! What the hell? You having the vapors or something?"

Lola yipped with another laugh.

Jen groaned beneath her breath. *Kill. Me. Now.*

She meant it, and even considered begging her ginger King Arthur to do it, but the only sound that emerged when she opened her mouth was another ridiculous whine. Why that made the hunk only smile wider and hold her tighter was just as irrational, if not fully dysfunctional—which of course, only made him more irresistible. Holy hell. *A lot more...*

"*Och*, Tremaine." The guy copied Cat Five's scowl, only with a shake of his head to rid his eyes of the thick highlander waves smacking into his eyes. "The *vapors*, man?"

"What?" Cat Five spread his hands, palms up. "*You* taking full credit, Braw Boy? What, so the lasses are now falling at your feet before you even meet them? Cocky sonofabitch."

"Lasses." It screaked softly out of Jen as she grabbed at the hem of her skirt, newly taunted by a fresh blast of wind. "Holy... crap. You're—You're him. The hotshot pilot from Scotland."

"Captain Sam Mackenna." He curled up his lips, which were a collection of bold lines emulating the cliffs of his native land. "Also known as the cocky sonofabitch." He offered a handshake. "And you are...?"

"Embarrassed as hell." Jen ducked her head, attempting to yank free from his grip. Though he was in civvies and she was no longer auditioning for the Victoria's Secret Angels, this was still a thousand kinds of inappropriate—an impropriety her whole body still begged her to continue. And though Sam allowed her to step free, he remained unusually close while issuing a quiet, easy reply.

"*Bah. Embarrassed* isn't fun at all. How about...mouse?" Though with his Highland drawl, it came out much closer to *moose*—which pulled a giggle out of Jen before she could help it.

"With the horrible squeak to match?"

He didn't return the laugh. Instead, with his hooded gaze dropping to her mouth, he murmured, "'Horrible' wasn't the first word that came to my mind, lass." As the parking lot was hit by another whomp of wind, making it hard to hear anything from more than a few inches from one's face, he leaned over and murmured close to her ear, "But adorable, hot, and sexy sure fucking did."

And now, the wind wasn't the only force walloping the crap out of her.

But maybe the gust had simply made her hear him wrong...?

One quick glance over. One stare full of his blatant flirtation.

Nope. Not a thing wrong with her hearing.

Jen concentrated on taking several long, steady breaths. But still, her heartbeat galloped. Her bloodstream still ran hot, then ruthlessly frozen. The wind kicked up again, mighty and merciless. *Dear God.* The man and his stance—and his rich nobleman's accent, and his easy ginger charm—could easily be the towering, dashing hero from the Highlander romance she'd finished last night.

Fiction, Jen. Fiction. *Remember? The fun little word bringing the reminder that strapping Scottish hunks* don't *come wrapped in kilts and romance and carnal promises in fluent Gaelic? And technically, this one's not even here for pleasure—*

though with Sin City right out the front door, he'll likely find
his way to it soon enough. Yeah, after talking rockets and guns
and blowing enemy jets out of the sky all day, he'll want some
recreation—not a night picking constellations out of the sky
from your apartment balcony.

"All right, all right." She held up both hands, managing to
insert a laugh that sounded halfway casual. "Why don't we just
try Jen?"

He tilted his head. The wind whipped hunks of whisky-
colored strands across his hewn features. She pretended to
clutch her Zapata's bag harder, helping her resist clearing the
brilliant strands away herself.

You: geek sandwich.

Him: alpha male filet.

The two don't belong on the same plate together.

As if she needed an even bigger reminder of *that* mental
sticky note, Cat Five strode over, clapping her on the back as
if he would one of the mechanics in the hangar. As Jen's teeth
found their rightful places again, he declared, "Thorne here is
your ace inside the office, Mackenna. She'll keep your ass in
line with the administrative song and dance, and since this air
combat cross-training program with the RAF includes twelve
of you Scottish jocks, there's going to be an assload of hoops to
hop through." He interrupted himself with a hissing grimace.
"Annnnd there I go, harshing the girl's Zapata's high. Sorry,
Thorne—but once you see what Braw Boy and his crew can
do with their planes, you'll be damn glad we invited these boys
over for a few months of friendly collaboration."

Lola, having locked and come around the car, broke in
with a snarky snort. "Oh, I think she already *is*, Major."

Cat Five acknowledged that with a grunt before spinning

back toward Jen and Sam. "So maybe the two of you should get together for a few minutes after Sam gets to know his way around the hangar."

Inwardly, Jen groaned. On the outside, she plastered a smile to her lips and said, "Sure thing. Whatever will make things easier for Captain Mackenna."

"That's my girl."

She was damn glad she'd kept her teeth clenched. One, it meant the man didn't knock any fillings loose with his new shoulder smack of "encouragement." Two, it helped cinch back the rejoinder that never failed to percolate when Cat Five used the pep talk.

I'm not *your girl.*

But that wasn't the biggest worry on her mind.

Already, Captain Sam Mackenna had upended her axis. Slammed a cosmic can opener on the lid of her composure, and made her inhale a scoop of pure, raw, chemical attraction from the inside. So how the hell was she going to see him—talk with him, interact with him, work with him—nearly every day for the next ten months?

The answer came in a strange but relieving rush.

She simply hadn't seen this coming. Hadn't known the superstar Scottish jet jockey would look—and talk, and smolder, and flirt—more like a kilt-clad warrior who'd walked right out of her favorite novel and onto her boring old blacktop. And because she was caught with her defenses down and her skirt flying up, she hadn't been prepared for the shock. And *really* hadn't anticipated what Mackenna himself would do with that vulnerability.

Decisiveness was good in a pilot.

So were ruthlessness, boldness, and dominant confidence.

So long as they were all focused on the strategies and the flying.

Along with that conclusion came Lola's wry chuckle—just before she ended it on a wistful sigh while joining Jen to watch the two pilots striding off to the hangars together.

"Ho. Lee. Fuuuuck," Lo muttered, twirling a couple of indigo curls around a finger. "That man's backside belongs in a G-string downtown."

Despite the weird curl of tension still lingering in her belly, Jen laughed. "It's...impressive."

"Ohhhh, girl." Lo patted her forearm. "Something tells me he's going to need the deluxe version of the talk."

"Hmm." It was more commiseration than consideration. "Which one? Keep-the-ego-in-the-cockpit, or keep-the-libido-in-the-locker-room?"

"Both."

Jen groaned. "That's what I was afraid you'd say."

This story continues in
Conquered: *Honor Bound Book Nine!*

ALSO BY ANGEL PAYNE

Honor Bound:
Saved
Cuffed
Seduced
Wild
Wet
Hot
Masked
Mastered
Conquered (October 23, 2018)
Ruled (Coming Soon)

The Bolt Saga:
Bolt (Summer 2018)
Ignite (Summer 2018)
Pulse (Summer 2018)
Fuse
Surge
Light

Secrets of Stone Series:
No Prince Charming
No More Masquerade
No Perfect Princess
No Magic Moment
No Lucky Number
No Simple Sacrifice
No Broken Bond
No White Knight

**For a full list of Angel's other titles,
visit her at www.angelpayne.com**

ACKNOWLEDGMENTS

Sometimes, it really does take a village. The journey to getting Rhett, Rebel, and Brynn onto the page took a pretty large one! Pushing into these uncharted waters was exhilarating, wonderful, and pretty damn scary! Thank you so much to my writing sisters for supporting every step of this one as I boldly "went there": Victoria "The Daily Rock" Blue, Shayla "Get Your Ass in the Chair" Black, Jenna "Sassy Sprinting Sistah" Jacob, Sierra "Eternal Cheerleader" Cartwright, Lexi "Yoda with Better Shoes" Blake, and Zoey "Eleventh Hour Savior" Derrick!

Elisa Mashal: You are something in French, and I believe that word is magnifique. None of these books would be what they are without you! I am so, so, so grateful!

From the bottom of my heart: A special thank you to everyone who writes, comments, and supports the "the boys." Your encouragement has meant the world!

And to the men and women of our military: a thousand thanks from deep in the heart of this grateful and humble citizen.

ABOUT ANGEL PAYNE

USA Today bestselling romance author Angel Payne loves to focus on high-heat romance starring memorable alpha men and the women who love them. She has numerous book series to her credit, including the Suited for Sin series, the Cimarron Saga, the Temptation Court series, the Secrets of Stone series, the Lords of Sin historicals, and the popular Honor Bound series, as well as several standalone titles.

Angel is a native Southern Californian, leading to her love of being in the outdoors, where she often reads and writes. She still lives in Southern California with her soul-mate husband and beautiful daughter, to whom she is a proud cosplay/culture con mom. Her passions also include whisky tasting, shoe shopping, and travel.

Visit her here:
www.angelpayne.com